D   FANTASY   94823

Drake, David
The sharp end.

THE SHARP END

DAVID DRAKE

THE SHARP END

This is a work of fiction. All the characters and events portrayed in this book are fictional, and any resemblance to real people or incidents is purely coincidental.

Copyright © 1993 by David Drake

94823

All rights reserved, including the right to reproduce this book or portions thereof in any form.

A Baen Books Original

Baen Publishing Enterprises
P.O. Box 1403
Riverdale, NY 10471

ISBN: 0-671-72192-5

Cover art by Larry Elmore

First printing, November 1993

Distributed by Simon & Schuster
1230 Avenue of the Americas
New York, NY 10020

Library of Congress Cataloging-in-Publication Data

Drake, David–
    The Sharp End / David Drake
    p.   cm.
    ISBN 0-671-72192-5 : $20.00
    [1. Imaginary wars and battles—Fiction.] I. Title

PS3554.R196S5 1993   93-10739
813'.54–dc20   CIP

Printed in the United States of America

DEDICATION

To our architect and builder Derwood Schrotberger

Writing a novel and moving to a new house are both stressful occupations. The fact that I was able to combine them is a comment on Derwood's consummate skill, which reminds me that architect originally meant Master Builder.

ACKNOWLEDGMENTS

Those of you who notice echoes of *The Glass Key* and *Red Harvest* by Dashiell Hammett in this book are correct. Those of you who don't should go off and read Hammett's splendid novels at your earliest convenience.

When I'm at a crux in my plotting, I tend to talk at those around me. When I did that this time on the way to the state fair with friends, my wife, Jo, and Mark Van Name made suggestions which were precisely on point. I adopted both.

NIEUW FRIESLAND

The room housing the Officers Assignment Bureau was spacious enough to have three service cages and seats for twenty around the walls of colored marble. Nobody was waiting when Major Matthew Coke entered, though a single officer discussed alternative assignments with a specialist.

Coke stepped into an empty cage. A clerk rose from her desk in the administrative area across the divider and switched on the electronics.

"Yes sir?" the clerk said pleasantly. "Is there a problem with your assignment?"

The Frisian Defense Forces reassigned scores of officers every week. Normally the operation was impersonal, a data transfer to the officer's present station directing him or her to report to a new posting, along with details of timing, transport, and interim leave.

This office handled problems. President Hammer, in common with other leaders whose elevation owed more to bullets than ballots, felt most comfortable with a large standing army under his direct control. Professional soldiers are expensive, and unless they are used, they either rust, or find ways to employ themselves — generally to the detriment of the established government.

Hammer's answer to the problem was to hire out elements of the Frisian Defense Forces as mercenaries. This provided training for the troops, as well as defraying the cost of their pay and equipment.

Sometimes the troops engaged were merely a few

advisers or specialists. When somebody, a planetary government or the rebels opposed to it, hired a large force, however, the OAB would be standing room only.

Officers on Nieuw Friesland knew that the only sure route to promotion was through combat experience. The Frisian Defense Forces had sprung from Hammer's Slammers, a mercenary regiment with the reputation for doing whatever it took to win . . . and a reputation for winning.

So long as Alois Hammer was President and the commanders of the Frisian Defense Forces were the officers who'd bought him that position in decades of bloody war, bureaucratic 'warriors' weren't on the fast track to high rank. You paid for your rank sometimes in blood, and sometimes with your life; but all that was as nothing without demonstrated success at the sharp end, where they buried the guys in second place.

Not everybody was comfortable with Hammer's terms of employment, but the Forces were volunteer only and the volunteers came from all across the human universe; just as they had to Hammer's Slammers before. A certain number of men, and a lower percentage of women, would rather fight than not. Alois Hammer's troops had always been the best there was at what they did: killing the other fellow, whoever he was.

A draft going out to a hot theater was a ticket to promotion. Officers would crowd the Assignment Bureau, begging and threatening, offering bribes and trying to pull rank to get a slot. Mostly it didn't work.

The Table of Organization for a combat deployment was developed by the central data base itself. Changes had to be approved by President Hammer, who was immune to any practical form of persuasion. The Assignments Bureaus were open because people prefer to argue with human beings instead of electronic displays, but that was normally a cosmetic rather than significant touch.

You could also appeal to Hammer personally. In that case, you were cashiered if you didn't convince him. Old-timers in the Assignment Bureau said that the success rate was slightly under three percent, but every month or so somebody else tried it.

There were no large-scale deployments under way at the moment, but there were always glitches, clerical or personal, which had to be ironed out. The clerk smiled at Coke, expecting to learn that he'd been assigned to a slot calling for a *sergeant*-major, or that he was wanted for murder on the planet to which he was being posted.

Coke's problem was rather different.

"I'm here to receive sealed orders," Coke said, offering the clerk his identification card with the embedded chip. He smiled wryly.

The clerk blinked in surprise. There were various reasons why an officer's orders would be sealed within the data base, requiring him or her to apply in person to the bureau to receive them. Coke didn't look like the sort to whom any of the special reasons would apply. He looked — normal.

Matthew Coke was 34 standard years old — 29 dated on Ash, where he was born, 51 according to the shorter year of Nieuw Friesland. He had brown hair, eyes that were green, blue, or gray depending on how much sunlight had been bleaching them, and stood a meter seventy-eight in his stocking feet. He was thin but not frail, like a blade of good steel.

Coke was in dress khakis with rank tabs and the blue edging to the epaulets that indicated his specialty was infantry. He wore no medal or campaign ribbons whatever, but over his left breast pocket was a tiny lion rampant on a field of red enamel.

The lion marked the men who'd served with Hammer's Slammers before the regiment was subsumed into the Frisian Defense Forces. Its lonely splendor against the khaki meant that, like most of the other Slammers veterans, Coke figured that when you'd said you were in the Slammers, you'd said everything that mattered.

Considering that, the clerk realized that Major Coke might not be quite as normal as he looked.

"Face the lens, please, sir," the clerk said as she inserted the ID card into a slot on her side of the cage. Electronics chittered, validating the card and comparing Coke's retinal patterns with those contained in the embedded chip.

A soft chime indicated approval. Coke eased from the stiff posture with which he had faced the comparator lens. He continued to smile faintly, but the emotions the clerk read on his face were sadness and resignation.

"Just a moment," the clerk said. "The printer has to warm up, but —"

As she spoke, a sheet of hardcopy purred from the dispenser on Coke's side of the cage. Coke read the rigid film upside down as it appeared instead of waiting for the print cycle to finish so that he could clip the document.

His face blanked; then he began to laugh. The captain at the next cage glanced at him, then away. The clerk waited, hoping Coke would explain the situation but unwilling to press him.

Coke tapped the cutter, then tossed the sheet across the counter to the clerk. "It says my new assignment is Category Ten Forty-seven," he said as the clerk scanned the document. "That's survey team, isn't it?"

The clerk nodded. "Yessir," she said. "You'll be assessing potential customers for field force deployments."

She didn't understand Major Coke's laughter. "Isn't this what you were expecting, sir?" she asked as she slid back the hardcopy.

"What I was expecting . . ." Coke explained, " . . . after the way I screwed up my last assignment on Auerstadt . . ."

He was smiling like a skull, as broadly and with as little humor.

" . . . was that they'd fire my ass. But I guess the Assessment Board decided I couldn't get into much trouble on a survey team."

He began to laugh again. Despite the obvious relief in Coke's voice, the sound of his laughter chilled the clerk.

Earlier: AUERSTADT

There was a party going on in the extensive quarters of General the Marquis Bradkopf, National Army commander of Fortress Auerstadt. Next door in the Tactical Operations Center, Major Matthew Coke of the Frisian Defense Forces was trying to do his job — and General Bradkopf's job — through a realtime link to the pair of combat cars in ambush position thirty kilometers away.

The combat cars were named *Mother Love* and *The Facts of Life*. They and their crews were Frisians; and the sergeants commanding them were, like Coke, former members of Hammer's Slammers, the mercenary regiment whose ruthless skill had transformed Colonel Hammer into Alois Hammer, President of Nieuw Friesland.

"We're getting major movement into Hamlet Three, sir," said 4-4 — Sergeant-Commander Dubose in *Mother Love*, stationed for the moment on a dike south of the three hamlets called Parcotch for administrative purposes. *"Nearly a hundred just from the direction of Auerstadt. Most of them are carrying weapons, too."*

The three clerks in the TOC with Coke were National Army enlisted personnel, two women and a male who looked fifteen years old. They were chattering in a corner of the open bullpen. One of the women had brought in a series of holovision cubes of Deiting, the planetary capital, where she'd gone on leave with her boyfriend, a transport driver.

There was a National Army officer listed as

Commander of the Watch, but whoever it was hadn't put in an appearance this evening. In all likelihood, the fellow was at General Bradkopf's party.

That was fine with Coke. The best a National officer could do was to keep out of the way of the advisor hired from the Frisian Defense Forces.

Though all the raw data was provided by the combat cars, processing by the base unit in the TOC added several layers of enhancement to what the troops on the ground could see. Coke checked the statistical analysis in a sidebar of his holographic display and said, "There's a hundred and seventeen up the Auerstadt Road. They're *all* armed, and ninety percent of them are in spatter-camouflage uniforms."

"*Bloody hell,*" said Sergeant-Commander Lennox from *The Facts of Life*. "*We've got regulars from the Association of Barons? Then it's really going to blow!*"

"And Four-Two has spotted another eighty-four coming down from Hamlet One and points north," Coke continued, watching his split-screen display. "The only thing I can imagine from an assembly this large is that they're planning to attack the fortress itself in a night or two."

Two companies, even of fully equipped regulars, weren't a threat to a base the size of Fortress Auerstadt; but Parcotch was only one village of the ninety or a hundred within comparable distance of the base.

The direct views from sensors in the combat cars filled the lower right and left quadrants of Coke's display. The top half of the screen looked down at an apparent 30° on a panorama extrapolated from the separate inputs and combined with map data.

Mother Love was a klick to the south and east of Hamlet 3. *The Facts of Life* was within 500 meters of the hamlet's west edge, and that was the problem. Lennox's vehicle was only 500 meters east of Hamlet 2 as well, where the incoming troops had parked a launching trailer full of short-range guided weapons.

The combat cars were in perfect position to do a number on the enemy concentration in Hamlet 3, but Coke wasn't willing to put Lennox between two fires.

"*Any chance the Nationals might send us some support?*" Sergeant Dubose said wistfully.

"*Any chance the tooth fairy is making a run by your car tonight?*" Sergeant Lennox retorted tartly. She was a lanky woman who shaved her head and was just as tough as she looked. "*Sir,*" she continued, "*let's do it. If we rip this one, the locals'll get their heads out of the sand.*"

"Not in your present location, Four-Two," Coke said. "If they salvo the full load of missiles, there's no way you're going to survive. Particularly with whatever's happening in Three."

"*Sir, look,*" Lennox said. "*The personnel are going to be in Three with the others, getting a pep talk or whatever the hell they're doing. The launcher's no threat!*"

"We don't —" Coke started to say.

A mortar fired just outside the TOC.

"Hold one!" Coke shouted, spinning from the console and grabbing the sub-machine gun he'd slung over the back of his chair. The National Army clerks jumped up also. They'd been frightened by Coke's reaction rather than the mortar's flash and hollow *CHUG!* through the TOC's doorway. The vacationer's glittering holoviews spilled onto the floor.

Cheers and laughter from outside the TOC told Coke there was no danger. The shell popped thousands of meters in the air, casting harsh magnesium light across Fortress Auerstadt. General the Marquis Bradkopf was using parachute flares to provide fireworks for his party.

Which suggested a way out of Coke's immediate problem.

In theory, Coke's console was linked to the National

Army net. Rather than go through the complicated handshake procedures, however, Coke turned to the rack system at the adjacent bay.

He switched the unit from standby to operations and waited a moment for it to warm up. When the light went from amber to green, Coke keyed the address of the heavy battery of the artillery battalion attached to the fortress defenses. The clerk responsible for the communications bay watched Coke in concern from across the room, but she didn't attempt to interfere.

Marquis Bradkopf began hectoring a subordinate outside the door of the TOC. Drink and anger slurred his words so that Coke couldn't make them out. A woman's voice wove a descant around Bradkopf's.

"Battery Seven," a man said. "Yeah?"

"This is Fortress Command," Coke said crisply. "I have an immediate fire mission for you." As he spoke, his left hand addressed a target information packet on the Frisian console. "This will require seeker shells, so I'm authorizing you to release them from locked storage."

"What!" said the soldier on the other end of the line. "What? Look, I'll get Chief Edson."

Theoretically, the Frisians were in advisory capacity without direct control of National Army forces. As with other large organizations, somebody who was willing to claim authority was more than likely to be granted it.

The mortar fired again, lofting a second flare into the night sky. There was static on the land line, masking a half-audible conversation at the battery end.

National Army heavy equipment was generally of off-planet manufacture, ranging from good to very good in design. The local personnel were of low quality, however, and virtually untrained. Coke didn't dare call an ordinary fire mission to support units within half a klick of the intended impact area. Battery 7's 200-mm guns were capable of nail-driving accuracy at thirty kilometers, but the crews were as apt as not to drop their heavy shells directly on *The Facts of Life*.

Technology could eliminate the problem. The battery was issued four Frisian-manufactured seeker rounds, one per tube. These self-steering warheads were designed for use against ill-defined or moving targets, and combined with satellite photos of Parcotch Hamlet 2 they would obviate the friendly-fire risk.

"Chief Edson," a businesslike voice said. "Who is this?"

"Major Matthew Coke," Coke said, "acting Fortress Command. Where's your battery commander?"

"Who the fuck knows?" said the chief, the battery's ranking enlisted man. "Look, Major, I don't care about your authorization — I flat don't have the codes to open the special locker. Maybe Captain Wilcken does, maybe the Marquis does — maybe nobody. Forget the seeker warheads, they're just for show."

"Prepare the battery," Coke snapped. "I'm on my way."

He dropped the handset onto its cradle and rose. More figures drifted through the shadows of the split screen. Lennox and Dubose held their silence, as Coke had directed them at last transmission.

Coke settled his commo helmet, slung the sub-machine gun over his shoulder, and started for the door. General Bradkopf and his entourage burst through from outside.

"Coke!" the Marquis roared. "Where's — there you are!" He pointed an index finger at Coke's face. "What's happened to my tanks?"

Bradkopf was in his mid-fifties. His body was fleshy but powerful, since swimming and exercise machines controlled the grosser results of the dissipation nonetheless evident on his face.

"Sir, you and I discussed using the combat cars for an ambush patrol," Coke half-lied. His mouth was dry, and his palm was sweating on the grip of his sub-machine gun.

This could get him reprimanded. If Bradkopf was angry enough, he could even have Coke recalled to Friesland.

The group oozing into the TOC behind the Marquis included most of the higher male officers of Fortress Auerstadt's complement. Among them was Captain Wilcken, a 20-year-old of excellent family and the titular commander of Battery 7.

Each of the men had a woman in train. The redhead on the Marquis' arm was approximately a third of his age.

"*You* said you wanted to send out one of the tanks with a patrol," Bradkopf said, his memory unfortunately quite accurate. "For communications."

For stiffening, actually, but the lie was a harmless one. When he'd gotten down to serious planning, he realized that he didn't dare saddle Frisians — *his* troops — with any of the National Army units in the fortress. The locals lacked noise discipline, fire discipline, and target identification skills. A Frisian combat car was the largest thing around and therefore the most likely target for the National troops who did manage to shoot.

Furthermore, the locals lacked guts.

"*I* said I'd think about it," Bradkopf said, "and now I find you've stripped me of all my protection! Are you a traitor?"

"No sir," Coke said, "I'm not a traitor. I —"

I screwed up badly, but Bradkopf wasn't the man to admit that to. Coke had taken the chance that the Marquis wouldn't notice the two combat cars — not tanks — normally parked near his quarters were missing. If Bradkopf hadn't decided to shoot off flares for his party, Coke would have gotten away with it.

If.

Coke couldn't quarrel with Bradkopf's assumption that the commander of an 8,000-troop base was unprotected if two foreign combat vehicles left his presence. It was just that protecting *this* commander was in no sense a military priority for Coke.

"*Six, this is Four-Four,*" Sergeant Dubose reported tensely through Coke's commo helmet. "*The troops are moving out of Three in civilian trucks and wagons. Over.*"

"General Bradkopf!" Coke said. "Association forces are maneuvering to attack this base tonight."

Not in a few days: in a few *hours*.

Fear of a bad rating in his personnel file had turned Coke's skin hot and prickly. The prospect of imminent combat washed him cool again. Major Matthew Coke was a professional and an employee; but first of all he was a soldier.

"What?" blurted the Marquis, sounding amazingly like the gunner on phone watch at Battery 7. "An attack *where*? Have you gone mad?"

"*Six, this is Four-Two,*" Sergeant Lennox reported. There was a lilt, almost a caress in her voice despite the flattening of spread-band radio communication. "*The rocket pod's moved out of Two. It's being pulled by a tractor, now. I'd say it was time, boss. Over.*"

The partygoers gaped without understanding at the multidirectional byplay. Most of them were drunk or nearly drunk. Captain Wilcken was white-faced but sober. The glance he exchanged with Colonel Jaffe, equally well-born and head of the garrison's supply department, held more terror than confusion.

Coke keyed his helmet. "*Six to Four elements,*" he said. "*Take th—*"

He didn't get the last word, 'them,' out of his mouth before the split display behind him ignited with gunfire and explosions.

"I'm sounding the general alarm," Coke said calmly as he turned his back on the Marquis. He uncaged and pressed one of the special-use switches at the side of his console's keyboard. The artificial intelligence sent an alert signal to every node on Fortress Auerstadt's communications network. The siren on the roof of the TOC began to wind.

The holographic display shimmered with the cyan hell engulfing Parcotch.

A Frisian combat car mounted three tribarrels in its open fighting compartment. Each weapon fired 2-cm powergun ammunition at a cyclic rate of about 500 rounds per minute. Because the barrels rotated through the firing position and had time to cool between shots, a tribarrel could fire sustainedly for several minutes before burning out. In that time, the powerful bolts of ionized copper atoms could peck halfway through the side of a mountain.

Nothing *Mother Love* and *The Facts of Life* faced at Parcotch had armor protection. The targets, unprepared Association soldiers and the civilian helpers driving the vehicles, wilted like wax in a blowtorch.

The Facts of Life's two wing guns hit the trailer of anti-tank rockets and the tractor towing it. That was overkill — a single tribarrel should have been sufficient — but the rocket pod was the only real danger to the Frisian vehicles, and Lennox hadn't survived to become a veteran by taking needless risks.

Cyan bolts licked the pod. The solid rocket fuel burned in a huge yellow ball, technically not an explosion but wholly destructive of everything within its 10-meter diameter.

At least one of the missile warheads *did* detonate. The white flash of 40 kilos of HE punctuated the saffron fireball. The tractor-trailer combination blew apart. Blazing debris rained across the landscape, igniting the houses of Hamlet 2 and the heads of the ripe grain in the paddies.

On the other side of the display, *Mother Love's* three tribarrels clawed the infantry packed into the civilian vehicles. Ammunition and grenades went off in secondary explosions, but the stabbing cyan plasma itself did most of the damage. The Association troops were too crowded to fight or flee in the first instants of the ambush, and those instants were all that remained to scores of them.

A stray bolt ruptured the fuel tank under a truck cab. Kerosine, superheated and atomized by the plasma, expanded into an explosive mixture with the surrounding atmosphere —

And flash ignited, just as it would normally have done when injected into the cylinders of the truck's diesel engine. Bodies and body parts flew up in the mushrooming flame, but most of the Association troops had already been killed by gunfire.

"You wanted to know what?" Coke shouted over the wail of the siren. He gestured to the screen which glowed with the light of the scenes it displayed. *"That's* what, General, and there's a lot more Association units out there tonight than those."

An automatic cannon opened fire from a bunker on the perimeter of Fortress Auerstadt. The gunners probably didn't have a real target. They were shooting at shadows or livestock.

That was the right response to the present circumstances. With the base fully alerted, any attack Association troops made would be fragmentary instead of coordinated and overwhelming. In all likelihood there would be *no* attack. At daybreak the National Army would be able to concentrate on scattered companies of their opponents.

"Why that's . . ." the Marquis said, staring at the console display. "That's a massacre!"

Coke was surprised that his nominal superior had enough military knowledge to make that perfectly accurate assessment of what was happening in Parcotch.

As soon as the shooting started, the combat cars' drivers fed full power to the lift fans. Howling like banshees as the fans sucked in vast quantities of air to pressurize the plenum chambers, spraying water and soupy mud in all directions from beneath their skirts, the 50-tonne behemoths accelerated toward Parcotch Hamlet 3 from two directions.

While her wing gunners destroyed the rocket launcher, Sergeant Lennox had opened fire on the community itself. Lennox didn't have a line of sight to the vehicles leaving the hamlet eastward from *The Facts of Life*'s starting position half a klick distant. Instead she shot up the buildings.

The structures had thatch walls and roofs of corrugated plastic sheeting, supported by wood or plastic frames. All the construction materials were flammable at the temperature of copper plasma. Houses, the school building, and the community center all burst into flame, spreading panic and confusing the enemy.

Everything moving this night was a foe and a target. The Frisians' only chance was to hit hard and keep on hitting before the enemy forces could organize their superior numbers. In the morning, every corpse in Hamlet 3 would be tagged as an Association soldier or an Association supporter. Like other forms of history, after-action reports are written by the survivors.

Mother Love bounced onto the Auerstadt Road from the dike which had concealed the vehicle in the darkness. The gunners depressed their tribarrels, raking the troops who'd jumped into the fields to either side of the causeway. A gout of steam flew up at each bolt, whether it hit a flooded paddy or super-heated the fluids within a soldier's body.

The flames enveloping the hamlet rolled in redoubled fury, whipped by *The Facts of Life*'s powerful drive fans. The combat car bellied through the blaze at a walking pace, firing continuously from all three weapons. Cyan bolts cut down the soldiers who had jumped from wagons and truck beds to run toward the fancied safety of the buildings.

Lennox made a point of destroying each of the stalled vehicles. Blazing fuel geysered over the paddies, igniting rice and troops alike.

"Good *Lord!*" the Marquis said. He turned from the

display to Coke and continued, "Get those tanks back here *now*, you fool! How dared you leave me at risk at a time of such danger?"

"Yessir," Coke said. "They're on their way back now."

The Facts of Life bulldozed burning wreckage off the causeway, clearing the route by which to return to Fortress Auerstadt. The driver was buttoned up within his compartment, using the curved bow slope to butt aside a truck festooned with corpses.

The tribarrels continued to fire. The visors of Frisian commo helmets could be switched to either light enhancement or thermal imaging modes. The latter could pick up bodies even through the shallow water of the paddies.

Captain Wilcken blurted something, clawed his personal sidearm out of a white patent leather holster, and pointed the small-bore projectile pistol at General the Marquis Bradkopf. Colonel Jaffe was drawing his pistol also.

Part of Coke's mind reasoned:

Wilcken and Jaffe were supporters of the Association of Barons. They intended to assassinate Bradkopf in conjunction with the attack, leaving Fortress Auerstadt leaderless at the moment of crisis. In panic, Wilcken has gone ahead with the plan even though circumstances have obviously changed. . . .

That was with the conscious part of his mind. Reflex thumbed off the safety of Coke's sub-machine gun as his left hand slapped the fore-grip and his finger took up the slack in the trigger.

The first bolt blew plaster from the wall above the TOC's doorway. The next four hit Wilcken in the chest and neck at point-blank range, virtually decapitating him.

Officers and their gorgeously clad mistresses screamed and threw themselves down. Coke body-checked the Marquis, knocking him to the side and clearing Coke for a shot at Colonel Jaffe. Jaffe's pistol was only half out of its holster. To Coke's adrenaline-speeded reactions, the colonel didn't seem to be moving at all.

The air stank of burned flesh and vaporized blood. Wilcken toppled backward, his head dangling onto his chest by a tag of skin. The pupils of the dead man's eyes had tilted up into the skull.

Coke's second burst winked cyan on Jaffe's corneas. The colonel's chest burst like a blood-filled sponge. The pistol in his hand fired a single shot into the floor. The bullet moaned away in sparks and a spurt of powdered concrete.

"Traitors!" gasped the Marquis, half-sprawled where Coke had knocked him, supporting his torso on the spread fingers of his right hand. "They were —*uh!*"

Coke was poised for a further threat, sweeping the bullpen over his sub-machine gun's holographic sights. The iridium barrel glowed white from the nearly instantaneous bursts. Heat waves trembled through the haze of powergun matrix and smoldering fabric.

Officers and their women hugged the littered floor, some of them with their hands crossed over their heads. The trio of enlisted personnel huddled behind the overturned table at which they had been sitting.

No one else was touching a gun. Jaffe's disembow-eled body thrashed, but he was as dead as the headless Captain Wilcken. Everything was safe —

Except that General the Marquis Bradkopf vomited blood onto the concrete floor, then pitched facedown into the bright pool.

The hilt of a narrow-bladed dagger projected from his back. Bradkopf's youthful mistress stared fixedly at the weapon. There was blood on her little finger and the heel of her right hand. Her tongue dabbed at it.

"Bloody hell," Coke whispered. He didn't shoot the girl, the third of the assassins. At this point, it wouldn't do any good.

"*Four-Two to Six,*" Sergeant Lennox reported

gleefully. *"We've done all there is to do here, boss, so we're heading back to the barn. Out!"*

Bradkopf's sightless eyes stared toward the split display of the carnage achieved by the troops who, by his orders, should have been guarding his own person. In that professionally significant aspect, Coke's gamble hadn't paid off after all.

TANNAHILL

Limping slightly, Lieutenant Mary Margulies entered the orderly room for the first time in seven months.

"Hey, El-Tee," called Kerry, the 305th Military Police Detachment's first sergeant. "*Good* to see you. You look like you're getting around okay."

Margulies grimaced. "Twinges, that's all," she said, "but the bastard medics put me on a profile anyhow. I'm being transferred out, Top. Stuck behind a desk, I suppose."

She was a stocky woman whose black hair was her only affectation. She'd removed padding from her commo helmet so that she could coil a longer braid when she was on duty. As a platoon leader in a war zone, she had been on duty virtually all the time, awake or sleeping, until a routine convoy escort went sour.

"Ah . . ." said Kerry. "You suppose? You got a copy of the actual orders, didn't you?"

"Oh, I got them all right," Margulies said with a wan smile. "Long enough to see I was being transferred back to Camp Able. Then I threw the chip and reader right through the window. *I* don't belong on Nieuw Friesland. Curst if I don't think I'll put in my resignation if that's what they want from me."

She nodded toward the detachment commander's door. "The Old Man in?"

"Ah . . ." Sergeant Kerry said. "No, Major Yates had an Orders Group at Tannahill Command this morning. Ah . . ."

Margulies smiled harshly. "Go on, Top, say it if that's what you're thinking. A crip like me shouldn't be in the field where she could get good people killed because she's hobbling around."

"No *sir*," Sergeant Kerry said. "*Hell* no, sir. What I meant — and I know that nobody but the recipient reads assignment orders until the recipient's signed off on them —"

Margulies laughed, this time with genuine good humor. "Top, you've got seventeen years in the FDF and the Slammers before them. Let's take it as read that you knew my orders before I did, all right?"

Kerry grinned. "For the sake of argument . . ." he said.

His fingers touched keys on his desk; the integral printer hummed. "I guess there's no harm in me giving you a hardcopy replacement of the assignment orders you lost, is there?" he said.

A flimsy spooled out of the printer slot. Kerry tore off the document and handed it to the lieutenant without looking at the contents. "I think you'll find," he continued, "that Camp Able on Nieuw Friesland is just a transit stop, where you'll join your new unit. You've been assigned as security to a survey team, El-Tee. You're not supposed to be in combat; but if things were peaceful, a survey team wouldn't be there trolling for business."

"Well I'll be hanged," Margulies said, reading the data through for the first time. "I was so scared they were going to stick me at a desk that I . . ."

Kerry affectionately scratched the corner molding of his desk as though the piece of furniture were a living creature. "Different strokes, El-Tee," he murmured. "Personally, I don't find I miss getting shot at in the least."

"Well, I'll *be* hanged," Margulies repeated with changed emphasis. "Do you know where this survey team —"

She blinked. "Oh," she said. "Oh, sure you know where we're going."

"Cantilucca," Kerry said, returning the smile. "I looked it up. West Bumfuck is more like."

His lips pursed in sudden concern. His fingers started to summon Margulies' personnel data, then realized doing so now couldn't help the situation. "Ah — don't tell me you come from Cantilucca, El-Tee?" he added.

"Not me," said Margulies with a broad grin. "But I know somebody who does. . . ."

Earlier: TANNAHILL

"Sarge . . ." Lieutenant Mary Margulies said as Angel Tijuca slid their two-seat air-cushion jeep between a pair of road trains. The huge vehicles had accelerated slowly, but they were maintaining 50 kph now and there was just enough clearance to spare the jeep's paint. "If you don't take it easy, you're not going to survive the last three days of your enlistment."

Margulies didn't sound concerned. Her eyes continued to search the roadsides instead of glaring at her driver.

Angel laughed infectiously. "Now, Missie Mary," he said. "Don't get your bowels in an uproar. And anyway, it's not three days, it's two and a wake-up."

In public Sergeant Tijuca was never less than deferential to his superior officer, but he and Margulies had gone through a lot in the year he'd been driving her. Angel was ending his enlistment in the Frisian Defense Forces, and Margulies was curst sorry to see him go.

"Only if you survive," Margulies remarked, but she wasn't serious. Angel's willingness to take chances was just as important a reason for her keeping him as her permanent driver as his skill at the joystick was.

Angel accelerated to 60 kph. The jeep passed along the right side of the road trains at an increment that was slightly faster than a man could walk.

The convoy consisted of ten articulated road trains, each of which had three track-laying segments with a driver in the lead cab. There was a gun tub crewed by Brigantian troops on the center segment of each individual train, but the convoy's real security was provided by the four combat cars manned by Frisian military police under Lieutenant Margulies' command.

The war was over, but the fighting might not stop for years. Brigantian regiments, spearheaded by armored companies of Frisian mercenaries, had swept across Tannahill's Beta Continent. The armies of the continent's local population, mostly Muslims of South Indian descent, had been smashed if they stood and run down if they retreated.

The guerrillas, supported by the local communities even when they weren't actually members of those communities, were a more difficult problem. They were controllable, at least for as long as the Brigantians of Alpha Continent could afford to pay their Frisian mercenaries, but Margulies suspected it would be decades if not generations before the locals accepted Brigantian domination.

That was somebody else's worry. Margulies had a convoy to take through 80 klicks of — literally — Indian Country.

"Yes *sir*," Angel said. "Inside a week and a half, I figure, I'll be back on Cantilucca with a forty-hectare gage farm of my own. Three more days here. Three days objective to Delos, that's the cluster's port of entry. Maybe a day to get transport from there to Cantilucca, another day's transit, and bam! I'm home, with a discharge bonus in my pocket. How long can it take then to buy some land, hey?"

Tijuca began to whistle a flamenco tune. Margulies smiled at his enthusiasm. She noticed that despite the sergeant's air of heedless relaxation, every time they overhauled a road train his eyes flicked left. He was checking through the gaps between vehicles to see what was happening along the far treeline.

Combat engineers had defoliated, then burned off, strips a hundred meters wide along either edge of the road. Ash flew out from beneath the jeep's skirts. It merged with the yellow dust which the trains' cleats raised from the gravel road surface. The breeze was slightly from the right, so for the moment the jeep was clear. Tijuca kept them ten meters out in the burned zone — comfortable, but by that amount the closest vehicle to the enemy if the guerrillas decided to start something.

"Take us back across between the second and first trucks," Margulies said. "I don't believe in giving anybody long enough to compute the lead on a full-deflection shot."

"Your wish is my command," Angel said. He goosed the fans, let the jeep settle into its new, higher speed, and angled the vehicle sideways across the line of heavy trucks. It was an expert job, as difficult as threading a needle blindfolded.

"My command is your command," Margulies grumbled. Her commo helmet slapped nose filters in place automatically, but she tasted the chalky dust on her tongue.

She wished that a battery of Frisian howitzers rather than Brigantian artillery was providing call fire for the run. Brigantian artillery was reasonably accurate, but Margulies didn't trust the indigs to react as fast as Frisian hogs would if anything blew.

The chance of an ambush was less than one in ten, but Margulies' platoon had provided security on this run fourteen times already.

"You ought to come to Cantilucca, Missie," Angel said, throttling back to 60 kph. "You'd love it. With a tract of top gage land —"

"Sarge," Margulies said, "I'm a city girl, born right smack in the center of Batavia. I wouldn't know which end of a hoe to use, and I don't even *like* gage. Alcohol works just fine for me."

When they crossed the road, Margulies hunched higher in the seat to view the left treeline over her driver's head. Angel watched the potential danger area also, navigating with his peripheral vision. A sub-machine gun was clamped beside his seat. Though it was ready for use, it didn't interfere with his driving the way a slung weapon would have done.

"Huh!" Angel said. "The only thing you can get from booze that you can't from gage is a hangover. The good stuff — the pure stuff, we're not talking about refinery tailings, sure — there's no side effects at all. You just go to sleep when you come down. Why would anybody want booze over gage?"

"Because if something pops, I can deal with it if I'm hung over and I can't if I'm in a gage coma," Margulies said tartly. That was true enough, but it wasn't the reason she relaxed with alcohol instead of stim cones of gage. It was all a matter of what you got used to —

Like everything else across the board. There was no question that a city was the most dangerous combat environment you could find: stone and concrete ate troops. Nonetheless, Margulies was always more comfortable patrolling or even fighting in a city than she was in the open air like this.

Not that it mattered. She was here to do a job.

This portion of the route was through lowlands. The soil was mucky, and there were frequent potholes where the treads of road trains had chewed through the gravel. The trees outside the cleared strip were five to ten meters tall. Their foliage was vaguely blue.

Margulies' four combat cars flanked the convoy front and rear, fifty meters out from the road. Because of the size of the road trains, the convoy was more than half a kilometer long even when closed up properly. The tribarrels of the combat cars could still sweep the full length of it on straight stretches.

They were coming to one of the route's few major curves, nicknamed Ambush Junction until the guerrillas hit what turned out to be a platoon of Frisian tanks instead of the Brigantian armor they'd expected. The route had been quiet as a grave since then.

Margulies keyed her commo helmet. "White Six to Rose One," she said, calling the driver of the leading road train. She glanced up at the cab looming beside her. Because of the angle, she couldn't see the Brigantian to whom she was speaking. "Can you crank up the speed a little? This isn't a place I want to hang around. Over."

A wash of hollow noise flooded Margulies' helmet, racket echoing from within the driver's compartment. The cab was lightly armored but not sound-proofed. A moment later the Brigantian said, *"All right, we'll see, but I don't want to put this sucker in the bog either."*

The background noise shut off. It was as effective a close-transmission signal as more standard commo procedures would have been. Presumably the Brigantian notched his hand throttle forward, though change came very slowly for mechanical dinosaurs the size of the road trains.

The leading combat cars pulled farther ahead and swung a little closer to their respective sides of the cleared strip. Margulies hadn't bothered to give her own people orders. They knew what the situation was and had been dealing with it for the better part of a month now.

There was new growth where Frisian tanks had blasted hundred-meter notches through the vegetation with their main guns. The flushes of new leaves were red and violet.

There wasn't enough silica in the soil to glaze when struck by powerguns, but steam from the high water content exploded main-gun impacts into craters that could swallow the jeep. During the ambush, one of the panzers had swept out into the forest, deliberating scraping its steel skirts across the dirt to uncover the guerrillas' spider holes. The arcing scar was still barren save for speckles of low growth.

Angel hung off the left front fender of the leading road train as the convoy squealed and rumbled into the long right-hand curve. He glanced at Margulies to remind her that this wasn't the position *he* would choose for a plastic-bodied jeep, though whatever the Lieutenant wanted . . .

"Yeah, ease back, let them pass us, and we'll cross to the right side between the second and third trucks," Margulies agreed. She was holding her 2-cm shoulder weapon at high port. Now her index finger pushed the lever at the front of the trigger guard forward, off safe.

She had a bad feeling about this spot. That was nothing new. She'd had a bad feeling about it every bloody time she crossed it.

Angel eased the fan nacelles closer to vertical, raising clearance beneath the skirt to slow the jeep as ordered. He kept the power up. The wasted charge was a cheap price to pay for greater agility in a crisis. Margulies rose in her seat to get a better view back along the convoy.

The lead road train's quad automatic cannon was swung to starboard, aiming at the inside of the curve. That was fine, but the crew of the second vehicle was doing the same cursed thing instead of covering the left side of the route as each alternate crew should do.

Margulies swore and took her left hand from the powergun's forestock to key her helmet — as a command-detonated mine went off under the third segment of the leading road train.

The charge buried beneath the gravel was huge, at least fifty kilos of high explosive. It lifted the segment, blew the track plates and several road wheels from the suspension, and dropped the 30-tonne mass on its right side.

The blast stunned the gun crew atop the middle segment and flung several of them out of the tub. The jeep flipped like a tiddlywink.

Margulies didn't hear the explosion. The shockwave gripped like a fevered giant's hand, crushing her in conditions of intense heat. She couldn't see anything but white light. Both her shins broke against the dashboard as she and the jeep spun in different trajectories. There was no present pain, but she heard the bones go with tiny clicks like those of fingers on a data-entry keyboard.

Margulies' world reformed as she lay prone on soggy ground. She wasn't sure whether or not she'd been unconscious. Her skin crawled, and all her senses were preternaturally sharp.

Twenty meters away the leading road train was skewed across the gravel. The rear segment lay on its side, but the coupling still held. The segment had acted as an anchor, bringing the huge vehicle to a dead halt. The cab door was open. A splotch of blue uniform marked the driver huddling in the ditch beside his abandoned charge.

The combat cars maneuvered violently, engaging the weapons shooting at them. Explosive shells raked the road train, igniting the two upright segments. Margulies thought part of the cargo was ammunition. Tracers or rocket exhaust trails fanned from a position at the treeline.

The second road train had tried to pass on the right side of its disabled fellow, but the ground to that side was apparently even softer than that on which Margulies lay. The vehicle sunk in over its running gear, hopelessly mired. The gun crew jumped from the tub and hid between the bogies.

The driver fired a pistol from his cab doorway. Machine gun bullets sparkled on the armor, starred the windscreen opaque, and punched the driver's lungs out through the back of his rib cage.

Margulies had lost her 2-cm powergun and her commo helmet. She didn't wear a pistol because it got in the way in a jeep's tight seating. Anyhow, she couldn't hit anything with a handgun. She wished she had one now. Her legs ached so fiercely that she had to look down to be sure that they hadn't been blown off at the knees.

Angel Tijuca ran toward her. A guerrilla machine gun combed for him, aiming low and making the black soil spurt upward. Angel tumbled, slapping at his pelvis.

Powerguns and automatic cannon fired at the rear of the convoy, out of sight around the curve. Small arms were probably involved also, but the sound was lost in the blasts of the heavier weapons.

Margulies tried to crawl toward the center of the convoy. Ash on the ground made her sneeze violently. The machine gunner shifted his aim toward her. The guerrilla wasn't very good, but it could be only a matter of time before he found the range.

Angel jumped to his feet, scooped Margulies up, and staggered toward the road with her in a packstrap carry. "Fucking ricochet," he said. "Knocked me — *down!*"

Margulies' toes dragged the ground. The pain in her shins was indescribable. Angel's normally olive complexion had paled to a jaundiced yellow, and his skin gleamed with perspiration.

"Not there!" Margulies cried. She wasn't sure if she was speaking audibly. "That truck'll blow any minute now!"

"That's —" her driver gasped "— the next — thing, m-missie."

He tumbled into the mine crater with his burden and released her. The pulverized soil was pillow-soft, but the reek of explosive residues clung to the pit chokingly. The machine gun sent a last spiteful burst of white tracer over the jeep's crew before casting off for other targets.

Angel had lost his helmet and sub-machine gun, but the butt of a pistol projected from the left cargo pocket of his trousers. He drew the weapon as he lurched out of the crater.

Margulies tried to follow her sergeant, using her knees and elbows for purchase on the loose soil. It was

like swimming through molasses. Every pulse tightened a red-hot vise on her lower legs.

Angel ran to the coupling which linked the overturned third segment to the pair whose running gear
was undamaged. The machine gun and the guerrillas'
light cannon traversed toward the motion, but the
Frisian was fairly well covered by the bogies of the
second segment. Cannon shells fanned the flames
already snorting through holes in the cargo box.

The coupling was torqued and immobile. Angel
aimed his pistol at it point-blank, covered his eyes with
his right forearm, and fired. The 1-cm powergun bolt
sprayed blazing steel in all directions.

Angel's battle dress smoldered in a score of places.
He squinted, fired again, and again, and again.

At the fourth bolt, the coupling parted with the
sound of a shattered bell. The overturned segment slid
a meter from the remainder of the burning vehicle.

Margulies knelt at the top of the mine crater and
waved her arms. She knew what Angel intended to do,
knew also that she couldn't stop him as she wished she
could. But if the guerrilla gunners concentrated on *her*,
then there was at least a chance Angel would succeed.

The light cannon shifted aim toward Margulies. It
had a three-round charger, so the tracers snapped out
in trios. They left tight gray helices in the air, like the
tailings of a metal drill.

Angel ran toward the road train's open cab. The
machine gun pursued him, bullets flickering against
the chassis and treads a half step behind. The cargo
boxes breathed blowtorch flames from every shell
hole.

An explosive bullet buried itself in the rim of loose
dirt beneath Margulies and detonated. The shock
threw her back as though she'd been hit by a medicine
ball. She lay at the bottom of the crater, wheezing and
blinking at the sky for a moment before she resumed
crawling upward.

When Margulies regained the crater lip, the only combat car she could see had been hit in the skirts by a shoulder-launched rocket. Air gushing through the jagged hole in the plenum chamber slowed the vehicle's motions to those of a half-crushed cockroach, but the tribarrels were still in action.

The two-segment road train staggered across the cleared ground like a drunken streetwalker. When one bogie or another found a soft spot the gigantic vehicle lurched, but each time inertia dragged it from the potential bog.

Angel was steering toward the guerrillas' automatic cannon.

Three buzzbombs like the one that had disabled the combat car burst on the road train's bow. The shaped-charge warheads went off with hollow *thocks*, like the sound of boards being slapped together. The cannon, the machine gun, and at least a dozen guerrilla riflemen were firing at the vehicle.

Ricochets and explosive shells danced across the cab like a fireworks display. The protective windows were starred white, the armor was holed in a hundred places, and gray smoke or coolant trailed back from the power plant to mix with the flames shooting from the cargo boxes.

The cab door opened fifty meters from the treeline. Angel somersaulted from the vehicle. He splashed into a muddy trench gouged by a main-gun bolt in the earlier ambush. He didn't move. A machine gun had hosed the side of the cab as the Frisian left it.

A guerrilla stood up in plain view to aim her buzzbomb at the road train. Smoke spurted from the back of the launcher as a rocket motor lobbed the missile into a near-side bogie. The warhead's pearly flash enveloped the running gear for an instant. The track broke, shedding links behind it and pulling the vehicle slightly to the left as it continued to trundle onward.

A single cyan bolt winked past the guerrilla's face. She dropped her useless rocket launcher and unslung the automatic rifle from her back. Angel's second pistol shot hit her in the chest. She spun as she fell to the ground.

The road train kept up a walking pace as its battered bow crunched through the stunted trees. A guerrilla leaped desperately for the cab, caught his sandal in metal torn by gunfire, and toppled screaming beneath the second set of bogies. It wouldn't have made much difference if he'd set his feet properly, because an instant later the munitions in the second segment exploded.

The first charge bulged the sides of the cargo box. Margulies ducked in time, before the shock wave compressed the mass of burning propellants and detonated them. A blast hugely greater than that of the guerrilla mine flattened vegetation in a hundred meter radius and sent tonnes of excavated soil skyward on an orange fireball.

The surface waggled, flipping Margulies like a pancake. She hit the ground again and bounced onto her back, stunned but no more severely injured than the mine had left her. Dirt rained down for tens of seconds.

All the shooting from the left side of the roadway ceased. A guerrilla, stark naked and bleeding from nose and ears, ran out of the trees. A tribarrel on the combat car roaring forward from the rear of the convoy cut the man in half.

The Frisian vehicle swung around the bogged second road train, ripping the right treeline with its full firepower. The guerrillas on that side were already disengaging. Hoses of cyan plasma devoured the few snipers trying to provide a rear guard for the main body.

Artillery shells began to land on both treelines. They were late as Margulies had feared, but at least they were accurate.

She saw a Brigantian carbine, dropped or flung on
the ash ten meters from the crater. She crawled toward
the weapon, ignoring the pain in her legs.

Halfway between her and the smoking gap in the
treeline, a man in Frisian khaki rose on one arm and
waved his muddy pistol at Margulies. Her eyes filled
with tears of joy, but she continued to crawl.

NIEUW FRIESLAND

The door opened and a full colonel stepped unexpectedly into the anteroom. Sten Moden rose to his feet and saluted crisply.

"Captain Moden?" the colonel said. "Could I speak with you for a moment?"

Which, when asked down a gradient of three steps in rank, was a rhetorical question if Moden had ever heard one.

"Yes *sir*," Moden said, sounding as alert and ready as he knew how. His tailored dress uniform was brand new; he'd had his hair cut that morning — he'd showered afterward to wash away the clippings; and for the first time in his military career he was wearing all — all but one — of the medal ribbons to which he was entitled.

Not even for this purpose would Sten Moden wear the most recent citation for bravery. That would be too much like drinking the blood of his own troops.

Moden followed the colonel, Dascenzo according to his name tape but not somebody Moden knew or knew of, into a comfortable office. One wall was a holographic seascape. Waves surged from horizon to horizon without a hint of land.

The view could have been from Dascenzo's homeworld. Moden's suspicion was that the view was intended as a soothing backdrop for interviews by an officer with a medical rather than personnel specialty.

Moden wasn't worried about his physical profile. If that was the only determining factor, the Frisian Defense Forces would give him a new assignment with no difficulty. The fact that he was talking to a colonel instead of an enlisted clerk proved what Moden was afraid of: there was a problem with his psychiatric evaluation.

"Please, sit down," Colonel Dascenzo said. He gestured toward a contour-adapting chair. "This isn't anything formal, Captain. I'd just like to chat with you."

The chair into which Moden lowered himself was the only piece of furniture in the office, save for Dascenzo's own console with integral seat. Moden wondered how many sensors were built into the chair or focused on its user from the surrounding walls.

Captain Sten Moden had given the Frisian Defense Forces valued, even heroic, service, so no invasive methods would be used on him. Apart from that, however —

The FDF would recompense its veterans for past service, but the organization had to look to the future as well.

"I've gone over your file, of course, Captain," Dascenzo said. "I must say I'm impressed by it."

Moden decided a slight smile was appropriate. "Thank you, sir," he said. "All I'm looking for now is a chance to continue serving Col-C-President Hammer for the foreseeable future."

"Well, that's what I wanted to check with you about," Dascenzo said. He looked serious, though he wasn't scowling. His expression was probably as calculated as Moden's own. "You do realize that you qualify for a pension at one hundred percent pay?"

"Yes sir," Moden agreed with a measured nod, "and I very much appreciate the honor implicit in that offer. But I'm still able to provide the FDF with useful service, and I'd like to stay on the active list for as long as that's true."

"The extent of your injuries . . ." Dascenzo said, letting his expression darken into a frown. His voice trailed off, forcing the captain to decide what the question really was.

Moden decided to take a chance. He rose slowly to his full enormous height. "Sir," he said as he gripped the arm of the heavy chair with his right hand, "my injuries were extensive. What remains of me, how-ever —"

Moden's biceps muscles flexed, threatening the weave of his uniform jacket. He pulled with the inexorable strength of a chain hoist.

"— is more than you'll find filling most of the slots in the FDF!"

The chair jerked upward with the sound of ripping metal. Only then did Moden realize that he'd been tugging against the conduits serving hard-wired sensors rather than merely gravity.

"Sorry, sir," he said ruefully, looking at the wreckage of a piece of very expensive equipment in his hand. He'd made the point he was trying to make. If he'd blown his psych profile off the map, then as well hung for a sheep as a lamb. "But strong and stupid has a place in an army too."

"Bloody *hell*, man," Colonel Dascenzo murmured. "Look, put that thing down before you drop it on your foot and do yourself some real damage."

His expression softened as Moden obeyed him. The chair balanced awkwardly on the ends of tubes which had stretched and twisted before they broke. "You really do want to stay in the service, don't you?" Dascenzo said softly.

"Yes sir," Moden said, standing formally at-ease. "I really do."

"There's a team being formed to survey a planet called Cantilucca," Dascenzo said. "They'll need an officer with a logistics background. Do you want the slot?"

"Yes sir," Moden said. "I'd like that very much." He heard his voice tremble with the relief he felt.

"You've got it," Dascenzo said matter-of-factly. He touched the keyboard of his console. "Assignment orders will be waiting for you in your quarters."

The colonel threw another switch, then looked up at Moden again. "Captain," he said, "you don't have to believe me, but I just turned off all the recording devices. Would you answer me a question, just for my personal interest?"

"Yes sir," Moden said. He flexed his right hand behind his back. Now that it was over, he too was surprised at the amount of force his body had been able to deliver to the task he had set it.

"*Why* do you want to stay in uniform so badly?" Dascenzo asked.

Moden smiled, amused at himself. "Because I screwed up," he said. "I therefore owe a debt. For a while I thought I should kill myself — I suppose you know that?"

Dascenzo nodded, tapping the data-gorged console without taking his eyes off Moden's.

Moden nodded also. "I decided that wouldn't pay anybody back," he continued. "I don't know *who* I owe, you see, but that wouldn't help anybody. I — I *believe* that if I'm given duties to perform, then someday I'll be able to . . . balance the account." He barked a humorless laugh. "Does that make me crazy, Colonel?" he asked.

"Captain Moden," Dascenzo said, "'crazy' isn't a term I like to use when discussing professional soldiers. What I do know, however, is that if all you want is a chance to do your duty — I'd be a traitor to Nieuw Friesland if I took you out of her service. You're dismissed, Captain."

Dascenzo rose and extended his right hand across the desk to shake Moden's hand. The psychiatrist was smiling sadly.

Earlier: TRINITY

The sound dived into the night of his mind, twisting deeper like a toothed whale hunting squid in the darkness a thousand fathoms down. It found him, gripped him, and tore him back to surface consciousness from the black gage coma in which he slept.

He didn't know his name. He didn't know where he was. But the whine of the base unit to which he'd plugged his commo helmet was the call of duty, and not even the half dozen stim cones of the past evening could deny his duty.

He stabbed the speaker button, cueing the unit to continuous operation. "Go ahead," he croaked.

He couldn't see anything. Existence was a white throb shattered by jagged bands of darkness.

"Cap'n, it's Filkerson," a man said, his voice pitched high and staccato. "That load of local-manufacture pyrotechnics that arrived today, I can *hear* the crates, they're *chirping*, and I don't like it a bit!"

Shards of light spun. They reformed suddenly into present surroundings and the past life leading up to them:

He was Captain Sten Moden, Base Supply Officer serving the regimental field force of Frisian troops on Trinity. He was in semi-detached quarters, three rooms and a bath connected by a dogtrot to the Base Intelligence Officer's suite.

The earthen berm surrounding Trinity Base's ammo dump was 400 meters to the west of the officers' lines. Filkerson was sergeant of the dump's guard detachment tonight, which meant this was a *real* problem.

"Right," Moden said. "Alert the emergency team. Start dousing the crates *now*, don't take any chances. Are they in a bunker?"

Spasms wracked his muscles, but the aftereffects of the gage would pass shortly. It was like being dropped into ice water while soundly asleep. Why in *hell* did a crisis have to blow up the one night out of a hundred that he overdid it on stim cones?

"Blow up" wasn't the most fortunate thought just now.

"No sir, there wasn't time!" Filkerson said with an accusatory tone in his voice. "This is the batch that came in after hours, and you told us to accept it anyway!"

"I know what I did," Moden said flatly. He'd donned his trousers and tunic while talking. Now he pulled on his boots and sealed their seams. He didn't bother with the strap-and-buckle failsafe closure. "Handle your end, Sergeant. I'll be with you as soon as I make a call. Out."

He broke the contact by lifting his commo helmet from the base unit. He settled the helmet on his head with one hand as he switched the base to local and keyed a pre-set.

As he waited for the connection, Moden shook himself to rid his muscles of the last of the gage tremors. He was coldly furious, with Loie Leonard and more particularly with himself because of what he'd let Loie talk him into doing.

"Yes, what is it?" a woman said. She sounded irritated — as anybody would be, awakened two hours before dawn — but also guarded, because very few people had this number.

"Loie," Moden said, "it's Sten. I need you here at the base soonest with manufacturing records for everything in that load of flares and marking grenades you just sent us. There's a problem, and part of it's your problem."

He squeezed the desk support hard so that the rage wouldn't come out in his voice. Tendons rippled over the bones of his hands. Moden was a big man, so tall that almost anybody else would have claimed the finger's breadth he lacked of two meters. He had difficulty finding boots to fit him, though now that he was in logistics, it was a lot easier than it had been with a line command.

"Sten, I'm at home in bed," Loie said in irritation. "I don't have any records here, and I don't see what there is that couldn't wait for dayli—"

"Soonest, Loie!" Moden said. "Soonest, and I mean it!"

He switched off the base unit so violently that the stand overset. He ignored the mess and started for the door.

Sten Moden had held his present position for thirteen standard months. Most of the field force's munitions were shipped from Nieuw Friesland. The expense was considerable, but powergun ammunition and self-guided shells for the regiment's rocket howitzers had to be manufactured to the closest tolerances if they were to function properly.

Supplies of other material were available cheaper and at satisfactory quality on Trinity. Because the local government had hired the Frisians at a monthly flat rate, cost cutting had a direct, one-to-one effect on President Hammer's profit margin. Sten Moden was responsible for procuring food, bedding, soft-skinned vehicles, and hundreds of other items on the local economy.

Trip flares and smoke grenades were high usage items for the field force. Forges de Milhaud had underbid other suppliers on the past three contracts. In the course of his duties, Moden had gotten to know Loie Leonard, the woman who owned the company.

Know her very well.

Moden didn't have a vehicle at his quarters, and he

didn't want to waste time summoning one from the motor pool. He began to jog toward the munitions dump, letting his long arms flap instead of pumping them as he ran. The floodlights illuminating the four-meter high berm emphasized the yellow-green cast of the local soil.

This afternoon Forges de Milhaud had delivered a load of pyrotechnics after working hours. Indig labor crews had to be off-post at sundown, so deliveries couldn't be properly sorted and inspected for quality.

According to standard operating procedure, Moden should have refused to accept the load until the next working day when it could be processed properly. This was an 8th Night, so delivery would take place after the weekend.

In normal circumstances, Moden might or might not have followed SOP. He didn't like red tape, but it was a fact of life in any complex organization. The field force had a twelve-day supply of flares and grenades on hand, so there was no duty-related reason for the supply officer to cut corners.

But Loie called him, explaining that she needed acceptance *now* in order to meet her payroll. Moden had called Filkerson, telling him to let the drivers dump their cargo where it could be sorted in the morning of 1st Night.

And Moden had visited Loie at a hotel near the Forges offices. Later she went home to her family, and Captain Sten Moden, exalted by gage, returned to Trinity Base.

"*Sir! Sir!*" Filkerson screeched over the helmet earphones. "*We've got a fire, a real fire, in the center of the pile. We can't get to it with the hoses!*"

Moden broke into a full run. He switched his helmet to override the carriers of all his subordinates. "Supply Six to all personnel in the dump area. Get outside the berm now! Run for it! There's nothing inside the berm that's worth your life!"

He wasn't sure whether the emergency team was on the same channel or not. He hoped so, or at least that they'd have sense enough to follow the dump staff when the latter started running for the entrance.

Still running, Moden keyed his helmet to a general Trinity Base push. "Supply Six to Base Operations!" he said. He was gasping with fear and exertion. "General alarm! We have an emergency situation at the ammo dump. If it blows, debris may injure personnel anywhere in the compound and start fires! Over!"

Moden was twenty meters from the separate outwork shielding the entrance to the dump. A burp of orange flame flashed momentarily above the berm. The ground shuddered, and Filkerson screamed over the unit channel.

A firetruck on a hovercraft chassis howled through the dump entrance, slid up on the outwork as it made the necessary 90° turn, and accelerated down the branch through which Moden was entering the dump.

Moden leaped sideways to save himself. The panicked driver hadn't noticed him. Four firefighters with airpacks and flame-resistant garments, and three of Moden's khaki-clad guard detachment, clung to siderails of the speeding vehicle.

The siren on the headquarters building began to wail. The floodlights around the dump flickered.

There was another explosion, much brighter and louder than the first. Shells and rocket motors emerged in sparkling parabolas from the fireball, screaming like banshees. The ground shock staggered Moden, though the berm protected him from whizzing fragments like those that sprayed overhead.

The entrance gate, cyclone fencing on a tubular framework, was torn askew. Two khaki figures ran out as Moden entered. The troopers clung to one another, though neither man appeared to be injured.

Moden grabbed them both in his huge arms. "Where's Sergeant Filkerson?" he demanded.

"Via, he's back there!" one of the troopers screamed. "The shack came down on him and we couldn't get him out!"

Moden flung the pair out toward safety. He'd thought of ordering them to help him, but they didn't look to be in shape to do that or anything else just now.

The guard shack had been to the immediate right of the dump entrance. It was constructed of dirt, stabilized with a plasticizer and compacted.

The locally made pyrotechnics had been off-loaded adjacent to the shack, as good a place as any since they couldn't be processed at the moment. When the pile exploded, the shock wave shattered the near wall of the building and collapsed the rest onto Filkerson, inside using the radio. It was hard to believe that anybody beneath the heavy slabs could be alive, but Filkerson's voice still moaned through the commo helmet. The sergeant had been — in a manner of speaking — lucky.

The floodlights went out. The dump glowed red in a dozen locations, bunkers where further material had been ignited by the previous blasts. Moden thumbed his helmet visor to light-amplification mode and began shifting the ruin of the guard shack, chunk by chunk.

The choice was speed or caution, and under the present conditions speed won going away. Moving the mass of shattered walls was much like playing pick-up-sticks. There was always a chance that when Moden's huge muscles bunched to hurl a block clear, the remaining slabs would shift and crush Filkerson like a caterpillar on the highway; but if Moden waited for specialized rescue equipment, blast shocks were going to make the pile settle anyway.

Besides, there was nothing else Sten Moden could do except watch helplessly the destruction caused by his failure to do his duty.

The edges of the crumbled guard shack were jagged rather than sharp. Moden should have been wearing gloves for the job. The pain didn't bother him, but the film of blood was slippery until it dried to tackiness.

Moden grasped a shard, found it set firmly, and stepped to the side to take instead the 80-kilo block that held the previous one in place. He lifted and threw the block aside. Filkerson's head and torso were beneath. The man moaned softly.

A bunker on the other side of the dump erupted in orange flame. The initial open-air blast had shifted the armored doors of some bunkers. With the volume of sparks and larger chunks of burning debris, it was inevitable that the fire would spread.

The Lord only knew how it had started. Perhaps a fuze had been defective, perhaps a ruptured membrane had brought two reactive compounds in contact. Perhaps there'd been no manufacturing flaw whatever, but one of the crates had been crushed with disastrous results when the load was dumped unceremoniously.

If lightning had struck the pyrotechnics, it would still have been Sten Moden's fault. The only reason the load was in the dump this night was that he had accepted it improperly.

Moden gripped the slab lying on Filkerson's legs, so that the whole weight wouldn't shear down on flesh like the blade of a roller mill. "It's okay, Sergeant," he murmured.

Only when Moden spoke did he realize how loud the background rumble was. The ground trembled at a low frequency that tried to loosen his bowels.

Filkerson's eyes opened. "Via, Cap'n," he said. "Get me out of here, right?"

He was still speaking on the unit push. Despite the radio augmentation, Moden understood the words only because he watched Filkerson's lips form them.

Another bunker blew up, belching the roof of steel planks and tonnes of dirt overburden. Moden staggered forward. He turned and lifted Filkerson onto his back. His left hand cushioned the man's buttocks while his right gripped Filkerson's arms, flopped over Moden's shoulders and across his chest.

Moden stepped carefully through the tumble of slabs and started for the nearby gate at a trot.

A bunker in the center of the dump detonated. The shock wave set off three more bunkers simultaneously. The cataclysmic blast hurled the two men over the four-meter high outwork protecting the entrance.

The sleet of debris riding the wave front chewed off Sten Moden's left arm, but Filkerson's body saved the captain's torso.

NIEUW FRIESLAND

Tech II Niko Daun was one of the tough jobs for the Enlisted Assignments Bureau. He'd rejected his automatic assignment, and the first live clerk he'd seen hadn't been able to help either.

That put Daun across the desk from Warrant Leader Avenial, the section head. Daun's quick gaze danced out through the clear wall at the open bullpen where most of the section's requests were processed, then back to Avenial. The technician looked nervous and very, very determined.

Avenial smiled. "Don't worry, Daun," he said. "If you get as far as me, the problem gets fixed. That's as true as if the Lord carved it on stone."

And it was. Not every disgruntled trooper got to the section head, but it was Avenial's truthful boast that he *never*, in seven years in the post, had needed to pass an applicant up the line to the Brigadier in charge of the Bureau.

Personnel files carried two kinds of carets marking a trooper for special treatment by Assignments. A white caret meant the trooper either had a valuable specialty or that the trooper had been noted as particularly valuable because of his or her behavior as a member of the Frisian Defense Forces.

A red caret indicated a trooper who'd had a service-incurred rough time, so Assignments was to cut an appropriate amount of slack. Treating veterans well is a matter of good business for a military force and the state which employs the force, though Avenial wouldn't have cared to be the person who stated publicly that Colonel — President — Hammer had no interest in the subject beyond good business.

Daun's personnel file bore both white and red carets.

The technician's complexion was dark — darker than Avenial's, though Mediterranean rather than African stock seemed to have predominated in his ancestry. He was short and slight, but the psych profile didn't indicate a dose of the Little Guy Syndrome that had made many of Avenial's assignment tasks harder than they needed to be. Most of that sort of fellow migrated to combat arms anyway, where they either learned to control the chip on their shoulder —

Or lost chip, shoulder, and life. Hopefully before they had time to screw things up too bad.

"I told the lady out front," Daun said, nodding toward the bullpen. "I won't serve with, with indigs. If that means changing my specialty, then all right. I don't care about rank, you can *have* that."

Avenial nodded. His eyes were on the screen canted slightly toward him from an open surface of the otherwise cluttered top of his desk. He wasn't reading the data displayed there, just using it as an excuse to be noncommittal for a moment.

The clerk who'd dealt with Daun — hadn't dealt with Daun — was new to the section. She might work out, but Avenial hadn't been impressed so far. The particular problem would have been a stretch for any of his underlings, however.

"Well, I don't think we want you to change your specialty, Daun," Avenial said mildly. "We need sensor techs, and it looks like you're about as good as they come. In line for a third stripe, I see."

He crooked a grin at the applicant. As an attempt to build rapport through flattery, it was a bust.

"I told you, I don't *care* about rank!" Daun said. "I'll resign before I serve with indigs. I'll resign!"

"Well, we don't want you to resign," Avenial said. "So we're going to fix things, like I said."

He gave Daun another kind of look — hard, professional, appraising. "You say you won't serve with indigs," Avenial said. "What other assignment requirements do you have?"

"None," Daun said, meeting the section head's eyes. "None at all."

Avenial smiled again. "Fine," he said. "That tells me what I've got to work with. Plenty for the purpose, plenty."

He touched his keypad, changing screens in sequence after only a second or two of scanning the contents of each.

"The lady said she could *assign* me to a Frisian unit," Daun explained, "but once I was out in the field, the needs of the service prevail. If the — the unit commander decided I was the only one who could do a job, it didn't matter what I thought about it. And in my specialty, they might well put me in a sector staffed by indigs who couldn't handle the hardware themselves."

"She told you the truth," Avenial agreed approvingly.

Enlisted people expected to be crapped on and lied to. It seemed to Avenial that some of them almost begged for it. It went with the image. He'd had troopers make false statements about a pending assignment, statements they *must* have known were false, in the obvious hope that by saying nothing Avenial would give their lie validity.

Avenial didn't do that, and nobody in Avenial's section did it more than once that Avenial heard about. He was funny that way; but then, he slept at night without knocking himself into a coma on booze or gage. Life has a lot of trade-offs.

Avenial's finger paused on the next screen key. "Umm," he said. He looked up at Daun. "What do you know about survey teams, kid?" he asked.

"I can learn," Daun said crisply. His expression changed slightly. "So it'll be out of sensors after all?"

"Hell, no, they need sensor techs," Avenial replied.

"Now, mind, everybody on a survey team better be able to do more than their base specialty. How's your marksmanship?"

Daun shrugged, smiled — a little wryly. "I've been practicing since my last assignment on Maedchen. Not great, but I'm getting better."

The lines of Daun's face flowed naturally into smiles, but this was the first time his nervousness had permitted one. He hadn't believed Avenial when he said that it was going to be all right. Well, they'd been lied to and lied to, why should they expect this warrant leader to be different?

"You see, kid," Avenial explained, "your specialty's too valuable for me to, say, reclassify you as a cook. Besides, if you're that good at running sensors —"

Daun smiled again. He'd loosened up, sure enough.

"— then it's what you like to do, so why should we fuck with it? Right?"

"No argument, mister," Daun said.

"So the trick's to put you somewhere that you're under Frisian command at all times," Avenial continued. "That's a survey team. Until the survey team makes its assessment, there's no indig employers *to* report to. Even if your unit commander's an asshole, he can't out-place you. You see?"

Daun nodded enthusiastic agreement.

"Now, the catch is," Avenial said, "you're out with —"

His eyes scanned for a figure on the screen.

"— five other guys, FDF troops. That's not like being in the middle of an armored battalion. There's not supposed to be any shooting going on, shooting at you, I mean. But I can't tell you it's safe."

He raised an eyebrow at the technician.

Daun shook his head and smiled. "Mister Avenial," he said, "I'm not . . ."

His hands flipped palms-up, then down again, in a *Macht's nichts* gesture.

"I could have gotten a job with a communications firm, I could have found something safe," he said. "I wanted the, you know, the travel."

Daun meant *danger*, but he was ashamed to say it. Smart enough to be ashamed that he was a young man who wanted to be able to say he'd been *there*, the place civilians hadn't been. Ashamed to be proud of being what he was, a member of the finest military force in the human universe.

But proud nonetheless, as surely as Jumbo Avenial was.

Daun swallowed. "I'm not afraid," he concluded. "But I won't be any place that I have to depend on indigs."

Avenial nodded. "Just wanted to be clear about the situation," he said.

His lips pursed, then grinned like those of a frog swallowing the biggest fly of its life. "There's one problem remaining," he said. "The slot in a six-man survey team is for a Tech Four. You're only a Two."

Daun looked stricken. "What does that —" he began.

His mind paused in mid-thought, then resumed smoothly like a transmission shifted from the lay-shaft to a front gear with only the least clicking of teeth. "If there were a way you could arrange for me to get the assignment on a provisional basis, mister, I would be personally grateful to you. I've got more saved up than you might think because there was no way to spend it —"

Avenial, still grinning, waved Daun to silence. There were times he'd been insulted by an attempt to bribe him, but this wasn't one of them.

"What I thought," Avenial said, "was that we'd just get you the extra stripes. Stripe, really. Like I said before, you're due for your third already."

"I —" Daun said. "I . . ."

He sat up very straight in his seat. "Mister Avenial,"

he said, "you don't need my money, I understand that. But some day you may need something from me. Let me know."

"Just doing my job, kid," Avenial said.

But someday it *might* be good to know a guy who could make walls talk and knew what anybody he pleased was saying, right up to the President . . . Yeah, that just might be.

Daun rose to his feet. "I'll wait for my assignment, Mister," he said. "Ah — do you have any notion when it might come through?"

Avenial touched another button. "It just did, kid," he said. "You're bound for a place named Cantilucca."

Earlier: MAEDCHEN

As Technician Niko Daun dealt the last cards, Bondo, one of the two Central States soldiers in the game, grumbled, "If I get a decent hand this time, it'll be the first tonight."

A dripping soldier entered the 20-man tent that served as living quarters for the battalion's technical detachment. His boots slipped in purple mud as he tried to seal the tent flap. He thumped the ground, cursing in a monotonous voice.

"You're only a rubber down," objected Sergeant Anya Wisloski, Daun's Frisian Defense Forces superior, partner, and — for the three months they'd been on outpost duty — lover.

"Yeah, but that's on Hendries' cards, not me," Bondo said. "I want some cards of my own."

Daun picked up his own bridge hand. Based on what the dealer had, everybody else in the game was looking at great cards.

"What *I* want," said Anya, "is some decent weather. I haven't seen the sun since we've been up here."

Anya was short, dark-haired and white-skinned. Her waist nipped in and her chest was broad, but the breasts themselves were flat. She was several years older than Daun's 21 standard — how much older she'd avoided saying — and had gone straight into the Frisian Defense Forces while Daun had four years of technical school.

Daun trusted his own judgment inside a piece of electronics farther than he did Anya's (or most anybody else's, if it came to that). There was never any question about who was in charge of a group when Anya decided to *take* charge, however.

Another gust pelted the tent as a colophon to Anya's statement. For the most part, today's rain had been a drizzle, but occasionally big drops splattered to remind the battalion outpost that there were various forms of misery.

Support Base Bulwark was almost as isolated as a space station would have been. Weekly convoys brought food, replacements, and very occasionally a team of journalists from one of the major cities.

The journalists never stayed long. Sometimes the replacements didn't either. Troops who shot themselves in the foot or, less frequently, in the head, during their first week at Bulwark were a significant cause of attrition.

The base was sited on a low plateau, chosen for its accessibility by road rather than for purposes of defense. Higher peaks surrounded it within a five-klick radius.

The sensors themselves were expected to alert friendly forces if the Democrats massed in numbers sufficient to threaten the outpost. Daun had his doubts, but he realized the Democrats might be just as sloppy as their Central States opponents.

Heavy construction equipment had encircled the perimeter of the base with an earthen wall. The same construction crews then dug bunkers into the sides of that berm. During the months of constant rain, the bunkers filled as much as a meter deep with water.

The infantry protecting the base lived in tents on the bunker roofs. They had no protection except — for the ambitious ones — a wall of sandbags. The tents weren't dry either, but at least the troops didn't have to swim to their bunks.

Conditions for support personnel within the base weren't a great deal better. Walkways constructed from wooden shell crates led between locations, but for the most part the makeshift duckboards had sunk into the greasy, purplish mire. The Tactical Operations Center was an assemblage of the high officers' four living trailers placed around a large tent.

The whole complex was encircled by a triple row of sandbags and dirt-filled shell boxes. The construction engineers had trenched around the protective wall to draw off water. Because of the lack of slope the would-be channel was a moat, but at least it prevented the TOC from flooding.

The 150-mm howitzers of the four-tube battery were on steel planking to keep them from sinking to the trunnions. The guns slid during firing, so it was impossible to place accurate concentrations when the sensors located movement. Because rain and the slick ground made it so difficult to manhandle the 45-kg shells, most firing was done at random when battalion command decided it needed more ammo crates for construction.

The remainder of the support personnel lived in tents and slept on cots. Most of the tents were sandbagged to knee-height, three layers. Higher than that, the single-row walls fell down when the slippery filling bled through the fabric.

The two Frisians' assignment was for six standard months. The indigs were here for a local year — twenty-one months standard, and at least three times longer than Daun could imagine lasting under such conditions.

"Oh, sure, it'll dry out in spring," Bondo said as he scowled at his cards. "Dry out, bake to dust, and blow into every curst thing from your food to the sealed electronics. You think equipment life's bad in this rain, wait until spring."

The purpose of this Central States Army outpost in Maedchen's western tablelands was to service a belt of sensors brought at great expense from Nieuw Friesland. In theory, the sensors and the reaction forces they triggered would prevent infiltration from the Democrat-controlled vestries on the other side of the divide.

Bondo was quite right about the sensor failure rate. The Belt no doubt looked impressive during briefings in the capital, but the reality was as porous as cheesecloth. Infiltrators had an excellent chance of penetrating the eastern vestries unnoticed, and an even better chance of evading the Central States Army's half-hearted reaction patrols.

"One club," Bondo offered.

Daun didn't blame the rain or the quality of the hardware for the rate of sensor failure. Quite simply, personnel assigned by the Central States government weren't up to the job of servicing electronics this sophisticated.

Central States field teams wouldn't follow procedures. For example, they regularly used knives or bayonets to split the sensor frames to exchange data cartridges. The special tools that would perform the task without damage were lost or ignored. They didn't understand their duties. At least a third of the cartridges were inserted upside down, despite the neon arrows on both casing and cartridge, and despite anything Daun could say to the troops he was trying to train.

And they didn't *care*. As often as not, a field team huddled in a sheltered spot within a klick of the base instead of humping through the rain to service the sensors for which they were responsible. In the morning, they returned with the circuit marked complete — and there wasn't a curst thing Daun or Anya could do about it.

"Three no trump," Anya bid. She grinned coldly around the table.

Daun had already drafted an assessment for the Frisian Defense Forces Maedchen Command, back in the capital Jungfrau. In it he stated flatly that the system wasn't working and could never work as presently constituted.

Nieuw Friesland should either withdraw support from the Central States, or the FDF should insist that the Central States hire a detachment of Frisians sufficient to perform all field as well as base servicing tasks. Otherwise, the inevitable failure would be blamed on Frisian technology rather than the ineptness of the Central States Army at using that technology.

Anya wouldn't let Daun transmit the assessment. It wasn't that she disagreed with him — quite the contrary. But she didn't believe anything a Tech II said could change the policy of bureaucrats on Nieuw Friesland . . . and there was a good chance Daun's opinions, once released, were going to become known to the Central States personnel she and Daun shared a tent with.

There are a lot of ways to get hurt in a war zone. Pissing off the heavily-armed people closest to you wasn't a good way to survive to a pension.

But the situation grated on Daun's sense of rightness, as well as making him feel he was a bubble in a very hostile ocean.

"Too rich for my blood," Hendries said. "I pass."

Daun stared at his cards again. They hadn't changed for the better. He had four clubs, three of each other suit, and his high card was the jack of hearts.

He knew his partner was asking where his support was greatest; and he knew also that the proper answer was: nowhere.

"I pass," he said aloud.

Anya grimaced.

"Pass," said Bondo.

Daun laid out his wretched hand. His partner's expression softened as she saw just what Daun had dealt himself. Hendries glared at his cards to determine a lead, a nearly hopeless task under the circumstances.

The tent flap tore open. "Hey!" called the Central States soldier who stuck his head in. "Smart guys! Your fucking pickup's gone down again. The screen in the TOC's nothing but hash!"

"Bloody hell," Anya muttered.

She laid her cards down. "My turn, I guess," she said to Daun. "You were out all morning with the satellite dish."

Daun stood up, waving his partner back. "Look, you were up the mast last night. Besides, I'm dummy. I'll catch this one."

"Hey!" the messenger from the Tactical Operations Center repeated. "Colonel Jeffords isn't real thrilled about this, you know."

That was probably true. The amount paid to Nieuw Friesland by the Central States government for Anya's services was comparable to what the colonel himself earned. Daun's pay was at the scale of a senior captain. The money didn't go into the two technicians' pockets, much of it, and if it had there was still no place to spend money out here on the tableland. It still provided a reason for some of the locals — Jeffords certainly, and apparently this messenger — to get shirty about off-planet smart-asses whose equipment didn't work.

"I'm on the way," Daun said. "Just let me get my gear."

He buckled his equipment belt around his narrow waist, pulled on his poncho, and tried to punch the larger working canopy down into its carrying sheath. He could only get it partway into the container, but that would hold it while he climbed the mast.

The slick fabric still shone with water from when Daun had to use it that morning. It didn't matter — to the job — if he got soaked, but rain dripping into an open box could only make a bad situation worse.

The messenger disappeared. Daun sighed and followed him. "I'll catch the next one, Niko," Anya called as Daun stepped out into the rain.

The flashlight strapped for the moment to Daun's left wrist threw a fan of white light ahead of him. He could switch the beam to deep yellow which wouldn't affect his night vision, but it didn't matter if he became night-blind. He'd need normal light to do his work anyway: many of the components were color-coded. The markings would change hue or vanish if viewed under colored light.

Rain sparkled in the beam. Reflections made it difficult to tell what was mud and what was wet duckboard. The crates were likely to shift queasily underfoot anyway.

Three months more. How the locals stood it was beyond him.

Daun couldn't blame the soldiers he tried to train for being apathetic. It was all very well to tell the troops that their safety depended on them servicing the sensors properly, but a threat to lives so wretched had little incentive value.

Daun and Anya complained, but professionalism and a sense of duty would carry the pair of them through no matter how bad things got. The vast majority of the Central States personnel were conscripts, and the conscripts with the least political influence in Jungfrau besides. Daun was sure that at least eighty percent of the outpost would have deserted by now, if there was any place to which they *could* desert.

Light through the walls of the tent turned the TOC into a vast russet mushroom, though the fabric looked dull brown by daylight. Daun could hear voices, some of them compressed by radio transmission.

It was conceivable that the problem was inside the TOC, either in the console or the connecting cables. Daun was tempted to check out those possibilities first, but he decided not to waste his time. The console was of Frisian manufacture and sealed against meddling by the locals.

The cables had been laid by the previous pair of FDF advisers. They'd done a first-class job; Daun had checked and approved every millimeter of the route the day he and Anya arrived. Unless somebody'd driven a piece of tracked construction equipment through the TOC, the conduits should be fine. The indigs were capable of doing something that bone-headed, but Daun would have heard it happening.

The thirty-meter mast was a triangular construct set in concrete and anchored to the trailer housing the battery commander. The unit telescoped in three sections. Daun could lower the mast to save most of the climb, but re-erecting it would require help to keep the guy wires from fouling. He didn't trust the indigs to do that properly even during daylight.

He squelched to the base of the mast, hooked his safety belts, and began to climb the runglike braces which bound the three verticals together. The mast was formed from plastic extrusions, not metal, but the rungs still felt icy to Daun's bare hands. They were also slick as glass.

The sensor wands' removable recording cartridges provided extremely precise information on all move-ments within the coverage area. If a human passed within two or three meters of the wand, the retrieved cartridge could determine the state of health based on body temperature and pulse rate. Such data were remarkable but useful only as the raw material for a historical overview.

Base Bulwark collected coarse sensor readings in realtime, via coded frequency-hopping radio signals. As the messenger had implied, this was the second miserable night in a row that the ultra-high gain antenna atop the mast had failed.

Last night a matchhead-sized integrated circuit had blown: the sort of thing that happened only occasion-ally with Frisian hardware, but always at a bad time. Anya had unplugged the blown chip and replaced it with a good one.

Anya, simply glad to have the antenna working again, had pitched the bad chip out into mud and darkness. If she'd instead saved the fried unit, Daun would have examined it to determine the cause of failure. Long odds the problem was due to manufacturing error, but there was always a possibility that a short within the box was causing a hot spot.

The chance to diagnose the underlying problem instead of merely fixing the symptom was much of the reason Daun had volunteered to climb the mast. Besides, he liked the hardware part of his work well enough that he preferred to be doing it instead of playing cards with strangers he couldn't respect and didn't much like.

There were guy wires on each of the three sections of the telescoping mast. When he reached each set of guys, Daun unhooked one of his two safety loops, rehooked it above the wires, and repeated the process with the second loop. At no time did he trust merely his boots and grip to keep him on the mast. Daun wasn't so much cautious as perfectly methodical. The notion of cutting corners to lessen his exposure to the chill drizzle didn't cross his mind.

Viewed from the top of the thirty-meter mast, the lights of Bulwark Base had a surreal innocence, like the gleam of will-o'-the-wisps in a nighted meadow. Rain softened the patterns and dusted glare into sparkle. The scene wasn't beautiful but it had a dignified tranquility, far removed from the muddy truth. The glowing canvas of the TOC could be the entrance to the Venusberg, and Daun could imagine that flashlights in the tents on the perimeter were cupids twinkling around the goddess of love.

The receiving antenna at the mast peak was enclosed in a weatherproof capsule about the size of a soccer ball. The covering was dull gray plastic which was reasonably sturdy but remained transparent over most of the electromagnetic spectrum. Wherever possible, the sensor wands transmitted over microwave frequencies, but those without a line of sight to the receiver used VHF or UHF as circumstances required.

Daun arranged the working canopy over the capsule. When he had it stiffened into position, the monomolecular sheeting blocked the rain completely. Before then, however, he managed to pour what felt like a liter of cold water down the back of his neck from the canopy's folds.

He sighed, clipped his light to a strut so that it shone down on the work, and opened the antenna capsule. Two of the micro-miniaturized circuits were black instead of the healthy gold color. That was neither surprising nor a problem. When one chip blew, it could easily have overloaded its neighbor. Daun's repair kit contained at least three replacements for every chip on the chassis.

He opened the cover wider as he prepared to pull the failed chips. An irregularity on the inner face of the cover caught his eye. The plastic had blistered and turned silvery on the side facing the chips that had failed.

The antenna didn't draw enough juice to heat the cover even slightly. A short circuit which blistered the plastic that way would have vaporized the circuitry, chassis and all, instead of popping a chip or two.

The energy that had caused the antenna to fail had come from outside. The most likely outside source was a precisely aimed X-ray laser on one of the enemy-held hilltops overlooking Bulwark Base.

Feeling colder than rain could make him, Daun reached up to key his commo helmet and alert the camp. The shock wave proved he was too late.

The warhead went off with a hollow *Klock!* that blew one of the TOC trailers inside out in a sleet of aluminum. The weapon, a laser-guided anti-tank missile, was configured to defeat heavy armor with a shaped charge. A straight fragmentation or HE warhead would have been better suited for the present task. This was along the lines of killing mosquitoes with an elephant gun.

On the other hand, an elephant gun *will* kill a mosquito. Little survived of the trailer, and nothing of anyone who happened to be in it.

The canopy flapped skyward in the blast. The antennas whipped violently and a guy wire parted, either overstressed or cut by flying shrapnel. Daun hugged the mast with both arms as his feet slipped from the rungs.

Buzzbombs and crew-served automatic weapons raked the bunkers on the north and west perimeter of the base. Tents collapsed or exploded, flinging out the corpses of troops huddled beneath canvas for shelter.

While the antenna was deadlined the previous night, the Democrats had moved an assault force into position in the gullies close to Bulwark Base. Tonight they had taken the antenna out of commission again in order to make their final approach through the rain. The Democrats knew they had nothing to fear from the garrison's patrols or the watchfulness of the troops on duty on the perimeter of the base.

Another terminally guided missile impacted, this time on furniture near the center of the TOC. The tent shredded in a reddish appliqué over the white flash at the core. Bits of missile casing, and fragments of equipment converted into secondary projectiles, riddled the three remaining trailers.

The mast swayed even more violently. Daun lost his grip. He was hanging by his safety belts. The broken guy wire whacked across his helmet and bound his outflung arm to the antenna mast.

Half a second later, a third missile detonated in the Technical Detachment's tent.

For an instant, the flash threw the silhouettes of the dozen startled occupants against the canvas. Then the tent was gone, the flash was a blinding purple afterimage on Daun's retinas, and Sergeant Anya Wisloski shrieked into her commo helmet like a hog being gelded.

Daun's legs flailed as he tried to find the rungs again with his feet. The mast had torqued and bent over so that he hung out in the air. Most of his weight was on his left forearm, bound to the mast. He thought the bones might have broken. The pain was inconceivable.

He didn't scream. His ears still rang with the sound of Anya's cry.

Figures, some of them waving weapons, lurched from tents. The TOC's instrumentation ran off a portable fusion power plant adapted from the drive unit of a Frisian armored vehicle. There was plenty of excess capacity. Most of the living quarters within the berm had electric lights run through a variety of jury-rigged conductors, with telephone line predominating.

The Central States personnel were backlit by their own illumination. Democrat troops had quickly crossed the skimpy wire entanglements by throwing quilted padding over the barbs. They opened fire from the berm, knocking startled defenders down like bowling pins.

Daun managed to grip a rung with his right hand and take some of the weight off his tangled arm. The mast swayed, dipping slightly with each movement. Sooner or later one of the twisted poles would snap and collapse the whole tower. Daun *had* to get free before then.

A ricochet moaned past his face. The bullet sounded lonely, like a dog unjustly kicked. Daun thrashed his lower body and finally hooked his right leg around the tilting mast.

In one of the gun pits nearby, the crew were trying to depress their 150-mm howitzer to fire directly on the attackers. A buzzbomb described a flat arc that climaxed on the gun's recoil compensator. The projectile burst with a white flash and a blast of shrapnel that was invisible except for its effect on the crew.

The gunners spun away and fell. Open powder charges sprayed across the gun pit and ignited in a fierce red flare. The gun captain crawled back toward her position through the flame, dragging loops of intestine. She pulled herself onto the trail and died, reaching vainly for the firing lanyard.

Trip flares attached to the wire on the south side of Bulwark Base began to go off. The sappers leading the Democrat assault had disconnected the flares on their approach routes. Members of the garrison stumbled over their own mines while fleeing into the night.

A truck, one of the few vehicles assigned to the base, drove south out of the engineer compound. Scores of troops clung to the cab and body. Some of them shot wildly.

Democrat riflemen and machine gunners opened fire. Bullets sparked on the frame and slapped troops from the vehicle. The truck continued to accelerate, skidding on the slick surface. Its eight driven wheels cast up a rooster-tail of mud, water, and duckboards.

Two buzzbombs sputtered toward the moving target. One missed high, sailing over the berm to vanish. The other went off close alongside. Would-be escapees tumbled from the bed, but the run-while-flat tires permitted the truck to keep going.

The gate to the road south from Bulwark Base was three X-frames connected by a horizontal pole and strung with barbed wire. A flangelike extension of the berm was intended to force vehicles to slow for a right-angle turn when entering or leaving the base.

The truck hit the gate, crushed it down, and roared over the berm's sloped extension in low gear. A Central States soldier ran along behind the vehicle, trying to climb aboard. He lost his footing on the berm and sprawled.

As the truck disappeared, the soldier rose to one

knee and tried to shoot at the vehicle. Mud clogged his rifle. He flung the useless weapon after the truck. A moment later, a Democrat machine gun nailed him into the berm with a burst of golden tracers.

The leg Daun had flung around the mast cramped because of the awkward angle. That pain was lost in the red throb of blood returning to his left arm now that he didn't dangle by it.

With no tools and one good hand, Daun couldn't unwrap the guy wire that held him. It was spliced into his safety belts and apparently pinched by a fold of the slowly collapsing mast. He'd lost the wrist light when the first missile went off.

He supposed that was a good thing, because otherwise he'd have been a lighted target. He giggled hysterically.

Daun heard a thump over the shooting. He looked down. A dark parcel lay on an expanse of softly reflectant aluminum. Someone had tossed a satchel charge onto the roof of the battery commander's trailer.

Daun clutched the mast with his free arm and tried to find footing for his other leg. He closed his eyes instinctively. Blood vessels in his eyelids reddened the yellow flash that streamed through them.

The blast flattened the trailer and flung Daun upward like a yo-yo shooting the moon. The guy wire broke again, but the safety belts held.

The mast toppled with the grace of a falling tree, slowly at first but accelerating as it neared the ground. Daun was underneath. Remaining guy wires zinged as they parted.

A Democrat parachute flare drifted down through the overcast to illuminate the encampment. The mast rotated as light bloomed. Daun stared down through the latticework at the ruin of Bulwark Base instead of up into the clouds that would otherwise have been the last thing he saw.

A pole in the base section had broken, causing the mast to twist on the remaining verticals before it hit the ground. Daun slammed into the mud, beside rather than beneath the structure to which he was bound.

The impact knocked all the breath out of his body. The antenna capsule snapped off and bounced twice before coming to rest beside the technician. He didn't quite lose consciousness, but the shots and screams around him faded into a thirty-cycle hum for a few seconds.

The rain had almost ceased. The flare sank lower. Vertical objects cast jagged shadows that cut like saw-teeth across the surface of Bulwark Base.

Daun lay with the mast on one side of him and on the other the low sandbag wall that had once protected the Technical Detachment's tent. The missile had destroyed the wall it hit and the structure beyond, but it spared the sandbags on the opposite side.

Someone just across the wall was moaning.

Daun tried to free himself from the tangle in which he lay. His left leg was pinned and his left arm was still tethered to the mast. He could move his head as far as his neck flexed, but he couldn't crane it high enough to see what was holding his limbs.

The bunched jacket held his right arm almost as tightly as his left. There was no possibility of tearing the tough, weatherproof fabric.

Daun heard voices nearby. He opened his mouth to call for help. One of the voices said, "Watch it! This one's alive!"

A machine pistol within the area the Tech Detachment tent had covered fired a short burst downward. The muzzle flashes were red and bright.

Daun wore a pistol as part of his required equipment. It was in a cross-draw holster on his left side, where it was least in the way when he was working. He could no more reach the weapon now than he could fly back to Nieuw Friesland under his own power.

"They were playing cards," said one of the Democrats.

"Hey!" said his partner. "We're just supposed to be taking guns and ammunition."

"So I'm searching their wallets for items of intelligence value," the first Democrat snarled. "If you're smart, you'll keep your fucking mouth shut about it, too."

The sky blazed orange as the light of an explosion reflected from the low clouds. The ground shock lifted Daun, the mast, and the sandbag wall an instant before the airborne shock wave punched across them. The ammo dump had exploded.

Daun hit the ground again. He was still tied to the mast. Sandbags collapsed over him.

Individual shells detonated during the next fifteen seconds, some of them at a considerable distance where the initial explosion hurled them. The first Democrat was cursing. The blast had knocked him skidding in the mud.

"There's one!" cried his partner. Two machine pistols fired together. Daun felt the whack of little bullets against the sandbags over him, but he wasn't the target. The moans of the soldier on the other side of the wall ended in a liquid gurgle.

"Hey, lookit!" shouted the second member of the Democrat clean-up team. He was standing beside Daun, but the Frisian could see only a triangle of cloud through the jumble of collapsed wall. "Look at *this*!"

"Bloody hell!" said the first man. "That's a bloody powergun. The Cents don't have bloody powerguns!"

"*I* do," said his jubilant partner. A bolt of cyan plasma lanced skyward.

"You cursed fool!" the first Democrat said. "Don't do that! Somebody'll shoot us! Besides" — His voice changed slightly into that of a hustler calculating his chances — "it's not worth anything much 'cause we can't get ammo for it. Look, though — just for the hell of it, I'll give you two hundred lira for it. For the curiosity."

"Fuck you," said his partner. "This is *mine*."

The two Democrats stepped onto the bags covering Daun. They hopped from him over the fallen antenna mast.

"Look," the first man was saying, "half of it is mine anyway. . . ."

Daun's lungs burned, but he was afraid to breathe. The detached part of his mind noted that the second Democrat should be very careful about standing with his back to his partner this night. Otherwise he might die for the trophy, as surely as Sergeant Anya Wisloski had died.

LAWLER

The platoon leader's door was open. Trooper Johann Vierziger paused in the day room and raised his knuckles to knock on the jamb.

"Come on in, Vierziger," called Lieutenant Hartlepool in false jollity. "You haven't been with us long enough to know, but we're not much on ceremony in this outfit."

Vierziger had been transferred to the 105th Military Police Detachment on Lawler as soon as he'd completed basic training with the Frisian Defense Forces. He'd arrived a week ago, and had seen action — with the FDF — only once according to his records. That action had occurred the night before.

"Thank you, sir," Vierziger said. He was a short man, dainty except for telltale signs like the thickness of his wrists. Pretty, Hartlepool thought when the fellow was assigned to his platoon, and a nance.

Hartlepool had nothing against queers, not so it got in the way of his duties, but this was ridiculous. The One-Oh-Fifth wasn't some parade-ground unit for show. They, and particularly 1st Platoon, A Company, were in firefights at least once a week.

Hartlepool couldn't imagine who'd thought his platoon was the place to stick an effeminate newbie. He'd liked to have met the bureaucrat in an alley.

"Sit down, sit down," Hartlepool said, gesturing to the seat in front of his desk. Malaveda, who now commanded First Squad, was in the room's third chair, backed against the wall to one side.

Platoon leaders didn't rate a lot of space at the best

of times. Hartlepool had a glorified broom closet, but he knew there were lieutenants in the 105th who *shared* comparable quarters. Accommodations in Belair were tight. Expectation of war brought people to the capital, either for its fancied safety or because they believed there was money to be made.

"Thank you, sir," Vierziger said. His face bore a slight smile, but he obviously didn't intend to volunteer anything unasked. He sat down gracefully without touching the chair with his hands.

Vierziger reminded Hartlepool of somebody, but the lieutenant couldn't place *who*.

"Well, we've got some good news for you, Vierziger," Hartlepool said. The cheerful tone was wearing thin, but he didn't know what other persona to adopt. "To begin with, *Sergeant* Vierziger. On the basis of Sergeant Malaveda's report —"

He nodded to the non-com. Malaveda's forehead glistened with sweat. He stared at the wall across the desk without acknowledging the remark.

Hartlepool cleared his throat. "Based on that," he resumed, "and my analysis of both yours and Malaveda's helmet recorders from last night's incident, I requested that Lawler Command grant you an immediate field promotion. I'm pleased to say that they've agreed."

"Thank you, sir," Vierziger said. He reached across the desk to take Hartlepool's proffered hand. His grip was firm and dry, almost without character.

"And thank you, Sergeant Malaveda," Vierziger added, glancing at the non-com. "I trust your promotion will come through quickly also. You deserve it."

He was perfectly appropriate in words, tone, and expression, but Hartlepool got the feeling that Vierziger was laughing at them. It was like watching a master artist accept the congratulations of a six-year-old on the quality of his painting.

Vierziger's faint smile made memories click into

place: another man, dark rather than blond, but small and *pretty* and queer . . .

"Ah, Vierziger?" the lieutenant asked. "Do you — did you happen to have a relative in the FDF? In Hammer's Slammers, actually?"

Vierziger shook his head easily. "Not me," he said. "No relatives at all, I suspect, though it's been a very long time since I was home."

Hartlepool thought of asking where Vierziger called home. He decided not to.

"I, ah . . ." he said. "I met Major Joachim Steuben once. He was an interesting man."

He raised an eyebrow, an obvious demand that Vierziger reply to the non-question.

Vierziger smiled wider. The expression was as unpleasant as a shark's gape. *The lieutenant had been playing games with him. The lieutenant would never do that again.* "So I gather," Vierziger said. "Hammer's hatchetman, wasn't he? Until someone shot him in the back."

"Bodyguard, as I heard it," Hartlepool said. He chewed on his tongue for a moment to stimulate the flow of saliva in his dry mouth. "Well, he's been gone for some while now. Almost since Colonel Hammer's accession to the Presidency."

"Seven years," Vierziger said. "Seven years to the day I joined the Frisian Defense Forces. Or so they told me."

Vierziger's battle dress uniform was perfectly tailored. That wasn't surprising, since Frisian MP units were traditionally strack, even on field duty. On Vierziger, however, the garb hung so perfectly that he might have modeled for the tailor.

Hartlepool cleared his throat again and tried on a brisk, businesslike expression. "Along with the promotion, Vierziger," he said, "you've been reassigned. You're, ah, quite remarkable. Of course you know that. Somebody seems to have decided you're too valuable for a line unit here on Lawler."

He was betting that Vierziger was too new to the FDF to know that the statement was utter nonsense. Nobody got transferred so quickly unless his commanding officer made a *"This or I resign!"* point of it with echelon.

From Vierziger's icy smile, he knew exactly why he was being transferred. Hartlepool had been shocked speechless by the images recorded by the new recruit's helmet cameras the night before.

Granted that Johann Vierziger was a valuable member of the FDF, the fellow was still too dangerous for Hartlepool to risk having him around. It was just that simple.

"Very well, sir," Vierziger said. "My service with you has been interesting. I wish you the best of luck in the future."

As if he were a commanding general speaking to his staff as he stepped down.

Vierziger stood up. "Am I dismissed, then, sir?" he added calmly.

"What?" said Hartlepool. "I, ah — I'd tell you your new assignment if I knew what it was, of course."

Hartlepool didn't know how he'd expected Vierziger to react to the notice of transfer, but he'd expected *some* reaction. The lieutenant felt as if he'd tried to climb one more step than the staircase had.

"It doesn't really concern me, sir," Vierziger said. "I'll serve in any capacity to which my superiors choose to assign me."

Vierziger's voice was without expression, and his face was a skull.

If the man was what he appeared to be, he was a tool like the pistol in his belt holster or the knife whose hilt projected from his boot top. . . . But guns and knives will not act of their own accord. Nobody could watch images of the previous night without wondering whether Vierziger was at heart as uncontrolled as he was unstoppable when he went into action.

"Yes, well," Hartlepool said. "Good luck in your assignment, wherever it is, Sergeant."

Vierziger threw him a crisp salute. He looked like a boy in uniform — or a girl — as he turned on his heel and left the office.

"He isn't human," Sergeant Malaveda said. He could have been remarking on the quality of the local beer. His eyes swung toward the doorway now that Vierziger was gone, though he hadn't looked at the man while they were together in the small room.

"He's a hell of a gunman, though," Hartlepool said, as if he were disagreeing. "Well, we'll see what they make of him on a survey team. He'll be going to Cantilucca as part of the security element."

Malaveda raised an eyebrow.

"Via, yes, I know what his assignment is!" the lieutenant snapped.

He looked toward the empty doorway himself. "Major Steuben was like that. From the stories, at least. And the same kind of eyes. But Joachim Steuben's been dead for a long time."

Sergeant Malaveda stared at him. There seemed to be a chill in the room.

Earlier: LAWLER

Though Vierziger, the trooper driving Sergeant Malaveda's air-cushion jeep, was a newbie to the Frisian Defense Forces, he obviously had a lot of time in other armies on his clock. Malaveda guessed he was on the wrong side of thirty standard, but it was hard to be sure. Vierziger had the sort of baby-faced cuteness that some men keep from early teens to sixty.

It was one more reason for Malaveda, who shaved his scalp to hide the fact his hair was receding at age 26, to dislike Vierziger.

"Pull up here," Malaveda ordered as they eased toward the mouth of the alley by which they'd approached the rear of the target building. "And *don't* get out where the street light'll show us up."

The newbie obeyed with the same delicate skill he'd shown while navigating the alley in the dark. In light-amplification mode, the visors of Frisian commo helmets increased visibility to daytime norms, but they robbed terrain of the shadings which the human brain processed into relative distances. Vierziger was a good driver, Malaveda had to admit —

To himself. There was no way he was going to praise the little turd out loud.

Vierziger switched off the fans. The hollow echo that filled the alley even on whisper mode drained away.

"Who the hell told you to shut down?" Malaveda snarled.

The newbie turned and looked at him. Vierziger's expression was blank but not tranquil. Malaveda felt ice at the back of his neck.

"Nobody did, Sergeant," Vierziger said. His voice was low-pitched, melodious, and just enough off-key to reinforce the chill Malaveda felt in his glance. "Would you like me to light the fans again?"

Malaveda scowled. "That's not what I said. Just remember, you may *think* you're something, but you're serving with the best, now!"

Vierziger faced the alley mouth again. He drew his 2-cm shoulder weapon from the butt clamp that held it vertical beside his seat and checked the magazine. "I'll keep that in mind," he said.

Malaveda scowled, but he didn't restart the discussion for the time being.

Lawler was a highly developed world with a population of nearly forty million. Even so there should have been enough room and resources for everybody.

The ostensible cause of — not-quite-war, but soon — was that the central provinces of the occupied continent wanted to retain links with Earth, while the coastal provinces wanted a Lawler that was independent and, coincidentally, ruled by coastal-province oligarchies.

The Junta of Central Province Governors had faced a planet-wide vote which would have been dominated by their opponents' political machines. They forestalled it by raising their own army — and hiring two armored brigades from the Frisian Defense Forces.

The Junta couldn't afford to pay the mercenaries forever just to stand around and look tough. Malaveda figured there'd be a riot pretty soon in one of the border cities. The Planetary Front — the thugs from the coasts — would kill people putting the riot down, or anyway the Junta would say they had.

And the Junta would respond, with FDF panzers the cutting edge of the blow.

For the time being, Malaveda and the rest of 3d Squad, 1st Platoon, A Company, 105th Military Police Detachment (Lawler), had a problem which didn't in the least involve local politics. A trooper named Soisson had been guarding a warehouse in Belair, the Junta's capital. Soisson shot the fellow on duty with him, then ran off with a truckload of powergun ammunition.

The ammo was probably an afterthought — the most valuable thing the bastard could grab after he'd nutted. It had to be recovered, though, and Soisson had to be brought back dead or alive. The tradition of the White Mice, the field police of Hammer's Slammers, was that dead was preferable.

Soisson was supposed to be hiding in a front apartment of the three-story building across the street. Malaveda waited in a backstop position thirty meters from the rear door. Lieutenant Hartlepool would take the main part of the squad in by the front and catch Soisson in bed — if everything went as planned. The lieutenant had stationed Malaveda there just in case.

Malaveda waited with a newbie who obviously thought he was hot stuff, even though he didn't actually *say* so. Malaveda lifted his sub-machine gun to his shoulder, aimed it at the apartment building's back door, and *clock*ed his tongue against the roof of his mouth.

He lowered the weapon and looked again at his driver. "I guess you think you've seen action, don't you?" he said.

Vierziger turned, raised an eyebrow, and turned back. "I've seen action, yes," he said softly.

"Well let me tell you how it is, buddy," Malaveda said. "You haven't seen anything till you've seen it with the FDF. Lieutenant Hartlepool, the Old Man? He was in the White Mice which Major Steuben commanded them. He was a friend of Major Steuben's."

Vierziger looked at him. "Joachim Steuben didn't have any friends," he said. His tone was as bleak as the space between stars.

Malaveda waited for the newbie to take his glacial

eyes away before saying, "You know a lot — for a guy who enlisted three months ago!"

"I know too much," Vierziger said, almost too quietly to be heard. "I know way too much. Now, let's just watch and wait, like we're supposed to. All right, Sergeant?"

As if a fucking newbie could tell a sergeant what to do! But Malaveda didn't feel like saying anything more. He'd had a creepy feeling about Vierziger from when the bastard was assigned to the squad. Vierziger made everybody's skin crawl. Being alone with him in a jeep was like, was like —

There was a sound in the alley behind them. Malaveda, keyed up, started to swing his sub-machine gun toward the noise. Vierziger —

Malaveda didn't see the newbie move. There was the sound, and Vierziger was —

standing in the jeep —

facing backward —

his 2-cm weapon in his left hand, held at the balance, out a hand's-breadth from his hip —

where it counter-weighted the pistol pointing in his right hand, a gleam of polished metals, the iridium barrel and gold and purple scrollwork on the receiver.

Malaveda hadn't seen the fucker move!

Vierziger slipped the pistol back into a cut-away holster that rode high on his right hip. It wasn't an issue rig, and it looked like it ought to be uncomfortable for driving; though he'd driven all right too.

He sat down again and smiled faintly at Malaveda. "Just a rat," he said. "Jumping onto the manhole cover back there. Where you have humans, you have rats."

Malaveda nodded in the direction of the pistol, now out of sight again. "Where the hell did you learn to do that?" he asked.

Vierziger shrugged. "Practice," he said. His face was unlined. He looked like a choirboy in this soft illumination, street lights shimmering from the damp brick walls of the alley. "And I had a — talent for it, I suppose you'd say."

"Bloody hell," Malaveda said.

A slow-moving car went by, the first traffic since the MP jeep took its pre-dawn station in the alley. The vehicle's windows were polarized opaque. They reflected the knife-edged whiteness of the hood-center headlight.

Malaveda didn't want to speak, but he heard himself say, "Could you teach somebody to do that? To — draw that way?"

"It's just practice, Sergeant," Vierziger said.

He looked at his companion again. Malaveda couldn't have explained what was different about the newbie's expression, but this time it didn't make him shiver to see it.

"It isn't hard to shoot people, you know," Vierziger said. "The hard part is knowing which ones. They don't always come with labels."

He smiled. Malaveda wasn't sure if the statement was meant for a joke. He smiled back.

The artificial intelligence in Malaveda's commo helmet projected a sudden emptiness through the earphones. The non-sound was the absence of the static which would otherwise have crackled when somebody opened the push but didn't speak.

"We're going in," a radioed voice whispered; Lieutenant Hartlepool or the squad leader, Sergeant-Commander Brankins. You couldn't tell in a brief spread-band transmission.

Malaveda threw the sub-machine gun to his shoulder again. Vierziger flicked him a side-glance and smiled faintly, but he didn't otherwise move.

Malaveda hadn't heard how they'd located Soisson. Chances were the tech boys had swept the low-rent district till they picked up the signature of the electronics in the powergun Soisson ran with. The deserter might have sold the weapon or traded it for something more concealable, but even so it was a link on the chain that would lead back to him.

Whoever had the sub-machine gun would be bent outta shape when a squad of armed men rousted him at this hour. Watching the back door wasn't necessarily going to be a tea party, but Malaveda was just as glad not to be in the snatch team.

All hell broke loose.

The initial gunfire was from the front of the apartment building. Malaveda couldn't see who was shooting, but the his*scrack!* of powerguns and reflected cyan light quivered over and around the structure.

It didn't sound like a raid, it sounded like war.

The back door opened halfway. A man peered through the crack.

Malaveda aimed his sub-machine gun. The holographic sight picture stuttered around the man. "Come out with your hands up!" he shouted.

The man started to duck back inside. Vierziger blew his head off in a flash of saturated blue.

The quality of light reflected from a third-floor window above the doorway changed. Malaveda noted the event subliminally, but his brain hadn't processed it into *somebody just slid opaque blinds open behind the polarized pane in order to see me/shoot me* when Vierziger fired again. The window shattered. The 2-cm round smacked a belt of powergun ammo slung around the man aiming a sub-machine gun. Hundreds of charged disks gang-fired, touched off by the 2-cm bolt. The blast must have cleared the room.

Soisson had made contact either with fifth columnists set up by the Front, or with a criminal gang that might as well be a government for the weapons in its arsenal. Either way, the snatch squad had walked right into a hornet's nest.

Malaveda ripped out half his magazine with no better target than the whole rear of the building. He hadn't expected things to blow up this way. It had spooked him.

Vierziger fired at another of the top range of windows. He must have seen something or he had the devil's own luck, because there was a man behind the disintegrated pane. The fellow had been pointing a shoulder weapon.

He'd been wearing body armor too, but that didn't help him against the energy a 2-cm bolt packed. The body hurtled backward, propelled by the shock of its colloid structure suddenly vaporizing. The victim's sleeves were burning.

The sub-machine gun recoiled against Malaveda's shoulder. That and the quivering gaps across his field of view, his visor blacking out the cyan dazzle to save his eyesight, combined to focus him on the job at hand. *It's not like this is my first firefight.*

The back door was still ajar. The first victim's feet stuck out of it. Malaveda sensed motion within the building. He aimed, squeezed. His three-round burst lighted the torso of a gunman. Vierziger center-punched the fellow with a bolt at the same instant, then fired again.

The second round was apparently to clear the magazine. The delicate-featured killer turned his weapon up with his left hand and stripped a fresh five-round clip through the loading gate. The gun's iridium muzzle glowed from the amount of plasma energy it had been channeling downrange.

Malaveda's commo helmet spluttered with clicks and hisses, sign of a lot of panicked activity that wasn't addressed to him. The people at the front of the apartment building — the survivors of the snatch team — were calling for serious back-up.

The hostiles inside must know that, and know besides that when a platoon of combat cars — or even tanks — arrived, it was all over for them. They had to break out fast, before the FDF came down with both boots.

When Malaveda was sure his partner had reloaded, he emptied the sub-machine gun into two windows chosen at random on the top floor. He thumbed the release button and reached down to his belt pouch for a fresh magazine.

Sirens and screams clawed what had been the night's stillness, punctuated with the slapping discharges of powerguns. A blast too loud for a grenade shook the opposite side of the apartment. Windows facing the alley shattered. Shards of the panes snowed onto the sidewalk.

Vierziger —

Malaveda's mind flashed with a montage of his partner in various stages of what had happened next.

First Vierziger's left hand lifted his 2-cm weapon up toward his shoulder, the girlishly perfect fingers of his right hand curving to the grip. *Then* Vierziger faced the back of the alley, the shoulder weapon out to his side and the pistol, again the pistol, pointing.

Three shots, strobe-light quick, winking on the face of the man lifting the manhole cover from beneath. Cratering the flesh, rupturing the skull itself with the pressure of gasified nerve tissue. The eyes blanking, the sub-machine gun dropping back into the utility passage converted to an underground escape route; the cover clanking down, catching the dead man's fingers for a moment before gravity tugged them loose.

Vierziger holstered the pistol. He bent, switched on the jeep's drive fans, and hopped out beside the vehicle. "Come on!" he ordered. "Watch our back."

"What?" Malaveda said. He jumped clear of the jeep. He felt as though he was partnered with a ticking bomb. He didn't understand what was happening, but he was afraid not to obey the newbie absolutely.

Vierziger revved the fans to full lift and reached for the steering yoke. The bottom half-meter of a second-floor window across the street blew outward, shattered by the muzzle blast of a machine gun firing explosive bullets.

Distortion through the window pane caused the gunner to aim his initial burst high. Chunks blew off the facades of the buildings to either side, hiding the alley mouth for an instant in a cloak of brick dust. Other projectiles burst in vivid red florets on the walls and among the garbage well behind the jeep.

The gunner didn't get a chance to correct his aim.

Surrounded by the *blam!blam!blam!* of projectiles and whizzing bits of casings mixed with brick chips, Malaveda spun and aimed. He walked a line of cyan flashes across ten centimeters of wall, up the transom, and into the window —

As Vierziger reholstered his glowing pistol. He'd drawn and fired twice in an eyeblink. His bolts had punched the gunner in the face, one to either side of the nose. The barrel of the machine gun tilted up and vanished as the gunner slumped.

"Watch our back!" Vierziger repeated. He slammed the jeep's control yoke forward. The little vehicle skittered ahead. It held its alignment but slid slightly to the right when it emerged from the alley and met a breeze down the main boulevard.

The manhole cover hadn't budged since Vierziger shot the man who'd lifted it. Malaveda kept the steel disk at the corner of his eyes as his conscious mind followed what his partner was doing.

Vierziger's holster was metal or a temperature-stable plastic, because it didn't melt or burn from contact with the pistol's glowing iridium muzzle. Judging from the way he'd drawn it both times that speed was an absolute essential, the richly decorated handgun was Vierziger's weapon of choice.

He nonetheless handled the heavy 2-cm powergun with an ease that belied his slight frame, as well as with flawless accuracy; and it was with the shoulder weapon presented that he waited now.

The jeep was too light to be stable without a man aboard. Its flexible skirts hopped on irregularities in the pavement, spilling air from the plenum chamber.

Vierziger fired twice as the vehicle bobbled its way toward the building. His first bolt ignited the interior of a room whose window had shivered away in the bomb blast. Malaveda hadn't seen a human target, but Vierziger probably had, and the baby-faced killer had hit everything he'd aimed at this night.

The flare of cyan plasma filled the enclosed space momentarily. An instant later everything flammable, including the paint, was a mass of orange flame. The transom belched a great fireball when something, munitions or an accelerant, added its energy to the inferno.

Vierziger's second shot was into the window from which the machine gun had fired. Malaveda hadn't noticed additional movement there until the bolt hit the muzzle of the automatic weapon just lifting back over the transom to fire. Plasma converted fifteen centimeters of the gun's steel barrel to gas. The superheated metal erupted in a red secondary flame as it mixed with air.

How had Vierziger hit a target so small at thirty meters, with an off-hand shot?

The jeep crashed into the half-open doorway at 50 kph. That was fast enough to crunch the front of the vehicle pretty thoroughly, though without doing serious damage to the building. The jeep's plastic frame fractured in a series of angry clicks.

Vierziger fired the remaining three 2-cm rounds into the wreckage. He picked his spots, blowing open a pair of fuel cells with each squeeze of the trigger.

The hydrocarbon fuel normally realized its energy in a cold process using an ion-exchange membrane. Now it blazed outward, enveloping the jeep in fire hot enough to involve the body panels and upholstery as well. The mushroom of flame rose roof high. It barred the building's rear street door as effectively as the presence of a tank could have done.

And that freed Vierziger and his partner for other activities.

Malaveda thought he saw the manhole cover move. He fired, rattling the disk in its coaming as the powergun bolts blew divots off the top of the steel.

Vierziger stripped in a fresh clip, then tossed Malaveda his bandolier of 2-cm ammo. "Follow me, swap guns and *load* when I tell you!" he ordered. "Now!"

The newbie had no business giving a non-com orders, but the present situation ignored what the Table of Organization might say. "Yes*sir*!" Malaveda shouted.

Vierziger wasn't wearing body armor; he'd claimed it would interfere with his driving. Now he reached left-handed into one of his tunic's front bellows pockets and drew out a red-banded grenade that he had *no* business carrying.

He struck the safety cap off against the side of the building with casual ease. Malaveda had seen troopers trying to arm a grenade that way, proving how macho they were. He'd never seen anybody succeed so perfectly, and with such little concern, as Vierziger did now.

Vierziger's right hand was on the 2-cm weapon's pistol grip, holding it like a massive handgun. He fired point-blank into the edge of the manhole cover. Sub-machine gun bolts made the steel disk stutter. The heavier charge flipped it like a tiddlywink. Vierziger tossed the grenade into the opening, put his back against the alley wall, and fired another bolt down the hole to disconcert anybody who might have the notion of throwing the grenade back up.

The lid hit the pavement a meter from the hole, spinning on edge with a nervous *clang-g-g-g* until the grenade went off beneath. It was a bunker buster. It atomized a mist of fuel through the air ten cubic meters of tunnel, then detonated the mixture in a blast that ruptured the pavement all the way to the mouth of the alley. Vierziger, poised with his knees flexed, rode out the ripple of concrete, but the unexpected jolt knocked Malaveda down.

Vierziger jumped into the pillar of gray smoke gushing from the manhole. "Follow me!" he shouted as he disappeared underground.

Malaveda followed. It didn't occur to him not to.

There was a ladder. Malaveda climbed down it, facing outward; clumsy because of the sub-machine gun in his right hand and the bandolier of 2-cm ammo swinging from his left. The helmet slapped filters over Malaveda's nose as he stepped into the noxious efflux from the grenade explosion. Four rungs down, he switched his visor to thermal imaging.

In thermal mode, the helmet converted temperature gradients to shapes. Malaveda hopped forward to keep from stepping on the pair of bodies scrunched at the base of the ladder. Another corpse lay on its back a few meters down the tunnel.

Vierziger moved ahead of Malaveda. The atmosphere swirled with blast residues which showed as pastels on the helmet visor.

The tunnel was purpose-built as an escape route, not a converted sewer main. It was round with a two-meter cross-section. The walls were monocrystal filament wound on a resin core. The matrix shattered when the fuel-air explosion flexed it beyond its resilient capacity. Swathes of monocrystal hung down like ancient cobwebs, but the structure hadn't collapsed as yet.

Vierziger fired his heavy shoulder weapon. Shock waves down the tunnel made Malaveda stagger, even though he was behind the shooter. Hot vortices spun off to both sides of the ionized track, expanding until they filled the cylindrical space.

The tunnel dead-ended at the ladder up into the alley. The lid on the alley end had locking dogs to avoid the risk of discovery by a utility crew. Either would-be escapees had undogged the lid, or the heavy jolt of plasma had flexed the disk enough to spring the bolts.

Vierziger broke into a run. The 2-cm weapon was butted against his shoulder. He fired twice more. Each jet of plasma heated the air like a mulling iron thrust into a beaker of wine.

"Feed me!" he screamed, still running, thrusting the shoulder weapon out behind him. Malaveda grabbed the gun by the forestock, too close to the glowing iridium muzzle, but he didn't drop it.

He slapped the receiver of the sub-machine gun into Vierziger's hand. Vierziger holstered the pistol that was pointing again as if by magic and presented the automatic weapon. He hadn't slowed.

Malaveda stumped along behind the killer. Sweat broke out all over his body. The filters kept his lungs free of ozone and the poisons streaming from empty cases which spun from the powergun's ejection port. His eyes burned and patches of bare skin prickled.

A corpse sprawled as a mass of indigo and purple in the midst of the tunnel's cool gray. The man had been partly dismembered by a bolt that struck at collarbone level. His right arm, tangled with a gun sling, hung by a few fleshless tendons; the spine was all that connected the head and torso.

Steep concrete steps led up from the other end of the tunnel. There was a handrail. Two bodies were tangled in it as they sprawled down the steps.

The armored door at the upper landing was open into the tunnel. Light flooded the passage. The panel started to swing shut. Vierziger triggered a burst at the doorway, perhaps hoping to ricochet a bolt into whoever was operating the powered mechanism.

Malaveda stopped and switched his visor to straight optics. He braced himself against the wall to aim the reloaded shoulder weapon past his partner. He was panting, drawing gasps of poisoned air through his mouth. Ozone burned the back of his throat.

He fired. Vierziger hunched at the base of the stairs, the sub-machine gun's muzzle questing back for the unexpected shooter. The door's upper hinge blew away in a cyan flash. The plating glowed white/yellow/red in circles concentric with the point of impact.

Malaveda ignored his partner's gun. The door sagged, kinking the lower hinge and freezing the panel half open. Tears blurred Malaveda's eyes, and the sight picture danced wildly. He fired anyway and hit the lower hinge squarely. The door toppled onto the concrete landing like a dropped safe.

Vierziger was already up the stairs. Malaveda followed. He could no more have made that pair of shots during a training exercise than he could have ripped the door loose with his bare hands.

In the newbie's company, Malaveda was operating at well above what he would have guessed his best day could be. He didn't know whether the cause was emulation or a justifiable concern for what Vierziger might do to him if he screwed up.

The steps were slippery with body fluids. Malaveda grabbed the left rail; the 2-cm bandolier clanged against the tubing.

Vierziger tossed a grenade left-handed ahead of him. It was an assault bomb with a contact fuze. The blast was instantaneous, but the glass shrapnel was safe beyond a two-meter radius. Vierziger was through the haze-veiled doorway while the echoes still sounded.

The sub-machine gun snarled out four separate bursts with only a heartbeat between them. Malaveda caromed off the transom as he followed his partner. He wasn't in shape for this. His body armor felt as though he were wearing a well-stoked oven.

Nobody was in shape for *this* except Johann Vierziger, who wasn't human.

"Feed —" Vierziger said.

Malaveda snatched the sub-machine gun away and replaced it with the 2-cm weapon. He tried to say,

"Only three in the magazine!" but his voice was a croak, and he didn't imagine the devil who led him didn't have the information already.

The room was an unfinished basement, open except for concrete support pillars. It held stacks of cased weapons and ammunition, as well as crates Malaveda couldn't identify at first glance.

Three bodies, two of them women in nightclothes, lay between the tunnel door and an elevator at the opposite end of the basement. Single-person lift and dropshafts couldn't have serviced the heavy goods stored here. A woman's legs wedged the cage doors.

The grenade had pretty well devoured a man holding a bell-muzzled mob gun near the doorway. Vierziger's powergun bolts had lifted off the back of his head anyway.

Malaveda didn't see a fourth corpse, but he knew there must be one. Vierziger had fired four times, after all.

Vierziger ran to the elevator. Malaveda reloaded the sub-machine gun as he followed. The barrel was badly burned by use. He'd have changed it for a new one if he'd been sure there was time. He wasn't sure of anything at all.

He saw something to his left, down a cross-aisle among the goods stored on pallets. He pointed the sub-machine gun but it was a corpse lying on its back, the face blasted away by a tight quartet of powergun bolts.

Vierziger drew his pistol and fired twice to his right, down another aisle. Cyan bolts chewed the ceiling above him as he shot, blasting gravel and a spray of calcium burned from the cast concrete.

The man in ambush had clamped his sub-machine gun's trigger as he arched backward in death. Vierziger had seen, drawn, and killed before the victim could react to the appearance of the target he'd heard running toward him.

Beside the elevator was a firedoor of mesh-reinforced

vitril, displaying a concrete staircase which led to the upper floors. No one was on the stairs. Vierziger tested the door to be sure that it opened from outside the smoke tower. It did. He tugged another grenade from his pockets, armed it, and tossed it up the stairs. He slammed the door shut.

Malaveda hunched aside. Vierziger grinned horribly at him. "Don't worry," he said. "It's gas."

The grenade bubbled open in waves of black haze that quickly filled the volume beyond the vitril. The doorseal, intended to prevent smoke from entering the stair tower, acted equally well to keep the contents of the grenade inside.

It was gas all right — KD nerve gas, which would oxidize harmless within two hours of use in an Earth-type atmosphere . . . and would paralyze the diaphragm muscles of anyone who breathed it or had skin contact before that time. Malaveda would have suffocated slowly and inexorably if a bullet had hit his partner's grenade during the firefight.

Vierziger ejected the nearly empty magazine from his pistol. To reload, he had to pluck a fresh clip from a belt pouch with the thumb and index finger of the left hand which still gripped the 2-cm weapon.

The woman jamming the doors had been very beautiful. Her filmy pajamas were of a natural fabric that had flashed like guncotton when the bolts struck her, leaving only a net of ash on the body.

Malaveda faced about to guard their backtrail. He felt as if he were in a bubble, he and Vierziger together; cut off from everything he'd for 26 years thought was the real world.

The 2-cm gun firing spun him around again. Vierziger had blasted the lock from the emergency hatch in the elevator's ceiling.

"Feed me!" he ordered crisply. Then, as Malaveda traded sub-machine gun for 2-cm weapon, Vierziger added, "Give me a leg up."

Malaveda made a stirrup of his hands. The dangling bandolier and sub-machine gun clattered on the cage floor, *Bloody hell it could have gone off!* but that was only a vagrant thought as he straightened his legs and boosted Vierziger through the narrow opening.

"Come on!" Vierziger said, thrusting a hand — his left hand — down toward Malaveda. "I need you to open the doors *now!*"

Instead of obeying instantly, Malaveda yanked open the latches of his ceramic body armor and shrugged the clamshell away. He probably wouldn't fit through the emergency access with it on, and he was already dizzy from the heat and confinement of exercise while wearing the armor.

He didn't try to explain what he was doing to Vierziger. Malaveda had to concentrate on *what* he was doing if he was going to achieve a fraction of what his partner expected. . . .

Re-slinging the gun and ammunition, Malaveda rose and took Vierziger's offered hand. He jumped and the little man pulled — like a derrick. Vierziger's physical strength was as shocking as everything else about the deadly man with the features of a child. Malaveda's right elbow scraped the edge of the opening and the sub-machine gun's muzzle rapped on metal, but Vierziger's tug was precise as well as effortless.

The sergeant knelt in the litter and lubricant sludge on top of the cage, then rose to his feet. A sagging cable brushed his shoulder. He had his second wind since he'd dropped the back-and-breast armor. A moment before, he hadn't been sure he could go on.

"Switch," said Vierziger, offering the 2-cm weapon. The elevator shaft was vaguely illuminated from above, but most of the light streamed up through the access port.

The little man was using Malaveda as a pack train; which was perfectly appropriate under the circumstances. Now that he was sure of the sergeant's obedience, the edge that had earlier promised, *"Do this thing, or I will kill you without hesitation,"* was gone from Vierziger's voice.

Vierziger nodded to the knife he'd already thrust into the juncture of the doors closing the elevator shaft from the first floor. He placed his boot along the edge, ready to thrust the door fully open as soon as Malaveda broke the seal. The top of the cage was eighty centimeters beneath floor level, not a serious problem.

The knife was a sturdy tool with a single edge on a thick, density-enhanced blade about 20 centimeters long. It could serve for a weapon, but it was obviously intended for more general purposes than killing. Here it made a functional prybar.

Malaveda gripped the knife with his left hand, crossed his left leg over the hilt to push the other door, and aimed his 2-cm weapon at the crack. Vierziger nodded approvingly.

The sergeant levered the knife with all his strength, using the thrust of his left boot as both anchor and supplement. The doors banged open to their stops. Vierziger was through the doorway like a lethal wraith, the sub-machine gun snarling. Malaveda heaved himself over the floor ledge, feeling like a hippo in comparison to his partner's grace.

But he got there without stumbling. The torso of a startled man in a business suit vanished in the huge flash of a 2-cm bolt, though Malaveda wasn't really conscious of pulling the trigger.

According to the plans and 3-D holograms with which the squad prepared for the raid, the apartment building's foyer faced the street through a wall of clear vitril. No longer. Armored shutters with firing slits had slammed down moments after the shooting started.

Vitril now covered the floor like a field of diamonds. Powergun bolts had shattered the former expanse into bits ranging from pebbles to dust. It was rough, but it didn't have dangerous edges.

A trooper in light-scattering Frisian battle dress lay

under the crystalline debris. Malaveda couldn't tell which of the squad it had been, because an explosive bullet had decapitated him/her.

Three men and a woman crouched by the slits, shooting outward or preparing to when the pair of Frisians appeared behind them. All four of them were dead by the time Malaveda stepped into the foyer. Vierziger had shot them in the back of the head. The purple-haired man on the left of the position was on the floor. His three companions were slumping in various stages of the same motion, like a slow-motion image of a single event.

The armored shield glowed in several places where it had absorbed plasma energy, but all those strikes had been on the outer face. Vierziger hadn't wasted a bolt.

A dozen more people of both sexes tumbled out the stairwell door. Despite being in various stages of undress, they were slicker-looking types than the shooters had been. Malaveda had killed the first of them. The woman behind that victim was shrieking, "The basement's full of gas!" when the 2-cm bolt sprayed her with the remains of her companion.

A tremendous blast shook the building. The shock wave down the stair tower projected the last would-be escapee into the foyer like the cork from a champagne bottle.

Nothing the snatch squad had on hand would have packed that wallop, and there hadn't been time enough for support to arrive. The residents themselves had planned to blow the place from the top down to cover their tunnel escape route.

The foyer lights flicked off, then on again but with a yellowish hue. The system had shifted to emergency power. The building was a *fortress*. It could have held out for hours against almost anything but what had arrived — the devil in the shape of a new recruit.

A woman knocked to the floor drew a pistol from the sleeve of a garment apparently too diaphanous to hide anything. Vierziger shot her hand off. Chips of vitril, now pulverized, erupted in the cyan jolts as the flimsy target vaporized at the first round of the burst.

Malaveda noticed movement and swung. A man threw down a carbine as though it were as hot as the white, glowing muzzle of Vierziger's sub-machine gun. "No!" he screamed. His eyes were closed.

"No," agreed Vierziger, touching Malaveda's hand on the forestock. He lifted the 2-cm weapon to a safe angle.

The armored shutters rang under multiple power-gun bolts. A 30-centimeter splotch went from gray to red to bright orange. The survivors of the squad were concentrating their fire, but the armor remained proof against small-arms.

"That's the, the s-s-switch," said a small man whose beige suit would have paid Malaveda's salary for a year. He pointed to a short baton. The man the sergeant shot had flung it onto the vitril in his dying convulsions. "To set off the bombs."

Vierziger nodded to Malaveda. Malaveda scooped up the device, careful not to touch the red contact points.

A grenade went off outside. The concussion lifted dust from the foyer floor without affecting the armor.

"Now," said Vierziger. "We'll need the controls to raise those doors. And we'll need a white flag, because our colleagues don't seem ready to accept my radioed assurance that we've captured the position."

He gestured to a man wearing a tunic that glittered as if diamond studded. "Your shirt will do, I think."

"The controls are here, right here, mister!" a woman whispered, tugging Malaveda's sleeve to get his attention. "Right here!"

She pointed to what looked like a trash chute in the wall between elevator and stairs. The cover plate was lifted to display a keyboard.

"Besides," Vierziger continued, smiling at the captive stripping before him, "I'd like a better look at your pecs, handsome."

He laughed. It was the most terrifying sound Malaveda had ever heard in his life.

MAHGREB

"I'm looking for a piss-ant named Barbour!" roared the stocky man who slammed open the double doors of the officers' canteen. "Lieutenant Robert Barbour? He thinks he's lifting out of here today!"

The man's gray hair was shaved into a skullcap. He wore his rank tabs field-fashion — on the underside of his collar, where they wouldn't target him for a sniper. His aura of command obviated the need of formal indicia anyway.

Barbour set down the chip projector he was reading and got to his feet. The projector was loaded with an off-planet news feed, nothing Barbour cared about one way or the other. It was just a means of killing time while waiting for the boarding signal of the ship that would return him to Nieuw Friesland. Killing time and taking his mind off other things.

"I'm Barbour," he said. His voice squeaked.

The dozen or so other officers in the canteen stared at Barbour when he stood up, then quickly looked in any direction except that of the two principals to the encounter. Conversations stopped, and the four poker players at a corner table huddled their cards between their cupped palms. The lights twinkling in enticement from the autobar looked *loud*.

"Do you know who I am, Lieutenant Barbour?" the stocky man demanded. When the canteen doors flapped, Barbour saw two nervous-looking aides waiting in the starport concourse. Unlike their principal, the aides wore scarlet command-staff fourragères.

Via! Barbour *did* know the fellow. Know of him, at

any rate. Tedeschi didn't spend a lot of time in the headquarters in Al Jain, where Barbour had worked until six days previous.

"Yes sir," Barbour said. He restrained himself from saluting. Field regulations again. In order to encourage his command into a war zone mentality, General Tedeschi, commanding the FDF contingent on Mahgreb, had forbidden salutes. "You're General Tedeschi. Sir."

"You're bloody well told I am!" Tedeschi snapped.

He looked around the canteen. From his expression, he'd just as soon have swept it with a machine gun. "You lot," he said. "Take a walk. Now!"

The trio nearest the doors were out before the order had been fully articulated. The cardplayers left their stakes on the table, and there was hand luggage beside several of the previously occupied chairs.

Hellfire Hank Tedeschi had no manners and no patience. He successfully completed campaigns in minimal time and with minimal casualties among his own troops, because there was absolutely nothing else in the universe that mattered to him. He would cashier an officer in a heartbeat, and he was rumored to have knocked down underlings who didn't jump fast enough to suit him.

Tedeschi believed in leading from the front. He'd killed people with his pistol, his knife, and his bare hands.

"What's this about you deserting your post, Barbour?" Tedeschi demanded. "The job here's not done, you know."

The anger previously in the general's voice had been replaced by menace. Barbour knew this was an act Tedeschi had practiced, but it wasn't *merely* an act. Tedeschi was a clever man as well as a violent one. As a means of intimidation, he let people see the raw emotions bubbling from his psyche.

"I'm not deserting, sir," Robert Barbour said. "I've

requested a transfer to another branch of the service."

He didn't add, "As is my right." That would be pouring gasoline on hot coals.

"Like hell you are," Tedeschi said. He gestured Barbour back into the chair from which the lieutenant had risen. "Sit."

Barbour obeyed. Instead of sitting down across from Barbour, Tedeschi put one of his boots on the circular table and leaned his forearms against the back of his knee. "The job here needs you, Barbour," the general said. "*I* need you. Are you hearing me?"

"Sir . . ." said Barbour. He didn't know how to continue.

Tedeschi wouldn't have given him the opportunity to go on anyway. "Look, what's the problem?" he demanded. "Is it me? Do you have a problem with the way I run things here?"

"Lord, *no* sir," Barbour blurted. Tedeschi could have been back at Camp Able for all the effect he'd had on Barbour up till this moment. Lieutenants in the headquarters bureaucracy didn't expect to have anything to do with commanding generals.

"Then your section CO, Wayney," Tedeschi pressed. "Trouble with her? Tell me, boy, tell me *now*."

"Sir," Barbour said. Tedeschi was leaning forward, compressing his cocked leg and bringing his brutal, swarthy features threateningly closer to Barbour's face. "Captain Wayney's — she's no problem, sir. She's fine."

Captain Wayney wasn't a brilliant intelligence technician. To tell the truth, she wasn't even a good one. But she was far too good an administrator to get in the way of an underling who *was* brilliant. Wayney not only handed Barbour the tough ones, she let him run with his whims. The result had been a series of striking triumphs for the section which Wayney headed.

"Look, I'll make you a proposition," Tedeschi said, leaning back a few centimeters. "You get an appointment on my personal staff. You report to nobody else, and I leave you the fuck alone. *And* you jump two pay grades to major. When this operation's over, which I expect to take another six to nine months standard, you have the choice of accompanying me to my next posting — as a light colonel. Fair, Barbour?"

Barbour stared up at Tedeschi. He didn't know how to respond. The whole thing was beyond belief.

Instead of reacting directly to the proposition, Barbour said, "Sir? Why are you doing this? There's eighteen people in Technical Intelligence. You don't need me."

Half of Tedeschi's face smiled. "Right, eighteen," he said flatly. "All of them can do thirty percent of what you do. Two of them can do about seventy percent. That a fair assessment, Lieutenant?"

Barbour swallowed. If he'd thought about the question — which he hadn't — he'd have figured that Hellfire Hank knew nothing about the operations of Tech Int. He was too busy running around in a combat car and biting the heads off Kairene guerrillas.

Dead wrong.

"Yes sir," Barbour said. "Wellborn's maybe better than that, but okay, that's about right."

"And not a cursed one of them can do the rest of what you do, the magic part," Tedeschi said, his voice like a cat's tongue, rough but caressing nonetheless. "I said six to nine months standard to finish the job."

He slammed the heel of his right fist into his left hand, a sudden stroke and *whop!* that made Barbour flinch back. "I don't need shooters, Lieutenant," the general continued. "I got shooters up the ass, I got shooters better than me, and that's *plenty* fucking good! The difference between six and nine is knowing where the bastards are to shoot. Do you see?"

"Sir," said Barbour miserably. "I can't do that any more. Target people to be shot. I can't."

"Do you want people to die, is that it?" Tedeschi shouted, his face ramming closer to Barbour's again. "If the operation goes the long way, it'll boost our casualties by fifty percent. You know that, don't you?"

Barbour nodded. Again, there was nothing wrong with the general's analysis. There was a pretty direct correlation between losses and the length of time people were running around, firing live ammunition.

"Also about double the number of local wogs get greased," Tedeschi added, "not that I give a flying fuck about that, but maybe you do?"

"I don't. . . ." Barbour said. "Sir, if I don't do it, it's not my responsibility. Sir."

"That last operation," the general said, "blitzing the headquarters of the Seventy-Three Bee regiment — that was fucking brilliant. That's the sort of thing I need to get this operation over, quick and clean. Right?"

Barbour's face formed itself into something between a smile and a rictus. He was afraid to speak.

"Come on, Barbour," Tedeschi said. He took the junior man's chin between a thumb and finger that could crush nutshells. He tilted Barbour's face to meet his hard blue eyes. "Tell me that you're going to stay with me till the job's done. Not for the promotion. For the *job*."

Barbour stood up carefully, lifting his chin out of the general's grip. "Sir," he said, staring at the wall beyond Tedeschi's left shoulder, "I'm sorry, but I can't do that job any more."

Tedeschi slammed his boot back onto the floor. He wasn't quite as tall as Barbour, but he had the physical presence of a tank.

"I'd spit on you, Lieutenant," the general said, "but you'd foul my saliva. Go to fucking Cantilucca, fuck around on a survey team. You're not fit to associate with the people doing *real* work."

Tedeschi slammed out of the canteen.

A few moments later, other officers returned to their drinks and belongings. They looked curiously at Lieutenant Robert Barbour, who remained where the general left him.

Barbour was crying.

Earlier: MAHGREB

The incoming shells screamed down on Lieutenant Robert Barbour like steam whistles pointed at his ears. *They're landing short!*

Barbour ducked in the fighting compartment of *High Hat*, the combat car in which he rode as a passenger. The regular crew, Captain Mamie Currant and her two wing gunners, didn't react to the howls overhead. Barbour raised himself sheepishly as the first salvo hit beyond the grove 500 meters distant.

Black smoke spurted. A sheet-metal roof fluttered briefly above the treetops. The blasts of the four shells with contact fuzes were greatly louder than the remaining pair which burst underground.

"Party time!" cried the gunner at the left wing tribarrel. He waggled his weapon, but he obeyed Currant's orders not to fire.

Currant's driver and the drivers of the other thirteen operational cars in her company — three were deadlined for repairs — gunned their vehicles out of the temporary hides where they waited for the artillery prep. The combiner screen beside Currant at the forward tribarrel showed the separated platoons closing in on the village of Tagrifah from four directions, but the crew — including the captain herself — was too busy with its immediate surroundings to worry about the rest of the unit.

The six tubes of the battery of Frisian rocket howitzers firing in support of the operation could each put a shell in the air every four-plus seconds during the first minute and a half. Reloading a hog's ammunition cassettes was a five-minute process for a trained crew, but that wouldn't matter today. The hundred and twenty ready rounds were sufficient to absolutely pulverize the target.

The second, third, and fourth salvos mixed contact-fuzed high explosive with cluster munitions, firecracker rounds. The outer casing of the latter shells opened a hundred meters in the air with a puff of gray smoke, raining down submunitions. Bomblets burst like grenades when they hit, carpeting a wide area with dazzling white flashes and shrapnel that drank flesh like acid.

Because the glass-fiber shrapnel had little penetrating power, the firecracker rounds were mixed with HE to blow off roofs and other light top cover. From a distance, the exploding submunitions sounded like fat frying. The effect on people caught in a firecracker round's footprint was also similar to being bathed in bubbling lard.

"C'mon, c'mon, c'mon!" the left gunner called, hammering the heel of one hand on the fighting compartment's coaming.

The two cars of 3d Platoon — understrength, so Currant was accompanying them — were to the immediate right, fifty and a hundred meters distant, approaching Tagrifah from the south. *High Hat* lurched repeatedly, throwing Barbour against the coaming. His clamshell armor spread the impact, but he still felt it.

Currant's driver kept the skirts close to the ground so as not to spill air from the plenum chamber as he accelerated the heavy vehicle. The meadow wasn't as smooth as the barley fields to the west and north of the village. Sometimes what looked like simply a flowering shrub turned out to be a rocky hillock against which the steel skirts banged violently.

Incoming shells drew red streaks across the pale dawn, plunging down at the targets Barbour had pinpointed in and around the village. The grove of deciduous trees swayed and toppled over. Rounds going off in the soil beneath the trees rippled the surface violently enough to tear their roots loose.

The whole mass heaved again in a gush of dirt and black smoke. Foliage and shattered branches flew skyward. A shell had detonated explosives stored in tunnels beneath the grove.

When the trees fell, Barbour should have gotten a glimpse of the village. All he could see were a few poles lifting above a roil of dust and smoke. In the far distance, the combat cars of 1st Platoon tore across the green barley, spewing plumes of chopped grain from beneath their skirts.

The fields and meadows serving the village weren't fenced. Three boys chatted on a knoll, watching the goats for which they were responsible.

The boys jumped to their feet to watch the first salvo scream in. When the combat cars appeared, two of the boys ran back toward the village, while the third threw himself face down and covered his head with both hands.

The local goats had long black-and-white hair. They circled in blind panic as the armored vehicles charged through them. The animals' mouths were open to bleat, but the sounds were lost in the shrieks and explosions of the artillery prep.

A goat sprang to the right, then tried to turn back to the left when it realized it had underestimated the combat car's speed. It tumbled directly in front of *High Hat's* bow skirts. The 50-tonne vehicle rode over the beast without a noticeable impact.

The shellfire stopped abruptly. The enormous howl of *High Hat's* fans, driving the vehicle and supporting it on the bubble of air in the plenum chamber, was quiet by contrast.

As the pall of smoke and dust drifted lower across Tagrifah, *High Hat* roared past the running goatherds.

One of the boys knelt, flinging his arms out and pressing his face in the dirt as a gesture of supplication. His companion simply stared at the huge vehicles. Tears ran down his cheeks.

Barbour looked back at the boys. He had to turn his whole body, because the back-and-breast armor held his torso rigid.

The combat cars braked as they neared the remains of the grove which had sheltered the south side of the village. Thirty-centimeter tree boles were scattered like jackstraws. They lay across one another, heaved up on the support of unbroken branches.

Barbour thought the tangle was impenetrable; the cars would have to go around. Captain Currant had a brief exchange over the intercom with her driver.

High Hat slowed to a crawl. The driver's head vanished within his separate compartment in the forward hull. The hatch cover clanged over him.

The car butted into a tree trunk, skewing it forward and sideways. The roots, dripping clods of yellow clay, locked with those of another fallen tree and jammed firm.

The fans howled louder. Dirt rippled up around *High Hat's* skirts. Air pressure was excavating the ground under the plenum chamber. The combat car shuddered, then leaped ahead, tossing fallen trees to left and right.

Munitions in the tunnel beneath the grove had shouldered the surface aside when they exploded. *High Hat* dipped into the long crater, blasting the loosened soil into the air. The car continued up the far side at a fast walking pace.

Tendrils of foul black smoke, the residue of stored explosives, rose where the combat car passed. Barbour thought he saw a human arm, but it could have been a twisted root instead.

The village Barbour had targeted was a ruin almost as complete as that of the grove.

A few minutes earlier, a casual observer would have taken Tagrifah for a harmless place, typical of this region of Kairouan. Even a patrol of the Frisian mercenaries in the pay of the Boumedienne government would probably have passed on, accepting the black looks and turned backs of the inhabitants as the normal due of an occupying army.

Robert Barbour had identified the village as a Kairene regimental headquarters without, until this moment, coming within fifty klicks of the place.

A few figures moved within the settling dust; women, an old man. A goat nosed a ripped grain sack with apparent unconcern for the raw wound on its left thigh.

With the fans at low speed, Barbour could hear scores of voices wailing. It was hard to believe so many people remained alive.

The houses of Tagrifah were wooden, raised a meter off the ground by stone foundations. Each crawl space served as a fold for the family's goats. Most of the foundations had collapsed from a combination of airbursts and the ground's rocking motion when delay-fuzed rounds went off beneath the surface.

"Via, Bob!" Captain Currant said, clapping her passenger across the shoulders. "It's a walkover! You're a fucking genius!"

Barbour had spent five years with the FDF, specializing in technical intelligence. He'd often surveyed the results line units obtained from his targeting information, but this was the first time he'd been in at the kill.

Literally at the kill.

"Didn't leave us much to do," the left gunner remarked. He turned and flashed Barbour a broad grin. "Which suits me just fine."

"It wasn't me," Barbour muttered. "It was the artillery."

He was holding the grenade launcher which Mamie Currant had handed him when he climbed aboard her car. He hadn't fired such a weapon since he'd gone through training so many years before.

As the wing gunner had said, there was nothing in Tagrifah left to fire *at*.

"Don't sell yourself short, Bob," Currant said. "Popping shells off into the brown doesn't do a curst bit of good. You told them where the targets were, and by the Lord! You did a great job."

She gestured over the combat car's bow. The driver had unbuttoned his hatch. "Like that," she said. *"That was the big one."*

That had been a circular pit a meter deep, surrounded by a fence of tightly bound palings and covered by a thatch roof. A shell from the first salvo had plunged through the roof and exploded on the target hidden within — an 8-barreled powergun, a calliope.

Calliopes could be used against ground targets, but they were designed to sweep shells and rockets from the sky. If this weapon and the three similar ones at the other cardinal points surrounding Tagrifah had been given time to get into action, they would have detonated all the incoming shells a klick or more short of the target. Company D would have had to fight its way into the village while flashes and dirty clouds quivered in the distant sky.

From the outside, the structure around the gun pit looked like a small shed, suitable for drying vegetables or holding community-owned tools. There was nothing about the shelter to arouse hostile interest.

The bodies of four Kairenes lay mangled among the calliope's wreckage. The victims were a boy, two young women, and a man in starched green fatigues. The Kairene regular had been in the gunner's seat, responding to an alarm from the calliope's search lidar. When the shell went off, the civilians had been trying to drop the poles that supported the roof of the shelter. The calliope would have been in operation in another five seconds.

Flight time for the 200-mm shells was less than seven seconds from the point at which they came over the calliope's search horizon.

Swatches of smoldering thatch lay around the shallow crater. The blast lifted the roof straight into the air, so fragments fell back over the same area in a burning coverlet.

One of the Kairene women had been stunningly beautiful. Her unbound hair was a meter long. The blast had stripped all the clothing from her upper torso. Her legs and body from the waist down had vanished.

The calliopes' laser direction and ranging apparatus was a low-emissions unit which worked in the near ultraviolet. It had been difficult to detect, even when Barbour knew from other indications that something of the sort must be operating.

Barbour had arranged for a utility aircraft fitted with broad-band detection instruments to overfly Tagrifah on an apparently normal hop between a Frisian firebase and a Boumedienne government post a hundred klicks to the west. The calliopes didn't fire, but two of them switched from search to their higher-powered targeting mode to follow the aircraft. That gave Barbour their precise location.

With those two in hand, he'd sent a van with a concealed high-gain antenna past Tagrifah at a kilometer's distance. The remaining calliopes gave themselves away by the electromagnetic noise of their loading-chute motors, one per gun tube, which ran at idle when the weapons were on stand-by. Barbour triangulated by plotting the signals — any electromagnetic radiation was a signal for his purposes — on a time axis calibrated against the van's route.

It was a slick piece of work, not something just any tech spec could have managed. Barbour stared at the lovely, naked half-woman as *High Hat* passed.

He'd accompanied the attack on a whim. Because

Barbour was the only person familiar with the target, Command sent him to Firebase Desmond to brief the troops told off for the operation — Company D, 3d of the 17th Brigade.

Barbour had met Mamie Currant during one of her visits to Frisian HQ in the capital, Al Jain. They'd gotten on well then, so it was natural for Mamie to suggest Barbour join the operation he'd set up in person, and natural for him to accept.

Tagrifah was nothing new for Robert Barbour. This was exactly what he'd done for a living during most of the past five years. What was new was seeing it as it happened.

A tribarrel fired on the other side of the village. Currant immediately keyed her commo helmet. Barbour wasn't in the company net, but the firing wasn't sustained. It couldn't have been a serious problem.

Barbour's nostrils were filtered against the dust, but the smell got through regardless. Smoke, earth ruptured upward by shells, explosive residues. And death, mostly human, from fire and disemboweling and flaying alive.

Tagrifah had a common well. The women congregated around it in the first dawn, drawing household water and exchanging gossip while adult males were still abed. Barbour hadn't targeted the well, of course, but one of the firecracker rounds strewed its trail of bomblets across the women and spilled them in a bloody windrow. Some of the corpses looked like bundles of rags rather than something once human; rags of predominantly red color.

One old woman, apparently unharmed, sat wailing in the middle of the carnage. Her blank eyes didn't react to the combat car, though the vehicle moved past close enough to stir her garments with the air vented beneath the skirts.

Mamie followed Barbour's eyes. She leaned close to him and said, "It's not us that did this, Bob. It's the sons of bitches who deliberately used civilians as a shield. We can't let them make up the rules for their own benefit."

"I know that," Barbour said. He didn't really know anything at all. He was pretending that he saw Tagrifah in a recorded image, with the camera lens between him and reality.

He pointed. "That was the headquarters," he said.

More accurately, the Kairene HQ had been concealed in a bunker beneath *that*, the mosque and the attached madrassah in which village boys were schooled in reading, writing, and the Koran. Girls as well as boys here in Tagrifah, and apparently a mixed class besides.

Kairouan had been settled three centuries ago from North Africa, where both Islam and Christianity had developed unique strains. Even so, Kairene society had departed to a surprising degree from its roots. Tagrifah could have been an interesting subject for study, before the shells hit.

The stone-built religious buildings had collapsed to rubble which barely filled the large bunker beneath. Gray smoke rose through the interstices of the jumbled stones. Mixed with the ashlars and broken roof beams were the bodies of the pupils, seated on the madrassah's floor at dawn to begin their lessons.

Some of the children were still moving. Captain Currant touched her helmet key again. Barbour heard the word "medics" in the request.

A preplanned operation like this probably had second echelon medical support laid on at the firebase already. The troops wouldn't need help, but the medics and their equipment would get a workout nonetheless.

The radio antenna serving the Kairene headquarters had run up the minaret. The vertical mast was still standing, pure and gleaming in the sunlight, though the building had crumbled around it.

The mast made a fitting monument for Tagrifah.

Barbour had initially identified the village as a hostile center because of the signals emanating from that antenna.

The Kairenes had limited themselves to burst transmissions: data collapsed into the smallest possible packets and spit out in a second or two instead of over minutes. They might as well have flown battle flags and set off fireworks for all the good their attempts at concealing their signals had done. They hadn't understood that they weren't dealing with hicks like themselves, they were facing the *Frisians*.

More particularly, the Kairenes faced Lieutenant Robert Barbour. Barbour's tuned instruments not only pinpointed the source of the transmissions, they ran the packets through decryption programs which spat the information out in clear faster than the Kairene units in the field would be able to process it.

"It wasn't a mistake!" Barbour said. "Tagrifah *was* a regimental headquarters!"

"Curst right it was!" Mamie Currant agreed. "Look at there."

She gestured this time by waggling the muzzles of her tribarrel. A hand and arm clutching a 2-cm powergun extended from beneath a collapsed house.

The weapon wasn't of Frisian pattern, though it might well take the same ammunition. The Kairenes had been well equipped with small arms. They lacked artillery and armor, but they would have put up at least a good fight if the Boumedienne government had attempted to reduce them with its own forces.

Guerrilla bands with powerguns, familiar with the terrain and dedicated to victory, could wreak holy havoc with an invader's lines of communications. Boumedienne's troops would have flailed blindly, destroying random villages but taking disastrous casualties whenever they tried to move in less than battalion strength.

The money cost to Boumedienne of a Frisian

brigade was considerable, but it was the difference between victory and the sort of bloody stalemate that is perhaps the only thing worse than losing a war. Tagrifah was proof the money had been well spent.

Four more combat cars approached from the east. The armored vehicles spun on their axes to extend the line on which 3d Platoon crawled through the village. The cars closed up. Another platoon was in sight to Barbour's left.

"Bunkers under every one of them?" Captain Currant asked/observed as she scanned the wreckage.

"Yes, that's right," Barbour agreed. The part of his mind that spoke retained its professional detachment.

In every instance, the foundations of the houses they passed had collapsed into a crater instead of mounding above ground level. Delay-fuzed rounds — there was no need for true penetrators, designed to punch through the plating and reinforced concrete of fortresses — had sucked the fieldstone foundations into the bunkers the houses had concealed.

Barbour had pinpointed the individual bunkers by having patrols set off small explosions in the ground, never closer than a kilometer from the village. Analyzing the hash of echo returns was more a matter of magic than science, despite the help Barbour's computers provided.

The results showed how perfectly he had succeeded. He wondered whether the villagers had built additional houses to conceal bunkers, or whether the Kairene military had limited their bunker locations to the existing buildings. Either way, there was a perfect equivalence.

The operation's planners had laid firecracker rounds down to follow the HE in order to catch soldiers stumbling from their shattered bunkers. It didn't appear that any Kairene regulars had made it that far.

Civilians lay individually and in groups near the doorways of their collapsed houses. An infant cried on the ground, between the bodies of its father and brother.

The car beside *High Hat* slowed. A gunner hopped from the fighting compartment, picked up the orphan, and remounted the vehicle.

Most of the dust had settled, but many of the house roofs burned sluggishly. Black smoke bubbled from the damp thatch. Occasionally the fans of a passing combat car would whip fires to bright flame, but mostly they remained glimmerings beneath an oily sludge.

The four-car platoon from the north of the village joined, bringing the company to full strength. Captain Currant spoke, switching her helmet from one sendee to another.

As a company commander, Mamie rated an enclosed command car with better communications gear and a specialist to run it. Like many other FDF officers, she preferred an ordinary combat vehicle.

Military doctrine for millennia had been that a commander's job was to command, not to fight. Aggressive officers had never accepted that formulation; and when the dust settled, the victorious side was normally the one whose officers were aggressive.

High Hat rotated 20°, then backed a few meters and settled onto its skirts. The remaining combat cars were shifting also, forming a tight defensive laager in what had been Tagrifah's open marketplace. The vehicles' bows faced outward, and their massed tribarrels were ready to claw.

They would have no target. Occasionally civilians blind with smoke and tears stumbled toward the laager. They ran as soon as the gleaming iridium shapes registered on their consciousness.

"There's a battalion of Boumedienne's boys coming on trucks," Currant explained to Barbour. "We'll wait for them, then head back to Desmond. There's nothing here the locals can't handle, now that we've done the real work."

She clapped Barbour on the shoulder again. "Now that *you've* done the real work, Bob. This one was all yours."

The dikes protecting Robert Barbour's mind crumbled, letting unalloyed reality wash over him. *The smoke and screams and the stench of fresh entrails . . .*

It hadn't been an atrocity. It was a necessary military operation.

And it was all his.

CANTILUCCA: DAY ONE

The sailor at the *Norbert IV*'s boarding hatch pointed to a row of low prefab buildings 300 meters from where the vessel had landed. The freighter's leave party — the whole crew except for a two-man anchor watch — had already stumped most of the distance over the blasted ground. The crewmen carried only AWOL bags, while the disembarking passengers had much more substantial luggage.

"There's the terminal," the sailor said. "The left one's Marvelan entry requirements. If there's nobody home, go to passenger operations beside it. Pilar'll be there, no fear."

"Not," said Mary Margulies, surveying the lighted buildings, "the fanciest-looking place I've ever been sent."

"At the moment," Matthew Coke said, "they aren't shooting at us. That's something."

It was late evening. The sky was purple. Cantilucca was supposed to have two moons, but either they weren't up or they were so small that Coke lost them in the unfamiliar stars.

The sailor snorted. "You want shooting?" he said. "Go on into Potosi. I guarantee you'll find somebody there who'll oblige you."

Johann Vierziger looked at him. "A tough town?" he asked.

His voice was delicate, effeminate. Coke didn't know what to make of Vierziger overall, but he'd watched the sergeant run the combat course at Camp Able. Whatever else Vierziger might be, he was surely a gunman.

"Tough enough, boyo," the sailor replied, eyeing Vierziger speculatively. "But it's a place a fellow can have a good time if he wants one, too."

"It appears that we're our own baggage handlers," Sten Moden said. He lifted his twin-width suitcase in his only hand. "Shall we?"

The big logistics specialist started down the ramp, drawing the others after him. Vierziger moved immediately to the front. Each member of the survey team carried a concealed pistol, but they were under Coke's strict orders not to draw their weapons unless he ordered them to.

Coke was uncomfortable. This wasn't either a combat operation or a routine change of station. He didn't know how he was supposed to feel.

Cantilucca's starport was a square kilometer bulldozed from the forest and roughly leveled. The earth had been compressed and stabilized.

There hadn't been a great deal of maintenance in the century or so since the port was cleared. Slabs of surface had tilted in a number of places, exposing untreated soil on which vegetation could sprout. The jets of starships landing and taking off limited the size of the shrubbery, at least in the portion nearer the terminal buildings.

There were twenty-three ships in port at the moment. Most of them were freighters of around 20 KT displacement, like the *Norbert IV*. Gage was big business, and Cantilucca grew the best gage in the universe.

Niko Daun chuckled. He was toward the rear of the straggling line — Lieutenant Margulies alone walked behind him, looking frequently over one shoulder, then the other.

"Here we all are in civilian clothes and everything," the young sensor tech said. "We look like a bunch of businessmen."

Coke glanced back at Daun. "That's right," he said

wryly. "We *are* businessmen. Or ambulance-chasing lawyers, that might be closer."

The survey team's luggage, two pieces for every member except the one-armed Moden, had static suspension systems. When the systems were switched on, they generated opposing static charges in the bottom of each case and the surface beneath it. The cases floated just above the ground and could be pulled along without friction.

On terrain as broken as that of the untended starport, that was only half the problem. Because of their contents and their armored sidewalls, the cases were extremely heavy. They wobbled on their narrow bases of support, threatening to fall over unless the person guiding them was relentlessly vigilant. The poor illumination didn't help either.

"Not bad training for life," Coke muttered.

"Sir?" Sten Moden said, turning his head back.

"Just talking to myself," Coke explained. "Sorry."

A bus pulled away from the terminal area. Its wheels were driven by four separate electric motors. One of the drives shrieked jaggedly as the bus headed toward the gate of the port compound.

"It's a lot easier," Sten Moden said without emphasis as he watched the bus go, "to replace a bearing than it is to replace a driveshaft *and* a bearing."

The bus didn't have headlights. A spotlight jury-rigged to the driver's side window swept the road and a stretch of the fence surrounding the compound. The forest beyond was a black mass. The sky had some color still in the west, but it no longer illuminated the land beneath it.

"Let's hope the soldiers aren't any better than the mechanics," said Robert Barbour.

Coke didn't have any more of a handle on the intelligence specialist than he did on Vierziger. Based on Barbour's personnel file, he was an easy-going man who was brilliant in his field. He had a bright career ahead of him, despite a lack of ambition outside his professional specialty.

There was no question about Barbour's qualifications. Coke had thought he himself knew his way around a sensor console, until he saw what Barbour could do casually with one.

In the flesh, though, the young lieutenant was withdrawn and apparently miserable. The file would have indicated if Barbour had survived a close one, as had happened to Daun. Maybe he'd had trouble with a woman. The Lord knew, there was plenty of that going around.

"They don't have soldiers here, Lieutenant," Johann Vierziger said. "On Cantilucca they have thugs, gangsters."

"We're not going to prejudge the situation," Coke said sharply. "Our report on the quality of potential allies and opposition is just as important as whether we recommend Nieuw Friesland accept an offer of employment here in the first place."

"Sorry, sir," Vierziger said. He didn't sound ironic, but neither was he making any effort to appear contrite.

The sergeant had made a statement which he knew, and which *Coke* knew, was correct on the basis of the score or more similar planets they'd both seen. Coke didn't know what Vierziger's background was — his file began at the point he enlisted in the FDF; but he knew the little gunman *had* a background. Nobody got as good as Vierziger was by spending his time at the target range.

Coke laughed. "Hold up," he called to Moden and Vierziger. He stopped where he was, set down the cases he was pulling, and motioned his team closer.

Lights from the terminal brightened that side of the faces watching Coke, but even there the flesh was colorless. Opposite the terminal, the team's features lacked detail.

"Look," Coke said, "we're here now, we're on our own. From this point on, we're on first-name basis."

Nobody reacted openly. Shutters clicked across the eyes of the more experienced trio, Moden, Margulies, and Vierziger.

"I don't mean," Coke explained hastily, "that we've suddenly become a democracy. Fuck *that* notion. You *will* take my orders, or I'll have you court-martialed on return to Camp Able."

A starship across the compound tested its landing motors. Plasma flared in an iridescent shimmer above the vessels, lighting the team members and the shattered ground about them. Vierziger grinned in broad approval.

"We're all good at our jobs," Coke resumed as the jet's rumble faded away. "And we'll be living in each other's pockets while the operation goes on. I trust that we can maintain real discipline without pretending we're back in base somewhere. Okay?"

The other members of the team nodded — Margulies with obvious relief. The last thing any sensible officer wanted was to serve under a commander whose first priority was that his troops *like* him.

Coke smiled and nodded. "Saddle up, troopers," he said. He switched on the repulsion units of his cases and resumed the last stage of his trudge to the terminal buildings.

Vierziger fell in beside him. "I'm not used to thinking of myself as 'Johann,'" the little man said with an unreadable substrate to the comment.

"Better get used to it, Johann," Coke said.

Vierziger's eyes were always on the far distance, the shadows which might be hiding an ambush. His cases tracked as nearly straight as the ground permitted, never tilting far enough to be in danger of toppling over. The little man's peripheral vision chose the best line possible across the field.

"People generally don't trust me," Vierziger said, as

if he were commenting on the magenta glow of the western horizon. "That's understandable, of course. But I want you to know that you could trust me, can if you want to."

A speck of light now at zenith had been 15° further east when Coke left the freighter. A moon, then, rather than a star; but merely a speck.

"I'll keep that in mind," he said aloud.

Vierziger laughed without malice. "The only difference between me and the pistol in your holster," he said, "is that you're more likely to hit the target if you aim me than if you aim it."

Coke looked at the little man. Neither of them spoke for a moment.

"Watch out for this," Vierziger said, gesturing toward a raw pit with the index finger of the hand gripping one of his cases.

The pit separated the two men by its width as they avoided it. "Why?" Coke asked.

"Because I think that's what I'm here to do, Matthew," Vierziger said.

He took two longer strides, then released his cases. They stood as sentinels to either side of the door as the gunman entered the terminal with his delicate hands free.

Coke walked through the doors a step behind Vierziger. Coke had been a combat soldier all his career, so he was irritated to be treated as an object for protection. Another part of him, though —

It was the job of the security element, Margulies and Vierziger, to protect the survey team's staff personnel. Coke, as team commander, couldn't object with even a frown at his people doing their jobs.

A hissing static broom shut off as the door opened. A woman, hidden until then behind the counter, stood up. Her lustrous auburn hair was caught in a braid and coiled on top of her head.

As Coke judged the mass, the hair would dangle to the floor if she removed the ornate silver combs pinning it up. Unlikely that she let it down often, though; the arrangement would take an hour to rebuild.

The woman wore black, relieved only by the massive silver crucifix hanging across her breast on a chain of the same metal. She was full-featured rather than fat and could have modeled for Rubens.

"Yes, gentlemen?" she said. Her voice held a touch of sharpness, a sign of uncertainty otherwise hidden. She appeared to be alone in the office. Two men had entered, well dressed but men and strangers, and there were further shapes looming outside the door.

"We're passengers from the *Norbert*, ma'am," Coke explained. "We're looking for the entry control office."

He hadn't forgotten the sailor had said that would be in the left-hand structure. The center building was the only one that was lighted, however.

"Oh, they should have told me!" the woman said with a stricken look.

Her eyes focused on the door. The panels had once been clear, but years of grit blown by nearby landings had blasted them to a pebbled surface. "How many of you are there?"

"Six," said Coke. "Is there a problem?"

"Not for six," the woman said. "I was going to take the operations van home anyway. My husband has our —"

She caught herself, flushed, and continued. "You see, the port bus just left with your ship's crew. They didn't say anything about passengers. I suppose they wanted to get into Potosi before dark."

Her skin was white, though from her dark lips Coke suspected she would tan to an umber color. She wore neither make-up nor, apart from the combs and crucifix, any jewelry.

"I'm Pilar Ortega," she said. "I'm the, well, I'm the

passenger services officer, but for the past few months I've been sort of running Terminal Operations — to the extent they're being run."

"What sort of entry formalities are there?" Coke asked. "Cantilucca is part of the Marvelan Confederacy, isn't it?"

The building was none too clean. From the sound of the static broom which the team's entry had interrupted, Pilar was doing not only the terminal director's work but also that of the janitor.

"Here, I'll log you in as well," Pilar said with a grimace. She turned to a console and brought it live. "Call your friends inside, will you please?"

Coke nodded to Vierziger, who moved to the door.

"The clerks in the Commission office next door have all gone home," the woman explained as she sorted through electronic files. Her fingers were tapering. They moved a light pen with short, positive strokes to control the holographic data. "High Commissioner Merian is . . . isn't as diligent as he might be. To tell the truth, so long as the port duties are paid, the Confederacy doesn't bother much about Cantilucca."

The team entered the terminal building in a smooth movement, forming a chain to slide all the luggage inside ahead of the personnel. Pilar looked up from her console to eye the cases. "It'll be tight," she murmured, "but we'll fit."

"Is the city far?" Johann Vierziger asked. His voice was calm and melodious, but his eyes never rested more than a second in one place. Watching him was like following a tiny, ravenous insectivore as it snuffled through the leaf mold.

"Two kilometers is all," Pilar said. "The usual separation in case of a landing accident. But sometimes the road —"

She looked up again. "There are people here who inject tailings from the gage refineries. It can make them dangerous. It's better not to be on foot when you're out of town. Potosi isn't anything more than a town."

Without changing her inflection she added, "May I see your identity chips, please?"

"Gage tailings are poison," Margulies said as she gave Pilar her ID chip left-handed. She and Vierziger were both nervous, though that wouldn't have been obvious to many outsiders. "Why use them when the whole planet's full of the pure stuff?"

"Poor people, of course," Pilar said primly as she fed the chips into a slot on her console. "Gage on Cantilucca is controlled for export. If you expected" — She glanced up sidelong, then back to the console — "to find it running free for the taking in the gutters here, I'm afraid you'll be disappointed."

"That won't really affect us one way or the other, Mistress Ortega," Coke said. "Ah — are there dangerous life forms on Cantilucca?"

"Only the human beings," Pilar said. "Some of them. Many of them."

The console popped the ID chips forth one at a time at half-second intervals. Pilar scooped them into her hand and distributed them to the members of the survey team. Though she scarcely glanced at the imprinted legends, she returned each to its owner on the first try.

"There," she said as she closed down the console again. "In theory, you should come in tomorrow when the clerks are on duty and go through this again. But I can't imagine anybody will mind. Half the time nobody shows up next door at all."

She took a deep breath and shook herself. "Are you ready to go?" she added.

"You bet we are," Margulies muttered, eyeing the translucent door behind her. A starship coughed plasma again, brightening the panels into feathery iridescence.

Pilar stepped into the office on the other side of the

counter and returned a moment later with a dark wrap. She opened the gate in the counter and said, "This way, then, please. The van is right outside."

Vierziger led again. He moved with serpentine grace, that one. He didn't appear to have hastened to get from one end of the room to the other ahead of his companions, but there he was.

Coke was impressed with Vierziger. Lieutenant Margulies' face was unreadable, but there was more to her expression than mere professional appreciation.

The night was as Coke remembered it, warm and muggy. He couldn't understand why the woman had bothered with an overgarment, until he noticed that it turned her into a shapeless blob without sex or individuality. He wondered whether that was more of a comment on Potosi or on Pilar's personality.

Beside the building was a four-wheeled van whose windows were broken out. Pilar got in while the team members wrestled their luggage into the back through the doors in both sides. The only seats were the pair of buckets in front.

Sten Moden opened the passenger door and swept his arm down in a courtly gesture toward Coke. "Rank hath its privileges," he said in a booming baritone.

"Bob, give me a leg up on top," Margulies called. "It's crowded inside, and I like the view from up there."

"I think perhaps I should ride there instead," Johann Vierziger said.

"I don't think so," Margulies snapped. Niko Daun chuckled.

Barbour made a stirrup of his hands. He grunted as he took the weight of the close-coupled woman, but she got a boot on the window frame and flipped herself neatly onto the vantage point.

Coke allowed himself a grin as he took his seat beside Pilar. The six of them had a lot of sorting out to do, with each other and with a job they were all new at. So far, so good.

The van was diesel powered. Pilar coaxed the engine to life with difficulty, and it ran rough after it caught.

"Are there aircars on Cantilucca?" Coke asked over the engine noise. From the amount of racket, there was no insulation in the firewall or body of the van to deaden sound.

"A few," the woman said. "It's hard to get maintenance on them. It's hard to get anyone to do *anything* in Potosi."

She engaged the torque converter. The van surged forward instead of picking up speed in a rising curve as Coke had expected.

"Except," Pilar added, "to swagger around with guns looking tough."

The van had a bar headlight across the upper hood. It worked, though its icteric cast suggested low voltage. The yellow light swept the gate of the starport compound, open and unguarded. Something hung from a pole just beyond the woven-wire fencing.

"Sir!" Margulies shouted.

"It's all right!" Coke called back. He'd seen the object as soon as Margulies did. "*He* isn't any danger, at any rate."

A corpse with its hands tied behind its back dangled by one ankle from a cross-pole. Either by chance or intention, the scene duplicated one of the arcana of a Tarot deck, *The Hanged Man*.

"Yes," Pilar Ortega said grimly. "That's also very popular in Potosi. Dying, I mean."

Either the breeze through the windowless van was unexpectedly cool, or the hormones flooding Coke's system were playing hell with his temperature regulation. He slid open the front seam of his dress jacket and let his index finger rest on the trigger guard of his pistol.

He began to smile. Survey work might not be as different from what he was used to as he'd feared.

✧   ✧   ✧

Coke had decided to enter Potosi quietly and not to arouse the locals' attention until he'd been able to view the situation on the ground. Frisian commo helmets with their array of vision-enhancing capacities would have marked the team even more clearly than would entering armed to the teeth.

Being able to see into the nighted forest would have been more calming to Coke than the weight of a 2-cm weapon in his hands. He supposed he'd made the right decision at leisure aboard the *Norbert IV*, but it didn't feel that way just now.

The van drove past a lean-to of brushwood and scrap sheeting. An open flame glimmered through the doorway. The shadow of an occupant ducked across the light.

"We're booked into a place called the Hathaway House," Coke said. "Is that near your house, mistress?"

"My *husband* and I have a suite on the other side of town," Pilar snapped. "Terence is in charge of cargo operations."

"I see," Coke said in a neutral voice. He saw, or thought he did, quite a lot. "I was only concerned that we were taking you out of your way, mistress. We're perfectly capable of making our way on foot. The cases are awkward, but the suspension takes all the weight."

The van rattled along at 45 or 50 kph, about all the pavement would allow. The vehicle steered with a pair of thumbwheels set on the arms of a control yoke. Pilar looked down at her hands for a moment, then raised her eyes to the road again.

"I have to go right past the Hathaway House to get home," she said. "Potosi has only the one street fit for a full-sized vehicle. There are alleys, but they're generally blocked."

"You're going out of your way to help us," Coke said, watching the woman with his peripheral vision. "I don't want to put you to needless trouble."

"Many of the people, the men, who come to

Cantilucca are a rough sort," Pilar said. She still didn't look toward Coke. "I shouldn't have reacted like that to you. I'm sorry."

"No problem," Coke said. "Were you born on Cantilucca?"

He knew what he was doing, and a part of his mind didn't like him much for it, but he was tense. This sort of game, this *hunt*, was a way to take his mind off wondering whether the next shadow was going to erupt in gunfire.

"Marvela," Pilar said. She wasn't a good driver; she had a tendency to overcorrect. At least she kept her eyes on the road while she talked. "We met when Terence was working in the port there. When he returned home to Cantilucca to run cargo operations, I —we married and I came with him."

From the glow in the sky ahead, the van was nearing the town proper. They passed a straggle of hovels like the first one. The dwellings weren't so much clustered as squatting in sight of one another, like a pack of vicious dogs penned together.

There was hinted motion, but no figure appeared in the open. There'd have been trouble had the team walked this way from the port. Nothing they couldn't have handled, but it would have gotten in the way of Coke's intention to start out with a low profile.

"Do you miss Marvela?" Coke asked. His eyes swept broad arcs though his head moved only slightly.

"No," Pilar said. "No."

She paused. "But I wish we hadn't come *here*. Cantilucca is a . . ."

She grimaced. Coke wasn't sure whether she was unable to find words to describe the planet, or if she was simply unwilling to voice them.

"There's too much nastiness here," Pilar said finally. "A man can go wrong anywhere. But on Cantilucca, it's very difficult to live decently."

Nothing wrong with my instincts, thought a part of

Matthew Coke's mind; and another part scowled at the smug realization.

The van came up the far side of a dip and rounded a slight curve. Potosi lay directly ahead.

The town had no streetlights, but the ground floors and occasionally one or two of the higher stories were dazzles of direct and reflected enticement. Instead of having common walls, the buildings were set separately, sometimes behind a walled courtyard. Barkers doubling as armed guards stood outside business entrances, shouting to the traffic through bullhorns.

Pilar slowed the van to a crawl. The theoretical right-of-way was fifteen meters wide, but hawkers and shills narrowed the street, grabbing at pedestrians. Coke saw a trio of crewmen from the *Norbert IV*. The sailors stayed together as they crossed from one set of premises to the next. Though the men wore pistols openly, they looked more apprehensive than dangerous.

There were no other vehicles on the street. A pink-haired woman with wild eyes stuck her head into the van on Coke's side. Her breath stank. She shouted something about the tray of electronic gadgets in her hand. The casings of gadgets, at any rate. Coke wouldn't have bet they had the proper contents.

He ignored the woman. She shouted a curse and spit at him. The roof post caught most of the gobbet instead.

The members of the survey team were in civilian clothing, but Margulies still wore her field boots. Her right leg described a quick arc, across the open window and up out of sight again. The hawker spun backward, tray flying as her eyes rolled up in their sockets.

It didn't seem to Coke that an action of that sort should arouse comment in Potosi; nor did it.

The ground floor of each building was walled like a pillbox, generally as a form of appliqué to the original structure. In some cases the strengthening took the form of sandbags behind a frame of timber and wire, but fancier techniques included cast concrete and plates of metal or ceramic armor.

In general, two or three upper stories were as-built. Many of the structures now had several additional stories added with flimsy materials.

Banners, lighted signs, and occasionally nude women or boys were displayed in second- and third-floor windows. There was always a screen of heavy wire mesh to prevent objects from being thrown in — or perhaps out. Music pumped from street-level door-ways, different in style at every one; always distorted, always shatteringly loud.

Every major starport had a district like Potosi. The difference here was that Potosi appeared to have nothing else.

As Pilar had said, no proper streets crossed the road from the port, but the set-backs between adjacent buildings created de facto alleys. One or more gunmen stood at each intersection, strutting arms akimbo or profiling on one leg with the other boot against the wall.

The gunmen weren't in uniform, but they wore swatches of either red or blue — a cap, an armband, a jacket — and never both colors. Most of them ran to crossed bandoliers, with knives and holstered pistols in addition to a shoulder weapon.

They eyed the van as it passed. A heavy-set, balding fellow with bits of red light-stripping twisted into his beard stepped after the vehicle, then changed his mind and took his former station. Coke relaxed slightly. He heard Vierziger sigh behind him, perhaps with disap-pointment.

"Are those your police?" Coke asked their driver.

Pilar sniffed. "There are no police in Potosi," she said. "None that count, at any rate. Those are toughs from the gage syndicates, Astra and L'Escorial. The Astras wear blue."

A leavening of ordinary citizens shared the streets

with the thugs, shills, and roisterers. Laborers; farmers in a small way, in town on business necessity but without money to spend as a few of their wealthier fellows had for the moment; clerks and office workers going home, hunched over and covered by capes like the one which concealed Pilar.

Somebody clanged a stone against the back of the van. Coke didn't react physically. He wondered if he should have put two of his people on the roof, so that Margulies wouldn't be clocked from behind. Too late to change plans now without precipitating the trouble he wanted to avoid.

"It isn't always this bad," Pilar said apologetically. Her hands were stiff on the control yoke. "Both the gangs have been hiring recently and bringing men in from the fields. It's, it's worse than any time in the six years we've lived here."

Coke didn't bother to ask whether "years" meant standard or the shorter Cantiluccan rotation.

"These are farmers?" he said, frowning at two bands of a dozen each, kitty-corner from one another at an intersection and only ten meters apart. The gangs glowered at one another as they postured.

A short man with a blue beret hopped up to the side of the van. He braced himself on the window ledge and shouted, "Dog vomit!" at the red-clad gang on the opposite corner.

Niko Daun clutched beneath his tunic. Sergeant Vierziger raised his left index finger to prevent his fellows in the back of the van from moving. His eyes were on the opposite side of the vehicle, however, ready to react if a L'Escorial thug decided to shoot through the vehicle at the challenger.

None of them did. The van rumbled on.

Pilar swallowed, showing that she too recognized how dangerous the past instant had been.

"I meant guards from the fields," she said, watching the roadway. "Some of them were farmers. Some of them were sailors who jumped ship or were discharged on Cantilucca for bad behavior. Many of them are just, just *badmen*. They've come to Cantilucca because word's out that the syndicates are willing to hire anybody who'll carry a gun and swagger."

"But there's no formed units of mercenaries on Cantilucca?" Coke asked.

"No," said Pilar. "No, we've at least been spared that."

So far, Coke thought. *But only so far.*

The van passed a three-story building on the right, set back in a walled courtyard. The structure was painted entirely blue, although several different shades had been mixed promiscuously. The whole facade was sheathed in concrete, and there were firing slits on each level in place of normal windows.

"Astra headquarters?" Coke asked. He thumbed toward the building, but he kept his hand below the level of the van's window so that only Pilar could see it.

"Yes," she said curtly — without looking toward the garish structure.

There were half a dozen guards at the courtyard gate, staring at everything which passed in the street. Their scrutiny drove pedestrians crowding to the left, the way a plume of cloud forms downstream of a hilltop.

Nobody looked at the guards. Nobody. Just for the hell of it, Coke turned deliberately to the right. His face wore a blank smile. The Astras glowered, but they were doing that anyway.

The guards were in full blue uniforms instead of wearing tags and scraps of the color. An elite force, then; and if those slope-browed slovens were the syndicate's elite, the Astras at least should be willing to pay for professional support.

"I'd think," Coke said in a neutral tone, "that there might be advantages to a dwelling closer to your place of work."

"Yes, I've thought of that too," Pilar said, giving Coke a brief smile. She was obviously glad of human contact. "But the part of Potosi past the two headquarter buildings is much quieter. The side toward the port is, well, you've seen it."

"Seen enough to imagine the rest," Coke agreed.

Somebody had sprayed scarlet paint on the pavement four hundred meters beyond Astra HQ. On the left side of the road, a group of twenty or so thugs sauntered from a heavily fortified building, also red, and surged across the street to form a cordon. They called to one another and jeered the civilians they blocked.

Pilar touched her crucifix with the tip of her right index finger and whispered a prayer. She stopped the van and cramped her wheels for a tight turn back the way they'd come.

"What is this?" Coke said. He opened his door and stepped out onto the running board. His eyes scanned front and to both sides, looking for the glint of a pointed weapon or the flash of a shot. His being was centered in his body, ready to send it in any direction.

The van's rear doors slid back as the rest of the team readied for action. Margulies' boots thumped on the roof.

"It's nothing, it's just a game they play every once in a while," Pilar said. She tried to ease the van into a turn, but the crowd recoiling from the cordon held the vehicle fast. "We'll have to go back and try to circle off the road — oh!"

"The idea seems to have caught on with our friends in blue," Margulies called from the roof of the van. "They've got the road blocked behind us now."

"Do you have any orders, Matthew?" Johann Vierziger asked in a voice as sharp and lethal as a cat's white eyetooth.

"No!" Coke said. *Not the guns, not yet.* "Mistress Ortega! What's the best way through?"

A three-wheeled jitney stopped at the cordon. The driver might have turned as more distant traffic did, but a thug pointed his sub machine gun at the little vehicle.

L'Escorial gunmen poked and prodded the passengers, a pair of sailors and their local whores. A gunman took the liquor bottle from a sailor, drank from it, and handed it back. The business wasn't a formal search, just harassment and almost good-natured — until the end.

A gunman lifted up the bandeau of one of the prostitutes to uncover her breasts. The woman's nipples were tattooed blue.

The gunman's quick feel turned into a vicious yank. The woman screamed. Another L'Escorial thug bashed her behind the ear with a pistol butt.

Half a dozen of the red-clad gunmen converged like soldier ants to the sound of an intruder. They kicked and punched, stripping the prostitute as she tried to crawl away from them. One of the men thrust the muzzle of his 2-cm powergun between the woman's legs.

Coke's vision focused into a narrow tunnel. His mouth was half open and his skin was cold.

He didn't know her. She was nothing but a whore and a stupid whore besides, a whore who took an indelible stand in favor of one gang of thugs over another.

But he was going to do it anyway, violate his own orders and he'd have had the *balls* of any team member who did the same —

The L'Escorial lifted his powergun, laughing, and kicked the woman instead. His nailed boots tore a double row of gashes in her buttocks; but that came with the turf. She continued to crawl, ignored now by the gunmen and other citizens alike.

The two sailors and the remaining woman slipped through the cordon during the incident. The driver left his jitney where it was. He ducked into a doorway marked DRINKS & ENTERTAINMENT.

Pilar shut off the van's engine. "There's no way through or around," she said. "No safe way. They —"

She closed her eyes and whispered something with her finger on the crucifix again.

"This doesn't happen very often," she continued in a resigned tone. "I suggest you take beds in one of these —" she grimaced "— places. That's what I'm going to do. It will be quite horrible, but . . . you can't tell what they'll take it into their heads to do. Many of them mix tailings and alcohol together. It makes them crazy. Crazier."

"This doesn't look like a great neighborhood a-tall," Niko Daun said, looking around at the dingy buildings.

He was right. The add-on levels above the original constructions were reached by rickety outside stair-cases. The signs reading BEDS or SLEEP or (in one case, and perhaps little more of a lie than the others) SAFE LODGINGS were always on these outside stairs.

"How far away is the Hathaway House?" Coke asked Pilar as he continued to scan.

"It's right across the street from the L'Escorial building," Pilar said, "but that's the problem. It wouldn't do you any good to walk around the, the armed *children*, because they're exactly where you want to go."

"Hathaway House may not be any better than these flops anyway," Sten Moden suggested. He didn't sound concerned.

"There's six of us," said Robert Barbour. "We ought to be safe enough for the night."

"The Hathaway is a decent place," said Pilar. "I mean really *decent*, the only one in Potosi. But you can't get there. It doesn't have any back door. That'd just be another point to guard."

"I would say," Vierziger said coolly, "that it's not too far to carry our luggage if the lady doesn't want to drive us."

"It's not *want*," Pilar burst out angrily. "It's not *safe* to cross that gauntlet, safe for you!"

People with great need or great confidence were getting past the cordon. A gunman in red cordovan boots cut a citizen's belt and sent him scampering away with his trousers around his ankles.

Women were fondled, generally roughly. A few people were relieved of small objects — a gun, a chip recorder; perhaps some money. For the most part the cordon was an irritation, not an atrocity.

But it could become an atrocity at any moment, Coke knew. The only apparent check on the gunmen's activities was their own desires. There was no sign of external control.

Coke glanced up at Margulies on the roof of the van. He'd order her into a firefight without hesitation, but this was something else again. At the start, anyway.

"Mary, it's your call," he said.

She shrugged. "I'm not thrilled either way," she said. "But we came here to get information. I guess we may as well go do that."

She hopped down, bracing her left hand on the van roof. Her toes took her weight, so that she landed as lightly as if she'd stepped from the side door.

"All right, that's what we're going to do," Coke said. "Whatever comes, we're going to take it. When we're in the hotel, we'll take stock — but not before then. Understood?"

Sten Moden shrugged. Daun said, "Yessir," very quietly, and Robert Barbour nodded. The intel lieutenant looked nervous, which was actually good: that meant he understood what was likely to happen. Coke thought he'd be okay.

"You mustn't do this!" Pilar said. "Please, just come with me."

She started toward stairs marked CLEAN LOCKED BEDS, rising from the unpaved alley beside where the van was parked. A man — or perhaps a woman within the ragged garments — lay supine just below the first landing.

"Nothing without orders, Matthew," said Johann Vierziger. "Nothing. I understand."

Coke nodded. "Let's do it," he said, hefting his own pair of cases from the van and starting toward the cordon.

"Please!" called Pilar Ortega. "Please, Master Coke! You don't know what you're doing."

She was wrong there . . . but that didn't necessarily mean that the business was survivable.

A few additional gunmen wandered out of L'Escorial headquarters to join the cordon. One of them brought a carton from which he tossed thimble-sized stim cones to his fellows.

Other L'Escorials left, bored by the lack of activity. Three of them headed for a ground-floor establishment whose doorjamb and transom were outlined in red glow-strip.

Many of the dives in the immediate neighborhood were marked red. None of them had blue anywhere on their signs or facades.

"S'pose they'd all go home if we waited a bit?" Daun asked.

"No," said Barbour beside him. There was tension in the voices of both technical specialists, but many things need to be tight to function. Neither of the men sounded as if he was about to break.

The 400-plus meter stretch of road between the rival headquarters had largely emptied since the cordons were established. The only traffic was of pedestrians crossing from one bar to another or climbing stairs to a flophouse.

A few drivers returned to their vehicles and ran them into the alleys. The jitneys had large-diameter wheels and often studded tires (though not all of them *had* tires). They could probably get along well enough off the pavement, though a serious pothole would overbalance them sideways. The little vehicles had narrow tracks and a high center of gravity.

The survey team, pulling its luggage toward the L'Escorial cordon, stood out like six sore thumbs.

The gunmen quieted speculatively. They didn't break their rough spacing across the width of the street, but there was a slight edgewise movement to concentrate in Coke's line toward the doorway of Hathaway House.

The door was metal-faced. It opened a crack. An orange-haired woman in her late middle age looked out. She closed the door after surveying the situation, but a triangular viewport opened immediately toward the top of the panel.

A blond man in his mid-twenties walked from the center of the line toward the end which the team approached. The fellow wore a crimson vest and cutoff trousers, high boots with rows of spikes around the calves, and a waist belt heavy with pouches of spare magazines for his sub-machine gun. His right arm and left leg were tattooed in patterns too stretched and faded to be identified in the bad light.

Coke paused a meter short of the blond man. Vierziger was a pace behind him; the rest of the team slanted back in precise echelon. Under the present circumstances, Moden instead of Margulies brought up the rear.

"Good evening, sir," Coke said to the presumed L'Escorial leader. He let go of the hand-grips of his luggage.

The blond man pointed his sub-machine gun into the air and shot off half the magazine in a single ripping burst. A cone of cyan bolts flicked toward the stars.

As their leader fired, most of the other L'Escorials in the cordon followed suit in a ragged volley. They carried a wide variety of weapons, though high-quality powerguns predominated. The night was a bedlam of *whacks*, hiss*cracks*, and propellant flashes of red, orange and yellow supplementing the powerguns' saturated blue.

Not all the gunmen aimed skyward. A burly, bare-chested man wearing garnet-studded nipple rings with a chain slung between them pointed his chemically powered fléchette gun at the front of Hathaway House. He fired twice.

The crashing reports of the hypervelocity weapon rattled shutters and screens against the windows they protected. The building's facade was concrete containing very coarse aggregate. The tungsten fléchettes blew out craters in sprays of yellow-green sparks. A piece of gravel the size of Coke's clenched fist flew back across the street. It smacked the wall fronting L'Escorial headquarters.

The gunman rocked with each round from his high-recoil weapon. He was lowering the muzzle for a third shot when the L'Escorial leader batted him across the temple with the sub-machine gun's barrel.

"Fuckhead!" the leader shouted as his henchman sprawled facedown on the pavement. The victim's hair, scorched by the white-hot iridium, stank obscenely. "You want to kill us all?"

He'd knocked the fellow unconscious. From the eyes of the man with the fléchette gun, he'd been flying so high on gage and other drugs that he probably wouldn't remember the lesson in the morning anyway, though he'd feel it.

The L'Escorial leader turned. He waggled the glowing muzzle of his powergun in Coke's face. "Where do you come from, dickhead?" he demanded.

"We're businessfolk from Nieuw Friesland," Coke said quietly. "Though the last stage of our voyage was through Delos."

"Everybody comes through Delos if they're coming here, dickhead," the leader snarled. He pointed his weapon one-handed at one of Coke's suitcases. "Open that. *Now!*"

"I'm sorry," Coke lied, "but they were hold baggage on shipboard, so they're time-locked. They can't be opened for another day and a half."

"Want to bet?" the gunman said. He fired.

The survey team's luggage was plated with 40-laminae ceramic armor beneath a normal-looking sheathing. The thin laminae shattered individually without transmitting much of the shock to deeper layers. A few rounds from a 2-cm weapon would have blown any of the cases apart, but the burst of 1-cm pistol charges from the sub-machine gun only pecked halfway through the plating.

Furthermore, the ceramic reflected a proportion of the plasma. The spray of sun-hot ions glazed Coke's trouser legs — the business suit was much more utilitarian than its stylish cut implied.

The L'Escorial gunman's bare knees blistered instantly, and the fringe of his shorts caught fire. He screamed, dropped his weapon, and began batting with his bare hands at the flames.

The case started to fall over. The burst of gunfire had smashed the forward static generator in a shower of sparks.

Coke grabbed the handle of the case. "Please, sirs!" he cried in a voice intended to sound terrified. "We're businessmen! Please!"

"Fuck you!" a tall man with a pair of pistols cried. "You're dancers, that's what you are!"

He fired twice into the pavement at Coke's feet. Glass and pebbles from the compressed-earth roadway spattered Coke's legs above his shoe tops. Coke staggered forward, lifting the front of the damaged case in his left hand. He squeaked in simulated terror.

The fear was real, but not terror, not anything that prevented Matthew Coke from acting in whatever fashion was necessary.

He didn't *know* whether or not the actions he'd set in motion were survivable. It was like a free-fall jump. Once you'd committed, you could only hope the support mechanism — static repulsion, parachute, or whatever — would work as intended. The team couldn't change its collective mind now.

A 2-cm bolt blew off the lower back corner of the damaged case and the rest of the static suspension. With the plating and the hardware inside, the case weighed nearly a hundred kilos. Coke lurched onward with it, bleating. He was through the cordon, but a bullet could flick through the back of his head and take his face off at any gunman's whim.

Mary Margulies touched the latch of her right-hand case with a finger so swift that the luggage appeared to have flown open by accident. Frilly underwear and lounging garments flew out onto the roadway.

"Hey lookee-lookee-lookee!" shouted a gunman. He grabbed a teddy and modeled it against his scarred chest.

The cordon collapsed into a rush for loot. The clothing had no value except as a matter of amusement, but that's all the cordon was to begin with: a way for men with a childish mindset to amuse themselves.

"Hey, sweetie!" a gunman cried. He grabbed, not very seriously, for Margulies' crotch. The lieutenant weaseled past with her remaining suitcase. "Stay with me! I'll give you more dick than all five of them pussies together!"

The door of Hathaway House opened in front of Coke. His left arm felt as though the shoulder tendons would snap with the weight of the case they supported. He stepped aside to check on his team.

"Get *in*, curse your eyes!" Johann Vierziger shouted. "I'll handle —"

Vierziger slid one of his cases into the doorway with a sweep of his left arm.

"— this!" and he sent the second case after the first, skidding like driverless cars.

Though the static suspension balanced the weight of

the luggage, its inertia was unchanged. Vierziger's movements, as smooth and practiced as those of a expert lawn-bowler, required strength that one wouldn't assume in someone as pretty as the little man.

A voice yelped from inside the hotel. The door started to close, but Barbour was there, using the mass of his cases to slam the panel fully open. He twisted aside. Niko Daun followed him in.

A pair of L'Escorial gunmen were dancing. One wore a pair of delicate panties as a crown; his partner had thrust his arms into leggings whose multiple shimmering colors shifted as they caught varied light-sources. Other L'Escorials cheered and clapped, or pawed through the open case for their own trophies.

Coke pointed Margulies *in*. She obeyed at a hasty rush, aware that her presence as a woman made the risk to every member of the team greater. The expression on her face was set and terrible.

Sten Moden tossed his huge case after her, picked up both of Coke's cases in his one hand and tossed them; and wrapped his arm around Coke's waist. Moden swept the major with him into the lobby of Hathaway House. Coke could as well have wrestled an oak tree for the good his protests did.

Somebody had to be last in; and yeah, that was probably a job for the security detail, for Sergeant Vierziger, but it didn't seem right . . .

The sixtyish woman with orange hair started to push the door closed. Daun and Barbour were already doing that. Vierziger danced backward through the opening.

The panel clanged against its jamb. It rang again an instant later: a L'Escorial had fired a powergun into the armor as a farewell. The door's refractory core, lime or ceramic, absorbed the discharge without damage.

The woman swept her hair out of her eyes. She was healthy-looking though on the plump side. A man of similar age with a luxuriant, obviously implanted, mane of hair stood to the side, wringing his hands.

Several tables stood in a saloon alcove off the foyer. A few men were seated in the shadows there. They stared pointedly at their drinks rather than at the newcomers. The silence within the hotel was a balm after the noisy violence of the street.

The woman planted her arms akimbo, fists on her hips. "Welcome to Cantilucca, mistress and sirs," she said. "Now, if you're smart, you'll head right back to the port and take the next ship *out* of this pigsty!"

"Oh, Evie, it's not so bad as that," the man said. "It's just with the, you know, with the syndicates on edge like they are, there's more, ah . . ."

"More murderous bandits in town than usual?" the woman snapped. "Yes, there are, and it's an open question whether they kill everybody else off before they kill each other or after!"

"I'm Georg Hathaway," the man said, bowing to Moden — probably because the logistics officer was the most imposing presence of this or most other groups. "This is my wife Evie, and I'm sorry for this trouble, usually things are better, it's just there are so many of the patrolmen in Potosi these last few months, and you know, the boys will let off steam."

"Usually things are *almost* bearable," Evie Hathaway said sharply. "That hasn't been the case since the bandits began gearing up to fight — and they *don't* fight, they just squeeze decent citizens harder yet. When will it stop, I'd like to know?"

"Evie, now, don't upset the gentlemen and lady," Georg Hathaway said. "They've had a difficult time already, we mustn't make it worse. Are you the Coke party, then, booking from Nieuw Friesland?"

Moden gestured, palm up. "This is Master Coke," he said. "You have rooms for us?"

"Oh, we have rooms, all right," Evie said. "What we don't have is patrons who can pay us for them. Since this trouble started three months ago, nobody with money and sense comes anywhere near Potosi."

She stared fiercely at Coke. "And we have *our* standards. Are you here on behalf of the gage cartel on Delos, Master Coke?"

"No," Coke said, "we don't have anything to do with gage."

Hathaway House was a two-story building. The lobby, saloon, and service quarters were on the ground floor, while the guest rooms were up a flight of stairs. Judged from outside, the protective concrete wall was of equal thickness all the way up, so Coke didn't see any need for special arrangements.

"Speaking of gage," said Niko Daun hopefully, "I don't suppose this would be a good time to have a cone or two?"

Moden looked at the younger man with an icy fury that shocked Coke. "No," the big man said in a voice as still as death, "it would not. Not so long as the operation is going on."

Daun blushed. "I'm sorry, sir," he said, looking toward the lower wall molding, gray against the lobby's general peach decor. "I just thought that since we had a break after, well, after . . ."

"There's no breaks until we lift out of here, T-tech, Niko," Sten Moden said more gently. "But I'm sorry, it wasn't mine to speak —"

He nodded formally toward Coke.

"— and I'm sorry for my tone. I — wouldn't care for others to make such a mistake as I made in the past, thinking I could let down."

Margulies and Vierziger had conferred briefly. The lieutenant trotted upstairs to check protection and fields of fire there, while Vierziger prowled the ground floor. The Hathaways watched him askance but neither of them spoke — even when he disappeared into their own quarters.

"Bloody hell," Coke muttered. He peeked out of the door's triangular viewport.

The cordons were still in place. The L'Escorials had

rolled an armored truck into the street to face the Astra line. It looked like a four-wheeled van covered with so many metal and concrete panels that it could barely move. The vehicle mounted tribarrels in a cupola and in a sponson to either side. There were firing slits as well, though Coke judged that they did little but weaken the already-doubtful protection.

Robert Barbour opened one of his cases. The interior was packed with electronics. He began to extend the case into a full-featured communications module.

"Come on, Daun," he said. "We need to get some information if we're going to do our job."

Niko Daun gave the room a bright smile. "We're going to need information if we're going to survive the tour, *I'd* say," he remarked cheerfully.

The sensor tech unlatched a case of his own. It too was full of gear. He took out a series of sensors, broad-band optical and radio frequency, whistling under his breath.

Clothing hadn't been a high priority for a team operating out of range of support — save for the suitcase Margulies had insisted on bringing as a decoy, and *that* thought had earned her a commendation if Coke lived to write it.

"Ah, would you gentlefolk not like some refreshment?" Georg Hathaway suggested. "We have what we like to think is a very good beer, I brew it on the premises myself, and there's local cacao as well, good enough to export, if it weren't that no one cares for anything but gage on Cantilucca."

"Gage and killing," his wife said bitterly. "And mostly killing. I don't think it'll stop before there's only one of the bandits left."

"About how many men do the gage syndicates employ, mistress?" Coke asked as he continued to look out the viewport. Barbour and Daun would give him much more precise data in a moment, but in some ways there was nothing to equal the naked eye.

"Too many," Evie said. "And they're hiring more every day."

Georg — eyeing the array of devices the tech specialists were assembling — said cautiously, "Sirs, I'd judge that Astra and L'Escorial have at least a thousand, ah, employees each. They aren't all in, ah, the patrol branch, but most of them are."

"Usually most of them are out in the fields, bullying the growers," Evie Hathaway said. "But they've been bringing them into Potosi since the trouble started."

She raised her arms and combed her fingers through her artificially bright hair. She looked tired and frustrated, a woman near the end of her tether. "I hope the growers are getting some benefit. Because it's *hell* here for decent folk."

The makeshift armored truck revved its air-cooled diesel engine. The separately bolted body panels vibrated at different frequencies, creating a grinding rattle. For the crew, it must have been like riding in a cement mixer — but maybe they were so stoned that they wouldn't feel the effects of their silliness until the next morning.

Niko darted up the stairs to arrange his equipment from high vantage points. Margulies came down, wearing a satisfied expression, and gave Coke a thumbs-up. The upper floor and roof were secure in her — expert — estimation.

"And there's no police force, I understand?" Coke said.

The tribarrel in the armored truck's cupola pointed up at 20°, probably its maximum elevation, and fired a two-round burst. The rich cyan of the high-powered 2-cm charges flashed in reflection from the facades.

"Police?" Mistress Hathaway crowed. She pointed into the saloon. "Police? Look at them there, afraid to go out without covering up so they won't be seen! Oh, we've got *fine* police here in Potosi!"

The two men drinking morosely at a corner table did, now that Evie called attention to the fact, wear white uniforms. Dingy white uniforms. They hunched their shoulders under the lash of her tongue. Drab capes like the one with which Pilar covered herself hung over the backs of their chairs.

"Evie, now, don't get yourself into a state," Georg murmured, wringing his hands again.

The gunman in the armored truck rotated his barrels manually, then fired another two rounds. The ill-maintained tribarrel jammed again at the third loading sequence.

One of the policemen turned and glared from deep-sunk eyes. "Look, what do you want us to do?" he demanded. He waved a shock baton, the only weapon he carried. "Go out and arrest them all, and for what?"

He made a face as if to spit, then thought the better of it. Sinking back over his mug of beer he added, "Better I should shoot myself. At least I could be sure it was quick if I did it myself."

"Find someone worth a bullet!" Evie Hathaway snapped, but she'd lost the edge of anger. Exhaustion reasserted itself.

A ripple — three pairs — of hypervelocity rockets cracked down the street in the opposite direction, well over the heads of the L'Escorial cordon. The Astras must have brought one of their own armored vehicles out, though Coke couldn't see it from his present vantage point.

The projectiles were aimed deliberately high, just as the L'Escorial tribarrel had been; but that sort of game could get out of hand as quickly as Russian roulette could. A red-clad gunman spread his fringed leather kilt and urinated in the direction of the Astra line.

"You gentlemen — and lady, of course," Georg Hathaway said cautiously, "are in the instrument business, then? You plan to sell instruments to the gage syndicates?"

"Not exactly," Coke said curtly.

"I've got a hook-up, sir," Barbour said. "Ah, Matthew. You can have a panorama here on the console or fed to your helmet."

Coke glanced briefly at the data console. A holographic globe a meter in diameter hung above the base. The image was a schematic of the center of Potosi. Buildings appeared as simplified versions of themselves, while vehicles and armed personnel were icons — red and blue, as indicated.

The L'Escorial armored car revved and backed slowly away, its tribarrels pointing toward the Astras. While turning to the courtyard, the vehicle's right rear fender bashed a gatepost. The engine stalled. The car rolled forward a meter.

Gunmen in the cordon hooted and catcalled at the vehicle's crew. The driver started his engine again with a cloud of black smoke. He advanced into the middle of the street and cramped his wheels to get a running start at the entrance. There was plenty of room, but the single side mirror wasn't adequate for backing so clumsy a vehicle.

The armored car lurched into reverse. It roared backward in a shower of sparks and concrete powdered from both the vehicle and the gatepost it scraped. The gunmen clapped and cheered ironically.

Johann Vierziger sat on a stuffed chair with his hands crossed in his lap, watching the scene in the holographic display. His face wore a grim smile.

The sensor tech had returned from upstairs. He shook his head and said, "I told them I'd never work with wogs again. Lord knows *that* was the right decision."

He grinned. Coke had read the kid's file. Daun was obviously as resilient as he was skilled in his specialty; but then, he was young too.

"Master Hathaway?" Coke said. "I under —"

"Georg," the host said, nodding. "Please, call me Georg."

"Georg, then," Coke said. "I understand that there are no professional military units on Cantilucca — no mercenaries, that is. Is that your understanding as well?"

"Well," Hathaway said, "both syndicates have Presidential Guards. They're mostly soldiers from off-planet."

"But not off-planet *units*?" Coke pressed. The guard forces in full uniform might be individually more skillful than the ruck of ex-farmers and ex-sailors carrying guns, but they obviously lacked the discipline necessary to carry out complex maneuvers.

"No, not that I've heard of," Hathaway said. "That would be much more expensive, surely?"

"That depends on what you're assigning values to," said Mary Margulies.

Coke had thought the cordons might disperse when the armored vehicles left, but a score of red-clad gunmen remained. Traffic was picking up slightly. The citizenry had decided that the gunmen didn't mean serious trouble.

"They can't bring mercenaries onto Cantilucca," Evie Hathaway said unexpectedly. "Because of the Confederacy."

"We'd heard the Marvelans left Cantilucca pretty well alone," Sten Moden said quietly.

"The Confederacy doesn't care anything about law and order here, so long as they're paid their money," Evie said. "*Blood* money, I call it. But they won't let a proper army onto Cantilucca. For fear they'd take over and the Confederacy wouldn't be able to drive them out."

Georg Hathaway looked at his wife in surprise. "What's that, Evie?" he said. "I hadn't heard that."

She turned slightly away. In a less forceful voice she said, "When the Marvelan delegation was on Cantilucca a year and a half ago, the overflow from the High Commissioner's residence stayed here. One of the aides explained that to me when, when I was complaining to him."

"Aides . . ." Georg repeated in a flat tone. "That would be young Garcia-Medina, I suppose you mean?"

"It might have been!" said Evie. "I was complaining about the horrible situation, that was all!"

"We have," Johann Vierziger said, "a war of sorts outside. I don't think adding one inside is necessary at the moment."

"No, no," Georg said. The innkeeper's forced smile quickly asserted its own reality over his personality. "That's old business and nothing to it, not really, not even then. Pardon me, mistress and masters, for letting the stress of the moment get the better of me."

The whole team was assembled in the lobby of the hotel. Coke grinned wryly at his people. With the corner of his eye still tracking developments in the street peripherally, he said, "Well, what do the rest of you think? Niko?"

The sensor tech grinned and flipped his hands palms-up in a non-committal gesture. "I can set you up to count the change in the pocket of anybody in town, sir. Just tell me what you want."

Coke nodded. "Bob?"

Barbour looked through the space occupied by his holographic display. His hands hovered over the console keyboard, not quite touching it.

"There's something over six hundred powerguns live in the three-klick radius," he said. "Given the ratio of powerguns to other weapons outside, that roughs in well with a total of a thousand shooters in town at present."

He looked at Coke; his eyes focused again. "What else would you like to know, Matthew?"

"That'll do," Coke said. He'd deliberately kept the parameters of his question vague. The team members were answering each to his own specialty, just as they should. "Sten?"

The logistics officer nodded twice before he spoke, as though his mind were a pump and he was priming it. "Yes," he said. "What Mistress Hathaway says rings true. If so, we'll either have to infiltrate the personnel or arrange a combat landing. I doubt we'll be able to get the Bonding Authority to cover either option."

"Is that a deal-breaker, then?" Coke asked. "Shall we just pack up and go home?"

Moden shook his head. "There've been precedents," he said. "They aren't talked about officially, but you hear about them in the bars around Camp Able. It affects the price and the size of the force to be risked, however."

"I don't like the idea of going in on a non-bonded operation," Margulies said with a frown.

"*We* won't be going in anywhere," Coke said. "And the decision isn't ours. We're just here to assess possibilities."

The Bonding Authority on Terra guaranteed that both parties to a hiring of mercenaries would perform according to the terms of the contract. That is, the troops would obey the orders of the contracting local party — whether the latter was a recognized government, a rebel movement, or an interstellar business conglomerate extending its holdings by force. And the troops would be paid, even if that meant the contracting local parties starved, or starved every civilian on the planet, in order to meet their obligations to the mercenaries.

The Bonding Authority didn't take a moral stand: money has no smell. Though one could argue that forcing adults to keep their word was itself a way of instilling morality on human weakness.

Margulies grimaced and nodded.

"Johann?" Coke said.

Vierziger sniffed. "A company of infantry, backed up by a company of combat cars," he said. He snapped the fingers of his left hand dismissively. "It could be done with less. These people are hopeless, quite hopeless."

"How about panzers instead of cars?" Margulies suggested. "This is a city of bunkers."

Vierziger shook his head. "There's too many hiding places for buzzbomb teams," he said. "Tribarrels can break up the facades almost as fast as a twenty-centimeter main gun could, and a car has twice as many eyes as a tank to watch for launchers. Even that's risky, but the infantry needs the firepower support."

Margulies pursed her lips. "We could use the local allies, whichever side, to unmask ambushes?" she said, the question implicit in her tone.

"Dream on," Vierziger said scornfully. Margulies shrugged and nodded agreement with her nominal underling's judgment.

"May I ask just what business you goodfolk deal in, please?" Georg Hathaway said in a cautiously distant voice.

Vierziger raised an eyebrow at Coke. Coke scratched the side of his neck. No point in trying to conceal matters. Theirs was, after all, a legitimate commercial operation.

"We're representatives of the Frisian Defense Forces," he said, nodding toward Mistress Hathaway to include her in the explanation. "Our superiors had been told that one or both gage syndicates here on Cantilucca might be interested in hiring high-quality mercenaries. The FDF are the best, period. We're here to assess prospects for doing business and to report back to our superiors."

Evie Hathaway's face hardened by increments as Coke spoke. When he finished, she said harshly, "I don't think you made a very positive impression when you arrived, *gentle*folk. I doubt either the Widow Guzman or the Lurias will be interested in paying for the services of more like yourselves."

"Evie, now, don't be that way," her husband begged. "I'm sure these —"

"No, no," Coke said. "Mistress Hathaway is right. I suppose we need to do something to correct the situation immediately."

"People are drifting away from the roadblocks, sir," Barbour commented.

Coke had seen as much through the viewport, but there were still twelve or fourteen L'Escorials in position. About right for the purpose.

Margulies raised an eyebrow. Coke nodded. Margulies and Vierziger unlatched another pair of cases.

"How thick are the walls?" Coke asked.

"You *won't* start a fight in here!" Evie Hathaway shouted. "You have to kill me first! This is a place of peace!"

"Ma'am, I wouldn't think of it," Coke said truthfully. "Anything that happens will be out on the street. I just want to be sure that none of the — side effects — will be dangerous to your structure."

Barbour adjusted a set of controls. A ghost of Hathaway House glowed as a sidebar to the schematic of the immediate streetscape.

He looked up at Coke. "The front wall is nearly a meter thick," he said. "Glass-reinforced concrete, and well shaken down. There's a slight batter, but nothing that should matter."

"Well, that's right," Georg said in surprise. "I thought, Evie thought, really, that we shouldn't spare expense on protection if we were going to get the kind of guests we wanted."

The innkeeper looked at the cases the security detail had opened. Like those of Barbour and Daun, they were filled with equipment. This time, all the equipment was lethal.

Margulies and Vierziger began handing out weapons to the rest of the team.

Vierziger handed each member of the survey team a vest woven from beryllium monocrystal. Moden and

Daun had carefully lifted the segments of ceramic plate from the exterior walls of the luggage. The plates fitted into pockets in the vests, forming body armor almost as resistant as the clamshell hard-suits which the FDF issued for normal field operations.

Coke took off his loose outer jacket and paused. "I don't think I want armor for this," he said. He was —

Well, of course he was frightened, a *turtle* would be frightened if it was about to walk into this one. It was his job, and anyway it'd be all right.

"I think you ought to wear it, sir," Margulies said.

She'd completely emptied the suitcase on which she'd been working. Weapons and ammunition lay in neat stacks on the tile floor around her. She stood up and latched the case, then twisted the hand-grip 180°. She slid the luggage over to him.

"I think he ought to wear armor also," said Johann Vierziger, "though I'll admit I wouldn't myself if it were me."

He smiled. His face was that of an ivory angel. "I prefer the freedom. But what I really think is that I should be the one to go outside, Matthew."

Coke shook his head forcefully. "It's my job," he said. "And anyway, it'll be all right."

He thrust his arms through the holes of the vest he'd prepared, then mated the front closures. His outer jacket was cut to hang the same whether or not there was armor beneath it. He pulled it on.

"Helmet?" said Barbour without looking up from his console display.

Coke shook his head brusquely. "The implant will do in a pinch," he said, tapping his jaw. The right mastoid contained a miniature bone-conduction radio transceiver. "They'd react to the helmet the same as they would if I went out in full uniform."

Barbour nodded without concern. It was his job to offer information to the action personnel. He didn't — couldn't — control what they did with the information.

Vierziger slid Coke a second case, emptied and prepared as Margulies had done with hers.

Coke looked down at the luggage, then at his security detail. "One's enough," he said.

"Two, Matthew," said Vierziger.

"Two," echoed Margulies. "What do you intend to save them for, sir?"

Coke laughed harshly at himself. There was a tendency in any combat unit, particularly with those which operated beyond resupply, to fear using up munitions which they might need later. At its worst, that attitude could mean a position being overrun because the defenders were unwilling to cut loose with everything they had, lest they be out of ammo when the next attack came.

Margulies and Vierziger were right. Unless Coke made the few next minutes *really* memorable for the L'Escorials, ten times the hardware the team had brought to Cantilucca wouldn't be enough.

"Right," he said. "Two." He took the suitcases.

Niko Daun put his hand on the door latch. Moden's strength would have been a better match for the mass of the armored panel, but the powerful officer's one arm carried a three-tube missile launcher. The unit was intended for vehicle mounting, but Moden held it as easily as a lesser man might have done a 2-cm powergun.

Margulies and Vierziger were in position to either side of the door, she with a sub-machine gun, he with his hands empty, though he'd slung a sub-machine gun for patrol carry along his left side. The embellishments of the pistol in the high-ride holster on Vierziger's right hip winked in the foyer lights.

Robert Barbour sat at his console, calm or comatose. Coke supposed the former but it didn't matter, not now, as he nodded to Daun and started toward the door, sliding the cases beside him.

Coke stepped through the doorway and shivered in

the warm, muggy air. L'Escorial gunmen turned in surprise to face him.

Coke set his luggage against the front wall of Hathaway House. Each of the big cases was a meter long and sixty centimeters high. They were thirty centimeters deep as well, but the volume wasn't important any more. Coke left the pair in a very flat V, end to end, almost parallel to the reinforced concrete facade.

He stepped quickly toward the cordon's leader, the blond man in vest and cutoffs. The fellow's legs were an angry color; he'd have blisters across the whole front of them by morning, if he survived that long.

A gunman with a bayonetted grenade launcher stuck his weapon toward Coke's face. The bayonet was a spike rather than knife-style. Coke swept it aside with his left hand.

"Excuse me, sir!" Coke called to the leader. "I believe you're in charge here?"

"Who the *fuck* do you think you are, you little prick?" the L'Escorial demanded in obvious amazement. He pointed his sub-machine gun like a huge pistol. The muzzle wavered, but not so much that the 1-cm bore ever drifted away from Coke's face.

"I'm Matthew Coke, my good fellow," Coke said. "I'm afraid I have to complain about the behavior of yourself and your friends."

The need to hold a persona protected Coke against his own fears. This wasn't *him* facing a gang of bored, drugged-out thugs, this was a prissy off-world businessman who couldn't imagine violence as raw as the norm of this hellhole.

A gunman whacked Coke in the back with the butt of a 2-cm powergun. Coke staggered forward, almost into the muzzle of the leader's automatic weapon. The armored vest saved his kidneys, but it did nothing to lessen the inertia of the solid blow.

Coke flailed his arms to get his balance. "Now that's

just what I mean!" he cried. "What sort of impression do you think that behavior makes on visitors? If you don't apologize immediately, I'll have to take action to bring this to your superiors' attention as clearly as possible."

"What the hell is he talking about, Blanco?" asked a gunman. He still wore a pair of lacy undergarments from Margulies' case over his scarlet beret.

What he's talking about, you moron, is the warning required by FDF regulations before FDF personnel use deadly force in a non-contractual context.

Blanco, the L'Escorial straw boss, stepped forward, poking his sub-machine gun toward Coke's eyes. The iridium bore was pitted from the long burst of a few minutes before.

Coke hopped backwards. Another gunman tripped him. Coke twisted like a cat as he fell, catching himself on his left hand instead of sprawling on his back. Blanco kicked him in the side with cleated boots.

Coke scuttled toward the doorway of Hathaway House, doubled over. He dabbed his left hand down like a deer running with a broken foreleg.

L'Escorials shouted and kicked. One of them swung his 2-cm weapon as a club. Because Coke was moving, the massive iridium barrel smacked him in the small of the back instead of across the shoulders. Again the vest saved him from crippling, perhaps fatal, injury, but the shock made Coke's mind go white nonetheless. He plowed facedown on the pavement.

The plated door flew open. Johann Vierziger stepped out, grabbed Coke left-handed by the back of the collar, and half-pulled, half-flung, the major into the foyer.

Sten Moden swung the door closed. A L'Escorial stuck his foot in the crack. Margulies kicked the gunman's knee, then shoved him clear of the opening with the sole of her boot. Several L'Escorials pushed from the other side of the panel, but Moden's strength overmastered them.

Someone emptied the 30-round magazine of a projectile weapon against the front of the door. A L'Escorial screamed, wounded by a ricochet or at least by spatters of the bullets after they disintegrated on the armor.

The door locked on three wrist-thick bolts worked by a single handle. When the panel slammed against its jamb, Niko Daun slid the bolts home into metal tubes set deep in the concrete.

"Open this —" Blanco shouted, his voice attenuated by the massive door and wall.

Margulies touched a thumb switch, detonating the pair of directional mines in the suitcases outside.

The lobby lights went out. Emergency lighting, glow-strips powered piezoelectrically by the structure's own flexing, drew pale yellow-green arrows down the staircase and from each doorway. Barbour's holographic display remained a ball of sharp-edged pastels. Dust, shaken from all the surfaces of the room, filled the air chokingly.

Georg Hathaway opened his mouth as if to scream, but no sound came out. Evie put an arm around her husband's shoulders and another on his nearer elbow.

Coke staggered to his feet. Margulies tossed him a commo helmet. The other team members were already wearing theirs. Vierziger offered Coke a 2-cm powergun, muzzle up.

The double crash of the mines had been terrible despite the wall's protection. Coke heard his own voice with ringing overtones as he said, "Right, open it."

Daun tried to obey. The blasts had warped the door and jamb together. The sensor tech braced a bootsole on the wall for a fulcrum. Despite his straining, it wasn't until Moden slung his missile launcher and tugged the handle that the panel swung open.

The huge doughnuts of dust and smoke from the blasts had spread and dissipated by the time Coke came through the doorway — third, after Margulies and

Vierziger, their guns pointing. Coke switched his visor to thermal imaging because the longer infrared waves penetrated the haze better than the normal optical range that light-amplification mode would have used.

A directional mine was built into one face of each suitcase, beneath the 40 ceramic laminae which the team had removed to use in its body armor. The outside of each mine was thousands of faceted steel barrels the size of the last joint of a man's little finger. The inside was a layer of cast explosive.

The mines went off like shotguns whose bore was the full plane of the cases containing them: six-tenths of a square meter. The pair, set to cross the edge of the L'Escorial cordon at a shallow angle, had swept the street like a gigantic buzzsaw.

All that was visible of Blanco was a left foot and left boot — from the ankle down. The mines' steel sleet hadn't had time to spread when it hit the L'Escorial officer. Blanco's torso must have been above the plane of the projectiles, but the shock wave had flung it indistinguishably into the bloody ruck.

Someone's right arm lay a few meters farther on. The radius and ulna were fleshless, but the hand and upper arm remained unmarked as a freak of the explosion.

Another gunman, still clutching a sub-machine gun, gasped on his belly in the middle of the street. He'd been at the edge of the area the projectiles cleared. Blood from a dozen pellet wounds pooled the pavement around him. The blast had stripped his clothes off. There was a ragged wound where his penis and scrotum should have been.

Vierziger glanced at Coke. Coke nodded. Vierziger shot the L'Escorial behind the ear, then reholstered his pistol. Coke blinked at the speed and smoothness of the motion.

Most of the gunmen's bodies lay against the wall fronting the L'Escorial compound. A L'Escorial wearing oil-stained coveralls and a short helmet — one of the armored truck's crew — ran out the open gateway. He gaped at the carnage.

Coke pointed his powergun at the L'Escorial and shouted, "Hold it!"

The L'Escorial carried a pistol in a shoulder holster where it would be out of the way aboard his vehicle, but he seemed to have forgotten he was armed. He didn't look so much frightened as dumbfounded, like a man who'd met a talking dog.

Holding his weapon with the muzzle pointed but the stock in the crook of his arm, Coke walked over to the L'Escorial. More gunmen scampered into and out of sight through the gateway. Nobody else left the courtyard. The armored vehicle's engine roared to life, then stalled with a clang as an inexperienced driver tried to operate it.

Coke lifted the muzzle of his 2-cm weapon. He reached into his purse with his left hand and removed a business card, which he stuck between the L'Escorial's pistol and its holster.

The card read:

> **MAJOR MATTHEW COKE**
> Frisian Defense Forces
>
>
>   Representative

The chip embedded within the card would project his image and description through a hologram reader.

"Go on back inside," Coke ordered. "Tell your leaders that we didn't come here to have a problem. We're here to do business on behalf of our principals, and that'll be *very* good business for the side that strikes the deal. Do you understand?"

The L'Escorial stared at the shoulder weapon, not at the man holding it. His eyes were wild, and he gave no indication of having heard a thing Coke had said.

Coke sighed. There was such a thing as making a demonstration *too* effective.

He put his left hand on the gunman's shoulder and rotated the fellow to face L'Escorial headquarters. "Go on," he said. "Tell your bosses that this just involved a few individuals — it wasn't important."

Coke pushed the man gently. The L'Escorial stumbled, then broke into a shambling run around the gatepost and out of sight.

Coke turned, though it made his skin crawl to do so. Backing away from the red-painted structure would have sent a signal of weakness to the gunmen certainly watching through firing slits in the upper floor of the building.

The street was a smear of blood and pulped organs. It reflected the light of advertising signs. Coke's bootheels shimmied as he stepped. He felt dizzy, and the stench of disemboweled corpses made him want to vomit.

A few of the bodies which the mines slammed against the courtyard wall were still alive, at least technically. Coke didn't want to think about that. There was nothing he could do now if he wanted to. He wasn't a medic.

He was a killer, no more and surely no less.

May the Lord give them rest; and may there be rest for the slayer, in his time.

The team, all but Barbour — visible through the open door at his console — waited outside Hathaway House for Coke's return. Daun blinked in amazement and a certain distaste. Moden and Margulies, the combat veterans, were grimly silent.

Johann Vierziger smiled.

"I gave a card to a citizen to deliver up the street, Matthew," Vierziger said in his liquid voice. He gestured with an open hand toward where the Astra cordon had been. "The mine blasts brought the blue-clad gunmen running a few steps toward the scene, then scurrying back into their compound to take stock. "Now what?"

"Now," said Matthew Coke, "you await developments here, and I take care of some personal business."

Coke stepped into the lobby of Hathaway House. He was shaking. He hadn't done anything to burn off the adrenaline with which his body had pumped itself in preparation for fight or flight.

The Hathaways stood with arms entwined about one another's shoulders and their other hands linked at waist level. Georg was blank-faced. Evie's expression was one of slowly dawning joy.

The three men from the saloon now stood in the broad archway where the alcove joined the lobby. One of the policemen opened and closed his mouth like a fish gasping silently on the dock. The third man, a civilian whose ragged clothing had once been of good quality, still carried his drink. He didn't look particularly interested, in the carnage or in anything else.

Coke tossed the 2-cm weapon to Margulies. She caught it at the balance. He still had a pistol in a belt holster beneath his jacket.

He thought of taking off the armored vest, but after a moment he decided not to waste the time. "You," he said to a policeman. "Does that shock baton work? Give it to me."

"Huh?"

Vierziger stepped behind the man and slid the 50-centimeter rod from its sheath.

"Hey!" the policeman cried. He and his partner jumped in opposite directions sideways, as though the little killer's presence were a bomb going off between them. "Look, what are you —"

Vierziger switched the baton's power on. He touched the tip of the slim rod to the inside of his own left forearm. The powerful fluctuating current crossed nerve pathways and flung his arm violently out to the side.

He smiled again, turned off the power, and tossed the baton to Coke. "Fully charged," he said.

Coke slid the baton beneath his waistband. "You'll get it back," he said to the policeman. Half his face grinned. "Or somebody will pay you for it."

He looked at Moden. "Sten, you're in charge till I return," Coke said. "I don't expect potential employers to react that quickly, but if they do, set up a meeting for tomorrow."

He touched his brow with one finger in a wry salute. "See you soon," he said and started for the door.

Margulies fell into step with him. "I'm coming," she said.

Johann Vierziger shook his head. "Three can be a crowd, Mary," he said in his cultured, mocking voice. "Matthew will probably be all right . . . and besides, as he says, it's a personal matter."

"Three?" said Niko Daun. Margulies nodded, turned, and leaned the extra shoulder weapon against the wall beside the door.

Barbour looked up from his console. "I'll be tracking," he said. If there had been any more emotion in the statement, it would have been a challenge.

Coke laughed out loud. The whole team thought he was behaving like an idiot — but he'd earned the right a few minutes before to do that. The *whole* team, himself included.

"See you soon," he repeated, and he stepped out into night fetid with death.

Scores, perhaps as many as two hundred, L'Escorial gunmen clustered around the windrow of bodies in front of their compound. An armored truck — not the one that had appeared before, but a similar design — illuminated the scene with its quartet of bumper-mounted headlights. One man sat cross-legged on the top of the wall, holding a liquid-fueled lamp, and other gunmen waved a variety of electrical handlights.

There wasn't much effort spent on caring for the wounded, assuming some of the victims were still alive. For the most part the L'Escorials stared, sometimes calling in wonderment. The sight appeared to touch them no more than a particularly vivid traffic accident would have done.

Coke expected the L'Escorials to react to him, perhaps to try to stop him. None of them seemed to notice that he'd left Hathaway House. The pool of light over the bodies acted as a curtain shrouding everything beyond the direct illumination.

A crowd of spectators aggregated quickly now that civilians realized the syndicate gunmen would pay them little attention. Coke noticed that a number of the onlookers covered blue garb with cloaks of neutral gray: Astras who wanted to see what was going on without themselves becoming causes of war.

Coke walked quickly up the street to where Pilar Ortega had abandoned the port operations van. Three filthy locals were in the vehicle now. One of them was trying to shoot something into his thigh with a homemade hypodermic. The injector's barrel was a hundred-centimeter length of hose.

The staircase to the flophouse Pilar entered was helical and of engineering-grade plastic extrusion. It had been salvaged from a starship. Despite hard use and lack of maintenance, the structure itself was solid and safe.

The stair's only attachment to the building was looped wire between it and external tubing — water pipes, electrical conduits, and a downspout from the gutter. The wire was of no particular type or strength. Baling wire alternated with insulated power cable and what looked like glass-core data transmission line.

The helix wobbled at Coke's every step and from any breeze or tremor. He didn't suppose it was going to collapse under him — and he could probably ride it down if it *did* break away; the staircase itself was plenty sturdy enough.

But it put the butterflies back in the pit of Coke's stomach.

The bum who'd been sprawled on the stairs when Pilar climbed them had vanished. Another man now lay halfway up, weeping uncontrollably and holding an almost-full bottle of clear fluid.

Coke entered clean locked beds, the building's fifth level. The salvaged staircase rose another two meters, but there was no doorway opening onto it from the level above.

The end of a counter protected by a hundred-millimeter mesh of barbed wire narrowed the doorway to half its designed width. A bar with a barbed wire apron closed the other half to prevent anyone from bursting into or out of the flophouse, though Coke wasn't sure why either should have been a problem.

No one was behind the counter; the gate into the flophouse proper stood open. The sign on the back wall read:

SPACE 5
BUNK 10
SOLO BUNK 25
LOCK 25

A board from which hung a dozen cheap keyed padlocks indicated the protection you got for the extra 25 pesos. Sten Moden could probably have twisted the barrels off their hasps . . . but men as fit and strong as Sten Moden didn't spend the night in a flop like this.

Coke raised the bar carefully and walked into the establishment. He'd had full immunization treatments before he left Nieuw Friesland, but there was no point in testing Frisian medical science against the filth that lurked on those rusty barbs.

The flophouse filled the entire level, an area of about ten meters by twenty. It was lighted by glow-strips, scraped and speckled but still able to provide a reasonable amount of yellow-green illumination. The good lighting was probably a safety feature — for the building's owners as much as for the staff and clientele.

A narrow aisle separated two banks of cubicles. Each contained a filthy mattress. Instead of solid panels, the cubicles had walls of coarse barbed wire netting.

The remainder of the flophouse was bare floor on which the lower grade of derelict sprawled and shivered and moaned. Twenty-odd were present tonight; varied in age and sex, but uniform in their utter degradation.

Something was going on toward the back of the big room. Men clustered around one of the cages, shouting and laughing in cracked voices.

Coke's face became still. He slid the shock rod from his waistband with his left hand and strode quietly down the aisle.

About half the cubicles he passed were occupied. Some of the men — few were women — in them were lost in their own worlds. Empty stim cones or cruder injectors lay on the mattresses with them.

One man was bent in a tetanic arch. His eyes bulged and his face was purple. Coke was pretty sure the fellow was dead, broken in convulsions by the wrong dose of gage tailings, but the fact impressed him as little as it did the flop's ordinary denizens.

Other caged occupants called or even tried to grab Coke as he strode by. None of them was coordinated enough to actually touch the Frisian. They didn't necessarily see him. The drugs and drug impurities with which they'd injected themselves were capable of turning any movement into a wild hallucination.

Pilar Ortega was in an end stall. She stood erect with her arms clamping her overwrap to her, as if by squeezing hard enough she could make herself vanish. Her eyes were wide open, but she didn't see Coke coming down the aisle toward her.

Seven or eight men gripped the mesh of the cubicle. One of them was the clerk who should have been behind the counter. They had all dropped their pants. They waved their penises at the woman as they jeered.

The clerk was a fat man, completely hairless. He wore a sleeveless black pullover; his overalls pooled around his ankles. As Coke approached, unnoticed in the drug-fueled hilarity, the clerk reached down into his trousers and came up with a key.

"Lookie what *I* got, Miz Fancypants!" he cried in a voice pitched higher than the size of his gross body suggested. "You think you rented the only key to your lock, did you?"

"Yeah, I wanna *see* them pants!" the man beside him cried. "I'll bite them —"

Coke whipped his shock rod across the bare buttocks of the four men directly before him.

The men screamed as they leaped convulsively into the wire. The cubicle swayed, but its steel-tube frame was strong enough to withstand the impacts. The men at either end of the cage, untouched by Coke's quick sweep, looked around in surprise, all but one fellow crooning and drooling in his own private dreamworld.

The clerk turned. He bled from a score of fresh punctures and gashes scattered from forehead to mid-thigh. "You —" he shouted.

Coke flicked the clerk with the baton, this time on the lower belly just above his genitals. Flailing limbs hurled the clerk against Pilar's cage a second time. The structure's resilience threw him facedown on the floor. Coke stepped aside to let him fall.

A derelict raised the jagged top of a bottle. Coke held his right arm crooked to the side. His hand hovered over the butt of his holstered pistol. To draw, he would shift his hips left while his hand swept aside the tail of his jacket. He wasn't Johann Vierziger, but it was a maneuver he'd made many times before. . . .

"Try me," he offered in a trembling voice.

The derelict dropped the bottle. He backed into the wall and pushed himself flat against it.

"All of you," Coke said. "Out ahead of me." He eased into an empty cubicle, permitting the men to pass without touching him. "Pilar, open your door and come out. It's all right now."

The clerk was whimpering. He paused on hands and knees to draw up his overalls.

"Did I tell you to do that?" Coke screamed. He lashed the clerk's buttocks again, reaching from the cage to take a full swing with the shock baton. The *whack!* and blue spark flashed terror across the derelicts' countenances.

"Go on! Move!"

The group shuffled and stumbled out, fettered as Coke intended by their dragging trousers; all but the wide-eyed fellow mumbling in his reverie about Maureen. Coke let him be.

Pilar came out of the cubicle. Her face was as still as that of a woman in shock, but her eyes moved febrily.

"It's all right," Coke repeated. He touched Pilar's shoulder to guide her down the aisle. "Ahead of me," he said.

He walked in lock-step behind the woman, reaching past her with the shock baton. Someone groped from a cage despite the warning. The baton's charge snapped him like the popper on a bullwhip into his cubicle's walls.

The clerk and the gang behind him had shuffled to the counter at the front of the room. "Stop!" Coke ordered.

The men cringed as they obeyed. The features of most of them would have looked leprous even under better lighting than that of the glowstrips.

"Now," Coke said. "Return the lady's money." In a gentler voice he added, "You paid fifty pesos?"

"Please *God* the money doesn't matter!" Pilar said, clutching the crucifix beneath her cape.

"That's not the point," Coke said. "You bastards! Make it a hundred pesos. Now!"

"But I can't," the clerk wheezed. His tears diluted the line of blood trickling down his cheek from the gouge in his forehead. "I *can't* get into the cashbox, only Master Delzine can open it!"

The box was a massive canister — too massive for a support structure as flimsy as the upper floors of this building — strapped beneath the counter. The inlet was a doubly-kinked tube with one-way gates, proof against any but the most sophisticated methods of drawing coins back along it. The clerk could hold out the clientele's fees, if he wanted to risk the owner's spot checks; but he couldn't retrieve money once dropped into the box.

"All right," Coke said. "Make it up yourselves. A hundred pesos."

"The money doesn't —" Pilar repeated.

"Shut up!" Coke snarled. "They're paying for what they did. Or else they'll do it again!"

The men squatted to rummage in their fallen trousers. Coke drew a figure-8 with his shock baton, touching the tip to cage supports on both sides of the motion. The sparks snapped loudly in the nervous silence.

Two of the men took off their shoes. The clerk, who'd found only ten pesos thus far, came up with an additional 50-peso coin.

The money lay in a ragged pile between Pilar and the men. Coke couldn't tell exactly how much there was; and anyway, the amount didn't really matter, Pilar was right there, though the principle mattered.

"All right," Coke ordered. "Head down to the street, all of you. Get going!"

He wasn't going to leave any of this lot ten meters above him. Maybe none of them could throw straight, but all they needed to do was get lucky with one brick or bottle. They shambled and crab-walked out the doorway.

Pilar relaxed so completely that Coke was afraid she'd fainted. He caught her. Her body was warm and trembling.

"I'm all right," she murmured, but it was a moment before she stepped forward. She bent, scooped the money into a pocket of her cape, and edged past the counter.

The men were partway down the staircase. The clerk had hiked up his overalls. When he saw Coke appear at the doorway above him, he dropped the garment again and hopped downward, holding the railing with both hands. The structure jounced violently. Several of the derelicts lost their footing. Half sliding, half stumbling, they made their way to the street.

Five steps up, Coke shut off the baton and slid it beneath his waistband again. When he moved, the men watching could see his holster, not that any of them had doubted it.

"I didn't bring you here to shoot you," Coke said in harsh, ringing tones. "But if I can see any of you thirty seconds from now, I *will* shoot him. Go!"

The clerk and derelicts stumbled into the traffic, pedestrians, and jitneys, that had resumed when the syndicate cordons terminated at the mine blast. Coke took a deep breath. His knees wobbled. He held the rail firmly in his left hand as he followed Pilar down the remaining steps.

"You wouldn't really shoot them, would you?" she asked.

"They're gone," Coke said, avoiding the question. "It doesn't matter now."

He massaged his left forearm with the fingers of his right hand. He'd been gripping the shock baton hard, harder than he'd realized until just now when he suddenly felt the ache.

"Look," he said, "is your husband at home? I can

take you there. Or we can get you a room in the Hathaway House; it seems to be a nice place. Like you said, a decent place."

Pilar shook her head. "I'll go home," she said. "I'll be all right, now."

She looked toward her van. She noticed the heads of bums silhouetted against the unglazed windows. Coke offered his left arm to her right hand.

"No problem," he said, whisking his tongue across the syllables like a blade over a whetstone. He walked beside Pilar toward the vehicle, flexing his left hand to be sure that it would obey his needs.

"Terry won't be home," the woman said stiffly. Her fingers lay in the crook of his elbow, light contact but warm nonetheless. "He's found quite a number of friends here since he learned to shake the money tree."

"He's smuggling, you mean?" Coke said. His tone counterfeited the sort of polite interest that he thought was appropriate to the statement. Below the surface, his mind considered alternatives with the icy logic of a bridge player assessing his hand.

Pilar stopped. A sailor walking behind them cursed as she blocked his path. Coke drew his pistol and pointed it without a word. The sailor started back and jogged across the street.

Coke reholstered the weapon. "Sorry," he murmured to Pilar.

"You work for the Confederacy?" she said tightly. She stood as though her feet had grown through the cracked pavement. "You're investigating port duties?"

"Not us," Coke said easily. "From what I've heard thus far, we're out of business if the Marvelan Confederacy learns that we're here."

By taking Pilar's hand in his, he made her meet his eyes. In a more sober tone than before he added, "We're with the Frisian Defense Forces."

"Oh," the woman said. The datum fell into place. "Oh!"

"We're not maybe the best thing that could happen to Cantilucca," Coke said, still looking directly at her though her eyes had lifted away. "But we're better than what I've seen here so far."

Pilar gave him a bitter smile. "Sometimes I think the best thing that could happen to Potosi, at least, would be a fusion bomb," she said.

Coke squeezed her hand. He stepped to the van, reached in through the window, and dragged one of the occupants out by the throat. The local squawked after Coke flung him on the pavement. He didn't say anything before he hit the ground, because the Frisian's fingers gripped too tightly to pass the sound.

The remaining two bums bleated. They slid to the other side of the open compartment. Instead of reaching for them, Coke pointed his pistol at the left member of the pair.

"You have five seconds," Coke said. "One. Two."

The local jumped up and stuck his head and torso out of the far window. Coke shifted his weapon's centimeter bore toward the other derelict. "Three. Four."

The local tried unsuccessfully to rise. His limbs were spastic with fear. He seemed afraid to turn and face the opening.

Coke pointed the gun muzzle sideways and said, "Go on, you're all right, I'll give you the time."

The local thumped out into the street and began crawling after his fellow. He was moaning about his bottle, but the only bottle the trio had left in the van was empty.

Pilar stood close beside Coke. "You're very direct," she said in a voice too neutral to be disinterested.

"Yeah," Coke said. He looked at her again. "What you see is what you get."

Pilar smiled wistfully. "No," she said, "I'm afraid that what *I* get is something else again. Perhaps I should have seen it, but I was younger then."

She opened the door of the van. The ignition card

clinked against the handle. "Thank you very much, Master Coke. I — I appreciate what you've done. I'd invite you home for a drink, but people might get the wrong impression."

Her face hardened. "And it would *be* the wrong impression."

Coke bowed formally. He wore a half smile.

Pilar suddenly leaned close and kissed him on the cheek. Then she was in the van, shutting the door needlessly hard.

Coke watched her drive away. He was smiling more broadly now. Someone watching him might have noticed the similarity of the expression to that which Johann Vierziger wore after killing.

The remaining five members of the survey team waited for a moment after Major Matthew Coke walked out of Hathaway House with a pistol and a commandeered shock baton. Georg Hathaway started to close the heavy front door. Margulies touched the innkeeper's arm to stop him.

Hathaway glanced around. The four Frisians besides Barbour stood in a concave arc, facing out the doorway so that among them they watched a hundred meters of the streetscape. All of them held weapons.

"Oh," Hathaway said. "Oh. I wasn't thinking of that."

Margulies nodded without replying, and without ever taking her eyes off the amazed clot of L'Escorials across the street. Her left hand returned to rest lightly on the foregrip of her sub-machine gun.

"There," Vierziger said with a slight relaxation of the drumhead tautness beneath his insouciant exterior. "He's clear of anything we can do — unless we want to follow him."

"Which we do not," Moden said. He set down the missile launcher with care. The weapon he carried comfortably was so heavy that if it dropped, the shock would seriously damage it.

"There's no organization," Barbour offered. He had directional audio from the spectators across the street, as well as a holographic view sharper than that of the others' naked eyes. "People run inside saying they're going to report to Raul or to the Old Man, but they don't come back with any orders."

"Raul Luria is head of L'Escorial," said Georg Hathaway. "With his son Ramon, and Ramon's son Pepe."

"Pepe is a weasel," Evie said in clipped tones. She looked at the Frisians and added, "We have rooms prepared for you. You'll share baths; I hope that's all right. But surely you'd like something to eat or drink?"

It was hard to read her expression. The sudden destruction of a dozen gunmen had opened a window on the woman's mind, but its interior was still thick with the dust of long depression.

"I wouldn't mind something to drink," Niko Daun said clearly. "You say you've got local cacao?"

"And I think I'll have a beer or two," Sten Moden added, quirking the younger man a smile. "It's been a long day. Not that it's over yet."

"Here, I'll serve you gentlemen," Georg said. "And lady of course. Evie, I wish you wouldn't say things like that, you know, in public. Though Pepe's off Cantilucca now, I believe."

The local patrons had returned to the alcove in which they'd been drinking. Vierziger walked to the table of the third man, the civilian, and said, "Good day, sir. My name is Johann Vierziger, and I'm a sergeant with the Frisian Defense Forces. May I ask who you are?"

The fellow looked up. His face was handsome in a hollow-cheeked fashion, but there was a gray glaze over him that was more an aura than skin tone.

"My name's Larrinaga," he said. He was younger than he'd looked; thirty years standard at the most. "And I'm nothing, that's who I am."

"Pedro's had a difficult time this past year," Georg

said; half-confiding, half in an attempt to forestall the wrath of the little stranger who made him *very* uncomfortable to watch. "His wife died. She was an artist in psychic ambiances, a very fine one, known all across the galaxy."

"Really?" said Niko Daun. "I've worked in PAs myself. Who was she? The wife."

His tone wasn't precisely dismissive, but there was a challenge in it. Daun didn't regard himself as a top PA artist, but he didn't expect to find a better one on this wretched planet.

Hathaway drew drinks. Larrinaga looked up and said, "My wife was Suzette. That was her working name. She was a saint. And there'll never be an artist like her. Never in all time!"

"Suzette was from here?" Daun blurted. "Blood and martyrs!"

Margulies raised an eyebrow in the direction of the sensor tech.

Daun turned his palms up. "She's —" he said. "Well there's taste. But the best PA artist in the galaxy, yeah, you can make a case for it. I'm amazed. . . . Well, I didn't think she'd have come from a place so . . ."

He looked at Larrinaga, who was staring morosely into his beer mug. "Suzette's work is so tranquil, you see," Daun said. "It's not what I'd expect coming from Cantilucca. From Potosi, anyhow."

Georg handed out beverages in rough-glazed ceramic mugs of local manufacture. The beer, for all his praises of it, had an oily undertaste that Moden found unpleasant. He'd drunk worse in the field, wine that had rotted rather than fermenting properly . . . and there were worse things in life than bad booze.

Daun sipped his mug of frothy, bitter, cacao drink with approval. His lips pursed as he considered Larrinaga and the situation. A Tech 4's pay didn't run to art the like of Suzette's, but there was always the chance . . .

"I wonder," he said, "if there's any of your wife's work still on Cantilucca? Some minor pieces, perhaps, that —"

The local man clutched his empty mug with both hands. He began to cry. He made a convulsive gesture that would have swept the mug against the wall to shatter.

Vierziger, who was standing arm's length away and didn't seem to be watching, caught the mug in the air. He set it on the serving counter.

Larrinaga lurched up from his seat. "I'm going to go piss," he said. He angrily wiped his eyes with his forearm. "That's fair, isn't it? I've pissed my life away!"

"Pedro?" Hathaway said. "Can I show them the draft? It's not the same, but they'll get the idea."

"Do what you please," Larrinaga called as he left the alcove.

"He leaves it here," the innkeeper explained as he opened a cabinet beneath the serving counter. "He doesn't have a place of his own any more."

Margulies returned to the saloon alcove. She'd taken a beer to Barbour at his console. "Trouble with the gangs?" she guessed aloud. "They robbed him?"

"Well, not quite that," Georg said. "You see, when Suzette died, Pedro sold his house to the factor of Trans-Star Trading on Cantilucca. His name's Suterbilt."

"Suterbilt is a criminal," Evie said from the lobby. She sat in an upholstered chair, knitting as her eyes stared into time. "He's no better than the thugs he bankrolls."

"Now, Evie, you know we shouldn't say things like that," Georg said. "But Suterbilt has, well, a financial stake in L'Escorial. That's personal, not TST."

The innkeeper was setting up a table-model hologram projector. Niko moved to help him. The unit had a lot of flash and glitter, but it looked clumsy compared to the trim projectors in use on Nieuw Friesland.

"So a shotgun sale?" Margulies pressed. The story would probably come out, from Mistress Hathaway if not from her husband, but Margulies didn't want to wait.

"Not that either," Georg said. He obviously felt uncomfortable speaking about the gunmen and their masters, though the chance to gossip with *these* folk had attraction as well.

"Not really, at least," he continued. "Pedro had been taking a lot of gage, mostly gage, because he'd loved Suzette so much. He wouldn't have sold at all if he hadn't been, well, if he'd been in better condition. Because Suzette's greatest masterpiece is a part of the home where they'd lived, you see."

"And then he lost the money," Evie added harshly. "He was drugged *silly*, and he gambled, and he lost every peso of the price."

"The price had been a good one, though," her husband said quickly. "Master Suterbilt didn't cheat him, not really, since the art can't be moved and its value's only what it's worth on Cantilucca."

"Suterbilt didn't cheat him in the notary's office, you mean," Evie said. "He left that job for his friends at the roulette table."

Her fingers clicked the needles with mechanical precision. Moden thought of the old women watching the guillotine; and realized for the first time how much, and how rightly, they had hated the aristocrats being beheaded.

"Why can't the PA be moved?" Daun asked in surprise.

"What?" said Georg. "Because it's built into the fabric of the room, sir. You'd destroy the whole thing to try to move it."

The technician frowned. He didn't argue, but it was obvious that he couldn't understand the problem.

"There," said Hathaway. "Watch this. It's the holographic draft Suzette did before she created the ambiance itself."

He dimmed the alcove lights. The policemen were watching from their table. Larrinaga reappeared from the rest room. He stood in the archway instead of reentering the saloon.

A psychic ambiance was just that, a recorded vision — a waking dream — capable of being transferred to recipients in the focal area. It couldn't be copied, because it depended on inputs too subtle to survive the duplication process. Though the PA was immaterial, the artist normally started with a visual or auditory sketch, just as medieval fresco artists drew cartoons on the wall before applying a coat of fresh plaster on which to fix the paint.

Suzette worked visually. The holographic sketch was of a verdant paradise, a mythic place in which fountains played and the geologic features seemed themselves alive though immobile.

No animals could be glimpsed, though the movement of plants hinted their presence. Above all, the shifting holographic image was suffused by light and a warmth for which the objects described could not themselves account.

The sketch began to repeat itself. The second time through, individual facets merged into a whole greater and quite different from its parts.

Daun frowned. He could *almost* grasp the unity to which the intersections of light beams were building in this holographic shorthand.

"It's her, you know," Larrinaga said abruptly. "It's Suzette. She did a self-portrait, she built it into our house so that I'd never have had to be without her. And I threw it away!"

He began to weep openly. Georg Hathaway shut off the chip projector; Margulies brought the lights back up. Though Hathaway House was a fortress, the bright internal illumination prevented the weight of the protective walls from crushing the souls of those within it.

"There, there, Pedro," Georg said awkwardly. "Maybe I shouldn't have done that. I know it bothers you."

"Everything bothers him," Evie said, knitting with tiny clicks unaffected by her words. "It's Pedro's life now, being bothered."

"It's still possible to see the PA, isn't it?" Niko asked, looking from Georg to Larrinaga and quickly away again.

Hathaway pursed his lips. He started to say something, then glanced toward the archway.

"Can I have another beer, Georg?" Larrinaga asked. "It'll have to be on credit, of course."

"Why of course, Pedro," Hathaway said enthusiastically. "You're not a patron here, you're our friend."

He gestured Larrinaga toward the serving counter instead of drawing the mug himself. A transaction had taken place, and everyone within earshot knew it.

As Larrinaga stepped past him, head bowed, Hathaway said, "The ambiance can only be viewed with Master Suterbilt's permission, and that's hard to come by. He's aware of its value, you see. He keeps — well, there are six L'Escorial, ah, security personnel in the house at all times. Suterbilt doesn't live there, but he visits frequently."

"The last time I went there and asked to see Suzette," Larrinaga said with his back to the others in the saloon, "they beat me unconscious and left me in the street."

He drank in order to create a pause for effect. "I think," he resumed, "I'll go back there tonight."

"Yes, I suspect you *will* do that," Johann Vierziger said in a voice like the purr of a well-fed leopard. He set down the mug of cacao from which he'd been sipping with evident approval. "It's the sort of thing a worthless bastard would do, after all."

The little man's enunciation was so precise that it was a moment before the words themselves registered on the others. Daun stifled a snort of laughter.

Margulies raised an eyebrow; Sten Moden pointedly failed to react.

"Sure I am," Larrinaga said loudly. "You bet, that's just what I am."

"Oh, you mustn't say that, sir!" Georg Hathaway blurted. "Pedro isn't that at all. You don't know what he's like inside!"

"Nor do you, Master Hathaway," Vierziger said with sneering intonation. "All we know is the side he shows the world. That side is a sniveling, self-pitying bastard."

The words wouldn't have cut as deep if there'd been emotion behind them instead of cold disdain. Larrinaga winced as though he'd been stroked with a barbed whip. The mug trembled. He set it down and walked to the outer door.

Barbour looked at the local man, calculating the door's opening against the movements of figures in his holographic display. There was no need to keep the armored door closed; but there might have been, and Barbour would have said so if there were.

The door closed behind Larrinaga. "Oh, I wish you hadn't said that, good sir," Hathaway murmured miserably, though he didn't look directly at Vierziger as he spoke.

"Why, Georg?" Evie Hathaway demanded. "Does the truth bother you so much? Has saying, 'Oh, Pedro just needs a little time to get straightened out,' made things better? For anybody?"

"Well, he blames himself for having sold the house," Georg said. "And it was Pedro's fault, I know, partying with Master Suterbilt who'd been trying for years to buy the ambiance and Suzette wouldn't hear of selling to him. But it's a shame that one mistake should ruin his life."

"The major's coming back," Barbour called from the foyer. He looked toward the policemen and grinned. It was the first smile any of his teammates had seen on his face. "He's returning your shock baton, gentlemen."

"One mistake can ruin more than a man's life,

Master Hathaway," Vierziger said to the innkeeper. "It can ruin all eternity."

He smiled tightly, terribly. "Of course, I've made many more mistakes than one."

Coke entered the lobby. He closed the door behind him, then rested his back against the cool metal surface.

"Any excitement, sir?" Margulies asked.

"Matthew, please, Mary," Coke said with his eyes closed. "And no, nothing to speak of. The usual run of port-city foolishness, nothing serious."

"What's the next order of business, Matthew?" Moden asked. "We continue to wait?"

"I could use one of those beers," Coke said, snapping alert again. He strode into the saloon alcove. From there he continued, "Yeah, we wait. I figure it'll be days before either side makes an approach. Two gangs may make this a tough place, but it sure isn't an organized one."

"Is organized better, Master Soldier?" Evie Hathaway demanded from her chair.

"Evie, *please*," said Georg.

"Yes, ma'am," Coke said, taking the mug the innkeeper had drawn him. "It is. Highly developed parasites see to it that the host body stays healthy. Less developed ones, roundworms and the like, are often fatal. Cantilucca has a bad case of roundworms, I'm afraid."

"And your prescription?" the woman said. She'd stopped knitting so that she could turn to look directly at the Frisian leader.

Coke drank, then shrugged. "Arsenic or the equivalent, Mistress Hathaway," he said. "The trick is to titrate the dose, of course, so that you only get the worms."

"In the short term, Matthew," Mary Margulies said, "would you have any objection to me doing a little sight-seeing in the countryside? Tomorrow, maybe?"

Coke shook his head. "No, we need to learn as much about the place as we can," he said. "Potosi may be the head of the planet, but it's not the whole place. Ah — I'd rather you didn't go any distance alone."

"I'll go along, sir," Robert Barbour said. "That is, if you'll permit me. I'll have the AI in this console dialed in to take care of ordinary business in an hour or two, now that you're back."

"No, that's fine," Coke said. "Just remember, we're in a fluid situation. Things might happen pretty fast. And I'm *Matthew*."

"My old driver came back here when he got out of service," Margulies explained. "He came from a place called Silva Blanca. It's supposed to be fifteen klicks away."

"Good," said Coke. He handed his mug to Hathaway for a refill. "It'll be good to get a professional's viewpoint about the situation here."

"I'm not sure there's enough arsenic, Master Soldier," Evie Hathaway said. She had resumed knitting. "Certainly there can't be too much."

CANTILUCCA: DAY TWO

The messenger at the door of Hathaway House flashed his gray cloak open toward the viewslit, displaying a blue uniform jacket with chromed buttons and frogs. By trying to look simultaneously self-important and inconspicuous, the man gave the impression of a rat tricked out in pheasant plumage.

"A lady wants to see Major Coke!" he hissed meaningfully, casting a wary glance over his shoulder toward L'Escorial headquarters.

Coke nodded toward Mistress Hathaway at the door. He was shrugging into his body armor. The location of Hathaway House wasn't ideally neutral, but the team hadn't been sent to Cantilucca to be fair. Just to strike a deal, and that seemed to be a practical proposition.

"A bit earlier than I'd figured," Coke said to his three fellows. "Niko, you're ready on your end?"

The sensor tech grinned brightly. He patted a magazine pouch on the right side of his waist belt, opposite the holster clipped for cross-draw.

"The bugs're here," he said, "not in my case." He waggled the attaché case in his left hand.

"Sten, you're comfortable with the hardware?" Coke went on, shifting his attention to the man who would remain behind in the hotel lobby.

"Quite comfortable," the logistics officer said. His arm swept across the terminal, changing the display from streetscape to a close-up of the Astra messenger's face, then back. "This isn't my specialty, but I've probably spent as much time at consoles as you or Bob have."

"Come *on*," the messenger whined. "Do you think I like standing out here?"

"Do you think we care?" Niko Daun snapped. The suddenness with which the young technician's smile broke and reformed indicated that he was jumpy, reasonably enough.

Johann Vierziger grinned at Coke. Neither man bothered to speak the obvious truths.

Coke settled a gray cape over his armor, his attaché case, and a slung sub-machine gun. "All right," he said. "Then let's do it."

The messenger scampered ahead. He was probably afraid to be seen with the trio of Frisians. It was late morning and the sun was hot. L'Escorials had removed the wrack of bodies from against their wall, but the stench of rotting blood was fierce even against the reek of garbage and human excrement.

The gates to the L'Escorial courtyard, vertical steel bars in a wall-height framework, were closed. Half a dozen gunmen sat beneath an awning inside, playing cards. The concrete around the titular guards was littered with gage injectors and empty bottles. None of the men paid any attention to traffic from Hathaway House.

The messenger was ten strides ahead of the Frisians. He turned around and waggled his hands toward them in a pulling motion. "Come on, come along," he urged.

"We'll get there, little man," Johann Vierziger said calmly. "And the more surely if we watch what we're about, not so?"

Though the messenger wasn't a prepossessing physical specimen, he was bigger than Vierziger. Nobody hearing the comment smiled at it, however.

A combat vehicle converted from a bulldozer was now parked in the entrance to the courtyard in front of Astra headquarters. Metal plates were welded to a framework around the bulldozer's sides.

The add-on armor didn't look to Coke as if it'd stop

much. The earthmoving blade which protected the front would originally have been tempered soft so that it wouldn't shatter if it hit a rock. The alloy steel *could* have been surface hardened during the conversion process, but he doubted that it had been.

The vehicle mounted a twelve-tube launcher for hypervelocity rockets. These could be extremely effective weapons, capable of penetrating more than a meter of ferroconcrete; but the mounting was fixed in azimuth, so that aiming a salvo required the vehicle itself be turned toward the target.

The messenger led the Frisians past the 'dozer's worn tracks. Astras on the vehicle and around it had their guns out. None of them spoke to the Frisians, but Coke heard several deliberately loud sneers about the pansies come to call. At least the blue-clad guards seemed to be more alert than their rivals down the street.

"The Widow's waiting for you, gentlemen," the messenger called, several strides ahead again. *"Do come along."*

Niko Daun stumbled twice while easing past the converted bulldozer. The first time he slapped his hand against the armor covering the commander's station on the right side of the vehicle; the next time he caught himself on the gatepost. He'd touched his belt pouch before either slip, but there was nothing noteworthy in that.

The sensor tech patted the jamb of the doorway into the headquarters building as well. Each time his hand touched, he left behind an irregular disk of self-adhering material, as unremarkable as a splash of clear lacquer. Each palm-sized swatch contained an audio pick-up and transmitter, powered by micro-flexions in the crystalline structure of its matrix material.

Though not precisely invisible, the bugs appeared to be merely areas of random gloss to anyone but an expert looking for them. Cantilucca wasn't a place where the survey team expected to find expert sensor technicians.

The front half of the ground floor was a single room, thronged now by fifty or sixty blue-clad gunmen. Men in full uniform formed a corridor, not quite a gauntlet, between the outer door and the inner one in the partition wall at the back. Astras in less formal attire were relegated to stand behind the elite.

Vierziger led. Daun, with another bug palmed and waiting, walked behind him, and Coke brought up the rear. The air stank of nervous sweat.

"These are the tough guys?" sneered a man as big as Sten Moden. A scar twisted up his cheek and forehead, filling one eyesocket with a mass of pink tissue. "Don't look much to me!"

"Now, boys, the Widow wants to see them," the messenger pleaded.

"This one looks like a fairy!" cried a man carrying a sub-machine gun and a slung grenade launcher. He reached out to pinch Vierziger's cheek.

Coke lifted his hand into the air, visible to everyone in the big room. Simultaneously, Vierziger's light cape ballooned as his arm moved.

The muzzle of Vierziger's chased and carven pistol bloodied the Astra's lips. The fellow yelped in surprise and would have lurched backward. The men behind hemmed him in too straitly to move.

"Does he indeed, my friend?" Vierziger said in a lilting whisper. "That's not surprising, is it? Since he *is* a fairy. Do you have a problem with that?"

The little killer punctuated each sentence by tapping his pistol forward, hard enough to chip the Astra's teeth. Blood smeared the iridium barrel.

Coke said nothing. His hand held the fat tube of a bunker buster. The grenade's red safety tab was lifted, and only the Frisian's index finger held down the arming spoon.

"Do you?" Vierziger's pistol lifted so that the muzzle centered on the Astra's right eye.

"No sir. *No sir!*"

"Just as well, isn't it?" Vierziger said conversationally. He tugged out the Astra's shirt with his left hand and wiped the pistol clean with it. The weapon vanished as suddenly as it had been drawn.

Coke put the live grenade back under his cape. Vierziger walked to the inner door. The corridor between the Astra lines was half again as wide as it had been before.

Nobody spoke for a moment, but pandemonium broke out in the anteroom when Coke closed the door behind him. Most of the noise seemed to be laughter, directed at Vierziger's battered victim.

Dark wood panelled and furnished the inner room. There were no windows, and the several lights were point sources which accentuated the darkness beyond the surfaces from which they glared.

An old man, a lushly attractive young man, and a woman in late middle age sat on the other side of a heavy table. The woman rose to meet the Frisian delegation. She had strong, handsome features, but she was trussed into clothing a size or more too tight for her soft weight.

"I am Stella Guzman," she said, extending her hand to Coke's touch. "The Widow, you may call me. I've been president of Astra since my husband passed on three years ago."

The woman's male companions stood up as she identified herself. The younger one put his hand on Widow Guzman's shoulder in a gesture of ownership. He smiled: appraisingly at Coke, disdainfully at Daun, and at Johann Vierziger with a spark of different interest.

Coke found the young man's warm glance at Vierziger to be utterly disorienting. Presumably wolverines can be considered sex objects also . . . but this Cantiluccan gigolo wasn't by any stretch of the imagination of the same species as Johann Vierziger.

"This is my friend and advisor Adolpho Peres," the

Widow said, covering with her own hand that of the man's on her shoulder. She patted it affectionately. Either she didn't see the look Peres gave Vierziger, or she was very complaisant.

"And on this side," she went on, extending a hand toward the other man, "is Simon Roberson, who has been of great help in Astra's business transactions. Master Roberson is a goods supplier with outlets all over Cantilucca."

Roberson wasn't, in fact, nearly as old as Coke had initially judged. Rather, he was sick with worry. The cause of the merchant's stress could have been any number of things; but given that Roberson was the man Evie Hathaway said bankrolled the Astra syndicate, Coke would have been interested in hearing the fellow's assessment of the relative strength of the sides.

The weaker party was usually willing to pay more for support. . . .

"Mistress, gentlemen," Coke said, bowing over the hand. "These are my associates Master Daun" — he nodded — "and Master Vierziger. As I'm sure you're aware, we're part of a survey team for the Frisian Defense Forces."

"This is a lovely table," said Niko Daun, stroking first the underside, then the top, of the piece. In fact, the wood was dented and ringed from long use. He beamed a smile toward the Cantiluccans.

Peres sneered at the sensor tech. "Sit down, gentlemen," he said to Coke. "I doubt we'll need help from mercenaries, but we're willing to listen to your offer. Will you try some of my private-stock gage? Or perhaps liquor?"

Roberson glared at the gigolo with impotent hatred. Widow Guzman winced, patted Peres' hand again, and reseated herself.

"Water for us, I think," Coke said. He unfastened his cape and hung it over the back of the heavy, leather-upholstered chair. The fuel-air grenade was clipped to his belt again, with the safety tab latched down.

"I wouldn't mind trying your gage, Master Peres," Vierziger said in his usual soft, cultured voice. Coke wondered where the little man came from originally. "A demi for a start, if you please."

"We don't have an offer for you, mistress," Coke said. "We're a survey team, as I said. We're here to observe conditions on Cantilucca and report on them. I'll be sending message capsules to Nieuw Friesland on a regular basis, probably daily, while we're here."

Vierziger took a pale green stim cone from the tray Peres offered him. "If you have proposals, we would of course forward them to Camp Able," Vierziger said as he set the injector against the inside of his left wrist and triggered it. "If not, well. We'd have to look for other interested parties."

It was useful to have two FDF negotiators present, though the team hadn't been deliberately structured that way. Vierziger was along simply as muscle, as a bodyguard.

Whatever the little man had been in the past, it wasn't merely a sergeant in the field police.

"Stop this nonsense!" the Widow Guzman snapped. "At any moment, it all could — burn, explode. What is it you're offering, Major Coke, and what price do you put on your . . . merchandise?"

"That depends somewhat on the circumstances," Coke said, nodding at the woman's candor. Peres hadn't brought the water Coke requested. He'd have liked something to do with his hands besides spreading them on the tabletop. "How many troops of your own are there?"

Peres frowned, then shrugged. "Eight hundred," he said. "Nine hundred, perhaps. And we have six tanks."

"And L'Escorial?" Coke said.

Peres and Roberson exchanged glances behind the Widow's head. If it wasn't an ulcer that grayed and twisted the merchant's features, he was sure on the way to giving himself one.

The Widow Guzman stared toward the far wall. Her eyes were empty and her plump fingers tented before her. Coke thought of Pilar Ortega touching her crucifix as she contemplated bleak horror.

"The same," Peres said at last. "About the same."

"Neither of your syndicates have tanks," Vierziger said with a lazy smile. "For the sake of discussion, let's assume L'Escorial employs, say, two hundred men more than Astra."

His smile broadened, sharpened. "Of course, that's twelve fewer than they employed at this time yesterday."

The merchant giggled nervously, then choked.

"Details like that make a difference, you see," Coke said mildly. "Not an insuperable difficulty, but a difference."

He paused. When he continued, his mind broke the stream of words into thought segments, each as precise as if Coke were taking aim instead of speaking.

"Based on my provisional assessment," he said. "I doubt my superiors at Camp Able would be willing to hire out any force smaller. Than a company of infantry and a company of combat cars. Fighting vehicles. To either of the parties on Cantilucca. And that will be expensive."

Roberson leaned across the table. "*How* expensive?" he rasped.

Johann Vierziger was examining his manicure. "As a matter of comparison . . ." he commented toward his almond-shaped fingernails, " . . . less expensive than being burned alive in your house, let us say."

"Approximately three thousand Frisian thalers per day," Coke said crisply. This was money, not lives. He was out of the mood of stark calculation which had gripped him moments before. "With add-ons, perhaps ten percent over. I estimate that the operation will take forty days, and as much longer as you dally about on your own end getting started."

"That's ridiculous!" Roberson blurted. The quoted figure had shaken him from his shell of despair. "That would make the cost of hiring your soldiers equal to the value of the gage the syndicate ships in a half *year*! Not the profit, the *value*!"

"In other words, a quarter's value of the gage shipped from Cantilucca as a whole," Vierziger said with a gentle smile. "Since control of the total would be in the victor's hands. Perhaps your hands."

"And you could reduce your in-house security force," Coke noted. His tone was flat, factual; not in the least cajoling. *This is the deal, people. If you aren't smart enough to take it, be assured somebody else will be.* "I know, man for man the cost is much lower; but what the FDF offers is victory, and what you're buying from those buffoons outside —"

His thumb hooked dismissively toward the door behind him.

"— is a stalemate that's about to collapse on you."

"It won't work anyway," said the Widow Guzman. She groped blindly to the side to grip Peres' wrist. *Hell of a thing to have to depend on that one for human warmth.* "You can't bring your armored cars to Cantilucca without the Confederacy learning, and for *that* they would react."

Peres bobbed his head at the beauty of the thought emerging from it. "How much for just the infantry, Master Coke?" he asked. "That shouldn't be very much, should it? We can slip men into the port in twos and threes, that won't be a problem. Marvela doesn't watch very closely."

"The cost of *three* companies of infantry," Coke said, "which would be the minimum I'd recommend — to my superiors — without armored support, is approximately the same. A Frisian infantry company isn't simply a hundred troopers, Master Peres; but I take your point about the need to infiltrate the units rather than bringing them in formed, on a single hull."

"That's too much money," Roberson moaned. He sat bent over, clutching his lower rib cage with both hands. "I can't possibly manage that. We're running at a loss as it is, with the force doubled and gage production down because we've squeezed the farmers so hard already."

The Widow looked at the merchant with a face as blank as ice ready to shiver off a warming window.

"Now I'm not sure the difficulty's as great as you suggest, Simon," the gigolo put in unctuously. "Perhaps if the three of us go over the books . . ."

He pressed the Widow's hand, then returned it firmly to her lap. This was Peres the Businessman, Peres the Wheeler-Dealer, not to be distracted by a woman's needs.

"I've *gone* over the books," Roberson retorted. "I've *been* going over the books. That's why I'm concerned, *Master* Peres."

Coke stood up, flanked by his companions in a motion so coordinated that it must have appeared pre-arranged. "We'll leave you to your considerations, mistress, gentlemen," he said. "Perhaps you'll have occasion to see us again before we leave Cantilucca."

Vierziger opened the door and stepped through it in the lead, as before. The anteroom had emptied except for ten or a dozen Astra gunmen. One of them threw the Frisians a mocking salute. The tension of the party's entrance was gone.

The door to the private office was thick. It thumped shut behind Coke, amputating all but the first syllables of the voices raised within.

Coke smiled. Lieutenant Barbour's software would polish and enhance the conversation into a form more clearly audible than it was for the three principals inside the office.

❖   ❖   ❖

The jitney driver, looking both puzzled and pleased at having reached Silva Blanca safely, went off in search of a bar. The two Frisians were paying him as much for a day trip as he'd normally have earned in a week.

Of course, they hadn't gotten back to Potosi yet; and it had taken the cold stare of Johann Vierziger (who'd wandered over "aimlessly" during the negotiations) to put the driver into a mood to deal. Margulies figured she owed her sergeant one for the help, not that he'd exactly *done* anything.

The Lord knew, though, she understood how the jitney driver felt. She didn't suppose she could have a better man to back her in a firefight . . . but she wasn't quite convinced Vierziger was human.

The village consisted of twenty-five or thirty buildings, constructed for the most part of local timber with shake roofs. Each house had its own chest-high fence of palings. A few chickens ran in the courtyards, though there weren't as many as there should have been. Most households had small kitchen gardens as well.

The driver had stopped his three-wheeled vehicle as directed, in front of a largish red-painted house. It was the only structure in town that wasn't naturally weathered wood, so Barbour had suggested the village headman likely lived there.

The intelligence officer was probably right. They couldn't be sure until somebody acknowledged the Frisians' presence.

"Hello?" Margulies shouted again. Nobody responded. Again.

She shifted the strap of her sub-machine gun. Probably not the best way to reassure the locals who were keeping indoors, but the gun was heavy, the sun was hot, and it had been a kidney-pounding ride in the curst jitney.

"The next time," she muttered to Barbour, "I check

to see if a planet's got aircars before I agree to take a mission on it."

"There's aircars in Potosi," Barbour said. "One at least, from the signature. It probably belongs to one of the syndicates, though. Like everything else bigger than these cyclos."

Barbour viewed the village with interest and less apparent irritation than Margulies felt. From what Barbour said during the ride to Silva Blanca, he'd been purely a staff officer before transferring to the survey service. Probably hadn't seen as many mud/stick/straw hovels as she had in the field police.

At least the intelligence officer was loosening up a little. Margulies had been a bit worried about him during training. Couldn't complain about his competence, but a six-man team was too small for somebody whose eyes always seemed focused on his memories inside.

Margulies pulled out a handkerchief and lifted her helmet to wipe her brow. She wasn't going to turn straight around and return to Potosi. She was too stubborn for that, and anyway she didn't relish an immediate fifteen klicks in the jitney.

But she *was* getting ready to kick a gate open, and kick down the door of the house beyond if it came to that.

An argument erupted from the house in the next courtyard over. At least three people shouted simultaneously. Each voice seesawed higher, building on the volume of its competitors. It was obvious that none of the speakers was listening to the other two.

The door opened fiercely enough to slam against the front wall of the house. A young man surged out, twisting his arm free of the older woman and man who had tried to hold him back.

"Sure, I'll stay here!" the young man shouted. "Stay here and starve, that's a *fine* idea! Why should I go to Potosi and live like a human being, hey?"

"Live like a filthy killer!" the woman shrieked. "My son, a killer like the killers who take everything we grow! Will you come back and rob us yourself, Emilio?"

She tore the front of her dress open. Her breasts sagged like banana skins. "Why don't you just shoot me now? Wouldn't that be easier than breaking my heart?"

Margulies motioned Barbour with her toward the gate into the adjacent courtyard. The low fence permitted them a full view of the events.

"Look, I'll be able to send money back to you, mother," the boy said. He glanced at the woman, then jerked his eyes away in horror at her histrionic self-degradation. "Look, we're all starving here!"

"Blood money!" the woman shrieked. "Blood money! I'd rather die!"

She flung herself on the ground. It wasn't an effective ploy, because it freed the boy's arm from her gripping hands. He half-ran, half-skipped toward the gate. His father followed, bawling, "Emilio!"

The door of the headman's house opened a crack. When those within realized the strangers were going next door, a little man scurried out. He wore red pantaloons, a loose shirt of unbleached cotton, and a red headband.

"You there!" the headman shrilled. "Strangers! You don't belong here! I've called for help, you know. You can't just come in here with your guns and order us around!"

The only thing Margulies had said since arrival was, "Hello?" Barbour hadn't said that much. The whole business was informative about the social structure of Cantilucca, all right.

As Emilio reached for the gate-latch, he noticed the Frisians for the first time. He recoiled abruptly. The boy's father grabbed his arm from reflex, but both of them stared over the fence at the strangers instead of carrying on their quarrel.

"You there!" the headman called. "Strangers! Come away from there at once!"

Margulies made a quick decision and turned toward the headman's compound. "We're here to see a friend of mine," she said. "Angel Tijuca. Can you tell me where he lives?"

Emilio snatched the gate convulsively open and darted into the street. His father gestured toward him, but the near presence of the Frisians kept him from following the boy. Emilio carried a short staff and slung his possessions from it. The bindle was so slight that its presence was better proof of poverty than nothing at all would have been.

"Blood money!" his mother cried. The boy bent forward, as though he were hiking toward Potosi against a sleet storm.

"We don't have any Tijucas here," the headman said. "You should go away now, before the guards arrive."

The fellow was short to begin with. He splayed his legs deliberately so that his eyes barely glinted over the fence. Margulies had the impression of a turtle peeping from a shell of palings.

"There's a vehicle with four driven wheels on the way, Mary," Barbour said. He looked doubtfully at the sub-machine gun she'd insisted he carry. His expression wasn't so much frightened as confused, that of a bachelor confronted with a squalling baby.

Margulies wasn't sure how Barbour had gathered the data — so far as she knew, the intelligence officer wore a commo helmet just like hers, with only the standard sensors. She'd have been willing to take Barbour's word for the situation, even without the headman's confirmation.

"That's no problem," she said, her voice reassuring. Though the implication was that there wouldn't be any trouble — and probably there wouldn't — Margulies' mind was considering the quantity of troops and weaponry carried by a patrol vehicle, and the degree to which she could count on Barbour for back-up in a firefight.

Not far, she was afraid. Of course, he might draw attention away from her by shooting himself in the foot.

"Angel was from Silva Blanca before he joined the Slammers," Margulies continued calmly to the headman. The local shifted his weight from one leg to the other, at a rate which increased with the intensity of Margulies' gaze. "And I got the impression he intended to return here after he retired. I just —"

An open car roared up from the other end of the town's only street. It had four oversized tires mounted on outriggers to keep the vehicle from tipping during off-road travel; a 2-cm tribarrel was mounted on a central pintle. There were four men aboard, one of them at the grips of the big gun. The muzzles swung as the vehicle swayed on its long-travel suspension.

The patrolmen wore red; red gloves, in the case of the driver.

Emilio's parents disappeared within their house. The boy was out of sight also, though Margulies thought he might have ducked behind a hedge. She didn't think there'd been enough time for him to have walked around the sweeping curve of the road to Potosi.

The vehicle shimmied to a halt. "Drop those guns!" shouted the man at the tribarrel. "Drop them right now or s'help me, I'll kill you!"

The driver was extending the collapsed shoulder stock of his sub-machine gun. The other two L'Escorials pointed weapons as well. The fat bore of the grenade launcher wavered between Margulies and Barbour without ever quite aiming *at* either one of them.

Margulies set her fists deliberately on her hips and faced the car, arms akimbo. "I'm Lieutenant Mary Margulies of the Frisian Defense Forces," she said in a harsh, hectoring voice. "An ally of L'Escorial *if* your Masters Luria can come to terms with President Hammer. Who in the hell told you to point a gun at me, *boy*?"

The driver's foot slipped off the brake. The car had a hub-center electric motor in each wheel. Their torque jerked the vehicle forward. The gunner fell back, lifting the tribarrel's muzzles. It was pure luck that he didn't manage to trigger a burst while he was at it.

The back of the vehicle was full of food and personal gear in wicker baskets. The tribarrel's gunner untangled himself from the clutter, awkwardly helped by one of his fellows. "Shut it off, Platt!" he shouted. "Shut it off, you dickhead! D'ye want to kill us all?"

The driver, a rabbity-looking fellow, cut the power. The motors' singing wound down against friction, leaving the village quieter than it would have been without that contrast.

The gunner slapped the grenadier on the shoulder to point him out of the crowded car, necessary so that the gunner too could step down behind him. The driver and the remaining gunman got out also. They stood on the other side of the vehicle; perhaps for the sake of cover.

The headman scurried out his courtyard gate to join the group in the street. "I told them they had no business here," he said. "And I called you right away, just like I was supposed to, sir."

"We do indeed have business here," Margulies said, frowning at the gunner, the apparent team leader. "I came to visit an old friend of mine from the FDF — Angel Tijuca. He was my driver for a year and a half."

The grenadier stared at the gunner. The gunner frowned in turn. "You know Angel, then?" he said.

"Yes, he was my driver," Margulies repeated. The L'Escorial didn't sound hostile for a change, so she didn't add a gibe to the statement. "He got me out of a tight spot. A really tight spot."

"Why's she here, then?" the driver asked plaintively. "Why this dungheap?"

Jalousies covered the windows of the houses. Corners of the slats tilted up as eyes peered from within. The Lord knew what the tableau would seem to people who couldn't hear the discussion.

A naked child opened the door of a house halfway down the street. An adult arm shot from the shadows and dragged him back inside.

"Look, if you're friends of Angel, then there's no problem you being here," the L'Escorial gunner said. He scratched his beard stubble in puzzlement. "But he's not here, lady, he's in Potosi."

"*Where* in Potosi is he?" Margulies demanded. She massaged the palm of her left hand with her right thumb.

"Well, he's in headquarters, I suppose, lady," the gunner said. He was unsure of himself and nervous of giving offense — under circumstances where, moments ago, he'd thought he and his tribarrel were the Lord God Almighty.

"He's our training officer, lady," the driver blurted. "He's training officer of the L'Escorial syndicate."

"Well, you missed the live show," Sten Moden said as Coke opened the door of Hathaway House, "but you're in time for the first rerun."

The logistics officer had been sitting at the console the whole time Coke's party was gone. He stretched, reaching up to the lobby's high ceiling. His lopsided figure looked like an archaeological treasure, an oversized monument dragged from the midst of ruins.

Evie Hathaway stuck her head out from the kitchen. She ducked back, though she could still overhear the Frisians' conversation.

The team had effectively commandeered the lobby, the only volume in Hathaway House big enough to serve them as an operations room. They had to treat the Hathaways as allies. Georg might be ambivalent, but Evie's support was willing. Coke and his team had proved they were willing to stand up to the syndicates — if only to get a better price for the FDF's services.

"Getting good signals?" Niko Daun asked as he stripped off his cloak.

"Clear as a bell," Moden agreed. "The guards on the tin can at the gate think Dobrynyev, who quit the poker game a winner, was cheating. Though they're not sure how."

"Dang!" Niko Daun joked. He was brilliantly cheerful from success, from the end of immediate danger, and from having been part of a dangerous and successful *team* operation. "Now I gotta go back and stick a personal shadow on Dobrynyev so we can be sure. Knew I should've done that!"

"Let's see how the leaders' conference went after we were gone," Coke said. His tone was a little sharper than he'd intended. The men had a right to be pleased; it was just that the job wasn't finished yet.

"Ready to roll," Moden said mildly. He touched a control.

"*We can't pay that!*" Roberson's recorded voice said in impotent fury.

"*I'd pay anything if I thought it would work,*" the Widow said. Despair made her empty, while it drove the merchant to frustrated anger. "*But if we hire them, then the Lurias will simply bring in more foreigners of their own. Thanks to Suterbilt, they have first look at possibles coming through the port.*"

"*You don't understand, Little Star,*" Peres interjected. His tone was disdainful, only lightly screened by a pretense of affection. "*In a fingersnap, these mercenaries will go through anything L'Escorial can put up. Spaceport toughs and petty criminals, that's all their best is.*"

"Good assessment," Coke murmured.

Vierziger gave the other men a lazy smile, like that of a cat awakening. "I don't like them with brains," he said. "But I'm not convinced that Master Peres has disqualified himself as yet."

"*A gun is a gun,*" Roberson muttered. "*And just how did you expect to fund these wonderful troops, Peres? Out of your purse?*"

"*I didn't expect to fund them at all, old man,*" the gigolo sneered. "*After all, the transaction can't go through the Bonding Authority.*"

"*Will they agree to that?*" the Widow asked.

"Smart lady," Niko said to show that he'd picked up something from the discussion among the officers earlier.

"Not smart enough just to hire us and be done," Johann Vierziger said. "Wait and see."

"*They'll have to agree to it,*" Peres insisted. "*They know as well as we do that the Marvelans would have to take action if they heard we were bringing in a mercenary regiment. If the Bonding Authority's informed, the Marvelans will hear about it. The Frisians are here to deal, so that means they're willing to go outside the normal channels.*"

"Maybe," Coke said. "*Maybe* we're willing."

"*I don't see how that follows,*" Roberson said, but his voice had lost its vehemence.

"*So our Frisian visitors arrive,*" Peres caroled, "*they clean up our problem. They board the ship* we *provide, though they don't know the ship's ours. And the ship never gets home. The credit chips are aboard the same vessel, so they're never presented for payment. End of story, yes?*"

"You see?" Vierziger said. "My type after all."

"*But can we be certain they'll agree to act outside the Bonding Authority?*" the Widow said. "*Surely they'll recognize the danger.*"

"*It's not our doing, you see,*" Peres insisted. "*The Marvelans really would quash the operation if they heard about it. We'll offer Master Coke a lagniappe of his own, five percent say. Enough to retire on happily,*" *if he sees matters the right way and explains them to his superiors."*

"I wonder," Sten Moden observed, "how carefully Mistress Guzman has gone over the contracts her friend lets on her behalf?"

Vierziger tittered. "Definitely my type," he said as he stretched his delicate, deadly fingers before him. "Dumber than dog squat."

Daun glanced at the gunman uneasily.

"I'm not sure. . . ." muttered Roberson, but he wasn't sure enough even of his objections to proceed. Generalized fear hung over the merchant, darkening his vision and blurring details into a miasma of formless danger.

"We don't have any choice," the Widow said abruptly. *"Every day our situation gets worse. I should have sold my interests to the Lurias when Pablo died, but it's too late for that now. I'll call Major Coke."*

"Not yet, Little Star," Peres said. *"We don't want to look too eager and make them suspicious. Wait for this evening and we'll say we've been able to raise the money after all."*

"In a way," Sten Moden said, "it *would* be surprising if clients understood just what they're buying from soldiers, and how much it's really worth to them."

As he spoke, he unconsciously kneaded his left shoulder with his remaining hand.

"All right," the Widow said. *"If you say so, Little Heart. That's what I'll do."*

Moden switched off the recording. Mistress Hathaway looked out of the kitchen again.

"And our move, Matthew?" Vierziger asked. He had his pistol out. He was rubbing the metalwork with a synthetic chamois which he carried folded in a pocket.

"L'Escorial doesn't seem to think they need us," Coke said, pursing his lips as he considered. "We should do something about that."

"Pepe Luria is off Cantilucca," Evie Hathaway

volunteered from the doorway. "He's the active one, though he's the grandson. Raul and Ramon are probably waiting for him to get back before they start the killing. In earnest."

Coke nodded. "Do we know where the syndicates' installations are?" he asked Moden.

The logistics officer grimaced. "I can make some guesses," he said. "For fine tuning, we're going to need Barbour. Though if" — he turned toward the kitchen doorway — "Mistress Hathaway is willing to provide some local knowledge, I think we can do a pretty good job right now."

"What are you planning to do?" Evie said crisply.

"Something very costly to the syndicates," Coke said. "Are you in?"

"Yes," the woman replied. Her voice was just as flat as Coke's had been.

"Get on with it, Sten," Coke said. He looked at Johann Vierziger. "Come along, Johann," he said. "You and I are going back to Astra headquarters to give helpful advice."

"Yes, I thought that might be the case," Vierziger said, rising easily from his chair.

His fingers twitched the pistol in and out of his holster twice, to be sure that it didn't bind. He was smiling.

"Patrol One to Base," announced the console. The voice was recognizably that of Margulies, despite the stitching and compression of spread-band radio. "We're coming in. So don't get nervous when the door opens, Johann."

Coke paused with his hand halfway to the latch of the front door. It swung in, pushed by Barbour while the security lieutenant watched the street in a would-be negligent fashion.

"When did you become Patrol One?" Moden asked.

"Well, it didn't seem right to identify ourselves in clear," Margulies said in mild embarrassment. "If you

like, sir, I can be Three from here on out. We don't
know who's listening in."

"On this benighted planet, nobody is," Barbour said
as he seated himself at his console.

He obviously didn't want to look like a mother
desperate to check her child after the first day of
school. Equally obviously, that *was* how he felt about
having handed his equipment over to somebody else,
however apparently trustworthy.

"Johann and I are going out," Coke said. "I'd like to
hear about your trip when we get back, though."

He reached for the door again.

"Just a moment, sir," Barbour said. "Let me find
Peres for you. He's left Astra headquarters."

Coke blinked at the intelligence officer. "You were
listening in on all this while you were gone?" he asked.

"Yes sir," Barbour said. "Through the console. Ah —
perhaps I should have asked your permission?"

He looked up in sudden concern. Barbour's sandy
hair and unlined face gave him the appearance of
being a boy at least a decade younger than he really
was.

"I won't tell you how to do your job," Coke said. "I
just — well, I didn't know you could do that from a
remote location. Without special equipment."

"Yes sir," Barbour said. He grinned suddenly, unexpectedly. "Commo helmets are more special than most
people realize. If you know how to program them,
which isn't any great trick."

Right, thought Coke. He'd heard exceptional cooks
talk the same way, in absolute honesty. *Oh, there was
nothing to it*. Nor was there, for them. As opposed to
99.7 percent of the people who might have attempted
the same dish, with results ranging from mediocre to
disastrous.

The console display shifted fluidly as Barbour spoke.
It locked into a section of streetscape five hundred
meters west of Astra HQ. "Here's where he's gone, sir,"

Barbour explained. "I think he's on the third floor."

Coke hooked a finger to Evie Hathaway to join the group about the display. "How in blazes did you determine that?" he asked. "How did you even know Peres had left the building?"

"Voice print," Niko Daun said/guessed.

"Right in one," Barbour agreed. "I told the software to analyze audio inputs and track Peres through it. He'd gone out past the bug at the courtyard gate a few minutes after you'd left, telling the guards he was going to the Bucket."

"The Bucket of Blood," Mistress Hathaway said. "Yes, it's in that building all right. It's an Astra bar. No worse than most places, not really."

"I tracked him through the external sensors here on Hathaway House," Barbour said in obvious — and justifiable — pride. "He was traveling with three companions, talking frequently enough that I could follow the audio after I lost video . . . though even with enhancement, I'll admit that there was a lot of guesswork at the end, sir."

"Your guesswork is what laymen call genius," Coke said. "You don't need to be modest with me, Bob. And Via! Call me Matthew, all right?"

"We need to place more sensors up and down the road," Daun said. "Visual, too. I'll get on that right now."

"Would you prefer to find Roberson, ah, Matthew?" Barbour asked. "Mistress Guzman hasn't left the building."

"No, no," Coke said. "Master Peres is the choice for this approach." He smiled tightly. "He's a gambler. That's what we need."

Niko Daun opened his case. He sorted through it with practiced fingers, pulling out items from several different pockets.

"Let me get something to drink," Margulies said, "and I'll give you some back-up, kid. No rest for the wicked, hey?"

She walked toward the saloon, rubbing the shoulder where the strap of her sub-machine gun had hung during the jitney ride. At the archway she turned and said, "When we all get back, Matthew, I'd like to talk to you about L'Escorial. I don't know how important it is."

Coke nodded. "Sure," he said.

"Shall we visit the Bucket of Blood, Matthew?" Vierziger said. "I wonder if the ambiance is as high-toned as the name."

He giggled as he opened the door.

The shill for the Bucket of Blood was a woman in pirate costume on whose shoulder perched either an aviform or a bird-featured robot (the thing/creature certainly wasn't a Terran parrot). She was bare-breasted, overweight, and seemed desperately tired.

From the way she kept trying to wipe invisible cobwebs from her face, Coke suspected that the woman had already overloaded on gage. Additional cones could no longer stave off the crash into near-coma that was due in an hour at the latest; they could only prolong its duration.

The outside stairs serving the third-floor tavern were wide enough for two to pass if they were careful. The burly Astra who came out while the pair of Frisians were midway above the second landing was deliberately clumsy. He lurched toward Vierziger, in the lead, in an obvious attempt to crush the smaller man against the railing for a joke.

Vierziger shifted stance and dodged past the Astra, right shoulder to right. Vierziger's hand moved too, probably with something in it, though even Coke couldn't be sure. Hand or object made the Astra's head *tunk* like a hammered melon. The man slid bonelessly down the stairs to the landing, where he sprawled.

The woman who'd accompanied the Astra out of the bar stared at the Frisians without speaking. Coke politely lifted his commo helmet as he passed her on the stairs.

The Bucket's waiters were husky, and the man in a protective cage by the door carried a beanbag gun. The big-bore weapon fired bagged shot at low velocity, giving the projectile an impact like the fist of the most powerful boxer who ever lived.

The beanbag gun could break bones, but it wasn't generally fatal. Coke presumed the intention was to avoid dangerous penetrations rather than to spare troublemakers' lives, however.

All the bar's staff and most of the clientele wore blue, though some of the patrons were obvious sailors who'd simply tied on a neckerchief of the correct color as a temporary measure. The music was loud and there was a life-sized holographic sex show going on in one corner, but the place wasn't exceptionally bad for its type.

Exceptionally tough was another matter. Most of the people, staff and patrons alike, carried guns. One wrong word and the bar would sound like Settlers' Day celebrations on a frontier planet.

Peres wore black, not blue. He and the three men with whom he'd left Astra HQ were in a corner booth with three women and a boy. Stim cones stood to attention on the table, with empties littering the stained floor beneath. Peres groped the crotch of one of the women beneath her dress, but his heart didn't seem to be in the activity.

Coke approached, Vierziger a pace behind to his leader's off side. An Astra with Peres looked up and grabbed for the machine pistol he carried in a shoulder holster.

There wasn't enough elbow room on the banquette seats for the fellow to draw. Peres saw the attempt, glanced blank-faced toward the oncoming Frisians, and broke into an oily smile.

"My friend Master Coke!" Peres called over the

glass-edged music. The gigolo reached across the girl he'd been fondling to lay a finger of restraint on the wrist of the henchman with the machine pistol. "And Master Vierziger as well! Can I hope that you're here for pleasure?"

"Business first, Master Peres," Coke said. "But if it goes well, then in a couple months we'll all have both time and a reason to celebrate. Is there a place you and we could . . . ?"

"Here," Peres said without hesitation. He chucked the girl under the chin. "You lot, get out of here. We need the space."

"Hey!" said the girl. "You told us that —"

Peres' three henchmen stood up. The boy and the other two women were leaving the booth without objection. Peres hit the protesting woman with the same hand that had been between her legs a moment before. Her head snapped back and she sprawled across the banquette.

The guard with the beanbag gun turned at the commotion. When he saw Peres was involved — and that Peres didn't need further help — he looked away.

One of the Astras with Peres carried gloves thrust through the epaulette loops of his sleeveless blue shirt. He took the pair out and pulled one of them on. It had fishhooks sewn into the back, points forward.

The other two women shrieked and grabbed their fellow. They dragged her out of the booth before the Astra was ready to punch her. He aimed a kick, but she was too groggy to react.

No bones broken, just a bruise or two.

Coke smiled at Peres. The escorts sat down again.

Coke thought of the ruck of blood and offal the mines had left of the L'Escorial cordon. This time he fantasized that the uniforms were blue, and that some of the pellet-torn faces were those of the men before him.

He sat on one end of the semicircular banquette;

Vierziger took the other end, across from his leader, so that they both had a way out of the booth. In a room full of guns and blue garb, that wasn't a free ticket home, but it was better than having to ask permission of Peres and his thugs before getting to your feet.

"What I was thinking, Master Peres . . ." Coke said.

"Adolpho, please," the gigolo said. "And Matthew and —"

He cocked an eyebrow toward Vierziger and smirked.

Vierziger smirked back, for the *Lord's* sake! "Johann, and of course you may," the little killer said.

"We realize that you're doubtful about committing so much money without certainty of the result, Adolpho," Coke resumed. "I'd like to show you that quite apart from armed force, we can help you through planning and — data collection."

He'd almost said "intelligence," meaning it in the military sense. Peres might have misunderstood by taking the word at its general meaning. That would have been correct also; but the wrong thing for Coke to have said aloud.

"What do you have in mind, then?" the gigolo said. Peres wasn't as stupid as Vierziger claimed while listening to the bugged conversation. Rather, he had no experience of the world outside Cantilucca, and he was too young to realize that Cantilucca was a *very* small pond.

"Your competitors warehouse their gage," Coke said. "With the information my colleagues and I provide, you can snatch the whole amount without any alarm being given. That's pure profit, a good quarter of the cost of the FDF's services."

"We could never do that!" said the Astra holding the hooked gloves. He looked as though Coke had told him to walk on water.

"Besides which," Vierziger said with a smile, "that will leave your L'Escorial friends with severe liquidity problems. They won't be able to bid for comparable services for several months."

Peres looked from one Frisian to the other. His right index finger sorted out one of the unused stim cones in the pile before him. He flicked it across the table to Vierziger. "Try this," he directed.

Vierziger rotated the thumbnail-sized gray cone. The casing didn't have the usual markings, lines, or spots to indicate the contents. "Gage?" he asked.

"Gage *and*," the gigolo said. "Go on, try it."

Vierziger shrugged and set the injector to his left wrist.

Peres wheeled and looked at Coke again. "*Why* are you offering me suggestions that'll handicap you in getting the Lurias to jack up your price?" he demanded harshly.

Coke smiled. "I'm not on Cantilucca to raise the price," he said. "I'm here to deal on the terms my superiors set me."

The smile broadened and grew as terrible as the one that played over Vierziger's lips in the aftermath of the mine blasts. "It may be that your L'Escorial friends think the way they greeted me cost them only a dozen dead. They would be wrong. It's cost them everything they have — so long as the Widow is willing to meet our minimum demands."

"The Widow is willing to do whatever I tell her," Peres sneered. "But how can I be sure you're not playing a double game? Let's you and him fight, hey? Astra and L'Escorial . . . and your troops land to loot the ruins."

A shudder rolled through Vierziger's frame. Coke looked at his companion with unexpressed concern. The little gunman waved a negligent hand when the spasm passed.

"What is it?" he asked Peres.

"Gage," the gigolo said. He smiled. "But cut with first-distillation tailings. Are you afraid now?"

Vierziger laughed. "Afraid of what? Dying? No, Master Peres, not me."

Vierziger flexed his hands above the table, showing that the nerves and muscles all responded normally. He laughed again. His voice sounded like snake scales scraping on rock. The nearest gunman groped toward his hip holster, then caught himself.

"There won't be a fight," Coke said to Peres. The pulse of the music overrode the discussion anywhere beyond the booth itself. The gigolo's decision to negotiate here had been a reasonable one. "There's only a few watchmen in the warehouse. I can show you how to get through the walls, and how to disconnect all the alarms before you start the operation."

"Are you afraid of a fight, Master Peres?" Vierziger asked in a voice too soft to be a gibe . . . and with a grin that could have sharpened knives.

"No," the Astra leader snapped. He looked at Coke. "Money in my purse so that there can be money in yours, hey? Very reasonable. So we'll do it — but you'll come along, Matthew, so that we can be *sure* the deal is that reasonable."

"All right," Coke agreed. "We'll go to your headquarters now and I'll brief you. I'll need a hologram projector — or I can get one from the hotel."

Peres' lips tightened. "We have projectors. We're civilized here, not some backwater, you know!"

Coke didn't laugh in the gigolo's face. Again, it wouldn't have been politic.

"Then let's go," he said, rising. "After I brief you, I'll send a message capsule to my superiors to update them. The operation itself will take place tonight, if you can get your end together that quickly."

"Yes, of course we can!" Peres snapped. He looked at Vierziger, rising also. "Are you going?"

"I wouldn't miss this for the world," said Johann Vierziger, stroking the inside of his left wrist with his right index finger, his trigger finger.

Coke viewed his surroundings from a cool vantage point above his flesh and prickling nerves. He would see Pilar when he routed the message capsule toward Nieuw Friesland. There would be time for dinner afterwards, and other things.

And it might be the last time Matthew Coke had.

Sten Moden emerged from the alley between a pair of six-story structures. Washed clothes hung by an arm or leg from poles thrust out of windows on the upper floors. The washing was the first sign of domesticity the Frisian had seen on Cantilucca.

The area behind the buildings along Potosi's single street was given over to garbage, storage, and living quarters. In a few places the forest had been cleared. Generally the trees had died when human activities stripped their bark or poisoned their roots. Derelicts used dead limbs for firewood and sheltered beneath the fallen boles.

This ten-by-twenty-meter space equidistant from the two syndicate headquarters was one of the formal exceptions. Four large trees had been left at the corners to support a roof of structural plastic. A metal post peaked the center of one end; the sheeting was rectangular, while the area it covered was a rough trapezoid. One of the corner trees was dead, but for the moment it seemed steady enough.

The fenced area under the rigid marquee garaged vehicles ranging from jitneys to the elaborate aircar beneath which projected the legs of a man in multi-pocket overalls. The four lift fans whined in different keys. They were spinning out of synchrony, obvious even to ears less trained than Moden's.

A boy of twelve or so was in the driver's seat, adjusting controls in obedience to orders which the man under the chassis shouted. The boy saw Moden and chopped the car's throttles. "Father!" he called. "A man is here. A big man!"

Moden waved to show that he was friendly. The fence around the garage was a combination of woven wire, barbed wire, and the body panels of wrecked vehicles welded to metal posts.

The chained and locked gate was metal plating on a tubular frame. Judging from the power cables, it could be electrified. Moden didn't feel a prickle when he passed the back of his hand close, but he didn't actually touch the panel to be sure that the power was off either.

The man who pushed himself into sight from beneath the aircar was dark-skinned and solid-looking; in his late thirties or maybe forty standard years, though Moden didn't consider himself any judge of age.

"Yes sir?" the mechanic called.

"I want to rent a vehicle," Moden replied. "Maybe several, there's six of us. We landed from Nieuw Friesland yesterday on business."

The man relaxed slightly. He wiped his hands carefully on a rag, giving himself time to consider both the request and the stranger making it.

"My name's Moden," the logistics officer went on, adding reassurance. "Besides, I've worked maintenance myself and I wanted to see what your operation was like. Who decided to bring a Stellarflow to Cantilucca?"

He gestured toward the aircar, its fans now at idle.

The mechanic's face changed again, this time to an expression of interest and even hope. "I am Esteban Rojo," he said. "I am the owner here, though not of the aircar."

He glanced over his shoulder and called to the boy, "Pito? Go on back to the house now. It's time for your lessons."

He unlocked the chain. Moden stepped aside so that Esteban could swing the gate outward. The boy darted through, following the one-armed stranger with his eyes until disappearing into the alley.

Esteban gestured Moden into the enclosure before chaining and relocking the gate. "You're familiar with the Stellarflow, then?" he asked.

"There's people who swear by them," Moden said, looking critically at the ornate aircar. "Not the people responsible for maintenance, though. And I wouldn't have thought you could get parts for one closer than Earth. Are there many aircars on Cantilucca?"

"This one," the mechanic said glumly. "Adolpho Peres, a friend of the Widow Guzman, bought it on Delos and shipped it here. He's given me a tennight to get it running properly."

"No spares, I gather?" Moden said. He didn't ask when the tennight was up, nor whether the Widow's gigolo had bothered to state the obvious "or else" at the conclusion of his orders to Esteban.

"Stellarflows are of the finest Terran engineering," the mechanic quoted in flat irony. "They never break down. This one must have been damaged in shipping. But it's up to me to fix it!"

He shook his head. "I can't get the fans to synchronize," he said. "Peres says the car was fine on Delos, but I don't believe him. I think the problem's electronic, not mechanical, but I couldn't have gotten control boards from Earth in time even if I'd ordered them five days ago."

Moden walked around the aircar, lifting and closing access plates. "You couldn't get parts on Earth either," he said. "From the serial number, this unit's older than either of us are."

"Stellarflows are of the finest Terran engineering," Esteban chirped. "They never wear out."

"Right," said Moden. He opened the side door and lay down on his back in the driver's compartment so that he could look under the dashboard. "Their engineers' stools don't stink, either. Just ask them."

The logistics officer carried a multitool. He used it now to loosen fittings behind the wood-veneer interior panels. His size and single hand made it difficult to work in the strait confines, but he proceeded without asking for help.

"I thought it might be the fans themselves," Esteban said, peering through the opposite window in an attempt to follow what was going on. "They'd been replaced in the past with standard units, Gurneys, instead of Stellarflow parts. I thought that might be the problem, but the fans synch fine when I jury-rigged a chassis from a ground car."

"You do a lot of work for the Astras, then?" Moden asked. His face was hidden, but his casual tone fooled no one.

"I work for whoever pays me!" the mechanic snapped. "Or doesn't pay, half the time. The cyclo drivers, it's their livelihood. They haven't got any money when they break down, and sometimes they forget to pay when I get them running again. Do you have a problem with that?"

"Quite the contrary," Sten Moden said. He folded the powered multitool into its belt pouch, then straightened with a flat plug-in module in his hand.

"This car has an autopilot," Moden said.

"Yes, of course," the mechanic agreed. "But we don't have guidance beacons on Cantilucca. You can't engage it."

"Right," said Moden. "And the board driving it is identical to the board driving the manual duct controls. Except with luck this one isn't shot."

He handed the module to Esteban, who took it with dawning comprehension.

"May the Lord bless you and keep you, Master Moden," the mechanic whispered. Relief flooded through the dikes of insouciant carelessness with which the man had tried to armor himself against the coming deadline.

"Well, we're not out of the woods yet," Moden said. "If this board's packed it in too, then we cobble together something from scratch. Refrigerator controls from big trucks — four of them in parallel, that might work. Do you have reefer trucks here?"

"I could never manage that in five days!" Esteban said.

Moden got out of the car. "We can do it in twelve hours," he said flatly. "I'm not looking forward to dialing in four separate units though, I'll tell you that. But chances are this one's going to work."

Esteban, holding the module as if it were his first grandchild, started to crawl under the aircar again. He stopped. "You want to rent vehicles, Master Moden? What sort of vehicles? Anything you please."

"We'll talk about that later," Moden said. "Right now, I want to get my hands dirty."

His face set, then smiled again. He took out his multitool. "I've been in admin too long."

The big Frisian sat down, lay back, and slid himself under the blocked aircar with the certitude of the tide coming in.

The man guarding the garage beneath the building holding the Ortegas' apartment wore brown trousers, a green shirt, and a carbine which fired fléchettes. He slid the gate closed as Pilar squeezed the port van into a space that was only wide enough by the thickness of the paint. Ten other vehicles, one of them a scarlet armored truck, had virtually filled the parking area.

"We'll have to get out through the back of the van," Pilar apologized to Matthew Coke.

Coke slipped between the seats ahead of the woman. "I've made low-level drops under worse conditions," he said, forcing a chuckle. He was keyed up and working very hard to conceal the fact.

You couldn't let your men know that you were as nervous as they were. Besides, the process of *acting* calm brought a degree of real relaxation.

"I appreciate you escorting me back, Matthew," Pilar said. "It's been . . . Until last night I could pretend it wasn't as bad as it seemed, but now I'm frightened to be out alone after dark."

"My pleasure," Coke said. "Besides, I could use the drink you offered."

The interior of the garage was painted half red, half blue. Both sides had staircases. Pilar walked toward the red one.

"Only a drink, you understand," she said. She didn't look at her companion as she spoke, and her left hand clutched her crucifix.

"I understand," Coke said in a neutral voice.

The guard smirked at the couple. He turned away when Coke gave him a flat glance from the base of the stairs.

"L'Escorial?" Coke said mildly. There was room to walk beside Pilar. He followed two steps back in order to keep his right hand clear of her if he had to draw.

"Not exactly," Pilar said. She paused just below the ground-floor landing to let a party of sailors exit noisily onto the street. They sounded happy, even the man who was reciting the Lord's Prayer in a singsong.

Pilar started up again when the way was clear. "The top floors, the fifth and sixth, are a, a brothel," she said. "They have the same — staff, I understand. But the entrances to the two floors are off different stairs so that there won't be fights. Our suite is on this side of the building, that's all."

The cape she wore for concealment draped her full hips and swayed as she moved. Coke smiled at the thought of Salome and the seven veils. Far more effective than just flaunting your bare tits over a railing . . . though that worked too; anything at all worked when a man was going into the red zone and needed to reassure himself.

Pilar had kept her explanation flat, purely informative. She cleared her throat and added with a touch of embarrassment, "It's actually a *good* location in Potosi, you realize. The security is so much better than at other buildings."

The door at the second landing had three separate lock plates, though they seemed to work from a single electronic key. As Pilar began to open them, a L'Escorial gunman turned at the floor above and continued down the stairs.

The man was drooling and wild-eyed from gage tailings. He held a 2-cm powergun. The loading gate was open, indicating that there wasn't a magazine in place, but Coke couldn't be sure whether or not there was a round in the chamber.

Coke walked up two steps and stood so that he blocked the stairwell. His hands were under his cape, the left one holding a needle stunner. Unlike powergun bolts, the little charged projectiles would penetrate the light film of the gray cape. "Good evening, sir!" he called. "L'Escorial forever!"

"Fuck you," the gunman mumbled. He braced himself against the wall and pointed his weapon at the Frisian's face.

"Inside quickly!" Pilar screamed as she flung the door inward.

Coke shot the L'Escorial in both knees. The gunman's legs splayed outward like those of a dancing marionette. His tailbone slammed violently down on the step behind him.

The powergun was pointing at the ceiling when it went off. Cyan light and the *wham!* of enclosed air superheated filled the stairwell.

The 2-cm bolt shattered the lower half of the cast-in-place concrete. It left a cloud of powder and the rusty squares of reinforcing wire across a meter-wide crater.

Coke lunged into Pilar's suite and slammed the metal door behind him. He held the panel shut while the woman reset the triple locks.

"Well!" Coke said, expelling a deep breath. He stripped off his cape and threw it down. He felt hot and trembly.

The floor was carpeted. Coke put the needle stunner on safe and dropped it onto the cape. His grip had been so fierce that his hand hurt. He'd trained himself to shoot ambidextrously, but using his left added a level of stress —

Necessary here so that he could have drawn the powergun with his master hand.

Pilar removed her own cape. Her face was calm until the composure crumbled like ice in a spring freshet. She threw herself sobbing into Coke's arms.

"I hate this place!" she cried. "This house and this town and this planet! Oh Lord, I wish I were dead!"

Coke stroked the back of her neck with his left hand. With his right he tilted her face and kissed her. Her lips were wet with tears.

"Don't wish that," he whispered. "It's not as bad as that."

"This place is Hell and I'm in Hell," Pilar moaned. "Oh, if only we had never left Marvela. . . ."

Coke kissed her again. He lifted her breast against his broad chest with his left hand.

"Please," she said. She put her hand to his and twisted her torso away. "Please."

The room was lighted by three globes, weaving a simple pattern as they hung unsupported in the air. The furnishings were of handmade wood rather than the plastic extrusions that Coke had seen everywhere else in Potosi. The syndicates preferred to import goods and even food rather than to turn the labor force into production of anything except gage.

Coke held Pilar by waist and shoulder. He kissed her again. "Your husband isn't here," he said. "You know he isn't going to be back tonight."

He thought of adding that Terence Ortega had gone to an apartment at the other end of town at midday. Barbour would warn them if Ortega left.

Coke decided not to explain that. Telling Pilar there was an electronic tag on her husband would have indicated the degree of preparation that Coke had made for this moment.

Coke was romantic — you didn't stay a soldier because of the pay and benefits. But you didn't survive as a soldier if you didn't plan each possible step, and that carried over to the rest of Coke's life as well. Women tended not to see things the same way.

Pilar snatched herself out of his grip again. "Terry's behavior doesn't affect *my* vows!" she said angrily to the far wall.

"Pilar," Coke said softly, "I'm — not real settled just now. Forgive me if I misspoke."

He put his hands on her shoulders and guided her around to kiss him again.

"Oh, Matthew," she said, "you could have been killed, I know. Because of me. But . . ."

Her fingers brushed his cheek, dusted by tiny fragments of the concrete ceiling. He kissed her, pulling her toward him without resistance.

"Matthew," she said desperately. She caught his hands as they rose again toward her breasts. "Matthew, I'm so sorry, please."

She stepped away, still holding his hands. "Let me get you that drink, but then I'm afraid you'd better go."

He lifted his chin and dipped it again. His face was as placid as that of a saint's statue. He lowered his hands to his sides. "That's all right," he said. "But I don't think I'll have the drink."

Pilar began crying again. She swallowed the sobs, but the tears pulsed down her glistening cheeks. She held her crucifix with both hands. "I'm sorry, I just can't," she whispered. "I want to, but I can't."

An internally lighted button controlled each lockplate from the inner face of the door. Coke thumbed the buttons in turn, switching them from green to red.

"No problem," he said without emphasis. He donned the cape again. His hands and the needle stunner vanished beneath the gray shimmer.

"Matthew?" Pilar said. "Please? Call me when you've gotten back to Hathaway House safely."

Coke looked over his shoulder at her. "I've got various business tonight," he said. "If it goes well, I'll probably see you tomorrow when I send another message capsule off from the port."

Pilar caught the door behind him and kept it from swinging to. She watched through the crack.

Instead of going down to the street, Coke started up the stairs toward the brothel.

Moden and Esteban Rojo could have finished the job in an hour and a half, if they'd had good luck and the right tools. They had neither.

Removing the Stellarflow's lower electronics module required either special equipment or great care. Moden was careful, but years of vibration had crystallized a plastic bearing. The joint snapped, and then they had to cut the other three straps as well because the clamps had frozen.

Four hours after they'd started — straps replaced with pieces cut from sheet stock, bearing freed in a sonic bath from the multitool, and journals cannibalized from one of the pair of redundant trunk-lid cantilevers — Esteban ran the fans up and down in perfect unison before shutting off the power.

"As good as new!" he announced.

Moden stretched mightily. "Which means," he said, "it's almost as good as a Frisian aircar that would have cost half as much free-on-board . . . but Via, some people have to have their Terran technology."

He'd acted in place of a hydraulic jack when the bow of the car had to come up 20 centimeters. Judging from the weight, Stellarflow had used iridium for the frame. Moden ached, but it felt good to have been doing physical labor again.

"Will you eat with us, Sten?" Esteban asked. He tossed a rag to Moden so that the big man could wipe his — hand. Esteban's mouth opened in embarrassment.

Moden pinned the rag between his knees and dragged his hand through it determinedly. "Got the big chunks off," he said.

He looked at the mechanic. "At your apartment, you mean, Esteban? I don't want to be in the way."

"We have a cafe," Esteban said with dignity. The Frisian had skirted as delicately as possible the question of whether Esteban could afford to feed guests, but the well-meant concern still rankled. "My wife and children run it, Pito and our daughter Annunciata; and I help when there's time. But I ask you there as a guest, not a customer, please?"

"Then I'd be honored," Moden said. He flicked the rag through the air, caught it in a fold; and folded it a second time, into a square, against his thigh.

Rojo's cafe was on the building's second floor, with the entrance and sign — The Sacred Heart — near the mouth of the alley down which Moden had walked to reach the garage behind. A dozen locals were present in the single small room, two families with children as well as individual adults. The food odors were piquant and wonderful.

The girl who shuttled plates from the serving window was in her early teens and strikingly beautiful. "My daughter, Annunciata," Esteban said proudly. "Nunci, I want you to meet Master Sten Moden!"

The girl dropped into a curtsy, though she carried a serving plate in either hand and there wasn't, Moden would have thought, space enough for her knees to dip as they did.

The patrons of The Sacred Heart sat at a single table supported on six pillarlike legs. The table was of native wood with a subtle grain, polished by use into an attractive brazen patina. Seating was on the pair of full-length benches. There was barely enough room between the cafe's walls and the ends of the table for patrons to edge by to the side away from the door — the side from which Nunci served.

"Rosaria!" Esteban called. A woman, older and much fatter than Annunciata, stuck her head out of the serving window.

The mechanic gestured to the cafe's patrons, all of whom were staring at him and his huge companion already. "Everyone! This is our great good friend, who repaired the aircar which had me tearing out my few remaining hairs. Rosa, your special chicken and rice for our guest — and plenty, he has the strength of ten men and no doubt he eats like ten!"

"Well, I'll be able to do justice to the meal," Moden said. The undoubted virtues of Hathaway House didn't include the cooking of Master Hathaway, who attempted that task.

Esteban led the Frisian to the open seat in the center of the table, facing the door. Moden's knees straddled the table's central leg. There was a general shifting and good-humored discussion to create a second place into which Esteban squeezed himself.

Pito popped out of the door to the kitchen and presumed living quarters, carrying a basket into which he dropped dirty dishes. They were plastic and crude, locally pressed from exterior sheeting.

Esteban whispered in his daughter's ear. She passed the message to her mother at the window and received two small glasses with a bottle of ruby liqueur, three-quarters full.

"From my father-in-law's farm," Esteban said as he poured. "That's where we get the food as well."

Annunciata reached past to put a serving platter, not a normal dish, of chicken with rice and a variety of heavily processed vegetables on the table before Moden. "Grandpa Mordechai won't grow gage," she said. "He says people must eat, mustn't they?"

"To your health!" Esteban said, raising his glass.

"And yours," the Frisian responded. He jostled the neighbor on his right in grabbing his glass. The liqueur was thick, almost a syrup, with a fruity flavor. Not unpleasant, and there was enough alcohol to bite the back of Moden's tongue.

"Both syndicates have been after Mordechai," Esteban said with a frown. "L'Escorial pushed him off his old farm, so he terraced a hillside that nobody claimed. I helped, the whole family helped, and his neighbors too. He's stubborn. I agree with him, but I worry."

The food was delicious. "Have things gotten worse recently with the sides arming?" Moden asked through a bite.

"No, no," Esteban said. "Since so many of the gunmen came here to Potosi, there's fewer left to bother the farmers. Most of the farms grow food for themselves, but they grow gage too for one syndicate or the other. So that they'll be protected."

A family got up to leave. The wife paid Rosaria with three separate credit chips. From the prices chalked beside the serving window, the five dinners totaled less than ten pesos — one and a half Frisian thalers. The citizens of Potosi didn't have easy access to credit terminals which could have combined the small amounts into a single chip for convenience.

The outer door opened. The chatter stilled. Three men wearing blue shouldered in. All carried power-guns: a pair of sub-machine guns and the third man festooned with four separate holstered pistols as well as a selection of knives.

Esteban stood up, awkwardly since he had to step over the bench to do so. Citizens — his neighbors — slid to either side, half-crouching toward the ends of the room.

"Gentlemen," Esteban said, "this is not a bar. I'm sure you'll find better entertainment elsewhere."

The leader of the Astra gunmen appeared to be the man with the pistols. "You got a red sign downstairs," he said. "We thought we'd check the place out."

"The sign is the sacred heart of our lord Jesus Christ!" Rosaria blurted from the serving window. "We have nothing to do with L'Escorial here!'

"Nunci," Esteban said in a low voice. "Go help your mother in the kitchen."

"She stays," ordered an Astra. He wagged the muzzle of his sub-machine gun to emphasize the point.

"They used to have a red sign," the gunman to the leader's other side tittered. "It had a little accident when we come by it."

The trio moved further into the cafe. The local patrons flowed behind them on both sides and out the door, like damping fluid when a shock absorber compresses.

Moden wore a pistol in a belt holster. He wasn't a particularly good shot. He certainly wasn't good enough to drop three men in the fraction of a second he'd have before the sub-machine gun aimed at him blew his head off.

"Please," Esteban said. "This is just a cafe. We have no sides, we are poor people."

The leader took the bottle of liqueur and drank directly from it, eying Moden past the plane of sluggish red fluid. He handed the bottle to the man aiming at Moden. "Who's the crip?" he asked.

"My name's Sten Moden," the Frisian answered calmly. His hand lay on his lap. The closed flap of his holster was in sight of the gunmen. "I'm from Nieuw Friesland, a businessman."

"He's a leftie!" said the Astra who'd warned Nunci not to leave. "Get it? A leftie!"

Without warning he triggered a single shot. The cyan bolt struck near the top of the kitchen door. Wood blew outward in blazing splinters, leaving a hole the size of a soup plate in the thin panel.

Rosaria screamed. Nunci stood transfixed, and Esteban's fists balled.

Sten Moden gripped the table's central leg. He lifted and hurled forward the massive piece of furniture with all his strength. Both sub-machine guns fired, into the tabletop and ceiling as the huge club pistoned toward the three Astras. Moden felt the shock of the bolts through his hand, but the table was too solid for the light charges of a pistol or sub-machine gun to tear it apart.

The tabletop hit the far wall, or almost, with a soggy thump. Moden pulled back, then slammed his weapon toward the wall again with his shoulder behind it.

There was a gurgling cry. When Moden withdrew the table the second time, sub-machine guns and other accoutrements clattered to the floor behind it.

Annunciata screamed. She threw herself into her father's arms.

Moden gave a convulsive gesture that slammed the table back down on its six legs. He was trembling all over. He had to brace his hand on the scarred top in order to continue standing. Powergun bolts had blown smoldering craters in the wood.

Moden didn't try to look over the table to see what had become of his victims, though he knew he ought to. One of the Astras might still have enough strength to pull a trigger. . . .

But probably not.

The Rojo family spoke or cried in four vocal ranges, all of them incoherently. The Frisian closed his eyes and opened them, drawing deep breaths.

The cafe's outer door flew open.

Mary Margulies lunged in behind a sub-machine gun. Niko Daun followed her with a set expression and another sub-machine gun.

The would-be rescuers looked at Moden, then looked at their feet. "Blood and martyrs," Niko said.

Margulies straightened from her crouch. She put her weapon on safe and cleared her throat. "Ah," she said. "Barbour, you know he monitors the audio from the helmets. He thought you might need a hand."

Sten Moden looked at his palm. His adrenaline-charged grip had left white valleys where it held the corners of the table leg.

"No," Moden said. "One was enough."

CANTILUCCA: DAY THREE

The outer fence surrounding L'Escorial's gage ware-house was woven wire, five meters high and topped with a Y of razor ribbon. The forest had grown to and entwined with the wire despite evidence of desultory attempts to burn it back. The diamond teeth of Coke's powered cutting bar opened a man-sized hole with one sweep of his arm.

The vegetation in the four meters between the fencelines was cut to knee-height scrub. There was a single row of buried toe-poppers, located so that the mower could straddle them. Daun marked a safe pathway with white tape.

The sensor-controlled directional mines placed every ten meters along the inner fence were even less of a danger. Daun turned them all off with a deactivation signal, just as the watchmen would have done while mowing or carrying out other maintenance operations.

"Who do these bozos think they're dealing with?" the sensor tech muttered disdainfully to Coke.

"Bozos like the Astras behind us," Coke replied.

Well behind them. Coke had decided he and Daun would breach the defenses alone. Vierziger wasn't happy to be a kilometer back in the forest along the road, but that was the only way Coke could be *sure* the Astras would stay where they belonged.

The last thing Coke wanted was a line of trucks to come driving up while he and Niko were in the middle of the wire. He'd seen relief in the sensor tech's eyes when they went over the plan the first time. Daun had more reason than most to doubt the competence of indig forces.

"Wait here, sir," Daun said crisply.

The sensor tech darted across the cleared area to the nearest directional mine, a lump against the inner fence. After a moment's manipulation there, he moved ten meters down the line to another lump. He tossed something to the ground.

"All right, sir," Daun said, this time using helmet intercom. "I've pulled the fuzes. I didn't want somebody turning them on again at a bad time. It can happen by accident, even, lightning or a plasma discharge."

"No, we wouldn't want that," Coke agreed under his breath.

He was smiling. He remembered he'd had doubts about how the kid would perform after the experience which got him transferred to a survey team. Just fine, so long as Daun could be confident of his back-up . . . and for that, so far, so good.

The warehouse was a huge hangar constructed primarily of structural plastic, but strengthened at the corners by pillars of reinforced concrete. A bank of lights on the roof was intended to flood the interval between the fencelines. Many of the bulbs had failed without being replaced.

It didn't really matter. The guards didn't patrol the exterior, and there were no windows in the building proper from which to observe their surroundings.

The gage syndicates had achieved parity of incompetence. That was fine until somebody arrived who knew his ass from a hole in the ground.

Daun set a small transducer close to the nearest of the inner fencepoles. He stepped swiftly toward the next support, holding a similar transducer and unreeling the thin cable which tied it to the box he'd set on the ground.

"Don't touch the fence yet, sir," the tech ordered;

needlessly, because they'd gone over the plan in the lobby of Hathaway House, and Matthew Coke knew better than to jump the gun in an uncleared detector field anyway.

"Right," Coke murmured. He preferred a subordinate who might irritate him with unnecessary warnings to one who let him walk into disaster because, *I thought you knew!*

Daun turned a switch on the control box. "There we go!" he said. "All right, sir. It'll think the circuit's complete even if you blow everything down between these two posts."

"No need for that," Coke said. He thumbed the cutting bar live and swept it up and down with his left hand in a nearly perfect catenary arc through the fencing. The blade whined and sparkled happily.

If L'Escorial's builders had used beryllium monocrystal or some other refractory material for their defenses instead of steel wire, the Frisians' task would have been more difficult. But if a frog didn't jump, it wouldn't hit its ass on the ceiling. . . .

Coke crouched in the opening as Daun sprinted for the building forty meters away. If Coke had to supply covering fire — he carried a sub-machine gun, with holstered pistol and a 2-cm weapon slung just in case — he didn't want to be so close to the warehouse that he couldn't cover both ends of the building with his peripheral vision.

Daun wrenched up a lid on the ground outside the building. It wasn't locked shut. The tech stretched on the concrete pad, holding a light down in the cavity with one hand and reaching in with the other. Bob Barbour claimed this fusion bottle was the sole power source for the warehouse.

Fusion bottles didn't fail, and the output of one was more than sufficient to power the building's lights, sensors, and motor-driven trackways. Coke still found it hard to believe that there wasn't at least a battery-

operated emergency radio, despite Barbour's assur-
ances. If Bob was wrong, well, he was also ready to jam
the transmission within a micro-second.

Niko Daun ran back, bent halfway over and flushing
with excitement. "Okay, sir!" he said quickly. "Okay,
whenever you want it."

Coke keyed his helmet to Channel One. "Go," he
said. "Out."

"Roger," said Johann Vierziger's voice, a whisper like
tendons rustling on dry bones. "Out."

Coke checked all his weapons. "Niko," he said, "why
don't you wait here. I'm going to wait by the door in
case they open it when they hear the trucks."

"No *sir*," said the sensor tech. "I'm part of this
team." He closed the case holding his equipment and
unslung his sub-machine gun.

"Glad to have you along," Coke said with a quirked
smile. He started around to the front of the warehouse,
walking just inside the inner fenceline.

It wasn't really true. Daun's combat skills were
coming along, but firefights wouldn't ever be the boy's
strong suit. On the other hand, he was probably better
than most of the guards they'd be facing in a moment.
And anyway, Coke wasn't about to tell the kid who'd
performed splendidly that he'd be a fifth wheel in what
came next.

Coke expected the first of the vehicles coming up
the road to be a flatbed truck configured as a ram with
a sloped steel bow and extra weight in back to add
momentum. Instead he heard the hum of a jitney, one
of those Sten Moden's mechanic friend had supplied to
the Frisians.

Coke frowned, but then he thought about it for a
moment. Vierziger had kept the Astras on their leash.
If the gunman wanted to arrive before the locals now,
there was no real reason he shouldn't.

Instead of coming to the first of the two gates on the
approach road, the jitney bounced off the pavement

and whined to the hole Coke had cut in the outer
fence. Though the Astra convoy was running without
lights, the twenty big flatbeds were audible by now.

Vierziger left the jitney at the gap in the fence. He
jogged the rest of the way to Coke and Daun. He wore
two bandoliers and a garrison belt hung with various
munitions, but none of the equipment jingled or
clattered as he moved.

"We were going to let the Astras take it from here,"
Coke commented mildly.

"No, Matthew," Vierziger said. "*We* were going to do
it right."

"We still have to wait for the ram," Coke said.

"I can open the warehouse doors if you'd like, sir,"
Niko Daun said. "So long as the power's still on, like it
is now."

Coke blinked. "You can?" he said.

Johann Vierziger smiled at him. The harsh illumination from the roof floodlights made the little man look
like a gnome, an incredibly vicious gnome.

"Sure," Daun said.

He reslung his sub-machine gun and fumbled in the
small tool pouch on his belt as he walked to the latch
plate beside the sliding doors. The kit Daun had left
back at the fence contained the special equipment he
needed for the outer defenses, but he wore what he
considered basic tools whenever he had his trousers on.

"I hope he remembered to put the curst gun on
safe," Coke grumbled.

"He did, Matthew," Johann Vierziger said. He faced
the door, but his eyes were far away. He flexed his
empty hands twice, then readied his sub-machine gun.
"He's a very careful lad. A credit to you as his
commander."

"I'm ready," the tech said. He'd pressed a flat disk
held by a magnet or suction cup to the latch plate. A
coil of thin flex ran from the disk to the squeezer in
Daun's hand.

"Just before the truck rams the first gate," Vierziger said softly. "Then cut the power when the door's half a meter open."

Vierziger hadn't said anything during the planning session when Coke proposed a battering ram to enter the warehouse after they'd shut off the building's power supply. If the sergeant had made this suggestion, Coke would have vetoed it as needlessly dangerous to members of the survey team. Now, with adrenaline surging through his blood, Coke couldn't imagine another way to have done it.

But Vierziger had *known* that all along.

The trucks were in sight, snorting and rumbling up the approach road. The ram plate on the lead vehicle was a V-shaped blade intended for a ground-clearing bulldozer.

"Don't the guards hear them coming?" Niko asked in a combination of wonder and nervousness. He had nothing to do but wait until Coke gave him the order.

"They're not guards," Coke murmured. He switched his visor to thermal imaging, then through light amplification and straight visual mode back to thermal again. Just to be sure. "They're employees who don't really believe there's need to guard anything. Drunken, stoned employees."

"Are we really going to put all this gage in the Astras' hands, Matthew?" Vierziger whispered.

The bastard had known all along!

"No," said Matthew Coke. "We're going to burn it here."

Daun squeezed, then dropped his clacker and grabbed the separate control clipped to his breast pocket. The double doors rumbled back. The lead truck slammed into the gate with sparks and a tortured squeal —

The lights on the warehouse roof dimmed and vanished, the doors froze the width of a man's shoulders apart —

And cyan hell broke loose as Johann dived into the building behind his blazing weapon.

Expanding echoes of Vierziger's bolts glowed in Coke's thermal optics. A man writhed on the floor, his face gone. Coke leaped the body, firing twice between his legs while he was in the air.

The warehouse offices were in three partitioned cubicles to the left of the doors. The remainder of the building's volume was a single room, ten meters high and stacked with drums of gage on pallets.

The car of the overhead rail and hoist system jogged forward on the inertia of the laden pallet slung beneath it. Because the building's power was off, circuitry hadn't shorted when Vierziger hit the control cage with a long burst. The operator lay slumped in his saddle, his clothing afire.

There was motion from the middle cubicle. A man stepped out. He lurched backward, shot simultaneously by Coke and Vierziger.

Coke dropped his sub-machine gun and aimed the 2-cm shoulder weapon instead. Vierziger ran down the center aisle. He would take any L'Escorials at the back of the building before they realized what was happening in front.

Coke fired twice through the open doorway of the center office, then twice into the door to its left. The bolts of sun-hot copper ions ignited the desk and furnishings of the first, and blew the extruded plastic door of the second into the cubicle's interior.

Coke loaded a fresh magazine. He was shifting his aim to the third office when a figure ran out of the burning center cubicle. He swung the heavy muzzle back as his finger took up slack on the powergun's trigger.

A woman, stark naked and screaming. She held a bandeau top in her left hand. No threat, no danger.

Coke aimed past her at the remaining office. He stroked his trigger twice to flush out anyone hiding there.

Niko Daun stepped alongside his commander. He fired at least half his sub-machine gun's magazine into the screaming woman. Gobbets of flesh and bone spewed away like wood chipped by the teeth of a router. She spun back into the flames of the office from which she'd fled.

"I got him!" Niko shouted. "I got him!"

The lead truck hit the opening hard enough to jounce the double doors nearly open. The driver managed not to stall his motor. He backed a few meters and accelerated again, cutting his wheels to slide the left door back against its stops.

Nobody else came out of the offices. A body lay in the corner away from the cubicles. As Vierziger entered the building, he'd dropped the fellow. Coke hadn't noticed him before.

Sprinklers opened above the burning offices. They were fed by standpipes in the roof, even though the pumped water system went off when the power did. Coke surveyed the ceiling, then put a bolt into the end of each standpipe where it joined the front wall of the warehouse. He fired until he'd emptied the 2-cm weapon's magazine, then reloaded again. Water gushed down the inner wall and splashed across the concrete floor. There it could do nothing to affect the flames.

"All clear in back!" Vierziger reported over Channel Three. Several quick bursts of sub-machine gun fire snarled from the rear of the warehouse. "All clear in back!" Vierziger repeated, simultaneous with another burst.

Steam and smoke billowed from the burning office cubicles. Another Astra truck drove into the warehouse. Its headlights brightened the gray mist but did little to illuminate the building's interior. The Astra gunmen didn't have night vision equipment. They shouted to one another in anger and confusion.

The gage was in double-walled 150-liter plastic drums. For shipment, the drug was dissolved in a matrix of ethyl alcohol. Because Coke knew what to look for, he could already see the fires started at the back of the warehouse where Vierziger had raked pallets with his sub-machine gun.

"I'm coming out!" Vierziger called over the unit push. "Do not shoot, I'm coming out!"

Coke grabbed the foregrip of Niko Daun's sub-machine gun and lifted the muzzle high. The sensor tech might not have heard the warning, might not have understood it — might have dropped his gun on the concrete and triggered a shot wholly by accident. Firefights weren't Daun's proper job, so it was the commander's duty to see that no accidents occurred.

Adolpho Peres swung down from the cab of the second truck. He wore body armor and a helmet that must have weighed nearly ten kilos. "Start loading the gage!" he bellowed. "We can't wait around here long!"

The gigolo waved his machine pistol. He turned his head as he spoke. Coke stepped toward him, releasing Daun.

Peres saw the motion past the edge of the helmet's cheek plate. He must have thought he was being attacked, because he tried to swing the gun onto the Frisian.

"I'm a friend!" Coke shouted as he lunged forward. Instead of directing the weapon upward as he'd done with his own trooper, he jerked the machine pistol out of Peres' hand. "We've killed them all for you!"

The office cubicles were fully involved by now, hammering the men in the front of the warehouse. The right side of the ram-equipped truck was only a few meters from the fire. The plastic body panels started to soften; bubbles appeared on the front fender.

"Who?" Peres shouted. "Coke, is that you? Manuel!"

The last call was for the gigolo's bodyguard, a man nearly as tall as Sten Moden and broad in proportion. Coke saw Manuel's vast, weapon-festooned bulk several meters away, groping in what was for him a gray fog. Vierziger's assessment of the big man was that a gun-jeep had more braincells and could carry even more weapons — but that choice was for Peres to worry about.

Johann Vierziger stepped up on the Astra leader's other side. "I'm here, Matthew," he said. "Now let's get out of these gentlemen's way, shall we?"

"Peres, we'll leave you to load the gage," Coke shouted in the gigolo's ear. "We'll meet you tomorrow morning to arrange contract terms!"

The warehouse had become a steambath because the heat boiled water off the concrete. The flow from the sprinklers had decayed to irregular dribbles, noticeable only if a drop happened to splash you from above.

"Yes, of course," Peres replied. He snatched his helmet off in frustration at its weight and the degree to which it limited his range of vision — not that he was going to be able to see much more without it. "Manuel! Sanjulio!"

The three Frisians broke for the door. Coke's finger on Daun's wrist gave the sensor tech guidance he might or might not have needed.

A third truck drove into the warehouse and collided with the second. The drivers shouted at one another, and the rest of the convoy stopped in confusion on the approach road.

Coke led his men toward the gap he'd cut in the fence. "I think we'd best stay in the woods and hump our way back," he explained. "I'm not thrilled about walking the six klicks into Potosi, but L'Escorial is going to see the flames before too long and come out with guns blazing."

"Does Peres realize that?" Niko Daun asked. The point had obviously escaped the tech himself.

"Here, wait by the jitney," Vierziger said.

"We can't drive it back through the forest," Coke

objected. "It's not a skimmer. We'll just have to abandon it."

"Sten's going to pick us up in a moment," the gunman explained. He looked at the sensor tech. "Niko," he went on, "the Astras don't know the gage is burning yet. Whether they'll realize that a fire here will call the owners' attention is an open question."

An unlighted aircar slid low over the treetops. Sten Moden was at the controls. He dropped vertically to hover on fan thrust directly behind the jitney.

Coke half-climbed, half-tripped his way into the vehicle's other front seat. Vierziger and Daun got into the back.

"Is there anything else you ought to have told me?" Coke demanded in a loud, generally directed voice.

"Well, you didn't want to walk either, did you, Major?" Sten Moden said as he pulled the joystick toward him to add power. "Esteban was still doing tests on the Stellarflow, so I asked if he'd mind me putting it through its paces tonight. Does pretty well, don't you think?"

The Stellarflow was too massive to accelerate quickly, especially with a load that included the logistics officer, but it had a good deal of power. Starlit glimpses of the treetops close beneath suggested their speed was 200 kph and rising. Moden swept them in a broad arc that would approach Potosi from the north, opposite to where all the commotion was occurring.

"Look, I'm not going to argue with success," Coke said after a moment. "But the next time, don't pull this sort of thing behind my back, all right? You guys act like a team, and I'll promise not to act like a little tin god."

He realized as he spoke that something very basic had changed in the structure of this survey team; and that he was pretty sure it had changed for the better.

They were out of sight of the warehouse at this altitude, but the whole sky behind them glowed red from the swelling inferno.

❖   ❖   ❖

Matthew Coke's bedroom had a window which opened out onto the alley beside Hathaway House. When he leaned his elbows on the ledge, he could watch the building across the street. As a result, he wasn't surprised to hear his commo helmet click, then warn in the voice of Lieutenant Barbour, "Matthew, two men are walking toward us from L'Escorial headquarters. There isn't any other exceptional behavior from that direction."

The breeze blew from the south. Even at this distance it carried with it a whiff of burned vegetation, burned plastic, and — present only if you knew it was there — burned flesh.

Coke lifted himself back from the ledge. One of the approaching visitors was garbed in an ensemble of scarlet and vermilion, a well-tailored outfit and clearly expensive. The two close hues made his plumpish figure seem to shimmer.

The other man wore a red beret, but the remainder of his clothing was khaki. The garments looked a great deal like Frisian battle dress.

"Right," Coke said as he snatched the gray cape from the hook by his bed. "Action stations, though I doubt there'll be trouble. I'm coming down."

The shooting had gone on south of town until nearly dawn. The fact that it hadn't spread to Potosi proper meant the syndicates really didn't want the lid to blow, despite all their deadly posturing. That might change when the L'Escorials realized just how badly they'd been hurt by the fire.

Margulies slammed down the stairs ahead of Coke. She slid her left hand along the balustrade against the possibility of her heel catching on a tread as she jumped the steps three at a time. Vierziger was already with Barbour in the lobby, his proper location.

Georg Hathaway stood by the door and wrung his hands. "I'm sure there won't be any trouble," he murmured. His voice sounded like that of a dying sinner claiming confidence in his salvation.

"Johann, take the upstairs today," Margulies ordered as her boots hit the tile floor.

Vierziger raised an eyebrow. He looked spruce and trim. Somehow he'd managed to scrub away all the soot and matrix residue which had settled on him during the firefight.

"This is —" he began.

"Not today, Sergeant!" Mary Margulies snapped. "We're trading today."

She flashed a near-smile of apology to her subordinate, then to Coke.

"I think I know this guy," she explained in an undertone. She pointed toward the streetscape in Barbour's display. "I think he used to drive for me."

Barbour didn't comment, but his right hand moved. Half the hologram screen became a facial close-up of the man in khaki.

"Via, that's Angel, all right," Margulies said. "Via, he looks bloody awful!"

Margulies' friend carried a sub-machine gun, but it was slung muzzle-down over his back. His cheeks were hollow and his skin looked flaky, almost mildewed.

His well-dressed companion raised his knuckles to rap on the door.

Hathaway shivered and smiled falsely. "Ramon Luria," he murmured with a nod toward the holographic display. "Raul's son, that is."

The knock was crisp and imperative — three short strokes.

"Let your guests in, Master Hathaway," Coke directed. "There won't be any trouble."

If one of L'Escorial's leaders had come personally, that was certainly true. For so long as he was here.

The door sighed open. Ramon Luria waved a hand expansively. "Hathaway!" he said. "It's been too long since I sampled your beer. And you, sir, you'd be Major

Coke, I assume? The very person I've come to see."

If you watched Ramon carefully, you could tell that he was nervous. His movements had a birdlike suddenness, and there was a tic at the corner of his left eye. At a casual glance, though, the syndicate boss was utterly relaxed.

"Hello, Angel," Mary Margulies said from a corner of the lobby. She stood with the sole of her right boot against the wall behind her. "I made a trip out to Silva Blanca just to see you the other day."

"El-Tee!" the man in khaki said. "Blood and martyrs, Lieutenant! What are *you* doing here?"

"Same as you, Angel," Margulies said, answering a more limited question than the one Angel asked. "I'm pulling security while my boss does business."

Coke suddenly realized why Margulies leaned back against the wall. That way she had an excuse for not offering her hand or her arms to her former comrade.

Angel's skin puckered and shook because muscles were twitching randomly in response to the commands of damaged nerves. He appeared to have been pulled from his grave to come here — and from the look in his eyes, his worst problems weren't the physical ones.

"Major Coke doesn't need security, El-Tee," Angel said. "We're all friends here. I was, I was —"

His eyes darted toward Ramon. The syndicate boss pretended not to notice him, instead eyeing the lobby with an avuncular smile.

"I'd been partying a little, I mean, when you guys landed," Angel rattled out, "or I'd have been over before. I've been telling Ramon here and the Old Man, if the FDF wants in, hire them. There's no better!"

"Angel's our training officer," Ramon said, deigning to glance at his companion. "And he assists my son Pepe, our . . . shall we say 'war chief'?"

He laughed, a throaty sound and as threatening as jovial. "Angel Tijuca," he added. "Since I gather that not all of you are familiar with our boy?"

"Rather than stand in a doorway," Coke said, "why don't we adjourn to the bar."

He nodded. "I'll buy the first round."

Ramon waved the idea aside. He wore rings on all four fingers and his thumb. The bands were set with rubies, diamonds, and what Coke judged was a large amethyst.

"I'm just the messenger, really," Ramon said. "I came to invite you back to our house to discuss future affairs with my father, Raul. I aid him, and Pepe even more so when he's home. But the Old Man still makes the final decisions."

"Your son Pepe isn't here, then?" Coke said with a bland smile.

"That's correct," Ramon answered with no smile at all. "But he'll be back soon, Major. And you will want to have come to a decision with my father before that time, do you see?"

He bent his lips up at the corners. The warning couldn't have been more explicit if he'd drawn and charged a pistol.

"I don't mind discussing my employer's business at any good location, Master Luria —" Coke said.

"Ramon, please, just Ramon," Luria said with another glittering arc of his hand.

"— but when we arrived, there was some difficulty with your men," Coke continued. "And since from the sound of matters last night, people are pretty worked up still, I don't know that your home would be the best place to talk business. For me, that is."

"Don't think anything of it!" Ramon ordered. "Those imbeciles you killed, you did me a favor. With so many in Potosi all together, the men need disciplining or they'll get completely out of hand."

"I'm not sure *they* feel that way," Margulies remarked from where she stood against the wall.

The veneer of bonhomie slipped from Ramon's face. "They feel whatever way the Lurias tell them to feel!"

he said. "If I, Ramon Luria, tell you that you can visit my home without concern, that is so. Will you doubt my honor?"

"The Old Man doesn't think it's a good idea for him to show himself with things like they are, Major," Angel Tijuca explained with desperate sincerity. "Out in the street, I mean. Like you said, things got pretty excited last night. You'll be all right, truly."

Coke shrugged. There wasn't really a choice about going. He just hadn't wanted to appear too eager. "All right," he said. "Mary, you want to tag along?"

"You bet," Margulies said as she shifted herself onto both feet. "Maybe Angel and I can catch up on things while you talk business with the important gentlemen."

Niko Daun stepped into the doorway from the kitchen. His action station was first floor, rear; Vierziger and Moden guarded the upper story for now.

"I wonder if I could go, sir?" the sensor tech asked. He already wore the ammo pouch filled with bugging devices. "I'd sort of like to see the place."

"No, stick around," Coke ordered. He didn't want to try planting hardware in L'Escorial HQ while Tijuca was there. Margulies' friend might recognize Frisian equipment, which could be embarrassing — or worse. "I won't need a gofer, since we're just across the street."

He grinned at the syndicate boss to draw attention away from the exchange which had just taken place. "You know," he said, "you could have just phoned yourself."

Ramon waved his hand. "Would you have accepted the invitation had I not shown myself willing to visit you?" he said.

"You've got a point," Coke said. He deliberately checked that his sub-machine gun was on safe. Slinging the weapon muzzle-down across his back, he added, "Let's go talk to the Old Man, sir."

❖   ❖   ❖

Ramon Luria ushered Coke ahead of him through the door marked BOARD ROOM. An old man in red and a middle-aged one wearing a business suit of Delian cut were already seated within.

Instead of wood paneling, the walls of the sanctum in the basement of L'Escorial headquarters were covered with holographic screens. If the equipment had been perfectly tuned, an observer would almost think he was standing at ground level and the building didn't exist.

In fact, the hardware had all been installed at stock brightness and coverage settings, which varied from unit to unit. One of the thirty-odd screens was dead and three others operated at less than half their proper resolution. The set-up made Coke think of a diorama viewed through distorting mirrors.

Ramon waved proudly at the walls and said, "My son Pepe brought these back with him from Delos on his last trip. Pepe is very up to date, very civilized."

There was no sign on the streets of the gunmen who had been omnipresent throughout Potosi since the survey team arrived. Civilians moved in nervous spurts, like birds on the verge of a violent storm.

The table in the center of the room was a black synthetic oval. There were thumb controls at eight points around its circumference. Each was a shallow dome paired with a shallow depression.

Coke casually fingered the bump nearest him. Nothing happened. If the system had been operating, his touch would have brought live a workstation linked to the data bank within the table.

"I am Raul Luria," the old man at the head of the table said without rising or preamble. "Potosi is mine, *Cantilucca* is mine. For too long I have allowed the Guzman syndicate to exist — out of affection for the late Pablo, so close a friend of mine. But after last night —"

Raul Luria rose with the staggering difficulty of a

ship's mast being stepped by amateurs. The man seated to Raul's left looked alternately bored and disquieted by the rhetoric.

"— after last night, I have no more compassion. They must be crushed!"

The old man — the Old Man — pointed a crooked index finger at Coke. "Where do you stand in that, foreigner? Shall we crush you too?"

"I represent a business firm, sir," Coke said mildly. "We can supply personnel and equipment that will permit you to achieve your stated goal faster and more cheaply than you could in any other manner. I don't see why we can't strike a deal that will benefit both parties."

"One of the possible problems, Major," Ramon Luria said with his back to the door behind Coke, "is the sort of arrangement Friesland has already made with the Astras."

"And what you had to do with the raid last night," Raul Luria grunted as he bent, joint by joint, back into his chair. "If you're working with those pigs, I'll see to it that you're slaughtered with them. I swear it!"

"Father, we agreed there's no profit in discussing the past," Ramon said, his voice quivering between fear and contempt. "Isn't that so, Master Suterbilt?"

The businessman grimaced. "There'll be no profit in anything for the best part of a year," he said. "It'll take at least that long to rebuild gage stocks. And what is the Delos cartel going to say?"

"There's no arrangement between Astra and the FDF," Coke said. "Zip. Nada. Do you have a chip projector here?"

He glanced over his shoulder. Ramon looked blank. "I can bring one," he offered.

"Here, you can use mine," Suterbilt said. He slid a palm-sized belt unit across the table to Coke.

The businessman was stocky and probably no older than Coke, now that the Frisian had time to focus on him. At the moment, Suterbilt wore a scowl that amplified the angry appearance of his ruddy complexion.

Coke looked at the projector, then unclipped the one from his own belt instead. "That's all right," he said. "Mine will do."

The Frisian unit was half the weight of the older Delian projector Suterbilt used. Coke had hoped for a console model — the equipment built into the table itself would have been perfect, if the cursed thing had worked — but it didn't really matter. Cantiluccans probably wouldn't feel comfortable with the sort of crystalline images which the civilized universe took for granted.

Coke dropped into the reader the chip he'd prepared. He turned up the gain. "This is why we have no deal with the Astras," he said.

The negotiations in Astra headquarters shimmered in a hologram a meter across. The image had a gray translucence and there was considerable distortion toward the edges of the field, but it was both visible and audible.

"A *company of infantry and a company of combat cars*," said Matthew Coke's image. The scene was assembled from recordings made by the commo helmets of the three Frisians present at the meeting.

The image cut forward a few seconds. Barbour had spliced the data into the continuous form Coke wanted, but that meant the visuals were choppy. "*Approximately three thousand Frisian thalers per day*," the Coke hologram said, "*perhaps ten percent over.*"

Raul Luria was trembling with rage. His mouth worked, but no words came out. Ramon, who had moved to the side where he was visible out of the corner of Coke's eyes, wore a fixed smile. Suterbilt, the factor for Trans-Star Trading, simply frowned in puzzlement.

The Frisians vanished abruptly. The three *Astra* principals remained. Through the excellence of Barbour's editing, Adolpho Peres' lips moved in near synchrony with his words: "*So our Frisian visitors clean up our problem. They board the ship we provide, though they don't know the ship's ours. And the ship never gets home.*"

The bug Daun had left beneath the Astra conference table was audio only. You couldn't have told that when Barbour had finished mixing input from the bug with images culled during the two-party conference. When the Peres image "spoke" the final words, his face froze in a grin of murderous triumph . . . which was certainly true to the spirit of the plan the gigolo had outlined to his fellows.

Coke shut off the recorder and smiled at the L'Escorial leaders. "So," he said. "I've recommended to my superiors that we not do business with Astra. Shall my team and I go home, or . . . ?"

Raul Luria began to laugh. For the first moments, Coke thought the old man might be having a stroke instead. The paroxysm continued for nearly a minute.

Ramon pulled out a lace handkerchief and stepped to his father's side. He stood there, looking worried but unable to act. Raul hacked and wheezed and drooled from the corners of his mouth.

Suterbilt swallowed. His body tilted slightly away from the L'Escorial patriarch, and he was careful not to look to the side.

The old man finally regained his composure. "You're a right clever bastard, aren't you, boy?" he said. "What's your name? Coke, is it?"

Coke nodded.

"You planning to eavesdrop on us the way you did those Astra gutter-sweepings, then?" Raul demanded.

"No sir," Coke replied. "I am not."

Not in the same way, at any rate. The devices Daun and Margulies had emplaced all up and down Potosi's main street would keep an eye — and ear — on both syndicates.

Raul nodded. "That's good," he said. "So, that's your price for two companies of your Frisian Defense Forces?"

"That's an estimate," Coke said. "It's a good estimate, but the final figure will have to be determined at Camp Able."

Raul looked puzzled, glancing toward Suterbilt.

"FDF Command on Nieuw Friesland," Coke clarified. "Ah — and I gather it may not be possible to bring heavy vehicles like combat cars in through the port here without getting the Marvelan Confederacy concerned. The price would be comparable for three infantry companies."

"That's a *very* high price," Suterbilt said. He glared at the Frisian representative as though he'd like to throttle him. The factor's hands, Coke noticed, remained flat on the black surface of the table, spread wide and patently innocent.

"Compared to the losses you received last night?" Coke said. "Because your present personnel and equipment are of such low quality?"

Suterbilt tightened his lips. He gave a quick toss of his head. It could have implied either assent or disdain.

"Infantry and tanks is better than just infantry?" Ramon Luria asked. "And the price is the same?"

Coke nodded to the plump man. "Roughly the same daily rate," he agreed. "And combat cars aren't exactly tanks, but they're big. The folks down the street didn't think we could ship them in. If we could, the concentrated firepower would be better."

"*We* can bring in your combat cars," Raul said, looking at the factor beside him.

"There's excess capacity on all the TST ships that land on Cantilucca," Ramon amplified with a giggle. "Empty coming in, but it can be full if there's something we want to *bring* in."

"Don't talk about that!" Suterbilt snapped. He glanced from son to father, clearly angry but aware that the pair of gangsters didn't view the situation as he — a nominally honest businessman — did.

Quite obviously the factor was cooking Trans-Star Trading's records by showing lower cargo tonnage than the hulls' actual capacity. By so doing, he cheated his employers of shipping charges and — more important — permitted the L'Escorials to avoid port duties which should have been paid to the Marvelan Confederacy.

The ships that carried undeclared gage off Cantilucca traveled part-empty coming in. As Ramon had said, that unlisted volume could be filled with Frisian troops and equipment.

"If it's possible to bring in the cars, that would speed up the operation," Coke continued smoothly, as if the byplay among the locals meant nothing to him. "I'm estimating forty days with combat cars, but using infantry alone would add considerably to the completion time."

"A million-two in *thalers*," Suterbilt said, wincing. He stared at his hands.

"Roughly," Coke agreed. "With combat cars."

"The deal still has to be without the Bonding Authority," Raul said. "You know that, don't you?"

Coke gave a nod as tight and enigmatic as that of the factor a few moments before. "That does leave a problem, doesn't it?" he said.

Raul looked at Suterbilt. "Pay him," the old man said. "Pay him —"

He glanced back at Coke. "Ten days, that'll be enough, won't it? On account, an earnest of our good faith."

"I can't raise that —" Suterbilt objected.

"I can't commit my superiors," Coke warned. "I can only recommend by message capsule. . . ."

The Old Man waved at Coke. "Yes, yes," he said, "but with the money in hand, there won't be any trouble about the deal."

Ramon giggled. "'Money talks, nobody walks,'" he said, quoting an aphorism old when Croesus struck the first coin.

"I don't have," Suterbilt said angrily toward Raul, "*we* don't have that kind of money available now. The warehouse *burned*, don't you remember?"

"It's still collateral so far as TST is concerned," Raul said. He waggled a wizened fist in Suterbilt's face to emphasize the point. "Borrow the money from the company accounts on Delos, that's easy enough."

"And we'll repay it out of the Astra stockpile," Ramon added complacently. "Nobody will know the difference."

The factor grimaced but did not speak.

"We'll be kings with Astra out of the way once and for all!" Raul snapped. "And there's no choice anyway. If we don't move now, how are we going to pay the men with the gage gone?"

Suterbilt raised his hands to his face. He gripped his cheeks with a trembling violence that Coke watched in concern, wondering what the factor was going to do next.

Suterbilt slammed his palms back down on the table. "All right," he said. "All right! I'll raise the money."

He glared viciously at Coke and continued, "But it will take five days, maybe six, because of transit time to Delos. I *can't* write you a valid draft out of the funds available here on Cantilucca!"

Matthew Coke nodded calmly. "I'll inform my superiors of the pending circumstances," he said.

Coke should have been enthusiastic at the success of his mission. True, a survey team leader couldn't *commit* the FDF; but this was a perfectly workable deal, a *good* deal. Cantilucca would provide live-fire experience for relatively green forces, just the thing Camp Able was looking for.

The trouble was, Coke kept seeing the red-clad thug

with a powergun thrust against the cunt of the whore his fellows were beating. The gunman could have pulled the trigger as easily as not, *on whim*; and the next time, he or another of his sort likely would do just that.

Matthew Coke was making sure that the set of circumstances which made such behavior possible continued.

Angel's private cubicle was at the end of the bunk room filling most of the L'Escorial building's second floor. He paused with his hand on the doorknob.

"Look, El-Tee," he said, "it's not a palace I got here. Ah — maybe we could go somewhere else, find a bar or something."

Margulies snorted. "It could be pretty bad, Angel," she said, "and I'd still have lived in worse. You know that, because part of the time you were there."

"Yeah, well, this is no great shakes," the man repeated, but he opened the door.

She *had* seen worse. There'd been the militia barracks on Typer where the locals relieved themselves in one corner of the room in which they lived, slept and ate. That was the only military installation Margulies could recall being dirtier than this room of Angel's.

She hadn't regarded the Typer militia as being real soldiers. Neither, obviously, was her one-time comrade here.

No feces, and perhaps no urine. But the smell of sour vomit was overpowering, and the originally white sheets on the bed were so dirty that they had for the most part a gun-metal color. The common barracks from which Angel's room was set off was in far better shape, though the number of troops bunking in it had been doubled or tripled in the recent past.

"Look," Angel repeated. "We better —"

Margulies pushed him casually inside and followed.

"You were going to get me a drink," she said as she closed the door behind them. "Stop dicking around, hey?"

"Yeah, I . . ." he said. This must have been the first time in quite a long while that he'd been straight enough to appreciate the reality of his existence. His shoulders slumped as he looked at the fetid ruin around him.

The back and one leg of a chair protruded from a pile of garments. Margulies lifted the chair and shook it, then kicked the filthy clothing aside to make room for her to sit down. "When we last talked," she said in a casual tone, "you were talking about buying a tract of land where you grew up."

"Aw, fuck it, Missie, I'm no farmer," Angel said. He seated himself on the edge of the bunk and met her eyes for the first time since they came upstairs. "I left here when I was fifteen. Engine wiper on a starship, then I did some soldiering on Wellbegone. Got in with the Slammers, then the FDF. I don't know what I was thinking when I said I was going to raise gage. I think I just wanted to be fifteen again."

He bent and groped first beneath the bunk, then within the bedding proper. He came up with a bottle. It was unlabeled. The ten centimeters' depth of fluid within had a pinkish tinge.

"Ah . . ." Angel said. "Do you really want a drink? I don't have glasses."

"No problem," Margulies said, taking the bottle from him. The liquor was harsh. The pink color suggested flavoring, but the only taste she noticed was that of raw alcohol. She returned the bottle, wiping her lips with the back of her free hand.

"Or there's gage, of course," Angel offered with false perkiness.

"Naw, not for me," Margulies said. "But you used to prefer it to booze, didn't you?"

Angel got up and rested his hands on the window

ledge. The glass was painted black and reflected the light of the single fixture overhead.

"I really stepped on my dick, Mary," he whispered to the glass. "I went out, I looked at land, and it all came back to me, starving and scrabbling and bored, bored to fucking *tears* all the time I was a kid. That was why I left. And it's worse now, the syndicates take twice the bite they did when I left."

He turned and looked at his former lieutenant again. "And I looked around the security troops and I thought, these clowns, they're not fit to be *recruits* to the Slammers."

"You got that right," Margulies murmured. Her mouth was oily with the liquor's aftertaste.

"So I hired on, with the Lurias because my old village, it belonged to L'Escorial," Angel continued. "Not that it mattered. I thought I could make something out of them, give them some discipline. That'd make it better for everybody, you see that, don't you El-Tee? The farmers too, if it was just paying for protection they had to worry about. Via, what place doesn't have taxes?"

"You can't turn the lot out there into soldiers," Margulies said. "Any more than you can build a gun out of cat turds."

"Don't I know it," Angel whispered. He looked at the bottle in his hand, then drank greedily from it. His Adam's apple throbbed with three swallows, four, before he set the liquor down again.

"I tried, El-Tee," he whispered to the bottle. "But they wouldn't listen. I'd have had to shoot a couple of them to get their attention and Via, the rest would've greased me the next night. You've got to sleep sometime, and there wasn't anybody *but* me."

He looked up at her. She nodded, agreement without empathy. Angel had chosen, just as surely as the constant low-level pain in Margulies' rebuilt leg reflected choices she had made.

"The gage stopped working," Angel said. "I was using too much. The first dose would put me to sleep. My skin was crawling, I'd scratch myself bloody."

He swallowed. "So I switched to booze and that, you know, that helped some. And I found that mixed gage didn't put me to sleep the way the pure stuff did, so sometimes I used that."

"Refinery tailings are poison," Margulies said harshly. "The best you're going to do is grind down the nerve sheaths so that you're a spastic for the rest of your life. *Or* you'll go blind. Or you'll fry your brain and sit around drooling. Think your new buddies are going to want to change your diapers, Angel?"

"I know all that!" he shouted. "I said it was just a time or two with tailings, didn't I?"

He hadn't, and if he had said that, it would have been a lie. It was amazing that Angel had managed the effort of will required to get straight when he learned that an FDF survey team was on Cantilucca, but it was vanishingly improbable that he would be able to maintain that state for more than a few hours.

Angel sat heavily on the bed, clutching the liquor bottle to him as if it were the only warmth in a world of ice. "Look, El-Tee," he said to the wall, "I just want you to know I've got it under control now. I'm fine, and in a day or two I'll have all my gear strack. I just want you to know that."

"I'm glad to hear that, Angel," Mary Margulies said as she rose to her feet. "I'd better check on the major. I'll see you around."

Twenty-odd L'Escorial gunmen lounged in the open barracks, laughing and talking. The general volume lowered as Margulies left the cubicle, but she heard some pointed gibes.

She didn't look to either side as she walked to the stairs at the other end of the room. If she looked at the men, she would kill them all.

It wasn't the liquor or the stench of Angel's room

that made Margulies want to vomit. It was the vision of what her driver had become. . . .

And the warning of what might become of Mary Margulies herself, if she ever tried to reenter civilian life.

Wind kicked dust and litter down the street. The eastern horizon was a mass of cloud, though the late afternoon sun still shone onto Potosi.

Coke drove one of the rented jitneys to the street from the walled courtyard at the rear of Hathaway House. Margulies waited for him at the head of the alley. The angles of a weapon in a patrol sling distended her light cape.

Coke disengaged the torque converter and braked beside her. "I don't need a guard, Mary," he said. "I'm just going to run up to the port and send a capsule off."

Margulies squatted to put her face on a level with his. Her smile was crooked; she hadn't said much since the pair of them left the meeting in L'Escorial headquarters that morning.

"You could lower the top and squeeze your cyclo into the back of the port van," she said. "I guess that's what you're planning to do. But I could also drive it back myself and save you the trouble. What do you figure?"

Coke looked at the security lieutenant. "Yeah," he said. "That sounds like a good idea. Hop in."

The jitney had four seats in back, facing outward in pairs from the central spine. Margulies sat crossways, so that she looked forward over Coke's right shoulder.

"I felt like getting out of Potosi for a bit," she explained quietly. "This isn't much out, but it's out."

"What the hell is that?" Coke said. He had started to reengage the drive train. Instead, he took his hand from the knob and touched the 2-cm weapon he'd thrust muzzle-down between his seat and the spine in back.

Three red-painted vehicles drove down the road from the spaceport at 30 kph, their sirens blowing. The first and last were armored trucks of the sort the team had seen before. The convoy's pace was probably governed to their best speed.

An air-cushion limousine drove between the two escorts. The vehicle was fitted with appliqué armor — which couldn't have been very heavy or the battery-powered drive fans wouldn't have been able to keep the car floating on a bubble of air. A scarlet film darkened the windows so that they were nearly opaque from the outside, but Coke thought the driver was the only occupant.

Coke switched his commo helmet to Channel One, the command push. "Stand by," he ordered. "Over."

He didn't know what was happening. He didn't think it was an immediate problem, but by definition he couldn't be sure of that. There was a tiny click behind him as Margulies took her sub-machine gun off safe.

L'Escorial gunmen spilled out of the gateway, thronging the street from which the sirens had driven all civilian traffic. Engines started up in the courtyard of Astra headquarters, but none of the Guzman personnel showed themselves.

The wind gusted again, promising the storm would sweep over Potosi in a few minutes. The open-sided jitney wasn't much protection, but it wouldn't be the first time Coke got soaked in the line of duty.

He keyed the command channel again. "Bob," he ordered, sure that Barbour would be at the console. "Upper right quadrant, feed me a composite of what's going on across the street. Over."

"Roger," the intelligence officer replied. A quarter of Coke's faceshield brightened with the scene in front of L'Escorial HQ, viewed by miniature cameras Daun had emplaced on the other side of the convoy. "Audio?"

"Negative," said Coke, "but maybe later. Out."

The Lurias, father and son, walked stiffly through the gateway. Raul leaned on Ramon's arm and used a cane with his other hand.

The sirens wound down to silence. The leading armored car fired a warning burst up the street past Astra headquarters. The tribarrel functioned properly, chugging out twenty bolts of deep cyan before the gunner took his thumbs off the butterfly trigger.

The limousine's doors lifted simultaneously like gull wings. A slim man got out on the other side of the vehicle. Without being ordered to, Barbour manipulated the camera view to give Coke a close-up of the newcomer's face. The man was young and handsome, with features as fine-boned as those of a bird of prey.

"Pepe!" Ramon Luria called.

Raul walked/staggered two steps forward and embraced his grandson. "You've come at a good time, my boy," the Old Man said.

The sound of the wind rasped syllables away from the words the men across the street spoke. Lightning flashed behind the cloudbank, but there was as yet no audible thunder.

"Bob, patch in the audio," Coke directed in a whisper. "Out."

"Trouble with our neighbors?" said Pepe Luria with liltingly ironic tones that now came through Coke's helmet. "Well, it had to come sometime, didn't it? I brought some toys that may come in useful."

Pepe reached back inside the limousine. When he straightened again, the camera showed that he had buckled on a belly-pack controller. He was holding a sphere some twenty centimeters in diameter in his hands.

"Bloody *hell*," Margulies whispered. "That's a firefly. All we need is a few of *those* things flying around."

"Watch!" Pepe commanded triumphantly.

The sphere floated out of his hands. A corona of

purple sparks bathed its lower surfaces. Coke's commo helmet crackled minusculy in response to the discharge. The crowd of gunmen let out a collective wheeze of surprise.

"They won't last long," Coke muttered. "Who are you going to get to maintain fireflies on Cantilucca?"

"They're six to a set," Margulies said. "Do you suppose he'd have brought more than one set?"

"I can direct them. . . ." Pepe continued. He worked one of the tiny joysticks on his belly pack. The firefly danced and staggered nervously.

"He's not very good at it," Margulies said.

"Nobody can use those stock control sets," Coke said. "Not even one bird at a time."

"Bet Barbour could thread needles with it if he had to," Margulies replied.

"Or I can let them act for themselves on programmed instructions!" Pepe said.

He took his hands away from the controls. The firefly sailed up the street at a smooth walking pace, two meters in the air. The sphere kept the same face forward at all times. It only appeared to rotate because of the spinning static discharge which supported it.

"I hate those bastards," Coke murmured. "With a man, you can watch his eyes or his hands. I always refused to serve around the fireflies in the field."

The device was now a hundred meters up the street. It stopped and began to turn very slowly on its axis.

Pepe's belly pack projected a holographic view of what the firefly "saw." "I can watch things with them," he announced. He poised his finger on the control lever.

"And I can do more than watch!"

He pressed the lever in. The firefly lighted the facades around it with the rapid-fire flashes of five pistol-caliber powergun bolts. The bar adjacent to where the device hovered was The Blue Ox, an Astra hangout. The sign over its armored door disintegrated in flame and molten plastic.

The firefly turned another 90° and drifted purposefully back. A man stuck his head out of The Blue Ox, gaped up at the blasted sign, and ducked inside again.

Pepe Luria stood arms akimbo, facing up the street toward the returning firefly. "Widow Guzman!" he cried. "I have six of them, Widow! And I can tell them to attack men wearing any color I choose, just the color! Do you hear me, Widow?"

Only the wind answered.

Pepe linked arms with his father and grandfather. He walked with them into the L'Escorial courtyard, laughing with bubbling promise. A red-clad subordinate jumped into the limousine to drive it and its cargo within.

The firefly's ammunition was expended. It trailed along behind its master. The glow of its iridium barrel faded.

"Let's get to the port," Coke said, but he stepped off the driver's saddle and motioned Margulies to take his place. "You drive. I've got to make some additions in the message I'm sending home."

The first drops of the storm hit, cratering the dust. The temperature had dropped ten degrees, but Coke felt colder than the weather justified.

CANTILUCCA: DAY FIVE

The telephone in the Hathaways' private quarters rang. Coke, lying in a haze of almost-sleep directly above the sound, snapped awake.

Moments later someone hammered on the hotel's front door. "Quick, open up!" a man called from the street. "I have to see the Frisian major at once! The Old Man needs him!"

It was three hours before dawn. Coke pulled on his commo helmet and switched it to the command channel. "Stand to," he ordered, probably needlessly, as he slid his feet into his boots. "Out."

He keyed Channel Five, the push Barbour chose as a patch to Cantilucca's land-line communications. The transceiver Niko Daun had placed in the Hathaways' handset was the size of a matchhead and far more reliable than the phone to which it was attached.

Coke already wore his trousers and tunic. The night before was the first time on Cantilucca he'd taken his boots off to sleep. He guessed he'd return to field SOP from here on out.

"Hello?" Georg Hathaway croaked into the phone receiver. The innkeeper sounded both nervous and disoriented.

"Quick, you old fool and don't start arguing about it!" ordered the voice on the other end of the line. "Tell that hireling Coke that he's to come at once to Astra headquarters. At once! This is Adolpho Peres. And I warn you, little man, if there's any delay in Coke arriving, I'll take it out of *your* hide!"

"But —" Hathaway gasped.

"At once!" Peres shouted. He broke the connection with a bang.

Barbour had been sleeping beside his console in the lobby. Coke met the rest of the team, armed and ready, in the upstairs corridor. Below, Mistress Hathaway was talking to the L'Escorial messenger through the viewport in the door.

"I'll take care of the Astras," Johann Vierziger volunteered. Like Coke, he wore a cape over his weapons. "Peres feels we're soulmates, after all."

His smile was as thin as the corona of a collapsed star.

Evie Hathaway ran up the stairs. "Major Coke!" she called. "Major Coke!"

"Right," said Coke. "I'll take L'Escorial. Sten, you're in charge here —"

He flicked a quick finger at Margulies, forestalling the comment poised between her open lips.

"— and no, I don't want company, I want a reaction force. If both sides are calling us, there's probably no immediate danger, but I want all of you ready to move as needed."

The Hathaways had stopped at the head of the stairs as they saw the Frisians were up and alert.

"Please, Major —" Georg began.

Coke waved his hand. "It'll be taken care of," he said. "We're on our way." He slid between the locals with more haste than courtesy, though that would have been the Hathaways' choice had they been asked.

"There's an envoy from Delos," Bob Barbour called as Coke and Vierziger passed him. "A Madame Yarnell, from the gage cartel on Delos, and she is *not* amused. From the way the Astra leaders talk, she's the cartel's troubleshooter — with the emphasis on 'shooter.'"

"Why can't they do this stuff at a decent time of day?" Coke muttered as he helped the sergeant pull open the heavy door.

"Because they're not decent people, Matthew," Vierziger said. "Of course, neither are we."

"You're the major?" the L'Escorial messenger said as Vierziger pushed past him. Then to Coke, "*You're* the major."

"Right," Coke agreed, striding across the street. Vierziger headed for Astra HQ at a gliding pace, not quite a jog.

"What's he doing?" the L'Escorial bleated, running to catch up with Coke but glancing toward Vierziger.

"Minding his own business," Coke said. "Pray to the Lord that *you* never find yourself his business."

He'd expected to find the L'Escorial courtyard full of armed men. Instead, half-dressed L'Escorials were trying to back their armored trucks into the garage beneath the headquarters building. The second-floor barracks was lighted. Coke could hear Pepe Luria shouting for his gunmen to get out by the back way at once.

Ramon Luria stood in the building's doorway, looking alternately inside and out toward the courtyard. The messenger scampered up to him.

Ramon raised his hand to strike. "You idiot, Pierro!" he shouted. "I told you to bring the Frisian major!"

"He's —" Pierro shrieked.

"I'm here," Coke said. The courtyard was indifferently lighted, primarily by the headlights of the armored vehicles. The Frisian in his gray cape was a moving shadow.

"Coke!" Luria cried. "Thank the Lord you're here! Look, you have to stop your troops coming. At once! You have to hold them back until Madame Yarnell has left Cantilucca!"

"Nobody at Camp Able's going to make a decision until they have your money in hand, Luria," Coke said harshly. "According to your paymaster, Suterbilt, that's still several days. You needn't have kittens."

Despite his aggressive tone, Coke felt cold inside. His daily message capsules were shipped by first available transport to Nieuw Friesland, but there was at least a week between sending and receipt. Coke wondered what the Lurias would do to him if they knew he had recommended against taking the proffered contract, whether or not Suterbilt came through with the earnest money.

The Old Man lurched along the hallway toward his son. Gunmen, groggy with drink and gage, were being hastened onto the back stairs by their more alert fellows. Pepe Luria fought his way down the stairwell through them. He wore the firefly controller, but none of the spheres were themselves in evidence.

"She's coming!" a L'Escorial shouted from the courtyard gate. "She's coming!"

"Everybody into the basement!" Ramon screamed. He gripped the Frisian's arm, fiercely and apparently unaware of what he was doing. His hand bumped the muzzle of Coke's sub-machine gun.

"Oh my Lord!" Ramon cried. "You're carrying a gun! Are you mad? She said no weapons in sight, none! She'll —"

Pepe joined them. Ramon turned to his son and said, "He's carrying a gun, Pepe!"

The youngest Luria looked Coke up and down with the interest of a dog sniffing something dead. "So, you'd be the expensive Major Coke, would you?" he said. "I suppose I needed to meet you some time, since L'Escorial now employs you."

To his father Pepe added, "It isn't in sight. But" — Pepe's eyes were as black as cannel coal. They focused again on Coke. — "hold it so that it's less obvious nonetheless. I don't care what the good Madame does to you, but she might mistakenly think L'Escorial was involved in your bad manners."

The last of the L'Escorial armored trucks collided with a wall. The vehicle stalled on the ramp into the garage. The driver tried to restart his engine.

Ramon scampered over to the vehicle. "Leave it!" he cried. "Shut it down! And get out, get out!"

A car with a slim, armored body and four metal-mesh wheels on wide-spread outriggers pulled up in front of the L'Escorial building. Coke had seen similar vehicles used for ground reconnaissance where for one reason or another hovercraft were contra-indicated.

Raul Luria reached the doorway. Pepe put an arm around the Old Man's shoulders, more for solidarity than for physical support. Ramon skipped back to join his father and son.

Matthew Coke stepped aside, flattening himself in the shadows across the wall. He held the sub-machine gun vertically against his body, covered by the folds of the cape. He glanced at Pepe Luria, but only for an instant; and there was no expression on his face.

The door of the reconnaissance car folded down; the female passenger got out. Though the car's interior was more luxuriously appointed than was normal for the type of vehicle, it was still cramped quarters for those within.

The woman wore a white jumpsuit trimmed with silver, and a short, lustrous cape of some natural fur. She was by no means young, but surgery and cosmetics prevented Coke from trying to guess her age within two decades. She halted in the gateway where the lights of the stalled truck lit her brilliantly.

Raul Luria began hobbling toward her with his descendants a half pace behind to either side. "Madame Yarnell!" he wheezed. "You honor us with your presence."

"Don't bother, Luria," the woman ordered sharply. "I'm going to say what I have to and then go back and repeat it to the Astras, those *other* childish idiots. This must stop! Do you understand?"

"Madame —" Ramon said, "we of course —"

"No, it's not 'of course,'" Madame Yarnell snarled. "If anything were *obvious* to you morons, you'd get on with business instead of ruining it. Can you imagine how much trouble you've caused with your fighting already?"

"It wasn't us who —" Raul began.

"Shut *up*, old man!" the woman ordered. "I'm here to talk, not listen. The reason gage deliveries have dropped by thirty percent over the past two quarters, and the *reason* that the product my fellows and I need to fulfill contracts has burned to *ash* — the reason is that you and Astra are squabbling instead of doing business. That will stop, now! Do you understand?"

"Of course, we want nothing more than to do business ourselves, mistress," Pepe said with his eyes lowered.

"That's good," the Delian representative said, "because if there's any more trouble, *our* retailers will cancel contracts and find other sources of supply. Whereupon Cantilucca will become superfluous . . . and you *gentlemen* in particular will become superfluous. Do you understand me?"

Pepe's face tightened.

Raul laid a hand heavily on the youth's shoulder. "May we offer you the hospitality of L'Escorial during your stay on Cantilucca, madame?" the Old Man said.

"You may not," Madame Yarnell snapped. "I'll be staying in the cartel offices in the port reservation while I'm here. And if you're wondering how long that will be — it will be until I'm absolutely sure that you and your imbecile compatriots have heard my message and are acting on it. I regret to say that it may be *years* that I'll be stuck in this cesspool!"

She spun on her heel, whirling the cape out from her shoulders, and walked back to the recon car. As soon as the door latched, the driver slammed into a tight turn and headed back toward Astra HQ. Coke suspected that the cartel representative had bypassed the Astras initially because she feared that L'Escorial, as the more seriously aggrieved party, was likely to take the next escalating step.

The Lurias bent their heads together, all talking at once. Coke looked at them, pursed his lips, and sauntered across the street to Hathaway House.

He supposed he should have been pleased that peace might come to Cantilucca. The trouble was, he kept thinking that with the syndicates in unbroken control, the best ordinary citizens could hope for was the peace of the grave.

CANTILUCCA: DAY SIX

"The beer isn't any better than Hathaway's," Sten Moden said. The logistics officer watched the afternoon traffic over Coke's shoulder, as Coke did over Moden's. "But it's good to get out anyway. With Madame Yarnell in town, you could almost imagine Potosi was a normal place, couldn't you?"

Niko Daun returned from the bar, clanking three more mugs down on the sidewalk table. "They've got a dancer in the back room," he said indignantly. "They let the johns poke at her with shock batons. I don't care if she's stoned, they shouldn't do that!"

"There's a lot of things on Cantilucca they shouldn't do," Coke said. He drained the last mouthful from his current mug and set the empty under his chair to get it out of the way. "Madame Yarnell stopped people who'd be better dead from killing each other. That's about it."

He didn't see any guns on the street. Syndicate colors were muted as well. A red beret, a blue neckerchief — rarely anything more overt. Widow Guzman and the Lurias had sent most of their gunmen back into the farming districts for the time being.

"I wonder how Esteban's father-in-law's doing," Sten Moden said. "I'm afraid that the thugs that were swaggering around Potosi'll be looking for something to keep them occupied out in the sticks."

A woman screamed in a broken voice from the cafe's back room. Shouts and laughter greeted the outburst. A pair of men wearing red armbands got up from the table beside the Frisians and walked toward the back. They were fumbling in their pockets for the cover charge.

"Sir," Niko blurted. "Are we really going to help these guys? I mean, both sides, they're — they're animals, sir! The least we ought to do is say 'no sale' and go on back to Friesland."

"That still leaves the same people here," Moden said. "It's not an answer."

He swizzled a sip of beer around his mouth. He didn't appear so much to be savoring as analyzing the fluid.

"Oh, the beer's not that bad," Coke said. Without changing his tone, he went on, "I think if we wanted to . . ."

He paused, looked at his companions in turn, and resumed, "I don't think it would require much pushing from behind the scenes to get Astra and L'Escorial to pretty well eliminate each other."

In Matthew Coke's mind, the response was:

Daun: "*Sir, your proposal is clearly against the interests of Nieuw Friesland!*"

Moden: "*Major, I regret that, in accordance with the provisions of the Defense Justice Code, I'm going to have to relieve you of command for that treasonous suggestion.*"

Niko Daun's face split with a wide grin. "Lord, sir!" he said. "I was afraid you were going to burn me a new asshole for saying that."

"Yeah," agreed Sten Moden, setting his mug down hard enough in his enthusiasm to slosh. "We were all afraid to discuss it with you, Matthew. But I don't care what color their money is — *something* has to be done about these bastards, and the six of us are the only folks around who might be able to do it."

"We *all*?" Coke repeated. "You two talked to the others?"

Daun nodded. "Vierziger said that was what he was here for, he guessed."

"Johann said he *presumed*," Sten Moden corrected. He shrugged. "I don't know exactly what he meant by that. But Johann's willingness to shoot people isn't in doubt, is it?"

"Bob, he's not real comfortable with the business," Niko resumed. "He's not afraid of Camp Able, it's not that, but . . . Well, anyway, he finally said he was in."

The sensor tech shook his head. "He's a good guy, Bob is. I don't understand what's going on under the surface, but he's a *good* guy. And a fucking wizard with that console!"

"Yeah, he's good all right," Coke said. All five of his people were good, were about the best he'd ever seen. And he was talking about dropping them into the gears of a very powerful machine, in hopes that the machine would break before they did.

"Mary?" he added aloud.

"She's the one who brought it up," Moden said with a half smile. "I suppose we'd all been thinking about it, but she said it aloud."

"She said," Niko amplified, "that this was sort of like wiping your ass with a broken beer bottle — sooner or later, you were going to wind up in a world of hurt. But if she survived, she didn't want to remember that she hadn't tried to change things on Cantilucca."

Coke drank half his beer in a series of smooth swallows. Nobody spoke again until he stopped to breathe and brush his mouth with the back of his hand. "I'll work up a plan of action," he said. "We'll have to wait for the cartel representative to leave, but that shouldn't take long."

Daun frowned. "She said she might stay here for years, sir," he said. "We aren't going to . . . ?"

"No," Coke said. "No, Madame Yarnell isn't going to bury herself on Cantilucca for any longer than necessary. A few months at the outside. Her coming is actually better for our purposes. When she does leave, the lid's going to come off with a bang."

The red hovercraft Pepe Luria brought back from Delos whined slowly down the street. Its presence cleared a path through the mostly civilian traffic, even though the overt threat of guns and murder was held temporarily in abeyance. The vehicle stopped alongside the table where the three Frisians sat.

A red-veiled side window slid down. Pepe was in the driver's seat. His father and grandfather sat in back.

Ramon leaned forward to get a better view past Raul. "Come with us, Major Coke," he called. "We'll ride in my Pepe's fine new toy, shall we not? And we'll talk."

Sten Moden's face was blank. Niko Daun looked questioningly from the hovercraft to his commander, taut as the hammer spring of a cocked pistol. Moden, seeing the same danger that Coke did, put his hand firmly on the sensor tech's right wrist.

Niko was desperately eager to do the right thing, but he hadn't a clue as to what the right thing *was* under these circumstances. That was a bad combination. . . .

"Glad to learn there's something to talk about," Coke said easily as he got to his feet.

"He'll be okay, then?" Daun murmured to Moden as the hovercraft drove away with the major.

"He's got as good a chance as any of the rest of us," the logistics officer said. He finished his beer in a single mighty draft, then banged the mug down. "Another?" he asked.

Daun shook his head with an impish smile. "I'm meeting a friend in twenty minutes," he said. His expression segued into a frown. "Unless you think, you know, with the major and all?"

Moden shrugged. "He'll call us if he needs us," he said. "Don't get yourself so fucked up you can't function, that's all. But you can't be a hundred percent *on* all day forever."

"Yeah, well, this is nothing serious," the younger man said casually. "She's a nice enough girl, but it's just passing the time."

He glanced at Moden from the corners of his eyes. "Suppose the major's getting anywhere with the lady from the port office, sir?"

The logistics officer looked at Daun hard. "Do you suppose that's any of our business?" he asked.

Daun laughed without embarrassment. So far as he was concerned, there was no rank when guys talked about women. "Not business at all, sir," he said. "Though the Lord knows Potosi isn't short of that kind of business establishment."

Moden laughed also. "Yeah, well, we could ask Bob," he said. "But I think we won't, okay?"

The big man got to his feet. "Twenty minutes is time enough for a beer, kid. Sounds like you need to be slowed down some anyhow."

Pepe had raised the hovercraft's window even before Coke could open the passenger door. The youngest Luria's feelings about Coke were a complex blend of disdain, the hostility of a dominating male for a rival, and fear. Pepe was smart enough to know that Matthew Coke was someone he should fear.

Coke's feelings about Pepe were much simpler: Pepe was a scorpion Coke had found in his boot, to be dealt with directly — in both senses of the word.

The hovercraft wallowed into a turn and proceeded north, toward the spaceport. The chassis was a standard civilian model. With the full four passengers aboard and the armor added by some custom shop on Delos, the vehicle was seriously underpowered. It was a toy, just as Ramon had said.

"Here's the earnest money," Raul said abruptly. He extended a quivering hand between the front seats to pass Coke a credit chip.

"Now, how quickly can you get your gunmen here?" Ramon asked. "Madame Yarnell will be leaving Canti-lucca in six days, maybe seven."

Coke took the chip and held it in his hand.

A pair of jitneys was passing in opposite directions in the street ahead. There was room for the hovercraft to fit between them, but the vehicle's damping program hadn't been upgraded to take account of the weight of the armor.

Pepe steered left. The car had by now accelerated to 45, perhaps 50 kph. The back end swayed outward, continuing the vector of the directional change after the driver centered his wheel again.

The left-side jitney carried a farm family — two adults, four children, and a vast burden of produce piled on top. The hovercraft sideswiped it with a bang and screech of metal. Three-meter-long stalks of sugar cane slapped the car's windshield. They left syrupy blurs across the film-darkened glass.

Pepe cursed viciously. He continued to overcorrect for the next hundred meters. The car fishtailed up the street, its paint scarred beyond the capacity of anyone on Cantilucca to match.

"The times are the same they've always been," Coke said. "Seven sidereal days, plus or minus, to get the message to Nieuw Friesland. A day to load the companies. Five days to get them here since the troopship will come direct. Plus whatever time it takes Camp Able to decide whether or not to take the contract. *If* they take the contract."

"You'll send the message now," Pepe said in a rasping whisper. "We're carrying you to the port to do that. And you'll see to it that your mercenaries do arrive on schedule, Master Major, or it will be very unfortunate for you and your friends. You don't expect to leave before *all* the business with Astra is completed to our satisfaction, do you?"

"Now, Pepe," Ramon said nervously. "We don't want the major to think that we don't trust him."

"I trust him," Pepe sneered. "Because he knows he's a dead man if he doesn't do what he's promised to do."

"What the major has promised . . ." Coke said in a

thin voice as his spirit floated out of his body to observe. "Is that he'll inform his superiors of the situation on Cantilucca. I doubt they'll act as you desire. There's every reason to expect your Delian mistress will summon a large force of her own as soon as the FDF arrives. Camp Able isn't going to send two companies into a ratfuck."

"Madame Yarnell is going to be recalled!" Ramon said.

They were beyond the outskirts of Potosi. The hovercraft had accelerated to about 75 kph, probably its best speed with this load. The vehicle pogoed over the bad surface, but the ride was more comfortable than it would have been in a jitney or the port van.

"I heard you before," Coke said. "When she leaves, I will immediately inform Camp Able of the fact."

Pepe gave him a look of boiling hatred. The flexible skirts of the car's plenum chamber brushed a treebole. Contact sent the vehicle in a slow carom toward the other side of the road.

"A bomb will go off in a consignment of Astra gage after it arrives on Delos," Raul Luria said in a voice as jagged as a crosscut saw.

"Grandpapa —" Pepe said.

"I will handle this," the Old Man retorted. "There will be a fire, perhaps great destruction. It will be far more important to the cartel than anything happening on Cantilucca is. When Madame Yarnell goes to Delos to investigate, *that* will be the moment to sweep Astra away forever."

"And by the time she comes back," Ramon added complacently, "there will be peace all across the planet, just as we all desire."

"I see. . . ." said Coke as a placeholder while he thought. "You don't think the cartel might take a serious view of this bomb?"

The car was nearing the spaceport reservation. Warned by his previous control problems, Pepe started the braking process in good time.

The young man looked at Coke. "Do you think I'm a fool?" he said. "We have nothing to do with the business. It's Astra gage, and it's not traveling on a TST hull. If they do trace the particular drum back, they'll find it was placed in the shipment by a port flunky."

"Not one of our people," Ramon chuckled. "He knows nothing about it. He thinks he's working a scam to substitute tailings for pure gage. Even the whore we're working through doesn't know more than that."

The hovercraft pulled up in front of the passenger operations building. The idled fans imparted a low-frequency wobble to the vehicle as it rested on its skirts.

"Now will you send your message?" Pepe demanded.

"You bet," Coke said. "You needn't wait around — I'll find my own way back."

Coke waited until he'd closed the car door behind him before he keyed his commo helmet. Pilar Ortega would be inside at the desk, and he didn't want her to overhear either. She'd be glad to see him, as she always was. . . .

"Two and Four," he said, alerting Moden and Barbour. "I'm going to need information on a shipment of gage that went out yesterday or today. Somebody, probably a port official, doctored a manifest, and I need to know his name soonest."

Margulies stood at the front door, looking out through the triangular view port. The evening traffic was somewhat lighter than it had been with a thousand more gunmen in town, but civilians had reappeared on the street in nearly a great enough number to balance the loss.

The two police huddled in a corner of the saloon. At another table, Georg Hathaway chatted morosely with his friend Larrinaga.

"There we go," said Sten Moden with satisfaction. He expanded the sidebar into the main screen. "There's the anomaly, sure enough."

Bob Barbour sat in a folding chair beside the console. Moden had handled the equipment enough in his presence that Barbour no longer hovered like a mother hen when the logistics officer used the console.

The intelligence officer leaned forward to check the line Moden highlighted. "Serial numbers out of sequence?" he said. His doubt was evident only in the perfect neutrality with which he stated the evidence he saw.

"Not the Astra serial number," Moden explained with satisfaction. "That wouldn't mean anything. This is the *transaction* number, the slug the port computer gave the drum at initial processing. That ought to be perfectly linear, but see — this one appears in a sequence of drums delivered three days later."

"I'll be hanged," Barbour said. "I didn't know there were transaction numbers different from the manifest serials."

He looked at Moden. "Sten," he said. "You just taught me something."

The big man grinned. "A lot of people think supply is boring," he said. "I didn't find it that way."

Still grinning, though the expression took on a certain stiffness, he patted the scar of his left shoulder and added, "Sometimes it's way *too* exciting."

"Nothing's boring if it's in your soul," the intelligence officer said. "All right, do you want to run the check on who was on duty or shall I? When we cross-check the time the drum dropped out and the time it reappeared, we ought to have our boy."

"*I'm coming in,*" the console reported in the voice of Johann Vierziger.

Moden looked up at Margulies. "Was he out with the major?" he asked.

"Just out," Barbour murmured before the security lieutenant could respond. "The major's still at the port."

"Waiting for us to answer him," Moden realized aloud. He got up from the console. "Go ahead, Bob.

Do the personnel check. Two hands'll get the data out quicker."

He grinned. "And anyway, you're going to have kittens if I don't let you play with your lady, here."

When Margulies pulled the door a crack open, Vierziger entered the lobby of Hathaway House wraith-swift. He looked at the men at the console. "You're succeeding?" he asked.

"So far, so good," Barbour murmured as his fingers danced over the keys. He didn't look up from his work, the two parallel half-screens of data which he was correlating.

"I'm glad somebody's doing something useful," Vierziger said in a voice of bridled fury. He walked into the saloon alcove.

Margulies turned so that her sergeant was within the arc of her vision, though she instinctively avoided focusing *on* Vierziger. Tonight he gave the impression of a door glowing white with the fire behind it, restrained until something happens to destroy the panel's integrity. After that —

"You!" Vierziger said. "Larrinaga. What are you doing here?"

The local man looked at the dapper Frisian. For a moment Mary Margulies thought Larrinaga was going to make a smart remark. She knew she wasn't fast enough to stop Vierziger if that happened, she didn't think *any* human being was fast enough.

Larrinaga swallowed and said, "Nothing, I suppose. That's all I've done for a long time."

"Get up," Vierziger said. Larrinaga blinked at him.

"Get up!" Vierziger repeated, his voice cutting like a bread knife honed to a wire edge. His left hand reached for Larrinaga's throat.

Georg Hathaway rose from his chair and backed away, mumbling to himself. Larrinaga jumped to his feet. "Are you going to kill me?" he shouted. "Go on! That way maybe I'll see Suzette again!"

"Johann —" Mary Margulies said. Her arms were out to her sides; her hands spread wide.

Vierziger slapped the local man, an open-handed blow *only* to the cheek. It cracked like a pistol shot and knocked Larrinaga to the floor.

"Vierziger, slow down," Sten Moden said, stepping from the console into the bar alcove. His manner was neither threatening nor afraid. He moved like a storm blowing off the sea.

With the same hand he'd used to slap, his left, Vierziger reached into his purse. He tossed several credit chips onto Larrinaga's chest.

"There you go!" he said. "Three hundred thalers, enough to get you off this *cesspool* of a world and off to somewhere that you can be a man again. Do you want to do that? Do you *want* to be a man?"

Larrinaga got to his feet. "I am a man, Master Vierziger," he said in a raspy voice. He met Vierziger's eyes, and that took balls even if he really wanted to die. Margulies knew there were worse things than death, and she was pretty sure that Johann Vierziger had seen some of them.

Moden stood quietly, arm's length from the pair of men. The situation was under control. He didn't want to draw attention to himself by moving again.

Larrinaga gathered the credit chips in his hand and offered them back to the Frisian. Vierziger didn't move.

Larrinaga put the money on the table at which he'd been sitting. "Thank you for the offer," he said. "I don't choose to leave Cantilucca while . . . what remains of my wife is here. But I'm not going to buy our house back by sitting here and cadging drinks, am I?"

He stepped around Vierziger because the Frisian wouldn't shift to let him by. Larrinaga nodded to Moden and to Margulies. "Thank you for your hospitality, Georg," he called to Hathaway. "I won't return until I'm able to pay down my bill, though."

He pulled open the front door and was gone. The mark of Vierziger's hand on his sallow cheek blazed like a flag.

"Oh my goodness," mumbled Georg Hathaway. He set upright the chair that had fallen over. "Oh my goodness!"

Moden sat down beside Bob Barbour. When things were serious, the big man seemed more like a force of nature than a human being.

Margulies let out a deep sigh of relief. She looked at Vierziger and shook her head ruefully. "You know," she said, "I gotta hand it to you, Johann. You may just have saved that silly bastard."

Vierziger looked at her. She remembered what she'd thought about the things he'd seen. "Nobody can save another person," he said, so quietly that Margulies thought perhaps she'd imagined the words.

Vierziger walked to the staircase. "Niko!" he called. "Come down here, please, with your kit. We have work to do."

Sten Moden glanced at the security lieutenant. He raised an eyebrow. Margulies shrugged.

Daun appeared at the top of the stairs, trying to buckle his equipment belt one-handed. The other hand held his larger equipment case and the sling of his sub-machine gun.

"What's up?" he asked, jouncing down the steps.

"We're going to check out security for our new employers," Vierziger said. He opened the coat closet beside the front door and took out the attaché case he'd put there. The case was made of — at least covered with — reptile hide of some sort, black and shiny and as exquisite as every other part of Vierziger's ensemble.

The only weapon he carried was the pistol over his right hip.

"Driving or walking?" the sensor tech asked. He stopped in the lobby and fastened the belt properly.

"You're driving us," Vierziger answered. "I'll give you directions."

He nodded goodbye to the others as he closed the door behind him.

"Doesn't handle himself much like a sergeant, does he?" Sten Moden said to nobody in particular after the door closed.

"Yeah, I noticed that too," Margulies said dryly. "Sten, did you know Joachim Steuben? Colonel Hammer's hit man?"

Moden shrugged. "Saw him once, a long way away. I'd heard he was dead."

"He *is* dead," Margulies said. "I saw the incident report. Took a 2-cm bolt slap between the shoulder-blades. No trouble with the identification — head and limbs weren't touched. But there's *no* curst doubt he was dead."

The two officers looked at the armored door without speaking further.

"Bingo!" said Barbour. He'd gone on with his search while everyone else was focused on Johann Vierziger. "I've got what the major's looking for!"

"Well, call it in to him," Sten Moden said. "Sounded like he meant it when he said ASAP."

Barbour touched the Channel 1 button on the console.

Mary Margulies leaned over the intelligence officer's shoulder to see the highlighted name. "Cargo Supervisor Terence Ortega," she read aloud. She frowned. "The name's familiar for some reason."

"Now," said Johann Vierziger as the door to the underground garage quivered. Daun ran the jitney forward five meters, across the head of the ramp.

Suterbilt's armored four-wheeled van pulled halfway through the doorway. The driver slammed on his brakes in a panic when he realized the lighter vehicle was halted across his passage.

Vierziger stepped off the back of the jitney with the attaché case in his left hand and a bright smile on his face. The van's headlights fell across him. "Master Suterbilt!" he called in a cheerful voice. "Just the man we're looking for! We've identified a security problem."

The van's driver opened the door and stepped out onto his running board. He pointed a bell-mouthed mob gun through the crack at the Frisian. Vierziger walked over and extended his right hand to the driver. The local man aimed the mob gun skyward and shook hands, looking confused.

"Who are you?" Suterbilt called from inside the vehicle. After a moment, he got out and walked a step up the ramp.

"Johann Vierziger of the Frisian Defense Forces," Vierziger answered enthusiastically. "We've run a security check on L'Escorial — and yourself, of course, since you're really the most important —"

"I'm not a member of any local organization!" Suterbilt interrupted hastily. "I work for Trans-Star Trading."

"Of course you do," Vierziger agreed with a patently oily smile. "Of course. But — you can see how significant you are to us, to the FDF, surely?"

He waved his hand toward the street traffic. "That other lot, they're boobs with guns. They don't matter to professionals like ourselves, whatever color they happen to be wearing when we go to work. But *you*, Master Suterbilt . . . Anything that could affect our payment is a matter of serious concern."

The TST offices were on the second floor of the building Suterbilt was leaving on his way home. He glanced up at the block of lighted windows.

"We have a security system as well as guards," he said in dawning nervousness. "Do you think . . . ?"

"It's not here that we foresee a problem," Vierziger explained. "After all, an attack on TST doesn't affect you personally. We're more concerned that the work of art you have in an outlying dwelling would be targeted. You have a Suzette, do you not? A psychic ambiance that's probably worth close to the value of the warehouse which Astra has already destroyed."

Except for the pistol on his hip, Vierziger looked like an unusually well-dressed businessman from a highly developed world. The reptile-skin case caught the light of passing vehicles as he gestured with it. The shimmer drew attention away from his right hand — gun hand — which moved scarcely at all.

"What could they possibly gain by damaging the ambiance?" the factor asked in amazement. "Anyway, I've thought of that. There's six guards in the house at all times. As thick as the walls are, they could hold out for days if there was trouble."

Suterbilt's driver settled back into his seat. He shifted his gaze between his principal, standing beside the van, and Niko Daun seated in the saddle of the jitney with a vaguely positive expression.

"Precisely!" Vierziger said, leaving Suterbilt even more puzzled. "And what would you give to prevent the destruction of that valuable work of art, Master Suterbilt? Would you cancel the FDF's contract?"

"Well, I wouldn't —" the factor began.

"And more to the point," Vierziger said, steamrollering the reply, "does Astra *think* you might do that? They've struck unexpectedly once, you remember. That success will encourage them to choose the next weak point."

"There's nothing weak about it!" Suterbilt insisted. "I have guards and —"

"*And* an alarm system, just as the L'Escorial warehouse had!" Vierziger snapped. "If you don't mind, sir, why don't we finish this discussion in place — at the threatened location. I can point out the problems to you as well as the steps we'll take to solve them."

"I wasn't planning —"

Vierziger turned and gestured imperiously with the attaché case. "Specialist Daun!" he ordered. "Back up your cyclo, please. When the car pulls out of the drive, you'll be able to park in the garage and get in with us. I want you along."

He looked at Suterbilt again. "That is all right, isn't it?" he said. "I'm concerned that Astra sympathizers or even mere vandals will deface the vehicle if it's not protected. Specialist Daun's expertise is quite important for our assessment."

Suterbilt swallowed. "Well, I —" he said. "Yes, of course, park your car in space twelve. I'll drop you off here again when we're done."

He frowned. "This isn't going to take very long, is it?"

"Tsk!" Vierziger said. "Ten minutes, fifteen at most. But if it's not done, the damage could be irreparable."

He slipped past Suterbilt and into the back of the van as though he'd been formally invited to do so. After a moment, Suterbilt sighed and got in beside the Frisian.

It would be simpler to carry out the inspection than to continue the discussion. Besides, Suterbilt got an uncomfortable feeling when he argued with the dapper stranger. It was as though he was eye to eye with a cobra, or perhaps a shark.

"Roger," Coke said, looking over the counter at Pilar Ortega as he spoke into the pickup of his commo helmet. "One out."

The artificial intelligence in the helmet disconnected the circuit at the word "out."

Pilar glanced up with a smile that faded when she saw the set of Matthew Coke's face. They'd spent long enough together during the time the Frisian had been on Cantilucca that she was beginning to read even expressions meant to be noncommittal.

"Bad news?" she asked. Her voice quivered on the

second word. No one else was present in the passenger services building; Pilar had been in the process of shutting up for the evening.

Coke looked around, more to provide a moment to think than because he expected there would be anything to see. A freighter well across the field lifted in a rainbow of ionized atoms. Pilar had processed the two passengers, salesmen traveling in irrigation and cultivating machinery, through the boarding checks an hour before.

"Expected news," Coke said. He met the woman's eyes. "Bad news, yeah."

He took a deep breath. "Pilar," he said, "you've got to get off Cantilucca immediately. Pack a bag with enough clothes to wear, take any —"

She was staring at him in horror. Her right hand clasped the crucifix.

"— knicknacks that you absolutely have to have," Coke continued, plowing forward even though the woman looked as if he'd started to disrobe in the middle of the office. "You can go anywhere, except not Delos, and you've got to —"

"Matthew! Stop this!" Pilar said.

"— go *now*," Coke blurted. "Pilar, please, I don't want to say this —"

"*Stop*, Matthew!" she cried.

The rainbow curtain of light lifted rapidly. It raced across the terrazzo floor as the freighter climbed vertically from the port. The deep thrum of the starship's engines made the prefabricated building shudder with familiar vibrations.

Coke leaned across the counter. He hugged Pilar tightly to him so that he couldn't look at her face.

"Pilar," he said quickly, crisply. "Terry, your husband Terry, has screwed up really badly. He's done something that'll cost the Delos cartel millions of pesos, maybe tens of millions. When they investigate they'll spot him, just as my people did. They'll kill him and everybody close to him as slowly as they can make it happen. You've got to get out of the way now, before it happens."

He thought that Pilar would push him away, though they'd held each other past evenings in the privacy of her suite. Instead she pressed her hands against his shoulder blades. "Matthew," she said, "why are you saying this?"

"I'll give you money, money's not a problem," he said. "*Time* is a problem. If you're still around when the cartel comes looking, I don't know what, what your chances'll be no matter how I try."

"Please," Pilar said in a subdued tone. She straightened against his pull. He let her go.

"Matthew," she said. "Even if what you say is true, I can't abandon Terry. You know —"

"Pilar, he's abandoned you!" Coke shouted. "He hasn't been home to sleep for a week! Three days ago he picked up some of his clothes while you were —"

"Matthew! How did you know that?"

"While you were at *work*, curse it, and I know it because I'm having him watched, that's how I bloody know it!"

She turned her back. Her shoulders hunched over her sobs. "You don't understand," she cried. "What Terry does is between him and the Lord. *I* won't abandon him."

Coke threw open the gate in the counter and stepped inside. Pilar flinched away, but he grabbed her by the upper arms. "All right, Pilar," he said. "You won't go without your husband, so let's get him."

She didn't resist as the Frisian walked her toward the side door where the van was parked. The door opened ahead of them. A Marvelan, one of the clerks from the office next door, stuck his head in. "Hey, Pilar," he said. "Tomorrow will you cover for —"

He finally noticed Coke and Ortega in an apparent embrace. "Oh," he concluded.

Coke cleared the Marvelan out of their way by pointing a finger like a lance tip. "Go do your own job for a change!" the Frisian shouted. "Pretend you're good for something!"

He handed Pilar into the van and stepped around to the driver's side. The key was already in his pocket. He'd driven the pair of them ever since the first night he escorted Pilar home.

The freighter had vanished into orbit, preparatory to entering Transit space. The two moons were chips on the eastern horizon.

"Where are we going, Matthew?" the woman asked softly.

"I told you," he said. The diesel spun thirty seconds before it caught. He'd meant to have Sten's mechanic friend work the cursed thing over, but he didn't suppose it mattered any longer. "We're going to get your husband and I'll put both of you on the next ship *out* of here."

He revved the engine to keep it well above its lumpy idle while he dropped the transmission into gear. The van lurched forward. Only when they were twenty meters along the driveway did Coke add the load of the headlight to his demands on the stumbling engine.

"I hope the two of you will find a happy life in your new home," he added bitterly.

Suterbilt got out of the van in front of a one-story free-standing structure on the northern outskirts of Potosi. The walls were sheer and windowless, and the door would have done for a bank vault.

"You see?" the factor said with a sweep of his arm. "No common walls or floors to break in through. This is probably the safest place in the whole town. A fortress!"

"If it were a fortress," Johann Vierziger said as he followed Suterbilt from the vehicle, "it would have firing ports. That's the obvious first problem here."

He sauntered toward the door. Behind him, Suter-bilt wore a look of dawning concern.

"Larrinaga must really have been in the money to afford this," Niko Daun observed as he brought up the rear. "You wouldn't guess that to see him now, would you?"

"What?" said Suterbilt. "Well, yes, I suppose he was doing rather well. It was Larrinaga's competition that drove that old fool Roberson to tie in with Astra, to tell the truth."

The factor laughed with cruel humor. "Out of the frying pan and into the fire, that was," he added. "If I'm feeling kindly after we've cleaned out the Astras, I'll let Roberson go off-planet alive."

He pressed the call button beside the door. A melodious chime sounded, blurred by the thickness of the walls. Nothing else happened for a moment.

"*And*," Vierziger noted aloud, "none of the so-called guards are keeping a watch on the exterior display."

He nodded upward toward the miniature lens array above the door. The camera fed a surveillance display inside.

Suterbilt pursed his lips.

Locks within the panel chuckled liquidly as the mechanism drew them back. A man inside grunted and pushed the heavy door open. He wore a red headband and tried to stand at attention when he'd accomplished his task. Three other men stumbled into the entryway behind him, tucking in their clothes and checking weapons that they'd obviously just grabbed.

"Ah, g'day, sir," the guard with the headband said. "I, ah, we weren't expecting you tonight."

The last two guards appeared from the living area beyond. One of them was holding the other upright. The front of the latter man's tunic was stiff with dried vomit. His eyes were open, but they didn't focus.

"You normally call ahead, I gather," Vierziger said to the factor. A sneer was implicit in his dry tone.

"These gentlemen are security specialists," Suterbilt said harshly. "They're here to view the premises."

Vierziger walked into the house. "And to look at the ambiance itself," he said coolly.

He raised his attaché case, holding it between himself and the guard. The gesture was similar to that of a woman whisking her long skirt away as she passes dog droppings on the sidewalk. When he was clear, he set the case down beside the wall.

The interior of the house was pretty much of a pig sty. Liquor bottles and hundreds, perhaps thousands, of empty stim cones littered the floors. The building had a sophisticated environmental system to exchange outside air, but the filters had been unable to control the stench of human wastes, vomit, and unwashed bodies.

There was no sign of women, though. Apparently Suterbilt's orders that no outsiders should be admitted had been obeyed to the letter.

The factor rapped his knuckles on a wall to direct attention away from the state of housekeeping which he'd permitted. "See these?" he said. "The whole place is a ceramic monocasting, 20 centimeters thick on the outside. You could shoot straight into a wall and not so much as scar it!"

Vierziger sniffed. "Ceramics are all very well so long as you don't exceed their strength moduli," he said. He walked down the hall, deliberately shuffling his feet sideways to sweep litter out of his path. "One additional straw beyond *that* and you've got sand, not armor."

"Well, yes, but . . ." Suterbilt said. "Ah — the ambiance is at the end of the hall. It was the master bedroom."

"I assumed that," Vierziger sneered. "I'm glad you had sense enough to lock your guard *slugs* away from it. Otherwise there wouldn't be anything left for Astra to threaten, would there?"

Niko sniffed. "Not much of a lock," he said. It was an add-on, cemented to the panel and jamb. "I guess it's good enough, though."

The guards were restive and concerned. One of them had drunk enough to be obviously angry, but a pair of his fellows gripped his wrists. The group was armed with the assortment of shoulder weapons, pistols and knives that had been typical street wear for the gangsters before Madame Yarnell arrived.

"I'll open it for you," Suterbilt said, stepping forward with an electronic key. Vierziger's sneering superiority had reduced the factor to nervous acquiescence with every demand, spoken or not.

The room illuminated itself softly when the door opened. The fixtures in the portion of the house which the guards occupied had been dimmed over the months by a grimy miasma. Here the light, though subdued, had the purity of evening over a meadow.

"*Nice* installation work," Niko said as he surveyed the bare room. "Some artists, they think the hardware is beneath them. Not her."

"What?" Suterbilt said. "Are you joking? I had the furniture removed. Quite a nice bed. I'm using it myself."

"No, no," the sensor tech said. "The ambiance, of course. Look at these heads."

Daun walked into the center of the room. His focus on the psychic ambiance burned through the layers of good humor which made him easy to get along with. Niko Daun liked to be alone when he was working . . . and people who'd been around him while he was in work mode didn't care to repeat the experience.

"There," he said, pointing to a glint in the ceiling, a rubidium-plated bead the size of a man's thumbnail. "There, there, there, there" — the sidewalls — "and the main board here" — he pointed to the shimmering 15-centimeter disk in the center of the floor — "where the bed would keep people from walking on it. Though

I doubt that would have hurt the resolution, the way she's got the projectors bedded. Just *look* at the way she faired them into the matrix!"

"Yes, it can't be removed without destroying the whole thing," Suterbilt said. "And probably the house as well."

Daun turned on him with the casual prickliness of a cat. "Don't talk nonsense!" the technician snapped.

"Specialist Daun," Vierziger said smoothly, "we're here to —"

"Look," Daun said, the first time anybody who knew Johann Vierziger had interrupted him in a long while. "Since we're here, I'm going to try the ambiance. This is probably the only time I'll be around a genuine Suzette."

Nothing in the sensor tech's tone suggested he was willing to discuss the matter further. As he spoke, he took a flat, palm-sized device from his smaller toolkit and opened its keyboard.

Vierziger laid the tips of his left index and middle fingers on Daun's wrist. "Master Suterbilt will switch on the ambiance for us, I'm sure," Vierziger said.

"Yes, yes, but I'm in a hurry," the factor grumbled. He took another key from his wallet. He flicked the on switch in the air without result. "Let's see . . ."

"Stand over here," Daun said, gesturing Suterbilt to a point near where the head of the bed would have been.

Suterbilt frowned but obeyed.

"I could have turned it on easier," Daun grumbled under his breath to the other Frisian.

"You could remove the work so that it could be reconstructed?" Vierziger murmured back.

"Huh?" said Daun. "Course I could. Don't be an idiot. The adhesive'll powder at twenty-eight point nine kilohertz. Take about three seconds each. And realigning them afterward, *that's* no sw—"

The room shimmered out of the present and into a

golden timelessness. Suterbilt had finally managed to trigger the ambiance with his low-powered key.

Vierziger was in an individual paradise. Foliage waved slowly in breezes the viewer could not feel, and the air was perfumed with life itself.

Movement was thought-swift and effortless. The trees mounted like towers holding the sky, far taller than was possible for normal vegetation which fed its branches by osmosis against the drag of gravity. The viewers' minds could ascend the roughness of the bark, feel the single-celled microflora which gave texture and color to the trunks, or exist as the entire world — plant, animal, and the supporting soil beneath.

The ambiance was more real than the sidereal universe to those within its pattern of impinging stimuli. Through it all, informing it all, was the single warm presence of its creator.

" . . . all that remains of my wife . . ." Larrinaga had said. He was right, and he was perhaps right as well that Suzette was a saint.

That wasn't a subject on which Vierziger felt competent to judge.

The glow dimmed, vanished. Physical reality reasserted itself and memory of the ambiance sucked itself down a wormhole into the unconscious of the men who had experienced it.

Suterbilt shook himself. "I ought to come here more often," he said. "It relaxes me."

Niko Daun looked at the projection heads, shaking his head in delight. "Amazing," he said. "Absolutely amazing. I wish I could meet her."

"I think," said Vierziger, "that you just did."

The effect was no more than a mental hologram; not *life*, not even something alive. But Vierziger could understand why Larrinaga believed his wife was still present in the ambiance. He supposed that was all you really had of any artist, and perhaps of any human being: the things they had done.

"We can go now," Vierziger said aloud. His left hand gestured Daun and Suterbilt toward the bedroom door, as if he and not the factor were the host.

The guards had returned to the main living area of the house, an arc of floor raised three steps on one end to set off, without a vertical barrier, the kitchen/dining facilities from the relaxation area. A hologram display blared loud music to accompany a pornographic recording.

The furniture was cheap, obviously junk brought in for the guards when Suterbilt carried off the original furnishings. It had been wrecked — shot, slashed, and broken apart. Two of the men sprawled on the floor, filthy though it was. The man with the headband got up from a legless sofa when the factor reappeared.

"Sir?" the guard asked.

"Keep a better lookout, for one thing!" Suterbilt snapped. He looked over at Vierziger. "Do you have anything to add?"

"Not at the moment," Vierziger said coolly. "I'll make my recommendations in two days."

He looked around the mess and the men guarding it. "They will be expensive to carry out, *that* I can assure you. But necessary."

The three men walked outside. Suterbilt's driver switched on the pump which powered the van's four wheel-hub hydraulic motors.

Vierziger swung the house door almost to, then caught the panel just before it clanged home and locked. "Blood!" he snapped. "I've left my briefcase."

He pivoted back into the house, pulling the door closed behind him. The guard wearing the headband was halfway back to the hologram. He turned, opening his mouth to speak.

"I forgot —" Vierziger began.

The door rang against its jamb. The Frisian drew and fired his pistol eight times in a single flowing motion.

The man with the headband lurched backward, flinging his hands in the air. The first bolt had blown out the thin bones of his nose and emptied his eyesockets.

The chest of a burly, blond-haired guard vanished in a red flash and a deafening roar. Vierziger hadn't noticed the string of grenades the fellow was wearing beneath a light jumper. The bolt that should have ruptured the guard's aorta instead set off a secondary explosion.

The blast flung the remaining guards in four separate directions, complicating the Frisian's task. It saved the man still seated on the sofa — for the few hundredths of a second before a second bolt slapped his temple while the ceramic wall behind where his head *had* been glowed white from the previous round.

Each of the men sprawled on the floor before the shooting started took a round. One of them was faceless and screaming from the grenade blast. The bolt that ruptured his skull was a mercy.

The last guard — and it was all in a half second punctuated by the grenade — was turning with a fully-automatic shotgun. Centrifugal force made his long red hair stand out like a porcupine's quills. The cascade of hair caught the first bolt. It vanished in a red fireball, drinking the cyan plasma and dissipating its force.

Vierziger's trigger twitched a last time. His bolt punched the guard's scream back through his palate.

The shotgun fired three times before it jammed. Aerofoil projectiles, designed to spread wider than spherical pellets, zinged from the walls and ceiling. One traced a line as thin as a razor cut across the Frisian's right cheek.

The living area was bloody chaos.

A toolkit/ammo pouch on the left side of Vierziger's belt balanced the weight of the pistol he carried on the right. He took out a spanner and turned the white, shimmering barrel off the weapon's receiver and dropped it on the floor. Rapid fire had eroded the

iridium to half its original thickness. The remainder of
the refractory metal was so hot that it deformed when
it bounced on the cast flooring.

Vierziger fitted a fresh barrel — the kit held two —
and reloaded the pistol, then holstered it again. The
process of replacing the shot-out barrel had taken less
than thirty seconds.

The house stank of ozone and bodies ripped apart
and half burned. The plasticizer of the grenade had a
pungent reek, unpleasant and probably poisonous in a
confined space. Vierziger ignored it.

Some of the men's clothing was afire. An arc of
garbage centered on the grenade explosion burned
also, though all the fires seemed likely to smolder out
rather than build into a major conflagration.

Vierziger's attaché case was just inside the living
area, where he'd set it behind a pile of trash when he
entered the house behind Suterbilt. He opened the
case and took out a cylindrical blasting device 20
centimeters across and half that in depth. He peeled
the protective layer off one end, stuck the charge on
the front wall near the door, and twisted the dial of
delay fuze to one hour.

Vierziger had printed a message on a card before he
left Hathaway House. He stuck that to the wall just
below the explosive device, then surveyed the room for
one last time.

One of the bodies twitched like a decorticated frog.
The burning clothes had smothered themselves in veils
of bitter smoke. Behind the gray, the hologram danced,
more enticing for the partial coverage than it had been
when the performers' tired flesh was uncompromis-
ingly revealed.

Vierziger opened the door. The card on the wall
read:

REMOVE THE AMBIANCE AND GET BACK ASAP

"All right, I'll tell him!" the Frisian called over his shoulder as he stepped outside.

Standing with his hand on the door he held ajar, Vierziger said to the sensor tech, "Daun, they're having problems with the hue of their hologram projector. I told them you could fix it in three minutes at the outside."

He gestured Niko toward the doorway. "Get at it. I don't want to wait longer than I have to."

"Say!" said the factor. "*I* don't want to wait at all! I've already wasted half an hour."

Vierziger closed the door behind Daun and stood with his back to it. "Relax," he said. "Remember, you said you needed to use the ambiance more often anyway. Besides, if those turds don't have the projector to amuse them, who knows what they'll get up to?"

Suterbilt sighed. "Yes, I suppose there's that," he agreed.

He grimaced. The van's headlights were on. This far out of town, their sidescatter was the only illumination. "Do you really think expensive changes will be necessary?" the factor asked.

Vierziger shrugged. "It's really a pair of changes," he said. "Part of the guard force has to be outside. Not really to do anything — just to be a tripwire so that if they're killed, the men inside have warning of an attack. *But* you also have to provide firing ports for the guards inside."

"That's impossible!" Suterbilt said. "You can't cut holes in these walls!" He slapped one to underscore his point.

"It's not impossible," the Frisian said. The lighted half of his face drew up in a deliberate sneer. "It's simply very expensive — as I said. *And* necessary. I'll have a detailed plan for you in two days."

The door began to swing open. Vierziger stepped forward, moving Suterbilt back a pace. "Any trouble, Daun?" Vierziger asked over his shoulder.

Niko looked at his fellow Frisian. "No," he said. "No, I took care of my end."

He didn't say anything more during the drive back to the TST offices, and he only once looked directly at Johann Vierziger.

Vierziger smiled at him.

"Stay in the car," Coke ordered harshly. He thrust his sub-machine gun at Pilar. Her hands wouldn't close on the dense metal and plastic. The weapon slipped into her lap. "If anybody gives you trouble, shoot them. It's off safe and there's one up the spout. Just fucking *use* it."

He'd stopped the port operations van in front of a six-story structure on the spaceport end of Potosi. Except for the location, the building was very similar to the one which held the Ortegas' — which held Pilar's — apartment. The ground floor was a club, The Red Rooster, which was beginning to get underway for the evening.

The doorman/bouncer realized that Coke intended to leave the vehicle parked in front while he went up the stairs beside the club's entrance. The doorman stepped toward Coke and shouted, "Hey dickhead!"

Coke pointed his left index finger at the man's face. His right hand hung out at his side. The hand was crooked on a level with the butt of his pistol.

"Don't even think about it," the Frisian warned. The flat assurance of his voice was more threatening than a snarl.

The doorman backed inside the club. Coke went up the stairs two at a time.

The door off the second-floor landing was metal-faced. The jamb was wood, however, and the interior wall didn't look particularly sturdy either.

Coke hammered on the panel with his knuckles. "Ortega!" he called. "Front and center! This is an emergency!"

"Hey bud!" somebody called from below. Coke looked down.

A man close to two meters tall, wearing an electric-green jumpsuit, had swung out of the club entrance. He held a combination weapon, a pneumatic gun firing explosive projectiles through a 30-cm long barrel with a shock baton of twice that length mounted beneath the muzzle like a bayonet.

"Serafina's busy!" he shouted as he pounded up the stairs toward Coke. "Now, buddy, you can wait or I can line you up with somebody just as sweet. But don't you go —"

Coke judged his moment. He kicked when the pimp was three steps below him. The gun was pointed up and to the left in rhythm with the tall man's strides. Coke's boot caught the pimp's jaw and flung him down the stairs, limbs flailing.

Coke turned to the door. Instead of knocking again, he took a flat ring charge from a pouch on his equipment belt, peeled off the protective layer, and pasted the charge around the door latch.

He pulled the igniter wire and jumped several steps down the stairs to get clear of the blast. "Fire in the hole!" he shouted from reflex.

The charge went off with a flat *whack!* A fragment of metal whined off the opposite wall. The door jounced on its hinges and stood ajar in a haze of gray smoke.

Coke pulled the panel fully open but kept his body behind the wall. A stunner needle snapped through the dissipating smoke. It sparkled minusculy against the opposite side of the stairwell.

"Ortega!" Coke shouted. "The drum you substituted in the gage going off yesterday on the *Tellurian Queen* — there's a bomb in it. The cartel's stocks on Delos are going up in smoke three days from now, and when they do people are going to be looking for you. You've got to get off-planet now!"

"Get out of here," a man called. *"Get out of here!* I don't know what you're talking about!"

A burst of a dozen stun needles hissed and popped through the opening.

Coke fumbled at his equipment belt, feeling for a smoke grenade. He'd go in with his visor on thermal —

"Matthew!" Pilar screamed. Her sub-machine gun ripped cyan runs in the night.

Coke drew as he turned. The street door's jamb and lintel were a shower of shattered concrete from the cyan bolts. The tall pimp had gotten safe to the shelter of the stairwell before Pilar fired.

The pimp aimed his weapon. Coke shot him in the chest and face.

The pimp jerked his trigger. The pneumatic gun coughed, recoiling out of the dying man's grip. The heavy shell hit three steps above the landing and burst, showering the stairwell with shrapnel and orange light.

Coke, startled by the blast and prickles from the shell, sprayed three more bolts. He hit the pimp only once — in the ankle as he fell backward. The fellow was dead already, or at least he would be in the next minute or two.

"Ortega!" Coke repeated. His ears were ringing. "Come on out. I won't hurt you, and you don't have a lot of time.

"Matthew, you mustn't kill him!" Pilar called. She was at the bottom of the staircase. She tried to step past the tall man. His thrashing arm struck her calf. She came up anyway, her face pale and her sub-machine gun's muzzle shimmering brighter than the stairwell glowstrip.

"Go back!" Coke ordered. She climbed toward him anyway.

The explosive shell had flung the room door shut again. Coke reached for it with his left hand. The panel opened from the inside. A naked woman stepped out onto the landing.

Her name — the name she went by, anyway — was Serafina Amoretta. Coke had seen her image, but that hadn't prepared him for her youth. She couldn't be more than 14 standard years, though her breasts and hips were full.

"Who do you think you are?" she shouted in bright-eyed fury. Perhaps she was on gage or other drugs, though she seemed alert enough. "Do you think you'll get me by coming here like this? Well, you won't!"

Serafina stood with her fists on her hips, glaring at Coke on the step below her. There was no sign that the corpse of her pimp or the gun in the hand of his killer affected her in any way. She didn't shave or pluck her body, but there was only a halo of hair surrounding the lips of her vulva.

"I don't want you," Coke said. "I'm here for Terence Ortega, to keep him from being killed by your little game."

The pistol in his hand embarrassed him. He tried to holster it again. He was awkward now in the aftermath of the shooting. He managed to sear the side of his rib cage with the hot muzzle.

"You want Terry?" Serafina caroled in raucous delight. "So that's it, is it? His frigid wife sent you to get him back? Terry, come out here. Now!"

Coke risked a look over his shoulder. He prayed that Pilar would have returned to the van, but she hadn't, she was just below him. Her lips trembled, and her face had no expression.

The door behind Serafina moved. A man looked out nervously, then stepped the rest of the way. He carried a needle stunner in one hand and held his trousers before him as a veil. He hadn't managed to get his legs into the openings.

"See who's here, Terry?" Serafina said, cocking her head so that she could watch the man out of the corner of her eyes. "She's here to take you back with a gun!"

"That's nothing to do with it!" Coke said. "I tell you, there was a *bomb* in the drum you thought was refinery tailings. You've got to disappear before the folks on Delos learn what I already know."

"Lies!" Serafina cried. "All lies!"

Her gaze slipped past Coke to Pilar. "Do you want to shoot me, bitch? It won't get you Terry back, you know. He'll never go back to you now that he knows what it's like to fuck a real woman!"

Ortega had been a good-looking man once. He still had the face, but standing nude on the landing made his paunch and generally run-down appearance painfully evident. Part of Coke's mind found time to wonder at what Serafina Amoretta saw in the fellow.

"Look," the Frisian said desperately. "You can lie to me, but it won't do you a bit of good with the enforcers from Delos, you know that. And L'Escorial, it's L'Escorial that planned this, they'll be *curst* sure Delos learns who planted the bomb because they don't want suspicion falling on *them.*"

"You can't have Terry and you can't have me!" Serafina cried. She groped behind her and caught the hand with which Ortega held up his trousers. She jerked the garment from him, tossed it down the steps, and then drew his hand forward to cup her breast. "Do you see! Your lies get you nothing. Nothing!"

There was a clatter behind Coke. He glanced back. Pilar had dropped the sub-machine gun. She was stumbling down the stairs.

"Wait!" he called.

"You see!" Serafina said. She jutted her hips backward against Ortega's groin and wriggled. "You see!"

Coke backed down the stairs. He didn't dare turn away from the needle stunner.

His boot jarred the sub-machine gun. He snatched the weapon up. For a moment he imagined blasting the couple on the landing to doll rags. *No, the cartel would take care of that. . . .*

He reached the bottom of the stairs. He heard the van's diesel roar to life. Serafina turned, drawing Ortega with her back into the room. Coke ran out into the street. He was too late. The van was a block and a half away, still accelerating.

A crowd had gathered at a discrete distance, drawn by the shooting and the corpse lying half in, half out of the stairwell. The pimp's eyes were glazed below the ruin of his forehead.

"One, this is Four," Coke's commo helmet announced in the voice of Lieutenant Barbour. *"Something's happened at what used to be Larrinaga's house. I think you'd better be present when L'Escorial gets to checking. Do you have transportation? Over."*

"That's a negative, Four," Coke said, watching the port operations van disappear in the distance. "Over."

"Roger, somebody'll pick you up on the way," Barbour said. *"Four out."*

Matthew Coke stared into the night. Spectators shifted when his blank expression fell across them, but they were only blurs to his consciousness.

He tried to change the sub-machine gun's half-expended magazine for a full one. He had to give up the attempt, because his hands were trembling too badly.

Metal scraps and pieces of broken glass hung from an ankle-height string concealed in the broad-leafed ground cover. Despite his visor's light amplification, Vierziger would have missed the warning device if he hadn't been looking for something of the sort. He knelt and tugged the trip-line with his left hand, making the trash rattle.

The only response was greater stillness.

"Larrinaga," Vierziger called in a low voice.

There was a rustle from the bole of the fallen tree. "Who's there?" Larrinaga demanded.

Larrinaga was crouched in the opening, gripping a club with metal spikes. He wouldn't be able to make out Vierziger's crouching form against the background of the trees between him and the rear of Potosi's buildings.

"Vierziger," the Frisian said. He switched on the miniflood in his left hand.

Larrinaga jumped as abruptly as if Vierziger had shot him. His head knocked against the lip of his shelter, but the punky wood cushioned the blow.

Vierziger stood up. "Don't worry," he said with the touch of a sneer in his voice. "I'm not here to put you out of your misery."

The local man scrambled to his feet. The intense light made him sneeze. Vierziger slid the control down, dimming the glare to a yellow glow.

"What do you want then?" Larrinaga said. He seemed to notice the club for the first time. He dropped it at his feet.

Vierziger's lips quirked with wry approval. He clipped the dimmed light to his belt, then slid the strap of his attaché case off his left shoulder. His right hand remained free at all times.

"Here," Vierziger said. "Take it and get to the port. You're booked on the *Argent Server* and she lifts in twenty minutes. You'd better be aboard, because I suspect it's going to be a while before any later ship gets clearance."

"I can't —" Larrinaga said.

"There's money in the case," the Frisian snarled. "And there's a cyclo in the alley that'll get you there in time. Get *going*."

"I —" said Larrinaga, and his face smoothed in dawning comprehension. He knelt and thumbed the latches of the reptile-skin case.

The six portions of a psychic ambiance gleamed from the bed of sprayfoam which cushioned them and held them in place.

Larrinaga carefully closed the case. He began to cry. "You can find an expert to set it up again when

you've settled," Vierziger said harshly. "I'm told that
anybody good enough to do the job will be honored to
work on it, on a Suzette. Now get out of here before it's
too late!"

He grabbed Larrinaga by the shoulder and dragged
him upright with fingers that could bend steel. "Get
going!"

The local man stumbled toward the buildings of
Potosi and the vehicle that would take him away from
them forever. He turned at the edge of the lighted arc.

"Why are you doing this, Master Vierziger?" he
asked.

"I'm damned if I know," the Frisian said. "But then,
I'm damned anyway, not so?"

Vierziger began to laugh. The sound mounted
swiftly to a register suggesting bats and madness.

The laughter, if it was laughter, broke off. "Shall I
shoot you now?" Vierziger shouted. "Get going!"

"Thank you, sir," Larrinaga said. He turned and
jogged off through the familiar darkness.

"I don't expect it'll make the least difference in the
long run!" Vierziger called after him. "But try to make
a life for yourself this time. There's that one chance in
hell."

In a much softer voice he added, "Even in Hell."

One of the L'Escorial trucks mounted a bank of
floodlights behind the armored cab instead of a heavy
weapon. The floods weren't well aligned, but their
glare made the former Larrinaga house stand out like
the lead actor during curtain call.

The gap in the front of the building was a nearly
perfect circle, about two meters in diameter. The mass
of ceramic casting belonging there was a heap of black
grit, trailing off both inside and outside the dwelling.

Suterbilt and the three generations of Lurias stared
at the hole as Margulies drove up with Coke. Daun
and Moden were already present. Thirty or forty

L'Escorial gunmen and four armored trucks surrounded the site, and there were more men inside.

All six of the fireflies danced a complex pattern around the Lurias. Pepe wore the controller.

"How did it happen?" Ramon Luria demanded, shaking his fist at the hole. "How did they do this?"

"Either sonics . . ." Coke said as he walked through the line of L'Escorial guards unchallenged. "Which I doubt, because of the time it'd take, or —"

He pinched some of the shattered ceramic between his thumb and forefinger, then sniffed the vapors still clinging to the material. "Nope, that's what it was. A spalling charge. That's the danger with monocastings. You really need to have spaced layers to prevent this sort of thing from happening, though that degrades projectile resistance."

A four-wheeled L'Escorial patrol vehicle pulled up with two red-uniformed gunmen and Johann Vierziger aboard. The dapper Frisian sauntered over to the blast site.

Pepe Luria turned toward Coke. "Now tell me what spalling charge *means*," he said in a deadly voice. His hands gripped the edges of his controller. "Instantly!"

"It means a quantity of inhibited plasticized explosive," Sten Moden said calmly, "which is spread in a thin layer over the target surface by a precursor charge and detonated from the open face a microsecond later."

Moden ran his fingers carefully across the inner surface of the hole. The ceramic was rippled in a series of surflike conchoidal fractures.

"The shock waves," Moden continued, "reflect within the plate. A ceramic of this sort has virtually no elasticity. When the stresses peak, the material itself crumbles."

He raised a handful of the glittering black residue and let it dribble down through his fingers.

Niko Daun eased up beside Coke and whispered

directly into the major's ear. Coke's eyes blanked. He carefully looked away from Johann Vierziger.

"I don't believe it," Suterbilt said. "The house is a fortress, a *fortress*."

"You should have hired the FDF sooner," Vierziger said coolly. "Or perhaps Master Suterbilt and I should have stayed longer when we visited earlier tonight."

"What would a few more men have mattered?" shouted Pepe Luria. "There must have been twenty Astras, more even! Look there!"

The house's interior lights were on. The guards' sprawled bodies looked more like cast-off clothes and lumber than they did a scene of carnage.

Pepe's hands twitched. One of the fireflies above him suddenly pirouetted, firing its powergun as it spun. One bolt glared from the roof coping. Three more blazed out into the uncleared forest, lighting small fires. The last round snapped back toward Potosi.

Raul put a shaky hand on his grandson's shoulder to calm him. "Not that," the Old Man said. "We don't want Madame Yarnell coming down on us."

Raul looked at Sten Moden. "If the bomb was outside the house," he said, "why didn't it blow the wall *in* instead of out?"

"It didn't *blow* in either direction," the logistics officer explained. "The structure vibrated itself apart."

He pointed. "The fragments fell in both directions, you see?"

As Moden said, as much of the shattered wall was in the slope across the living area floor as was outside the wall.

Daun drifted away. Coke motioned Vierziger over by crooking his finger.

"Is there something you want to tell me, Johann?" Coke asked in a low voice.

"No," said Vierziger, "there isn't. But thank you for asking, Matthew."

"All right, they've had their game," Pepe Luria cried.

"Now we shall take the set. Tijuca! Tijuca! Where's the drunken bastard Tijuca!"

Pepe's expression was as furious as that of a weasel in a trap. "That's it, I'll —"

Mary Margulies stepped forward. "I told Angel I'd cover for him tonight," she said calmly. "We got used to trading off like that in the old days."

Pepe started to shout a curse in the Frisian's face. He looked at her more closely before the words came out. He settled back on his heels, then said, "Will you? All right then. We'll take eight men only, and two patrol cars."

"What are you going to do, Pepe?" Ramon asked nervously. He touched his son's wrist to draw the youth's attention. "We daren't anger the cartel."

Pepe's snarl melted into a smile even more cruel and terrifying. "In and out, gone before anyone knows there's been an attack, hey?" he said in a husky whisper. "That's the way the Astras do it, and they've had no trouble. We'll do the same."

"Their warehouse?" Raul asked, frowning.

"No, we'll kidnap Peres!" his grandson said. "And the price to get him back alive will be for him and the Widow to leave Cantilucca forever!"

CANTILUCCA: DAY SEVEN

A jitney filled with gunmen — Margulies thought they were L'Escorials, but the muted gang colors of the present didn't show up at night — rolled down the nearly empty street. The vehicle swayed from side to side. The passengers cursed and flung bottles. Before Madame Yarnell arrived on Cantilucca, they would have been shooting.

The L'Escorial acting as communications officer, still holding the radio handset to his ear, turned to face Pepe in the back seat with Margulies. "They've taken in another case of liquor. There's no chance she'll be moving before noon."

"Yarnell parties every night," Luria muttered angrily. "Imported food, wines from *Earth* to drink. And we pay for it! She acts like she's a queen."

"On Cantilucca," Margulies said, "she *is* a queen."

A pair of jitneys drove out of the garage beneath the building opposite. The structure's lower three stories were an Astra recreational center of varied capability. None of the men aboard noticed the pair of patrol cars in the alleys across the street.

"He'll be coming soon," Pepe said. He peered down at the firefly controller.

"No," Margulies said.

Pepe reached for the power switch anyway. The Frisian caught his hand.

"No," she said. "Fireflies are good for an area target —"

A lie as far as she was concerned, but the politic thing to say just now.

"— but this has to be precise. Let me handle the shooting."

Pepe's faced blanked in white fury, then relaxed again in a smile. The change was as sudden as a pair of eyeblinks. Margulies put her left hand back on the fore-end of the 2-cm weapon she'd brought for this operation.

"Area target," Pepe said. "Yes. But I've set them to attack blue, you see? They'll kill the guards, but Peres doesn't wear blue himself!"

"Peres *usually* doesn't wear blue," Margulies corrected. "You're betting that he won't come out of that whorehouse with his new girlfriend's blue bra around his neck."

She shrugged. "Likely so. But why risk it?"

The radio set crackled. "He's coming!" warned the commo officer.

Margulies stepped out of the car and took her position at the mouth of the alley. The wall against which she stood blurred her outline, but she had no real concealment beyond the darkness. She held her heavy shoulder weapon diagonally across the front of her body.

The garage's automatic door rose with a series of rhythmic bangs. The gigolo's newly repaired aircar howled up the ramp.

Peres himself was driving. He misjudged the slope and struck the street lip. The plastic landing skids flexed and bounced the nose high.

Margulies fired. Her 2-cm bolt stabbed the right front fan nacelle. The blue flash sent blades and fragments of the shorted windings in all directions, like shrapnel from a bomb burst.

The vehicle yawed right, hit the pavement at 30 kph, and cartwheeled.

The armored garage door started to close automatically. While the aircar was still spinning, flinging off bits of body panel, Margulies fired at where the edge of the door mated with the track along the jamb. The plasma bolt vaporized a section of the track and hammered the door panel like a collision with a speeding truck.

The door skewed in its frame and stuck. Nobody was going to get out of the garage to aid Peres unless they wanted to crawl through the 25-centimeter gap beneath the lower edge of the jammed panel.

Both L'Escorial four-wheelers accelerated from their ambush positions. Pepe Luria stood, clinging to the back of the commo officer's seat. He held an automatic carbine in his free hand.

The aircar landed upside down. It continued to rotate slowly, driven by the vibration of the two fan nacelles still spinning at full revs. The right rear installation had torn itself apart when that corner of the vehicle slammed down violently and drove the side of the housing into the blade arc.

The L'Escorial cars skidded and stopped on opposite sides of Peres' vehicle. The roof of the aircar was compressed but not flattened to the level of the car's body.

A youth crawled from the passenger side. He wore a blue posing suit, blue sandals, and nothing else. He was crying and the crash had bloodied his forehead.

Pepe Luria pointed his carbine from the hip and triggered a burst. The weapon fired large-bore explosive bullets, rocket-assisted to keep the recoil manageable. The rocket exhausts were red sparks across the night. Two of the projectiles hit the boy in the chest, blowing him backward into the wrecked aircar.

The quartet of L'Escorials from the other four-wheeler dragged open the driver's side door of the aircar. One of them smashed the warped support pillar with the butt of his 2-cm weapon to make it release.

Peres screamed in terror. Two of the men pulled him out. A third threw a restraint net over the prisoner, and the fourth L'Escorial — the man with the 2-cm weapon — swatted him with the flat of the gun butt to silence the blubbering cries. They tossed Peres face-down into the back of their vehicle and got in themselves.

Mary Margulies stood at the edge of the alley, looking down the street toward Astra headquarters and the jitneys full of gunmen who'd driven that way moments before. The only thing moving in the night was the aircar, quivering on its back like a half-crushed bug.

"Get in!" Pepe Luria called to her.

Margulies glanced aside at him. She waved. "Go on," she said. "I'll walk, thank you. You've got what you came for."

The pair of patrol cars made tight low-speed turns and accelerated together up the street. The L'Escorial gunmen shouted to one another in glee.

There was a brief squeal of metal from the underground garage. Somebody was trying to free the door with a prybar. An argument broke out inside, identifiable from the timbre of the voices though the words were inaudible.

Margulies changed her magazine's weapon for a fresh one. She set off toward Hathaway House, staying close to building fronts and trying to look in all directions. She was nearly home before she heard the wail of sirens from Astra headquarters.

The Roberson & Co. trading post in the hamlet of Veridad was separate from the Astra patrol base there, but loud music from the stockade housing a score of gunmen pulsed through the walls. Roberson shivered, clutched his arms around himself as if against a cold wind.

"He's not coming," he said to the Widow Guzman. "It's some sort of —"

The door at the back of the trading post gave onto a

fenced storage area, inaccessible from the outside. The door opened. A tall, nervous-looking Frisian soldier, not a man the Astra leaders had met before, stepped out.

"Barbour?" the Widow said in surprise.

"How did you get there?" Roberson gasped.

"I'm Barbour," the Frisian said. "And don't worry about how I got through your fence, I *did*, that's all. Did you bring the money?"

The merchant glanced reflexively at the case on the floor beside him, behind the counter. They'd expected Barbour to arrive for the meeting he'd arranged by the post's front door.

There was a pistol in the case as well. To Roberson's surprise, the Frisian appeared to be unarmed.

"You claim you can free Adolpho," said the Widow Guzman. "If you can do that, you'll have your pay. You'll have any pay you ask."

"In open-remitter chips, so there's no way they can trace back where it came from?" Barbour warned. He looked as skittish as a roach when the lights come on.

"Yes, yes, just as you said," Roberson snapped. "Now, how are you going to release Peres?"

He couldn't keep the distaste from his tone as he spoke the gigolo's name, but he hadn't even attempted to argue with the Widow when the Frisian made his offer. Barbour had called on what was supposed to be a private direct line between Roberson's office and Astra HQ. That in itself lent credence to his proposition.

"I didn't say I'd get him out," Barbour said defensively. His gaze shifted quickly around the big room, but he didn't make eye contact with the Astra leaders. "I said you could get him with what I'd give you."

"Well go on, then, man!" the Widow said. "How? Tell us!"

She stepped close to the Frisian and caught his chin between her right thumb and forefinger. He jerked his face away. Her ornate silver rings traced glittering arcs as she slapped him hard.

"Tell us!" she shouted.

Barbour turned his head away. "Look, they'd kill me if they knew I was doing this," he whined. "The major would say it was treason!"

"Via, boy!" Roberson cried. "Where —"

"It's the TST offices, you see?" the Frisian blurted. "They aren't guarded like L'Escorial bases are. You go in there and pull the core from Suterbilt's private data bank, you see?"

They didn't see. Guzman and the merchant looked blankly from Barbour to one another, then back.

Barbour shook his head in disgust. "Don't you see?" he repeated. "Suterbilt's cheating both TST and the Confederacy, faking the amount of gage that goes out of here. If the Confederacy learns they're being done out of port duties, they'll clean L'Escorial out of here, right? And it's all there in Suterbilt's private data bank, it's *got* to be!"

The music from the patrol stockade paused. For a moment, the only sound within the trading post was the breathing of the three occupants.

Barbour had chosen the meeting place, an Astra-controlled village twelve klicks from Potosi. He'd demanded that no one be inside the post save himself and the two principals. The Widow agreed and held to her agreement, overruling Roberson on the point. It was now evident to the merchant also that the Frisian would have noticed guards, no matter how well concealed.

"He'll have the information coded," Roberson said cautiously. "We won't be able to read it, will we?"

"What does that matter, you fool?" Barbour snarled. He appeared to be a man clinging to the ragged edge of his sanity. "The Marvelans can decrypt it, can't they? And anyway, it doesn't matter — Suterbilt won't dare take the chance."

"We're not using the information," the Widow Guzman agreed in a distant voice. "We're trading the information for Adolpho. But if Adolpho's been harmed or they won't give him up —"

Her voice had been bleak. Now it became as cold as the heart of a comet.

"— then I will give it all to the Marvelans. And they will gut this planet when they learn how they've been cheated."

"Now, Stella," Roberson said nervously. "We don't want *that* to happen. If the Confederacy really takes direct control here, it'll put a crimp in our operations too. Or worse."

The Widow looked at him. "Do you think I care?" she whispered.

"Look, that won't be necessary," Barbour said. "Look, I've got to get out of here. I'll give you the codes to get through the TST security system and you give me the money."

His moods appeared to change as abruptly as a rat's did. He was whining again.

"No," said the Widow.

Roberson looked at her in surprise.

"What do you mean?" the Frisian said. "You need the codes or you won't be able to get into the offices without setting off alarms. If L'Escorial comes in, you've got a war!"

"You'll come with us," the woman said. Her combs shimmered. Glowstrips covering most of the ceiling illuminated the post's interior. The light was diffuse but considerable in total, like that of a clear sky as the sun sets.

"I can't!" Barbour whined. "Via, you'll have me killed to save the money!"

"We'll messenger the payment to Hathaway House in your name," the Widow continued in icy determination. "You understand the security system better than we do. You'll get us through it with less chance of a mistake."

"We?" Roberson said, hugging himself. "I'm not going on a *raid*."

"I am," said the Widow. She gestured in the direction of the music coming from the patrol stockade. "We'll take those men. Twenty should be sufficient. And we'll go now."

Barbour covered his face with his hands. "Oh Lord, oh Lord," he whimpered.

He looked up. "All right," he said. "Let's do it quickly before, before . . ."

He covered his face again. "Oh Lord, don't let the major learn about this!"

In the lobby of Hathaway House, Sten Moden looked up from the console. "Do you think Bob's going to need help, Matthew?" he asked.

Major Matthew Coke looked at the four soldiers waiting with him. All were fully kitted out with weapons and extra ammunition.

"If he does," Coke said, "then we're ready to give it to him."

CANTILUCCA: DAY EIGHT

Robert Barbour projected a hologram for Kuklar, the Astra chosen to remove the guard. The monochrome display was a schematic of the back of the building which held the TST offices. The building itself was a dark blob fifty meters away. Stella Guzman watched over his shoulder.

The night sandwiched them with human sounds from Potosi and, behind the Astra force, forest noises. Despite Barbour's desperate orders for them to keep silent, the gunmen talked, cursed the scrub they'd tramped through from where they left the vehicles, and injected stim cones.

The Frisian gestured with his light pen. "You see, there's only one guard at the back staircase," he whispered. His pen dabbed twice again. "There's two more inside, but they're asleep on the couches in the waiting room."

"Where?" demanded Kuklar. He looked from the display toward Barbour, then the Widow. "I don't see nobody."

Kuklar didn't understand that the icon Barbour pointed out on the display, a jagged lightning bolt that slowly pulsed, indicated an armed man. It wasn't certain that he understood what a *map* was. Barbour took a deep breath.

Somebody on the top floor tugged open a window.

"Hey!" shouted a voice from ground level. "Don't you —"

A bucket of waste slurped its way down anyway.

"Fucker!" The L'Escorial guard bawled. He fired his sub-machine gun upward.

A few of the bolts slapped the back of the building; most of them vanished as quivering sparks among the stars. The burst didn't hit whoever'd thrown the slops, because the window closed again a moment later.

"Oh, there he is," Kuklar muttered. "Why din't you say he was down there? I thought you said he was *here.*"

Kuklar started to crawl forward. He unlimbered a weapon from his belt as he moved through the garbage and scrub. Barbour couldn't be sure of the sort of weapon, even with his visor amplifying the ambient light to daytime levels.

"Get a fucking move on, won't you?" a gunman said at nearly normal volume. "I'm supposed to be off duty tonight."

Barbour winced.

"They were the first men available!" the Widow Guzman said. "You were the one who chose Veridad!"

"I didn't say anything," the Frisian muttered.

"Hey?" called the L'Escorial guard.

There was a sound like a melon hitting from a height. Somebody squealed. Violent thrashing punctuated Kuklar's shout, "I got — come on — I got —"

Astras ran toward the building, jostling one another and cursing as they stumbled over garbage in the darkness. None of them had night viewing equipment, even though they were supposed to be a patrol unit.

Barbour shut off his projector and jogged along behind. He noticed that about half the score of gunmen *didn't* move forward until others had reached the scene of the fighting.

Guzman kept up with him, though she wore a dress and was as blind as her troops in this starlight. "Leave most of them down here to cover our retreat," the Frisian ordered her. At this stage in the proceedings, the task overrode his desire to appear a cowardly buffoon. "I'll take three with me. That'll be plenty. The guards upstairs probably won't wake up till long after we're gone."

Kuklar had used a brush knife with a hooked blade as long as his forearm. He was levering the hilt back and forth. The heavy blade was buried in the guard's skull, as deep as the orbit of his right eye.

Barbour swallowed as he started up the stairs. The staircase actually served the building's upper three floors, but it angled past a window at the back of the TST offices. Barbour felt the treads flex as Astra gunmen followed him.

It would have been easier simply to walk up to the L'Escorial guard and shoot him. The burst of shots the man had fired didn't arouse any attention.

Barbour was used to Frisian standards. He began to appreciate Niko Daun's bitter scorn of "indigs."

The window was locked, barred, and in the beam of a microlaser across the room. If the glass pane stopped reflecting a calibrated amount of laser light to the receptor above the tiny emitter, alarms would go off here, in Suterbilt's apartment, and in L'Escorial HQ. The system had a lifetime charge so that it remained independent of the building's power supply.

Barbour knelt, placed the drill, and felt the diamond bit whine happily as it spun a one-centimeter disk out of the pane. Hands-on work wouldn't usually have been an intelligence officer's task, but the team had thought it might come to this. Daun had trained Barbour patiently until they were both convinced he could use the equipment successfully.

He replaced the drill in his borrowed belt kit and fitted the mimicking emitter to the hole. It was self-adjusting: when Barbour switched it on, the micro-laser aimed and brought itself into sequence with the security sensor. The telltale at the back of the little unit glowed red, then amber as the Frisian bent over it.

Somebody's chin bumped Barbour's shoulder. Barbour whirled around, poising the laser's carrying case to strike. "Fucking *fool!*" he snarled. "Do you —"

The Widow Guzman started away from him. Kuklar stood behind her, idly wiping the hook of his knife with his shirt-tail.

Barbour swallowed. "Don't do that," he muttered. He set the case down and smoothed the top of it with his fingertips. "Please, you'll get us all killed."

"Yes," she said. "Yes, I see."

The telltale was green.

Barbour took the cutting bar out of his toolkit. Unlike that of a standard brush-clearing blade, this one was only ten centimeters long and a millimeter thick. The diamond teeth sang through each of the four vertical bars in a few seconds. When Barbour had the top severed, he cut the bottom of the first bar, holding the shaft as he did so.

"Here," he said, handing the bar to Guzman. She took it, then yipped as the friction-heated end touched the inside of her wrist.

Barbour ignored her. The powered blade gave a high-pitched whine as it spun into the steel. It was a tortured sound, certainly loud enough for the guards to hear through the closed door to the lobby. They must be in the throes of gage comas. Why did Suterbilt even bother having such *people* present?

The Frisian handed the last bar behind him. He hadn't been able to practice the next part, but Daun assured him it would work.

Barbour set the end of the cutting bar's blade at an upper corner of the window and pressed inward. There were sparks and an angry sputter from the wire-cored glass; then the blade was through. Barbour drew the bar across, shearing the reinforced pane like tissue paper. Flakes of glass pattered against his wrists and visor.

He cut the other three edges of the pane as easily. When he made the final cut, on the left side, he remembered to angle the cutting bar. The blade levered the glass out where the Frisian could catch it, rather than letting it drop onto the floor. He wasn't worried about the sound, particularly, but the glass would interrupt the mimicking laser if it fell across the beam.

"There," he said. He set the pane down. "There!"

As Barbour climbed through the opening, he happened to look over his shoulder. The Widow stared at him with a puzzled expression. He supposed his obvious competence had surprised her.

If it came to that, he'd surprised himself. Barbour had always been somebody who *helped* people who did things.

The locks on Suterbilt's desk were electronic bio-sensors. Rather than try to duplicate the patterns of the factor's brain activity, Barbour zeroed the settings, then changed the combination to his own patterns. It was childishly simple.

The owner was supposed to scramble the access codes after he or she set the locks. If Suterbilt had done that, even the computing power Barbour could call in through his commo helmet would have required ten minutes to get to this point. Most people, Suterbilt included, didn't bother to proof their locks properly. It was as if the equipment were a magic talisman which need only exist to be effective.

The desk popped open. Barbour leaned under it and began unhooking the computer itself.

Several Astras entered the office behind him. "Keep quiet," he whispered, "and keep away from the waiting room. Let them sl—"

He heard the anteroom door open quietly.

"Don't —" he rasped.

A sub-machine gun lighted the office cyan with reflected light. The gunman emptied his entire magazine into the sleeping L'Escorials. The air roiled with ozone, hot matrix from expended powergun ammunition, and fires the bolts started in the upholstery.

"Shut the door," the Widow Guzman ordered. "Keep the smoke out."

Barbour closed his eyes and whispered a prayer. Then he got back to work. He had the computer out in three minutes, but by then the stench of feces from the men disemboweled in the anteroom had oozed under the door to bathe him.

He sat up and handed the fist-sized unit to the Widow. "There," he said hoarsely. "They'll trade your friend back to you for this, never fear."

She nodded her head crisply. "Yes," she said. "The chips are waiting in your name at your hotel."

Gunmen were leaving the office through the window, as they'd come. The waiting room door was beginning to glow from the heat of the fire enclosed behind it.

Barbour looked at the door. Unwilling to speak but unable to help himself, he said, "Did you have to do that? They were asleep!"

The Widow frowned at him. "What does that matter?" she said. "It's better that they're dead, surely?"

Robert Barbour looked at her in a sudden epiphany. For the first time in his life he realized that there really were people who should better be dead.

It gave meaning to his life.

CANTILUCCA: DAY NINE

Matthew Coke and Johann Vierziger watched from chairs set on the sidewalk in front of Hathaway House. The breeze followed Madame Yarnell's reconnaissance vehicle up the street and out of Potosi. Bits of trash lifted as if waving goodbye for the evening.

It was midnight. If past practice continued, the cartel representative would remain in the spaceport compound for the remainder of the night.

The gangs began to come out. An armored gun truck maneuvered from the L'Escorial courtyard. Down the street, the converted bulldozer grunted forward to lead the Astra contingent.

Vierziger chuckled. "The best show in town," he said. "And we're the only ones interested in front row seats."

"They're watching, though," Coke said, glancing at the facades of the nearby buildings. "For that matter, we could get a better view at the main console inside."

All the windows were shuttered, curtained, or blocked with makeshifts like the side of a packing crate, but there were hidden viewslits in the screens. The citizens of Potosi didn't want to call attention to themselves, but they were afraid not to watch.

"Something I've noticed about war zones, Matthew," Vierziger said. "The people who live in them either act as if they're in danger always, or they act as if there's no danger at all."

Three more L'Escorial armored vehicles followed the first. They puffed and snarled as they lined up side by side to block the street. The same thing was happening in front of Astra headquarters.

The escape hatch in the back of one L'Escorial truck was open. Suterbilt huddled inside, mentally clinging to both armor protection and freedom of movement.

Coke glanced at his companion. "Look, I know it's dangerous," he said. "I just didn't want to be cooped up inside if something popped."

Somebody on the Astra side signalled with a bosun's whistle. The L'Escorial gunmen who followed the vehicles on foot stared goggle-eyed, looking for signs of an ambush.

"The rest of the team can handle security for Bob," Coke said. Vierziger's comment still rankled. It wasn't the whole truth, but . . . And nothing was the *whole* truth. "Via, I know we might get shot out here."

"The difficulty isn't in being killed, Matthew," Vierziger said. His smile was as unreadable as that of the "Mona Lisa." "The difficulty's in what comes after."

Pepe Luria sauntered from the courtyard of the L'Escorial building. His galaxy of fireflies looped and spun ten meters above him, each outlined by the purple haze of the static discharge which supported it.

Adolpho Peres stumbled along behind his captor. A L'Escorial gunman walked a meter to either side of the gigolo, but from a distance Peres did not appear to be tethered.

Coke raised his visor's magnification to x40, then doubled it again. A glint joined Peres' face to the short batons which the men beside him held. Trickles of blood had dried on the back corners of his jaw.

The L'Escorials had poked a length of piano wire through the gigolo's cheeks. The men escorting Peres held the ends wrapped around their batons. If Peres tried to run — if he did *anything* except walk in precise unison with his escorts — the wire would rip his face open like a razor blade.

A L'Escorial with a handheld radio sat on the back deck of an armored car. He held his free hand over his ear as he spoke, then listened, to his radio. He looked up and waved to Pepe. Pepe waved back.

The four armored vehicles roared and staggered forward in clouds of black smoke. The men behind them followed, squinting through the dust and exhaust fumes. Overhead, the fireflies sailed in a figure-eight formation that advanced just ahead of the armored cars.

The breeze had died. The Astras moved up also, in a pall of their own raising.

Roberson clung to himself and shivered at the gates to Astra headquarters. The Widow Guzman walked behind the snorting armored vehicles. Kuklar was beside her, wearing a blank expression and carrying a drawstring sack. The bag held the data base looted from Suterbilt's private office.

Vierziger laughed. He leaned his chair back against the building wall. "What do you suppose they'd do if Madame Yarnell returned to town just now?" he asked.

"Both sides are watching her," Coke said. "They'd scurry to their holes like mice when the cat comes home. There'd be enough time."

The L'Escorial radioman kept the armored cupola between him and Astra guns while he watched Pepe. When the lines of opposing vehicles had advanced to within fifty meters of one another, Pepe pointed his index finger.

The radioman spoke into his mouthpiece, turned, and closed his eyes. He jumped upright in plain view of the Astras, waving his arms like a semaphore.

The armored lines halted. The radioman lurched forward. He almost slipped off the side of his mount. He caught himself to crouch again in the shelter of the cupola.

Pepe gestured forward the men holding Peres. They worked their way carefully between the flanks of two of the armored cars, paying more attention to the hot exhaust louvers than they did to the man whom they were escorting. The wire twitched and quivered, drawing drops of fresh blood at every motion. The gigolo was crying.

Kuklar stepped in front of the armored bulldozer. The vehicle's rocket launcher was depressed to sweep the street ahead. If Kuklar realized that, he didn't seem to care. He walked forward stolidly, the sheath of his hook-bladed knife swinging in synchrony with his right leg.

"You know?" said Vierziger idly. "If something went wrong right now, they might all kill each other."

Coke shook his head. "Not all of them," he said. "Besides, we'd likely catch something ourselves, you and me."

"There's that," his companion agreed.

Suterbilt got out of the armored car and scuttled forward behind Peres and his escort. The factor was terrified, but he was the only one who could identify the stolen data bank so that the exchange could be completed.

The banks of lights on the opposing vehicles cast multiple faint shadows from the men converging between the armored lines. The Widow Guzman stood with her left hand on the blade of the bulldozer. Her right was extended toward Peres as the gigolo approached haltingly. Her visage trembled between fear and longing.

The engine of an Astra vehicle stalled. The driver restarted with a roar. Men on both sides jumped. Pepe Luria raised his face to the sky and laughed.

When Kuklar was almost halfway between the lines, Suterbilt ran to him. The TST factor tugged open the bag holding the computer core while Kuklar continued to grip one of the drawstrings. Suterbilt nodded his head furiously toward the L'Escorial line, invisible behind the blaze of headlights.

Kuklar looked at the Widow. She waved. Kuklar let go of the drawstring.

Peres' escorts dropped their batons and ran to the

armored vehicles. The gigolo, weeping with pain, staggered toward Widow Guzman. The ends of the wire trailed from his face like the barbels of a catfish.

The exchange was complete. Either side's gunmen on foot — Coke was unwilling to think of them as infantry — streamed toward the safety of their headquarters.

The armored cars backed with greater difficulty. Two of the L'Escorial vehicles crunched, fender to fender, as they swerved in opposite directions at the start of the maneuver. The drivers rose from their cabs and screamed curses at one another. In ten minutes, even the vehicles had vanished from the street, however . . .

"Show's over, I suppose," Vierziger said. He let his chair drop onto its front legs. "No excitement at all." He giggled. "Nobody killed."

Coke looked at the little man curiously. "Is that the only kind of excitement?" he asked.

Vierziger stood up. "Well, there's sex, I suppose," he said. "But that's a bad second for me." He smiled. "What do you think about that, Matthew?"

Coke rose to his feet. Backblast from the directional mines the day the team arrived had left black starbursts across the reinforced concrete. He opened his mouth to speak.

The door of Hathaway House opened. Georg peeked out, then stepped into full view. "Major Coke," he said. He cleared his throat. "There was just a message for you, a Mistress Ortega. She'd like you to call on her at your earliest convenience. She, ah, she said she was at home."

Johann Vierziger chuckled. "I'll give you a night to consider your answer, Matthew," he said.

Pilar's door opened as soon as Coke reached the landing. That meant not only that she'd been watching the surveillance screen for his arrival, but that she'd kept the door unlocked.

She shouldn't take chances like that. Coke didn't think she had a gun in the suite, not even a needle stunner like the one her husband carried.

He stepped inside. Pilar was wearing a strapless black dress with a mantilla of white lace over her bare shoulders. She closed the door without looking at him and began setting the multiple locks.

"You shouldn't take chances like that," Coke said. She turned and threw herself into his arms.

"Terry's gone," she said against Coke's shoulder. "He went off on the *ND Maru* this evening. I guess he listened to you after all. Or she did."

Coke tried to kiss her. She wouldn't lift her lips to him. Her arms clamped him fiercely.

"He came to see you before he left?" Coke asked. He stroked her auburn hair with his right hand; she'd let it down for the first time since he'd met her. It was amazingly thick and fell below the pinch of her waist.

"No," she whispered. "I — I recognized the number of the account to which the passage was charged. It was one of Terry's, I suppose one I wasn't supposed to know about."

She nuzzled Coke's shoulder for a moment before she added, "They traveled under the name Sanchez. Master and Mistress Sanchez."

"I'm sorry," Coke said softly. He *was* sorry. It surprised him. Sorry for her pain, though his body was very well aware of the implications of the new state of affairs.

"I need somebody to hold me, Matthew," Pilar said. As she drew him toward the bedroom, he noticed that tonight she was not wearing her crucifix.

CANTILUCCA: DAY TEN

Dawn was red with a promise of storm. The sky was bright enough to mute the lighted advertising signs, but too dim to bring out the color of paint.

At night Potosi looked tawdry. This morning the city was a dull waste; steel rusting on dirty sand.

Hundreds of men, all the members of both gage syndicates who remained in Potosi, lined opposite sides of the street. The gunmen looked sleepy, sickly, and sullen. Most of them would barely have gotten to bed when Madame Yarnell called, demanding that they be assembled to hear her.

The leaders of Astra and L'Escorial faced each other with only the width of the right-of-way between them. Both groups were nervous. Coke's magnified view of their faces suggested that while the Widow Guzman and her companions felt uncertain, an air of monstrous glee underlay the Lurias' twitchiness. The L'Escorial leaders knew, or they thought they knew. . . .

The sound of Madame Yarnell's reconnaissance vehicle preceded the car itself. The driver was winding out his motors, and the active suspension set up an audible keening as it smoothed the high-speed ride over the spaceport highway.

"As pissed as she was to come to Cantilucca," Margulies said, squatting on the roof of Hathaway House beside the major, "you'd think she'd be happy to be going back to Delos. Doesn't seem like she is, though."

"There's folks that'd bitch if you hanged them with a golden rope," Coke said. He kept his tone light, but he knew that very shortly the survey team would have to fish or cut bait.

The Hathaways stored building materials on their roof. The team had converted the crates, lumber, and barrels into a temporary refuge against need, but it couldn't hide them for long.

Madame Yarnell's car didn't slow until it reached the center of town. It skidded to a halt from a hundred, hundred-and-ten, kph. Pebbles and a stoneware bottle, miraculously unshattered by the *poot!* the tire gave it, flew out like langrage from a cannon.

The charge pelted the gunmen who hadn't ducked away when they realized what was about to happen. The bottle dished in the sloped forehead of a L'Escorial gunman; two Astras leaped back with their hands to their faces, screaming that they'd been blinded.

The car's passenger door lifted while gravel from the crash stop still clicked and pattered. Madame Yarnell got out. Her headgear was similar in design and purpose to a Frisian commo helmet. She surveyed the crowd that had gathered at her orders.

"You filth!" she said at last. Her voice boomed from the omnidirectional speaker on top of her helmet. "You cretins, you hog feces!"

The cartel representative turned as she spoke, so that all those present could receive her direct contempt. Lightning traced the eastern clouds. A gunman injured by the gravel whimpered brokenly.

"I'm going off-planet now," Madame Yarnell announced abruptly.

Peres seemed alternately frightened and exultant. The face of the Widow Guzman didn't change, but she wrapped her arm around the gigolo's waist and held him tightly. Roberson simply looked terrified, as he had since he appeared in obedience to the summons.

The Lurias' suppressed glee suggested — correctly — that they knew more about Madame Yarnell's recall than she did herself. Coke guessed that the cartel representative was too furious at this moment to take much notice of the gangsters' expressions; but she wasn't stupid, and she wasn't the type to limit the basis of her judgments to hard facts.

When Madame Yarnell returned to Cantilucca it would be obvious who had gained by her absence. Coke believed it would be very, very bad for those same parties.

"You *will* keep the peace," Madame Yarnell said. "*While* I'm gone, *when* I return — forever! All of you!"

She looked around the segregated assembly. "If there's any problem, *any* problem with the supply of gage from Cantilucca, may the Lord have mercy on you! For I will have none."

"I wonder how much she knows about what's been going on while she's here?" Margulies said.

Coke shrugged. "Not a lot," he said. "She doesn't have any local sources she could trust, and she didn't bring the sort of hardware Barbour and Daun deployed for us. She's probably pretty frustrated with what she must guess."

Madame Yarnell threw herself into the reconnaissance vehicle. The driver began his hard turn before the passenger door had finished closing.

"How do you feel, boss?" Margulies asked. She lifted her eyebrow.

Coke smiled grimly. "A little antsy," he said. "Not frustrated, though. We may or may not be able to pull this off, but we sure as *hell* know what we're doing."

The Delian vehicle screamed up the street, shimmying as hard acceleration unloaded the front wheels. One of the electric drive motors sent occasional sparks quivering out into the night.

"Ramon Luria's coming this way," Margulies said as she peered over the roof coping.

"Yeah, he's probably wondering when the FDF is going to arrive on Cantilucca," Coke said.

"And?" Margulies asked.

"And the answer's, 'Never, if Camp Able takes my recommendation,'" Coke replied. "But I'll say something more neutral than that to hold him for the time being. Sooner or later, though . . ."

He started for the trap door and the ladder down into Hathaway House.

"Sooner or later," Mary Margulies said, "everybody dies. When that happens, I wouldn't want to remember that I helped keep either group of these bastards in power."

CANTILUCCA: DAY SEVENTEEN

The youth's facial make-up made him look like an actor in a Noh play. His body was slim, supple, and completely hairless. The room's score of mirrors reflected all angles of his perfect beauty as he stretched.

"I'll get some more wine," he said. "The same vintage?"

Johann Vierziger turned on the blue satin bed. "Yes," he said. "It wasn't bad."

Vierziger arched his chest upward, supporting himself on toes and the tips of his fingers extended backward. The mattress's resilient underlayer undulated softly in reaction.

"But don't be long," Vierziger added with a chuckle.

The youth opened the door concealed behind one of the brothel's floor-to-ceiling mirrors. A pair of fireflies drifted in past him.

"Shall we have a friendly talk, Master Vierziger?" Pepe Luria called from the corridor. "You and me and my friends?"

The fireflies halted a meter to either side of the bed, balanced on their hissing violet spikes. Another pair followed them.

"Get out of here, boy!" Pepe snarled to the youth who'd frozen in the doorway. He struck backhanded.

The youth darted past Luria, whimpering. Blows thudded as he ran the gauntlet of Pepe's coterie further down the hallway.

"Would you mind if I relaxed, Luria?" the Frisian asked from the tight arc in which he balanced. His erection of moments before had subsided, but his voice was calm.

Pepe stepped into the room, flanked by the last pair of fireflies. He wore the belt-pack, but he held his left thumb down on a separate remote control. "Do you know what this is?" he asked in place of answering.

"A dead-man switch," Vierziger said.

Pepe giggled. "Just so you know," he said. "If I release the button, poof! My little darlings do — what I've directed them to do. Are you faster than an electronic switch, Frisian?"

"I'm faster than some of them," Vierziger said. There was no sign of strain or emotion in his voice.

"You're not faster than six at the same time!" Pepe snapped, obviously angry at the lack of response to his murderous banter. "All right, you can sit up."

Three L'Escorial gunmen followed Luria into the room. Two carried widemouthed mob guns, the third a sub-machine gun. They looked relieved to see the Frisian nude and unarmed.

Vierziger lowered himself flat, then turned to swing his feet onto the floor as he lifted his torso. His movement was smooth but not as quick as it would have been under normal circumstances. He didn't want to startle the L'Escorials.

"Something puzzled me when I went through Suterbilt's house," Pepe said. "The house he took from Larrinaga. The psychic ambiance was missing. And that night Larrinaga, who didn't have a pot to piss in, lifted on a starship to Mahan. Interesting coincidence, no?"

Vierziger shrugged. "Maybe Larrinaga helped the Astras with their attack," he said. "You say it was his house, after all."

"I thought of that," Pepe agreed in a falsely reasonable tone. "But that didn't answer all the problems."

The Frisian's chased and carven pistol hung in its

holster from a chair backed against the head of the bed. Pepe nodded toward the weapon.

The sub-machine gunner jumped as though prodded with a shock baton. He snatched the pistol away. The Frisian commo helmet continued to rest on the seat of the chair.

Johann Vierziger smiled faintly. He looked at the constellation of fireflies encircling him.

"Is that fellow Daun your gunsel?" Luria demanded sharply.

Vierziger shook his head. "Niko wouldn't be in the least interested," he said. "Even if I were a woman, I'd be too old for him."

He shrugged. "Besides," he added, "I prefer professionals."

Pepe reached into a pocket with his free hand. "But sometimes amateurs, isn't that so?" he snarled.

He held out his open right hand. On the palm was a shot-out pistol barrel. The iridium had been so hot when Vierziger dropped it inside the Larrinaga house that the cylinder had deformed when it hit the floor.

"I thought to myself," Pepe continued. "There were very few shots fired. All the guards *could* have been killed by a single man. But it would have had to be a particular man, isn't that so?"

He let the barrel fall toward Vierziger's shrunken genitals. Vierziger's right hand, flat on the mattress beside him, moved as a blur. When the motion ended, the iridium was a bump raising the knuckles of the Frisian's hand — palm-down again, beside him.

Vierziger's lips held the faintest quirk of a smile. He said nothing.

"Ass is cheap in Potosi!" Pepe Luria shouted angrily. "But I can't imagine why else you would have bothered to help a wretch like Larrinaga!"

Vierziger looked up at the L'Escorial leader. "No," he agreed. "You wouldn't be able to imagine it, Luria."

"Take him!" Pepe said.

Johann Vierziger didn't move or cease to smile, even as the butts of the mob guns swung toward his head from opposite sides.

"Scramble!" Bob Barbour shouted. "L'Escorial's picked up Johann!"

Margulies snatched the 2-cm weapon she'd slung from the back of the chair beside hers in the saloon alcove. She'd been ready to drive Coke on his normal evening run to the spaceport to send a message capsule.

Coke was on his way down to the lobby. He paused, midway on the stairs, and asked, "Are they coming here?"

"Not yet, the bloody fools," the intelligence officer said. "Either they're not that organized, or they don't realize that we're keeping an eye on things."

Barbour watched his console as he spoke. The main screen showed Johann Vierziger surrounded by L'Escorials and fireflies on a brothel bed, but graphic and numerical sidebars reduced the main image by sixty percent.

Barbour's shouted warning drew Georg Hathaway's head from the family apartment. Coke heard the door open beneath him.

"Hathaway!" he said, leaning over the balustrade to make eye contact. "Is anybody in the building but us, you and Evie?"

"No sir," Hathaway said, staring at Margulies by the door. The security officer was pulling her armor on one-handed while she held the shoulder weapon with the other and looked out the peephole in the front door. "No sir, there's only you two gentlemen and the lady, that's all who are present in our establishment."

The innkeeper's voice singsonged, as if he were chanting to himself in private. He was so frightened that his hands were still rather than washing themselves.

Evie Hathaway appeared behind her husband. She laid a hand on his shoulder.

"Sten's on the way back," Barbour noted. "He's picking up Niko on the way."

"Via, they shouldn't risk it!" Margulies muttered from the doorway.

"They'll be all right," Barbour said. Tension clipped his tones, but his enunciation remained perfect. On the main screen, a pair of gunmen clubbed Vierziger unconscious. "Pepe guessed Johann sprang the ambiance for Larrinaga. There's no evidence it's occurred to him to come after the rest of us yet."

Coke walked down the stairs and turned to face the Hathaways. "Georg, Evie," he said. "If you can handle it, we'll go up to the hide on your roof now. If you can't, we'll head for the woods. Either way, tell Pepe or whoever comes looking that an Astra messenger came for us twenty minutes ago. We left with him. All right?"

"Sten and Niko're back," Margulies called. The whine of a jitney's motor came through the peephole and, faintly, through the building's thick walls. "They're going around to the lock-up."

"Go upstairs, then," Evie Hathaway said. "That's what you want, isn't it? Go!"

"Master Hathaway?" Coke said.

Georg finally met the Frisian commander's eyes. He patted his wife's hand on his shoulder. "Yes," he said. "You are our guests. We will do what we can for you, despite, despite . . ."

Hathaway's face settled into unexpectedly firm lines. "Your friend helped Pedro, returned Suzette to him and got him away from here. You'll want to do what you can for your friend. We'll hide you until you can."

"There's about forty men leaving L'Escorial HQ," Margulies warned from the peephole. "A couple armored cars are coming up from the garage, too."

"Sten and Niko have gone up the ladder to the back," Barbour said.

"Shut it down, Bob," Coke ordered, putting a hand for emphasis on the intelligence officer's arm. "Everybody up to the —"

He heard the trapdoor open. "Stay where you are!" he bawled to Moden and Daun, who'd climbed the rope ladder from the locked parking area behind Hathaway House. "We're on our way!"

Barbour blanked the console. His hesitation at abandoning his equipment was obvious in the longing glance he threw over his shoulder when Coke tugged him way.

"They're crossing the street!" Margulies warned. She hadn't moved from her position.

"Come *on!*" Coke shouted. He gave Barbour a push toward the stairs and skipped up after him, charging his sub-machine gun as he moved. The security lieutenant backed from the door, covering the rear.

"Twenty minutes ago!" Coke called from the top of the stairs.

The Hathaways couldn't hold out against torture — nobody could if the stress was properly applied, though Coke doubted any non-Frisian on Cantilucca was competent at *that* either. Whether or not the Hathaways would blurt something when L'Escorial gunmen knocked them around, as would inevitably happen, was an open ques—

"We will stand it!" Evie Hathaway called. "For your sake, and for Cantilucca!"

"Blow the fucking door down!" shouted a gaunt, one-eyed L'Escorial gunman at the front of Hathaway House. Georg Hathaway was already pulling the door open as quickly as its mass would allow.

The five Frisians waited silently beneath piled lumber and the barrels on the roof. Enough of the twilight leaked through cracks in their concealment that they could see one another as their eyes adapted.

So long as the console in the lobby operated as a

base unit, the commo helmets could access sounds and images from any of the sensors Daun had placed — including those in the hotel. There were no peepholes to look out through directly.

Six gunmen bulled into the lobby, deliberately slamming the innkeeper against the wall. Evie Hathaway stood at the doorway to the family apartment, glaring at the L'Escorials.

Ramon Luria entered behind his men. He looked at Evie, then Georg. "Where are the Frisians?" he asked.

"They're gone —" Georg began.

Ramon nodded. Two of the gunmen grabbed Hathaway by the wrists.

"— twenty minutes ago when —" Georg said, his voice climbing a note with every syllable.

Ramon punched the innkeeper in the belly with all the strength of his pudgy body. Georg's breath whooped out; his face lost color.

"The Astras sent for them!" Evie cried. "They went to the Astras with nothing but their guns!"

Ramon turned from the husband and slapped the wife. It was a full-armed blow which Evie could have dodged had she wished to. Instead she accepted the *whack*, knowing that there was no escape but death from whatever Luria chose to do.

Three scarlet armored cars were in the street, their armament pointed at Hathaway House. Several score gunmen milled around the vehicles. If the tribarrels and rocket launcher ever opened up, shrapnel and fragments of the facade would kill more of the L'Escorials than the Frisians could in the first few seconds.

Evie's head rocked back. She put a hand to her cheek, then snatched it away as a sign of weakness.

"Go on," she said. "Go on! The Astras came for them twenty minutes ago. Hitting me won't change that!"

Ramon panted from his exertion. "Search the place," he ordered his men generally. "Search it all!"

Four men of the group who'd entered with him scattered. Three went upstairs while the last entered the kitchen with his sub-machine gun outstretched like a cattle prod.

More L'Escorials stamped through the outer doorway, multiplying the number of searchers without adding organization to the process. One gunman began opening the console's access panels, though only a child or a midget could have fit into the enclosed volume.

"Hey, there's a ladder up to the roof!" a man called from the top of the stairwell.

The Frisians faced the barrels that formed the side of their concealment nearest the trapdoor. Each of them but the intelligence officer held a weapon ready.

Barbour started to pick up the sub-machine gun on the floor beside him; Coke laid a hand on his and shook his head. Barbour nodded understanding and let the weapon lie. The chance that the intelligence officer would do something noisily wrong was greater than any help his unskilled shooting would provide if the situation blew up.

Sten Moden carried three shoulder weapons, two slung and the last in his hand where it looked like a pistol by comparison to his size. There wasn't room in the narrow hide for the rocket launcher he favored, and the big missiles would be useless in a point-blank shootout anyway.

Three L'Escorials came out onto the roof clumsily. Each of them climbed with one hand and waved his weapon through the trapdoor ahead of himself. The first man out shouted in alarm as the next prodded him in the back with a fléchette gun.

"They been up here," a L'Escorial noted. "Hey, look at this!"

He'd found the panoramic camera Daun glued to the coping of the facade weeks before. It was a relatively large unit, about the size of a clenched fist, and Niko hadn't tried to conceal it. The camera provided a view of the entire streetscape — distorted at the edges, but correctable into normal images by the console's processing power.

"It's a bomb!" cried the man with the fléchette gun. Why he thought so was beyond imagining, especially since the next thing he did was put the muzzle of his weapon against the camera and fire.

If it *had* been an explosive device, it would have detonated and killed all three L'Escorials. Instead, the gun's enormous muzzle blast blew the camera across the street in tiny fragments. The osmium fléchette left a split and a crater in the facade of L'Escorial headquarters.

"What's that?" a gunman in the street screamed. Another man emptied an automatic shotgun upward, scarring the reinforced concrete of Hathaway House. Dust and sparks flew past the coping.

"You bloody fool!" a L'Escorial snarled — correctly — at the man with the fléchette gun.

"Hey!" called a man through the trapdoor. "You dickheads up there? Come on back, we're moving!"

Two of the L'Escorials moved quickly to the trapdoor. The third demanded, "What do you mean, we're moving?"

"I mean we're going to take out the Astras once and for all!" cried the man below. "Pepe just gave the order!"

The last of the three gunmen jounced down the ladder. Coke waited another thirty seconds, then reached for the latch holding the side of the barrel closed. Bob Barbour touched his hand. "Not yet," the intelligence officer whispered. "I'll tell you when they're all clear of the building."

Barbour's faceshield would be taking the input of up to a dozen of the visual sensors in and around Hathaway House. Coke couldn't have kept that many locations straight, quite apart from needing a clear view of his immediate surroundings in event of a firefight.

Coke grinned and nodded to his intelligence officer.

"Now," Barbour murmured. "They're gone."

Margulies swung open the door; Coke was out onto the roof first. He kept his head below the level of the roof coping. The sun had fully set, but the afterglow was vivid to eyes that had been covered within the hiding place.

"They took the weapons they found," Sten Moden said. "They carried my launcher and the reloads back across the street."

"We've got what we need," said Coke. "First we'll do something about Johann."

Mary Margulies looked at him. "We're going to take them all on, then?" she said.

"Yeah," Coke said. "All that're left after they get done with each other."

Margulies shrugged. "Suits me," she said, checking with her fingers the pouches of 2-cm ammo on her crossed bandoliers.

Niko Daun slapped another panoramic camera onto the coping, a centimeter from where the previous one had been blown to atoms.

Coke stared at him. "You carried an extra one of those when you ran for cover?" Coke asked.

The sensor tech looked defensive. "I've got two of them, sir. Well, they're real handy."

"It's all right," Barbour said, responding to a threat before his fellows were aware of it. He positioned himself so that his body was between the trap door and the other members of the team. "It's Hathaway."

Georg Hathaway stuck his head up through the opening. It certainly hadn't occurred to the innkeeper that without Barbour's warning, somebody — very likely Coke himself — would have blown him away.

"Sirs," he said. His normally pudgy cheeks looked sunken, though the fact he'd climbed the ladder spoke well of his general condition. "They've gone for now, all of them. They say they're going to attack Astra. You can escape now."

"I'm checking my equipment," Bob Barbour said, the last syllable spoken as he slipped past Hathaway. He let himself drop to the corridor since the inn-keeper's body blocked the ladder. Hathaway recognized the problem and scurried down also, puffing and wheezing.

Coke started for the ladder. Margulies touched his arm. "Sir?" she said. "What's the drill? Do we break Johann out now?"

"We check the situation on the big screen," Coke said. "And then we break Johann out, yes."

Wild gunfire erupted from the street.

Both syndicates had moved gunmen back into Potosi as soon as Madame Yarnell left, though the gangs kept a lower presence than before. Instead of loitering in opposing groups at every corner, men of the two sides kept generally to one end of town or the other — spaceport side for Astra, the eastern half for the L'Escorials.

Though the Lurias were acting on the spur of the moment, Pepe's sudden decision was tactically ideal. Three red-painted armored cars were already in the street. The remaining vehicles rumbled out of the garage beneath L'Escorial HQ even as the first phase of the battle began.

The gateway into the Astra compound was blocked, as usual, by the converted bulldozer. As the L'Escorials swept unexpectedly toward their rival's headquarters, the blue-clad guards started the dozer's engine.

Pepe's fireflies stooped like hawks with violet pin-ions. The short powergun barrel in each firefly spat cyan death at the startled guards. The side hatch to the cab of the converted bulldozer was open. A firefly slid in, lighted the vehicle's interior with its five-round magazine, and curved out again.

The bulldozer stalled in a cloud of black smoke. The Astra guards sprawled on or around the vehicle, mangled by concentrated gunfire. The fireflies hissed back toward their controller. Pepe had told off a pair of his henchmen as assistants, to reload the fireflies' magazines when they returned.

Civilians vanished from sight. A few Astra gunmen opened fire on the advancing L'Escorials. The Lurias' armored cars raked the street with their tribarrels and a salvo of 10-cm bombardment rockets. The latter blew up on building fronts with huge red flashes, hurling shrapnel and broken concrete in every direction.

Astras dived for cover in doorways and alleys. Counterfire stopped instantly, though only a handful of Astras were hit by the wild volley. The sheer volume of fire which the vehicles put down was too much for undisciplined troops to face. As more armored cars joined the initial trio, the gunmen who'd been chased to cover tore off their blue accoutrements and disappeared into the night.

The only Astras still fighting after the first exchange were those in the headquarters building with their leaders — and they were trapped like mice in a bucket of water. By taking the initiative, Pepe had won the battle.

A pair of L'Escorials, stoned on gage and bold to the point of lunacy, leaped aboard the converted bulldozer. Astras fired wildly from ports in the headquarters building, but most of the shots were aimed at fireflies which existed only in the gunmen's minds.

Powergun bolts traced magenta afterimages across unprotected retinas; terror turned the shudder of color into the fireflies' static suspension system, though all the little devices were at the moment being reloaded.

The bulldozer grunted to life. One of the L'Escorials jumped from the hatch again. He was immediately shot in half by gunmen from both syndicates. The remaining man backed the converted vehicle with a skill that its regular driver couldn't have managed with leisure and full daylight.

The door to the underground garage was open; an armored truck was driving up the ramp. The bulldozer crashed into the flimsier armored vehicle, blocking the exit completely.

The L'Escorial driver jumped out and scampered away, miraculously unhurt by the sleet of bolts and bullets which pursued him. A L'Escorial armored car nosed through the opened gateway. Its three tribarrels fired point-blank at the rocket pod mounted on the converted bulldozer.

The dozer was armed with hypervelocity rockets which didn't have explosive warheads. The rocket fuel deflagrated with what was only technically a fire rather than an explosion.

A ball of yellow light enveloped the front of Astra headquarters and the vehicles in the garage beneath the building. More fuel and munitions went off in a second blast a heartbeat after the first. The building's protective facade lifted as a piece, then settled again in slabs and pieces that crumbled away.

A L'Escorial armored car raked the courtyard wall with fléchette rockets. Almost all the hundreds of osmium penetrators punched through the cast concrete, each drilling a finger-sized hole on entry and blowing a divot the size of a soup plate from the inner face as the projectile keyholed out. Backblast from the powerful rockets incinerated dozens of L'Escorials who had sheltered behind the launcher.

Wreathed in smoke from its rocket exhausts, the vehicle that fired the salvo drove into the weakened portion of concrete. Metal shrieked, but a ten-meter stretch of wall collapsed inward.

A cloud of white dust enveloped Astra headquarters. Scores of L'Escorial guns fired with no target beyond the silent building itself. Another armored car rumbled through the gap. Its sole functioning tribarrel ripped a rich cyan line across and through the building's inner fabric. There was no return fire, but ricocheting projectiles spun several of the red-clad gunmen.

"About now, I'd say," Mary Margulies prompted. She gripped the large hasp to open the unlocked front door.

"Not yet!" Coke ordered. His mind tried to fill the immediate future, encompassing every possible event and side effect. The task was beyond his conscious intellect, but instinct told him that the moment was not —

A white flag — a scrap of sheet — waved from a hole on the ground floor of Astra headquarters. Bob Barbour gestured minusculy to the keyboard of the console at which he sat.

The holographic screen split. The lower half showed the interior of the building. Audio was from one of the laminar bugs Daun set during the initial visit to Astra HQ. Visuals came through miniature cameras at roof level across the street, processed to an illusory slickness by the console's artificial intelligence.

"Luria!" the Widow Guzman shouted through a bullhorn, toward a hole torn into the wall by powergun bolts. "We surrender! We're coming out!"

Three Astra gunmen and Adolpho Peres crouched with the Widow in what had been her private office. In the outer area, another gunman stood behind the thickest remaining portion of the building's facade, waving the white flag. There were dozens of bodies around him, most of them mangled beyond recognition of their species.

The fireflies, their magazines reloaded, curved toward the riddled building like swarming hornets.

"Bob, you're control," said Matthew Coke as he stepped to door of Hathaway House. "The rest of us — now!"

Margulies put her weight against the inertia of the door, then stepped out behind her commander.

The Lurias had left a six-man guard at the gate to their headquarters. By this stage in the fighting the gunmen stood in the middle of the street to watch the battle in the near distance.

Coke didn't make the mistake of using his sub-machine gun as an area weapon when he had individual targets. Three-round bursts spun two of the L'Escorials an instant before Margulies blew a third nearly in half with her 2-cm weapon. The last three syndicate gunmen went down in a ripple of cyan as all four Frisians fired simultaneously.

The brief fusillade didn't arouse the attention of the fighters half a kilometer away, locked in the death throes of the Astra syndicate. Coke and his team sprinted across the street and through the open door into L'Escorial headquarters.

The smoldering body of Angel Tijuca lay faceup in the center of the entryway. He'd been shot in the chest, twenty or thirty times at close range. The 1-cm powergun bolts had burned most of his torso away. He still held the pistol he'd managed to draw in the last instants of his life.

"Fireflies," Margulies said softly. "He wouldn't have liked it when Pepe brought Johann in."

"I'm sorry, Mary," Coke said.

She looked at him. Her face was freckled by the overlay in one quadrant of her visor, echoing the image from Barbour's console. "Don't be," she said. "We all die. He didn't — die a bad way after all."

Coke nodded. "Sten," he said, "Niko — check the barracks upstairs and rejoin when it's clear. Mary, Johann ought to be —"

Margulies had already swung herself into position beside the heavy door to the right of the anteroom. It was ajar, though it had a lock.

"Go," said Coke. He had the automatic weapon, so he would be first through.

Margulies pulled the door open. The room beyond

was the armory. Weapons lockers lined the walls, most of them emptied or nearly so for the sudden attack. The cases of Frisian equipment that Ramon's men had taken from Hathaway House lay on the floor among the remains of the L'Escorial hardware.

A restraint cage stood against the far wall. Johann Vierziger was in it. The probes touched his nude body at a dozen points including his genitals, sending fluctuating currents through his nerve pathways.

A fat man, naked to the waist, sat on an ammunition case beside the prisoner. He was mopping sweat from his face with the red bandanna tied around his throat. He jumped halfway to his feet between the time the door opened and the moment Coke's long burst disemboweled him.

Margulies fired into the control box at the top of the cage. The electronics disintegrated under the jolt of plasma. Droplets of metal and silicon shards sprayed a wide area. Some splashed on Vierziger as the cage released him to topple forward, but the prickles were nothing to the pain from which he'd been freed.

Coke started toward Vierziger. A young L'Escorial, scarcely a boy, stepped into the room behind the Frisians. He was buttoning his trousers. *"Wha—"* he cried as Margulies turned, bringing her heavy weapon to bear less than arm's length from the gunman's breastbone.

He didn't have a gun. That wouldn't matter, but as her finger took up slack on the trigger she recognized —

"Emilio!" she said. "Your name's Emilio and you come from Silva Blanca."

The muzzle of the 2-cm weapon shimmered yellow. The iridium was cooling slowly from the five rounds she'd put through it in the street a moment ago. Coke glanced back at the lieutenant, but his real attention was on Vierziger. Margulies' situation was under control, though he wasn't sure what she meant to do.

The young L'Escorial swallowed. He leaned back, afraid to move his feet and unable to take his eyes from the 2-cm mouth that would swallow his life with another millimeter of trigger travel. "How did you know?" he whispered. "How did you know me?"

An automatic carbine leaned against the wall by the doorway, probably Emilio's weapon. Margulies doubted the boy would have been able to grip it if she picked it up and put it in his hands.

"Go home to your parents, Emilio," Margulies said. The boy wore a red armband. She ripped it off while her right hand continued to steady her weapon on the youth's chest. "Farming's better than dying. You've got *no* talent for this business."

"You'll shoot me if I turn," Emilio whimpered. Tears dribbled down his cheeks. "Oh, Mama, Mama . . ."

Margulies thrust the 2-cm weapon toward Emilio's face. The heat of the muzzle made him flinch away. He turned and ran into the night, still crying.

Moden and Daun strode into the armory. "All clear," Niko called. He was bright, spiky with hormones and eagerness.

The logistics officer lifted the triple rocket launcher and checked it with a critical eye. "Who was that?" he asked Margulies in a low voice.

Margulies grimaced. "A civilian," she said. "Somebody who didn't have any business here."

Coke helped Vierziger rise cautiously from the floor where he'd fallen. The little gunman waved him away.

"Find me some clothes," Vierziger said. His eyes were open. He looked straight ahead and held himself stiffly. "They cut mine off me when they put me in there."

Niko Daun turned and sprinted up the stairs to the barracks without formal orders from anyone. The dead torturer's pants wouldn't have fit, even if they'd been in better condition than the corpse which wore them.

"They had the cage's power turned all the way up,"

Coke said in a quiet voice. "They put him through hell."

Vierziger looked at Coke and managed a shaky smile. "No, Matthew," he said. The lilting insouciance was back in his tone. "That was somebody else entirely. And it can't have been Hell, can it? Because I still have a chance to do penance."

He flexed his hands with apparent approval.

"Here you go!" Niko Daun called as he returned with boots, a pair of gray trousers and a camouflaged tunic. The items were all small enough to fit Vierziger. If they weren't particularly clean, they at least offered the spiritual protection which clothing gives a civilized man.

Coke frowned as Vierziger drew the garments on. "I don't understand, Johann," he said.

Vierziger chuckled. "Neither do I, Matthew," he replied. "But we're not required to understand, you realize."

Heavy fire roared from down the street. Coke switched his visor to give him a quarter overlay view of the console display. He chose another sub-machine gun from the selection available in the armory.

The three Astra gunmen in the office with the Widow and Peres stumbled out through a hole torn in the facade by L'Escorial fire. They'd thrown away their weapons. One of the Astras had even stripped so that he didn't show any blue garments in the lights bathing the battered headquarters.

Fireflies dropped from the night sky, circled the men, and stabbed them with multiple cyan bolts. The Astras screamed and died in the rubble of their fortress. One man flung out his arm to fend death away. Bolts blew the limb off at the shoulder before another round finished him.

"Come out, Widow!" Pepe Luria called. His father and grandfather crouched behind the courtyard wall, but Pepe stood in the gap between two L'Escorial armored vehicles. "We'll treat you with full honors!"

"I'll take the roof," Sten Moden said, hefting his launcher and a case holding three additional missiles. "Niko, will you load for me?"

"The roof?" Coke said. "That's not great if you've got to displace."

Moden shrugged despite the enormous weight he carried on his one arm. "A good vantage point," he said. "And the backblast of these — it'd be almost as bad in an alley as inside. The cost of power, you know."

"Go on," Coke said. "But be careful."

L'Escorials had refilled the tubes of the car mounting fléchette rockets. Pepe stepped to the side. This time his henchmen were careful to avoid the lethal wedge of exhaust behind the vehicle.

The gunner inside closed the firing contacts. The twelve rockets rippled off in four nearly simultaneous trios. A fraction of a second after they left the launching tubes, the casings split open and unleashed hundreds of dense arrows, finned to spread slightly along their trajectory.

The fléchettes hit the facade of Astra headquarters like osmium sleet. The pillar sheltering the flag-waving gunman disintegrated, as did what remained of the wall of the office beyond. Dust rose, dazzlingly white in the lights of L'Escorial vehicles.

"Come out, Widow!" Pepe shouted gleefully as he stepped into view again.

Johann Vierziger draped himself with bandoliers and two slung weapons, a sub-machine gun and a 2-cm powergun. He slid a pistol into the pocket of the tunic he wore.

"Pepe must have kept my rig," he said wryly. "Well, it's only a tool. Like the flesh itself. The tools aren't what matter."

"You and Margulies stick together," Coke ordered. "I'll take the opposite side of the street myself."

Vierziger shook his head and smiled. "The two of

you take the other side," he said/ordered. "I prefer to work alone."

Vierziger began dropping grenade clusters into various pockets of his garments. His body armor lay where it had been dumped with the other Frisian suits.

Coke looked at the little man, then said, "Okay, Mary, let's get into position. It'll be party time any moment now."

They stepped from the building and crossed the courtyard, covering one another's movements alternately. Fires lighted the interior of a dust pall to mark Astra headquarters and the street before it. Hundreds of L'Escorial gunmen capered about the site, silhouetted like insects by a lamp.

Adolpho Peres, an overlay on one corner of Coke's visor, bawled, "I surrender! I surrender! I'm coming out!"

The gigolo staggered through the curtain of dust and smoke. Debris fouled his outfit, a ruffed doublet and tights of black velvet. His eyes were slitted.

Peres negotiated the rubble of the protective facade without falling, only to trip over the riddled bodies of the gunmen who'd preceded him from the building. He tumbled to his knees and clasped his hands in prayer. "Oh, dear Lord in heaven Luria I'm your friend you mustn't —"

The fireflies drifted within a meter of Peres before they one at a time emptied their magazines into him. When the last unit fired, only scraps of bone remained of what had been the gigolo's muscular torso.

"Four to team," Lieutenant Barbour said through the silence on the scene his console projected. *"Are any of you wearing visible red garments? Report ASAP, repeat ASAP! Over."*

Coke sprinted across the street under cover of Margulies' shoulder weapon. He took cover at the corner of the next building up from Hathaway House to avoid involving Barbour and the Hathaways themselves. "One negative," he called.

"*Two negative*," from the logistics officer, breathing heavily with the exertion of his climb to the roof of the L'Escorial building.

"*Three nega— Five negative*," Niko Daun stepping on Margulies' report, but they were both clear and that was what mattered.

"*Six negative*," said Sergeant Johann Vierziger, by pay grade the lowest-ranking member of the survey team. "*And it is time that we act, Matthew. Out.*"

"*Negative!*" Bob Barbour snapped. The command was as unexpected as seeing a nun aim a rocket launcher. "*This is Four. I'll tell you when I'm ready, but do nothing till then. Four out.*"

"Roger that," Coke said, crouching at the corner of the building. He wasn't sure what the intelligence officer had in mind, but he knew Bob well enough now to trust his judgment. Hell, he trusted every member of his team. "One out."

The town of Potosi was locked and unlighted. Civilians huddled beneath furniture, praying that their homes would be spared by the heavy weapons that could shatter walls and bring down upper stories in an avalanche of brick and timber.

On Coke's faceshield, the image of Stella Guzman stepped through the curtain of dust. Her combs gleamed in the glaring lights. She stood like a wraith. The ruin of her fortress wound a shroud about her.

"Luria!" she cried. Her eyes stared straight before her, as though she were unaware of her lover's corpse at her feet. "I will wait for you in Hell, Luria. You'll join me this night! Do you hear me? *You'll join me this night!*"

Pepe's assistants were still reloading the fireflies' magazines. The youngest Luria let his controller hang at his belt and rose to face the Widow. "Why, Stella!" he called. "How shameless! Making an assignation and your lover's body still —"

He drew a pistol and pointed it. From the purple highlights it was indeed Vierziger's weapon.

"— warm!"

"I'll wait for you in —"

Pepe shot her in the face. The Widow turned. Luria continued shooting as the body spun onto the rubble and bounced. The Widow's hand was out-stretched toward Peres, but their dead fingers did not touch.

The last of the fireflies rose from the hands of the attendant servicing it. The six deadly constructs wove a violet corona above the L'Escorial leadership.

"Now," the intelligence officer said. *"But don't harm the fireflies, they're mine. Four out."*

Pepe Luria noticed that his constellation of fireflies moved without his ordering them to do so. He reacted instantly, diving to cover under one of the armored cars flanking him.

"Take them!" said Major Matthew Coke, and the darkness ignited.

Vierziger fired his 2-cm weapon into the side of the vehicle. Even at a range of nearly 500 meters, the powerful charge turned a chunk of steel armor into vapor and white flame rupturing outward.

Molten and gaseous metal sprayed Pepe beneath the opposite car. Luria jumped up screaming, his hair and clothing afire. Vierziger's second bolt blew his head off in a cyan flash.

Sten Moden launched a missile. The roof of L'Escorial headquarters reflected some of the back-blast straight up, so the building itself appeared to have exploded in red flames.

Before the launcher operator fired, he locked a missile on by snapping an image with his guidance laser, then designated it as a point or object target. In the latter case — a maneuvering armored vehicle, for example — the missile guided itself to the target without updates from the operator.

The missiles had a ten-kilometer range, or even farther if they were launched from a level higher than the chosen target. Here, at half a klick, unburned rocket fuel added to the already cataclysmic effect of the powerful warhead.

An armored car disintegrated in a flash so bright that it seemed to shine through the steel. A red-orange mushroom mounted a hundred meters in the air, raining debris. The blast stove in the side of the car nearest the target vehicle and set it afire. The spray of fragments killed scores of L'Escorial gunmen, shredding some of them from knee height upward.

Matthew Coke chose targets — anybody moving on the street this night — and spun them down with short bursts. Margulies fired her 2-cm weapon from a door alcove five meters ahead of Coke, and Vierziger's weapons slapped with mechanical precision from the alley west of L'Escorial headquarters.

On targets so distant, a sub-machine gun's 1-cm bolts were near the low end of their effectiveness. Coke preferred an automatic weapon to the wallop of a 2-cm powergun, particularly at the short ranges he expected before this night was over. He could have carried weapons of both styles, as Vierziger did, but when he got tired he might have grabbed the wrong ammo for the gun he was trying to reload. Even the most experienced veteran could screw up that way . . .

Part of Coke's mind wondered if Johann Vierziger ever screwed up. Not when it involved killing something, he supposed.

The second missile hit. The launcher was intended for vehicular use. The thrust of exhaust against the sides of a launching tube pushed even a man as big and strong as Sten Moden a pace backward, so it took a moment to recenter the sights between rounds.

This time the target was the vehicle which carried bombardment rockets. The launching rack was empty, but Moden guessed there might be reloads within the armored hull. He must have been right, because the secondary explosion shattered the concrete facade protecting the building across the street and swept away all the external staircases.

The carnage among L'Escorials still stunned by the first blast was immense. The gunmen literally didn't know what had hit them.

Coke changed magazines, then slung the first sub-machine gun to cool while he fired the back-up weapon. Anything moving was a target. They weren't human, they weren't even *alive*; they were merely motions in his holographic gunsights. He supposed a few of his bursts missed, but he was carrying over 2,000 rounds of ammunition. . . .

"Three, cover my advance!" he ordered. He sprinted past Margulies to the alcove that had served a ground-floor brothel at the west end of the building. The strapped and plated door was firmly closed.

Gunmen — L'Escorials now, like the Astras before them — would be seeking shelter in the buildings. There was none. Those inside would not open their doors to the violence beyond, and the lawlessness of Potosi in past days meant the locked portals would withstand the efforts of panicked thugs to break in.

There was only the forest; and, for those who stayed in Potosi, death.

Two figures — a pudgy man and the aged one clinging to his arm — staggered toward the armored cars straddling the hole in the wall before the Astra compound. A tribarrel on one vehicle raked the night, but its bolts slashed at mid-height across the facades across the street.

The gunner didn't have a target despite the flaring backblast of Moden's launcher, which Coke thought would have fingered the rocket team across a five-kilometer radius. The fellow was blind with fear, shooting the way a devotee of Krishna might have chanted to bring himself closer to God in a crisis.

Coke aimed at Raul Luria. If he shot Ramon first,

the Old Man would fall out of the sight picture as the son who supported him twisted down in death.

Moden's third rocket hit the armored car as Coke took up the slack on his trigger. The gunner found whatever god he worshipped, and the expanding fireball engulfed the Lurias.

Something tapped Coke's helmet. He spun, slashing empty air with the butt of his weapon. Shock from the blast had flung bits from the wall above him, nothing more.

The L'Escorial vehicles were all out of action, either hit by missiles or wrecked by the explosion of neighboring vehicles. Fuel fires spread a lurid illumination across the scene in place of the harshness of headlights a few minutes before. The wreckage of Astra headquarters was ablaze also, a pulsing, bloody glow that erupted from among the fallen walls.

Fireflies coursed the alleys, working outward from the killing ground about Astra headquarters. Occasionally the little machines dipped and stabbed the darkness with a single shot. They had been under Barbour's direction since he broke, then changed, Pepe's control codes.

A violet spark trundled purposefully down the street at a hundred-meter altitude, then dived to waist height directly in front of Matthew Coke. A hatch in the rear of the hovering device popped open. The firefly had expended its ammunition on L'Escorial gunmen and needed refilling.

Coke thumbed five rounds from a sub-machine gun magazine and fed them into the firefly. The hatch closed and the device curved back into action. *Better machines clear the alleys like ferrets in a rabbit warren than that men should have to do so. . . .*

The fireflies weren't armored, and their corona discharges marked them for hostile gunmen. Like tanks, however, the machines had a psychological impact on untrained troops that went far beyond the physical threat they posed. Thugs ran screaming or closed their eyes and sprayed the sky blindly.

The fireflies put their pistol bolts into the center of mass. They dropped each target with the cool precision of hunting wasps stabbing the nerve ganglia of the prey that will feed their larvae.

Coke and Margulies advanced past one another twice more. There were few targets for their guns now.

Moden put a missile into the center of the Astra courtyard, blasting a crater in the scattered rubble and flushed several figures. One of them sent a short burst of automatic fire in the direction of the launcher's signature. Coke, Margulies, and Vierziger all spiked the L'Escorial shooter; Niko Daun's submachine gun spattered the vicinity of the target a moment later.

Coke paused just short of an alley mouth. *"Cover my —"* Margulies began.

"Three, this is Four," Barbour broke in. *"Don't advance just yet, I want to run the alley. Over."*

"What do you —" Coke said.

A blast of shots and powergun bolts glanced from within the alley. A man screamed. Three gunmen — an Astra and two L'Escorials, each unaware of the others' presence until that moment, burst onto the street. Coke cut them down arm's length from his muzzle in a single long burst.

Two fireflies which had expended their magazines but were still lethally threatening drifted into sight above the men they had chased to their deaths. The devices' static suspension sputtered faintly, like hot grease.

Across the street, Vierziger's bolts lit a gunman who'd been similarly chased into sight. The fireflies turned and rose to comb the next pair of alleys in similar fashion.

"Two to One," Sten Moden reported. *"We've run out of missile targets, so we figured we'd work east from where you started. Is that a roger? Over."*

"One to two," Coke said. "Roger, but use the fireflies for the action, keep them loaded. Break. Four, put half the fireflies at Two's disposal. One out."

Neither Daun nor Moden was properly combat material, but Sten was right: a few L'Escorials would have kept away from the battle on their end of town. They weren't the hardcore gunmen, obviously. Nonetheless, they couldn't be simply ignored.

The trio on the ground were nearing what had been Astra headquarters. The stench of blood and death was overpowering. Heat from a burning vehicle — plastics and the rubber tires blazed long after the fuel had been consumed — drove Coke into the center of the street. His boots slipped on blood and flesh pureed by the explosions.

A man who breathed in rhythmic gasps tried to stuff coils of intestine back into his belly. Coke sighted on the dying man's head, then shifted his weapon back to the search for possible threats.

He knew it would have been kinder to finish off the L'Escorial. He just didn't have the stomach for that particular mercy on top of so much other killing.

A figure running, its limbs jerking like those of a wind-whipped scarecrow.

The man turned as Coke fired. Coke moved on. At every further step, his mind flashed the terrified visage which his bolts had lighted and blown apart.

Coke and Margulies leapfrogged again. Across the street Vierziger kept pace. Coke's bare hands prickled. Ozone and flakes of matrix plastic, spattered molten from the guns' ejection ports, had eaten away the outer layer of skin. Thirst was a red furnace within him, and his feet dragged with the effort of walking.

A man in a red vest with a leather fringe, kneeling and moaning a prayer at a locked doorway as a firefly made passes toward him.

Coke shot, then shot again as his bolts flung the man

into the door and the corpse caromed back. *Not men, not things; merely motion.*

One of Coke's sub-machine guns jammed. He'd replaced the barrel twice, but the light-metal receiver warped from the heat of continuous firing. He threw it away and picked up a similar weapon which lay beside a man Margulies had decapitated.

The weight of Coke's ammunition had lessened. He'd emptied the pouches of two of the three bandoliers he'd belted on before the start of the action. . . .

The three Frisians reached the western end of Potosi. There were no more targets. Coke didn't know how much time had passed. His hands were swollen. They felt as though they were twice their normal size.

"Pretty well does it, s-s-Matthew," Margulies croaked. "I was wrong about fireflies. They come in handy s-sometimes."

Two of the fireflies had vanished while working the alleys ahead of Coke and his partners. Hit by lucky shots or mechanical failure, it didn't matter; they'd served their purpose.

The remaining unit hung close above the Frisians, hissing like a restive cobra. Coke hated the fireflies even more than he had before he'd operated with them. It was as bad as being allied to people who ate the men they killed.

Cyan flashes quivered across the forest in the direction of the spaceport. A moment after the shots, the Frisians heard the blat of a diesel engine being pushed.

The port operations van, its headlight flicking up and down like a conductor's baton as the vehicle flew over the washboard surface, raced toward Potosi. A circle of cooling metal on a quarter panel indicated that a fleeing gunman had hit the van when it failed to stop for him.

"Bloody *hell!*" Coke said as he lurched into the

middle of the roadway. "Why did she take a chance like that? She could have been killed!"

"Sir!" Margulies warned. She dropped to a kneeling position with her back braced against the building as she aimed her 2-cm weapon. "That may not be your friend!"

Coke waved the sub-machine gun in his right hand. It felt immensely heavy, as if he were waggling a full-sized tree to get attention. The sky behind him was bright enough to cast his fuzzy shadow toward the oncoming vehicle.

The van fishtailed to a halt. The engine lugged but caught itself again without dying.

Pilar stuck her head out the side window. "Matthew!" she called. "Madame Yarnell's back, and she's come with a regiment of mercenaries! She says they're going to clear the syndicates off Cantilucca and set up new factors before Marvela has time to react. Matthew, get in! They'll kill you too, I'm sure of it!"

"Bloody hell!" Lieutenant Barbour blurted over the commo net. *"One, this is Four and she's right, I wasn't monitoring the port. Four transports have set down and there's another requesting landing instructions. It's the Heliodorus Regiment and I'd estimate —"*

A pause for instant mental synthesis of data that a normal interpretation team would have required an hour to complete.

"— over two thousand troops. I don't know the equipment standard; it isn't in my data base. Over."

"Mary, you drive," Coke ordered as he got in on the passenger side of the van. "Pilar, get into the back, it'll be safer. How much fuel is there in the tank?"

"Matthew, I'm really sorry," Barbour added. The needless and unprofessional comment showed how nervous he was. *"I should have been watching the port. Four over."*

Barbour had run up to six fireflies simultaneously

from a console that hadn't been built for the purpose. Who did he think he was? The Lord God Almighty, that he should be omniscient?

"The Heliodorus Regiment's light infantry," Johann Vierziger said as he swung open the van's rear door and sat, cradling his 2-cm weapon. The van now had a sting in its tail. "Wheeled transport, no fighting vehicles; coil guns with explosive bullets."

"The tank's about half full," Pilar said. Instead of getting into the back as ordered, she slid to the middle of the front seat where her thigh pressed Coke's. "The gauge doesn't work, but there should be enough fuel to go a hundred kilometers or more."

"And there're about three thousand bodies on the TO and E," Coke said to Vierziger as Margulies gunned the van forward. Data that hadn't been downloaded into the intelligence officer's console for lack of need bubbled to the surface of the combat veterans' minds. "Not that anybody ever landed with his complete table of organization strength."

Verbally keying the AI in his helmet, he continued, "Four, this is One. We'll pick up you and the eastern element, then keep going as far as we've got fuel for. Which apparently isn't very fucking far, the roads being what they are, but maybe we can improve our transport on the way. Break. Two and Five, do you copy? One over."

"*One, this is Two,*" Sten Moden replied. His voice was breathy. "*We'll join you at L'Escorial HQ. We left the launcher there, and we may need the rounds we've got left. Over.*"

"*One, this is Four,*" Barbour said. "*I'm packing the console for travel now. Out.*"

The intelligence officer shouldn't have been able to override his commanding officer's transmission — which is what he'd done, stepping on Coke's attempt to protest about Moden's plan. On the other hand, if Barbour couldn't control the net, he wouldn't have been as good as he'd repeatedly proved himself.

Coke sighed. "Roger both of you," he said. "One out."

He'd intended to run with a minimum of equipment. They would hide in the forest — if possible — until the situation changed or at least became more clear. If the survey team dropped off the map, Camp Able would send a follow-up mission.

In three weeks or a month, the FDF would send a follow-up mission. And while the Heliodorus Regiment was an organization of professionals, they were low-end professionals and the Cantilucca operation had to be handled without Bonding Authority oversight.

The Heliodorans just *might* carry out an order to execute captured Frisians. And there was no question in Coke's mind that Madame Yarnell would give such an order.

Pilar's hand lay beside his on their joined thighs. Coke squeezed it, then resumed compulsively counting the loaded magazines in his remaining bandolier. A moment before the van came in sight, Coke had wanted to find a hole and curl up in it for a week of sleep. Now he had a second wind, but he felt as though something could snap at any moment and leave him a pile of constituent atoms. . . .

Margulies stopped in front of the L'Escorial building without killing the van's engine. Daun and Barbour ran from Hathaway House across the street. Both men were heavily laden. The intelligence officer carried his console, packed again into its integral case, while Niko staggered along ahead of the lieutenant with a wicker hamper.

"Daun, we don't have room for your . . ." Coke called. *Clothing? Housewares? What in hell* did *the kid have in the basket?*

"Beer!" Niko shouted as he slammed the hamper down in back of the van. "Master Hathaway's best!"

And if you're as dry as I am, it's better than ammo!"

Sten Moden, carrying so much equipment that he looked like a forklift, waddled from what had been L'Escorial's courtyard. Besides the launcher with two tubes ready, his hand gripped a pair of ammunition boxes. He'd slung additional weapons from his shoulder.

Coke jumped out to help his logistics officer. The team was going to need all the munitions, all Barbour's electronics, and mere thought of the beer was a cleansing shower for Coke's mind. But they were going to *need* a hundred times anything they could bring, so loading the van to the point of breakdown was bad tactics.

Particularly they were going to need troops. And the troops didn't exist on Cantilucca.

The beer was in earthenware bottles. Daun handed Coke one which he'd opened by digging the wax stopper out with a screwdriver blade. The cool lager slipped through the major's being like a blessing from the Lord.

"Let's get going," Coke said as he seated himself again beside the white-faced Pilar. He dropped the empty bottle out the window and took the fresh one Daun offered.

Margulies accelerated with care, but the vehicle wallowed anyway. It would be worse when they reached what passed for rural roads on Cantilucca.

The team couldn't run far enough on a planet where it had no friends, any more than the six of them could successfully fight a regiment. But they would run as far as they could; and then they would fight, because sometimes a bad choice is the only choice there is.

Coke reached an arm around Pilar. His hands were black with smoke, ammunition matrix, and iridium redeposited when plasma charges sublimed it from the bores of his weapons. Pilar snuggled close anyway.

Coke started to laugh. Margulies glanced over, and

he felt Pilar stiffen. "It's not over yet, friends," Coke said in partial explanation.

Dawn was beginning to break over Potosi. The intelligence officer switched channels on his commo helmet intently, using its limited resources while his console was in traveling mode. He saw Coke looking back at him and flashed his commander a tight smile.

It was a hell of a thing to think under the circumstances, but Major Matthew Coke was glad to be alive.

The van rumbled eastward out of Potosi. According to the map Coke momentarily overlaid on his visor, the nearest hamlet had been owned by L'Escorial. The Lord only knew what the situation in the sticks was now, since both syndicates had lost their command groups and much of their rank and file.

Coke took only a glimpse at the map overlay, because he still had to watch for possible ambushers. Most of the gunmen who'd escaped Potosi alive would hide in panic when they heard a vehicle approaching, but a few might take potshots at strangers lucky enough to have transport.

Of course, bushwhackers would probably wait for the van to pass. That meant they'd be trying conclusions with Johann Vierziger.

"Heliodorus is just now putting out patrols," Bob Barbour reported. Niko had placed a variety of sensors throughout the spaceport one evening after driving Coke to the terminal. "Madame Yarnell is furious. She's told Colonel Shirazi that they should have been moving an hour ago."

"If she wanted professionals . . ." said Sten Moden. He was picking with a knifepoint at matrix congealed around the ejection port of a 2-cm weapon. " . . . she should have hired us."

"Direct rule by the Delos cartel's probably more efficient than leaving it to local thugs," Margulies said.

"More of the locals might starve to death, but they wouldn't be as likely to be shot for the hell of it by some yo-yo having a night on the town."

"*Frisian Vessel* Obadiah *to FDF commander Cantilucca*," crackled an unfamiliar voice through Coke's commo helmet. "*Come in FDF Cantilucca. Over.*"

The members of the survey team stared at one another in surprise. Pilar didn't have a commo helmet. She clutched Coke fiercely, then snatched her hand away lest she interfere with his movements. She knew something had happened to startle her companions, but she couldn't imagine what it might be.

"It's coming from orbit," Barbour reported.

"*Frisian vessel* Obadiah *to FDF commander —*" the voice repeated. Coke cut the signal off so that it didn't interfere with his thinking.

"The Heliodorans?" Niko Daun suggested.

"Negative, they couldn't crash our frequencies," Barbour insisted. "This is on a general purpose push, but it's encrypted normally."

"The Heliodorans are trying to get us to give away our position," Margulies insisted stubbornly. "They'll home on the transmission if we respond."

"There is an *Obadiah*," said Johann Vierziger as he watched the rear and sides of the van for possible dangers, "on the FDF naval list. She's a Class III combat transport."

Coke stared at the back of Vierziger's neck. The information Vierziger just stated wasn't secret — but it wasn't something Coke knew, or that a newbie sergeant was likely to have known. Coke didn't doubt that the statement was true, however.

Sten Moden released the blade catch and slid his knife back into the sheath on his belt. "I don't see that there's a downside to responding, Matthew," he said. "If the Heliodorans are good enough to mimic our codes, then they've got us anyway."

"The Heliodorans," Johann Vierziger said toward

the landscape rumbling past the back of the van, "aren't good enough to hit the floor with their hats. Though numbers count for something."

Coke grimaced. "Bob," he said, "will my helmet raise them, or do we need to put up a beam?"

"You'll do better if you're out of the van," replied the intelligence officer. "But if they've got their antenna array extended, and I'm sure they do, they'll pick it up anyway."

"Pull off —" Coke began. Margulies swung the wheel and braked before he got to, "— the road, Mary."

Coke was out the door before the vehicle had come to a complete halt. The immediate area had been cleared around a shack now tumbled to moss and ruin. The van's other doors opened as suddenly as Coke's, the guns of his team facing the chance of attack. Even Margulies was scarcely a heartbeat slower than her commander in jumping from the vehicle she drove.

"— *FDF Cantilucca. Over*," as Coke switched on the transmission from orbit again.

"Survey team commander to FDF vessel *Obadiah*," Coke said. "We're glad to hear from you, boys, because we've got the Heliodorus Regiment looking for our scalps. Can you drop a boat to pick us up? The Heliodorans have secured the spaceport. Over."

Margulies had shut down the diesel when she stopped. Either she didn't choose to run further, or she was more optimistic about chances of restarting the beast in a hurry than Coke was. Metal pinged as the engine cooled.

"*Obadiah to FDF Cantilucca*," the helmet responded. "*You bet we'll drop a boat. Hold what you've got, troopers. Help is coming in figures one-five minutes. Obadiah out.*"

"Well I'll be hanged!" Niko Daun said in pleased amazement.

"That depends on whether the extraction boat reaches us before Madame Yarnell does, kid," Moden said, but the big logistics officer was smiling also as he pointed his missile launcher back down the road toward dawn and the Heliodorus Regiment.

"Thirteen point six," Bob Barbour said with satisfaction. "Minutes, that is."

The intelligence officer's hearing must have been that much better than that of his commander, because it was another five or six seconds before Coke heard the first whisper of the vessel's landing motors.

Pilar stood beside him, a hand on his hip beneath the edge of his body armor. She didn't have armor of her own. Via, he should have grabbed Vierziger's suit for her since the sergeant wasn't using it. They brought every other cursed thing from Hathaway House when they —

Niko Daun looked up, toward the sound of the incoming boat. Coke, suddenly fearful that Pilar would follow the direction of Daun's gaze, shot his hand over her unprotected eyes. "His visor will darken automatically," Coke said.

Pilar pulled his hand down with a firm motion. "I've worked in spaceports for twelve years, Matthew," she said. "I know that plasma exhausts can be dangerous to my eyesight."

In a slightly sharper tone she added, "And I'm *not* fragile."

She squeezed him to take the edge off the rebuke. He remembered that in previous times of crisis she clutched her crucifix. She no longer wore that symbol.

"Sorry," he muttered, meaning more than his conscious mind really wanted to dwell on.

"Blood and martyrs, sir!" Niko said. "It's not a boat, it's the whole *ship*! They're coming straight in and there's no *port* here!"

"Class *III*?" Coke snapped to Vierziger as the penny dropped.

The little gunman smiled, though his eyes continued

their ceaseless quest for a threat — or a target, it was all the same thing. He was holding a sub-machine gun now.

"That's right, Matthew," Vierziger agreed. "The *Obadiah*'s a battalion-capacity combat lander. She's got pontoon outriggers, so she doesn't require a stabilized surface to set down. And armor, in case the landing zone's hot."

The transport swept overhead at a steep angle. The roar and glare of her engines were mind-numbing. Foliage at the tips of trees beneath her track curled and yellowed.

The vessel's exhaust was a rainbow flag waved at Madame Yarnell and the Heliodorans, some ten klicks to the west. Either the *Obadiah*'s commander expected to lift again before anyone could react, or —

Or the commander didn't care what a regiment of light infantry might attempt. The *Obadiah* was coming in with her landing doors open. The troops she carried were ready to un-ass the vessel as soon as the skids touched, or maybe a hair sooner.

"Bloody hell!" Mary Margulies shouted over the landing roar. "She's coming in loaded! She's coming in with troops!"

The *Obadiah* landed a hundred meters away, like a bomb going off in the forest. Her exhaust and armored belly plates cleared their own LZ. Dirt and shattered trees flew away from the shock. Coke caressed Pilar's head closer to his chest to protect her from the falling debris.

Lift fans howled through the shutdown sizzle of the landing engines. The rounded prow of a combat car burst through the fringe of forest which remained between the survey team and the LZ. The vehicle's wing tribarrels covered the sides, but the commander's weapon forward pointed straight at the van.

Coke stepped clear of the others, waving his sub-machine gun butt-upward. The combat car dropped to idle a meter from his feet. The legend on its scarred bow read *Cutting Edge*.

More vehicles deployed through the forest to either side. They were accompanied by squads of infantry riding one-man skimmers.

The commander of the leading car tilted up his tribarrel and raised his visor so that he could face Coke directly. "I'm Captain Garmin," he announced, "with my C Troop, First of the First and L Troop, Third of the First for infantry. I'm in acting command, but I'm supposed to turn the force over to Major Coke if he hasn't been incapacitated when we land. Are you Coke?"

You're supposed to fucking what?

Aloud Coke said, "I'm Coke, but what are you *doing* here?" *With a company of combat cars and a company of FDF infantry!*

Garmin grinned broadly. Coke remembered him vaguely from back in the days of the Slammers, a non-com who'd gotten a field commission.

"The Colonel took your initial reports and cut a deal with the Marvelan Confederacy," Garmin explained. "We're to clean a couple gangs off Cantilucca for them. Orders didn't say anything about the Heliodorus Regiment, but I don't guess that'll change anything important."

"I'll be . . ." Coke muttered. He didn't finish the thought because he didn't know what the finish should be. "You've got just the two companies?"

"Yessir, but we're not cadre and trainees," Garmin said. "Most everybody in both troops wears the pin."

The captain tapped the left side of his breast with an index finger. His clamshell armor didn't show citations, but his meaning was clear: the expeditionary force was made up of Slammers veterans and soldiers with whom the veterans felt comfortable to serve. That was still true for much of the 1st Brigade of the Frisian Defense Forces.

"Right," said Coke as the next sequence of actions cascaded through his mind. "Your troopers are ready to go, Captain?"

"My troopers are gone, Major," Garmin corrected with justifiable pride. "Both troops have completed disembarking."

He coughed and added, "The *Obadiah* is armed and has her own security element, sir. I'd figured to get to work with my entire force — if you hadn't been around."

"Right, hit them before they get organized," Coke agreed. "Bob, set up in —"

He looked to his side. The intelligence officer had already re-erected his console, backing it against the parked van.

Barbour glanced up from a display of the Potosi area including the spaceport. Mauve icons denoted the Heliodoran forces. A platoon-sized Heliodoran detachment was probing Potosi, but the bulk of the regiment milled around the vessels on which it had landed.

"This'll do, sir," Barbour said. "I'm already patching data to the main com room of the ship. You can access it from there."

He nodded up to Captain Garmin. "We've got sensors throughout the area of operations," Barbour explained to the newcomer. "I'll hand you targets on a plate."

Garmin blinked in surprise. The officer who'd unloaded two troops inside of three minutes could appreciate professionalism in another man too.

"Niko, stay with Bob as security and a gofer," Coke ordered. "The rest of us'll need a car."

Who ever heard of running central intel from a shade tree? But Barbour was right, so long as he had a link to the nearby ship, it was as good a place as the next. "You others —"

"I'll drive," said Johann Vierziger. "It's not my favorite slot, but I'm good enough at it."

"I'll give you my XO's command car," Captain Garmin said. "It's —"

"Negative, Captain," Coke interrupted. "You will give me a *combat* car. The one you're in will do fine. If you want to ride into a firefight closed up in a can, be my guest — but I don't."

Coke hopped onto the skirts of *Cutting Edge*. "ASAP, Captain!" he prodded. Moden and Margulies were beside him — the logistics officer still shouldering his brace of heavy missiles. Vierziger mounted the bow slope and thumbed out the car's surprised driver.

"I —" Garmin began, then swallowed a protest that he knew wasn't going to do the least bit of good. "Yes *sir*," he said as he swung over the far side of the fighting compartment. He took with him only his personal weapon — a grenade launcher — and an AWOL bag of possessions.

A good man. And willing to be a good subordinate.

Niko Daun looked up in disappointment as the team's combat veterans crewed their new vehicle. Somebody had to keep an eye on the immediate surroundings while Barbour concentrated on his console. The sensor tech was the right person for the job . . . but he'd rather have been going along.

Coke checked the action of his tribarrel. It moved slickly on its gimbals, and the multifunction display beside it already glowed with enemy dispositions as reported by the survey team's sensor array. The Heliodorans flat wouldn't know what hit them.

Coke used the attached light pen to sketch the plan of action onto the display screen, from which it was echoed to every vehicle and helmet visor in his command. "C Troop, First and Second Platoons, north of Potosi. Flank speed, you'll hit the port from the east. Third Platoon and HQ element, south of the town to the south side of the port. Bypass the town! We don't want fighting there."

He was setting up a dynamic version of an L-shaped

ambush, in which the attacking elements moved
against a static target. Fields of fire shouldn't endanger
friendly troops . . . much.

Coke rubbed his forehead before he continued. The
only way to do this was headlong. If the Heliodorans
had time to spread, it'd be the devil's own job winkling
out each squad with their buzzbombs and explosive
bullets. He was afraid to *think* beyond the level of
reflex, so he'd go with reflex.

"Infantry commander" — Coke didn't even know
that officer's name — "leave a squad in blocking
position at either end of town on the east-west road.
Remainder of your forces, conform to the movements
of their opposite numbers in C Troop. Captain
Garmin, take operational control of the eastern element. I'll handle the south."

Via, he didn't even have a call sign!

"Team One, that's Tony One, over."

"*Charlie One, confirm, out*," said Garmin's voice.
Coke wondered where the cars' CO had taken himself.
Another combat car, he supposed.

"*Lima One, confirm*," said a female stranger. "*Do
you want the mortars here, where the ship provides a
base of fire, or shall I put them on line? Over.*"

Bloody good question.

"Bring them along, Lima," Coke decided aloud. Ten
klicks was within the effective range of the troop's pair
of 10-cm automatic mortars, but he might want to use
shellfire to prevent the Heliodorans from displacing
west when the nutcracker of powergun bolts started to
close. He'd best keep them near the target area. "Team
out."

He looked around at the vehicles and mounted
infantry already in line with his car. "Let's roll!" he
ordered —

And noticed that Pilar Ortega squatted against the
bulkhead of the fighting compartment, between Coke
and Moden who manned the starboard tribarrel.

Vierziger poured power to the fans. He had as certain a touch with the fifty-tonne combat car as he did with a pistol's trigger.

"Not you, Pilar!" Coke said. "Blood and martyrs, not you!"

"Me," the auburn-haired woman said coolly. "I won't stay behind, Matthew."

She was holding a sub-machine gun, one of those Moden had brought aboard. She'd proved in Potosi that she could use one, would pull the trigger at least . . .

C Troop's Headquarters Squad — *Cutting Edge* and the XO's enclosed command car which carried additional commo in place of weapons and munitions — fell into line behind the five cars of 3d Platoon. Ten-man squads of infantry, each accompanied by a two-place gun jeep mounting a tribarrel, followed as the armor blazed a path through the scrub forest. Map data downloaded from the orbital scans provided a course for the lead driver, and the sensors Barbour monitored kept close watch on the Heliodorans.

"Bloody hell," Coke repeated. He couldn't very well throw her over the side of the car, could he?

Garmin's crew had left two suits of back-and-breast armor behind when they evacuated the car so suddenly. Coke sighed.

"Sten, show her how to get into her armor," he said, and he went back to planning the imminent battle.

The port's facilities — maintenance sheds and the terminal buildings; thank the *Lord* Pilar had gotten herself clear — were on the north side of the fenced reservation. The south was unobstructed, though there were twelve ships scattered over the ground in addition to the five from which the Heliodorus Regiment was slowly disembarking.

Coke had put the weight of his main thrust on the side toward which the newly landed regiment was moving, but the shock of ten combat cars and two infantry platoons was likely to drive the Heliodorans back. When they realized their south flank was being raked by a lesser force, they'd fight like raging hell to blow a way clear.

It was going to be interesting.

Coke's helmet AI filtered out all but Priority 1 messages. Margulies leaned close to him and said, loudly enough to be heard if her commander wanted to, "Barbour's told Madame Yarnell that the *Obadiah's* a freighter that lost gyro control during normal set-down."

"She's not going to believe that, is she?" Coke said in surprise.

"Via, no!" Margulies agreed. Overlays projected across the inner surface of the security lieutenant's visor distorted her hard smile. "From what they're saying through the bugs in the terminal building, they're sure we're smugglers who picked a bad time to land and try to undercut the Delos cartel. Yarnell figures to take care of us smugglers just as soon as she's got Potosi secured."

Matthew Coke's mind flamed with blood and cyan light. He laughed. The sound made Pilar's face go blank in an expression closely akin to fear.

The south column burst from scrub into bottom land planted with gage. The leading car boosted its speed to 60 kph, three times the rate at which it had picked its way through the heavy growth. The combat cars were capable of doubling that in open terrain, but the infantry wouldn't have been able to keep up.

The gage crop was a month or so short of harvest. The reedy stems were a full meter tall, but the heads where the drug concentrated hadn't taken on the orangish tinge of full ripeness.

At Captain Garmin's orders, the cars spread from line-ahead formation to line abreast. As directed, Vierziger placed *Cutting Edge* on the left of the formation while the platoon leader took the right.

There was an officer in position if the force had to displace suddenly toward either flank, and Coke was at the hinge of the attack.

"There's shooting in town," Margulies murmured, relaying data from the intelligence officer. "The Heliodorans ran into a couple dozen Astras who'd gone to ground and came out as the patrol arrived. The Astras just want to surrender to somebody, but the patrol leader's calling for heavy backup."

"I'd as soon," Sten Moden said, "if there wasn't fighting in Potosi. Civilians are bound to get hurt."

"When we take the main force," Coke said, "the rest — Heliodorans and syndicate both, the rest'll die on the vine."

Civilians weren't his concern at the moment. His task was to defeat hostile troops. . . .

The column blasted by a dozen farmers' huts in fenced courtyards. Occasionally a shiver of movement indicated someone watching through the palings or from a shuttered window.

A squad of infantry dropped off to cover the community until the force was safely clear, but there was no real threat. A syndicate garrison might still occupy the loopholed stone building, but the flag was gone from the pole on the roof peak. Surviving gunmen didn't want to be identified with either of the losing parties.

"If there's ever to be peace on Cantilucca," said Pilar Ortega with a harshness at variance with the soldiers' professional calm, "it'll come the way you're bringing it. No other way."

Coke's eyes danced from the actual terrain to dots crawling across the combiner screen of his multifunction display. "Team One to Team elements," he ordered. "Take preliminary attack positions with at least five meters of screening between you and the perimeter fence. Out."

The south column was back in brush again,

uncultivated country that was too dry to raise healthy gage. Vierziger slowed their car and pulled it off the general line of advance. The spaceport perimeter and all the structures within it were directly north of them but out of sight.

The local vegetation averaged three meters tall. A few trees rose half again as high before they flared out like golf tees. The trees had whippy, thin trunks, but their crowns were of straw-colored foliage which provided a complete visual screen. Someone in the spaceport tower could conceivably notice that the vegetation waved with the passage of the armored vehicles, but the chance of anybody being that alert was vanishingly slight.

Besides, the Frisians weren't going to be waiting very long.

A squad of infantry dropped off its skimmers and wormed its individual way into the scrub. The infantry could get much closer to the start line than the combat cars without risk of being observed. The squad's air-cushion gun jeep halted back with the cars.

The mortars were jeep-mounted also. By themselves they could keep up with the infantry easily, but the jeeps carried only two 4-round ammo chargers. The remainder of the ammunition supply rode in a wheeled caisson behind each jeep.

Pulling a trailer with an air-cushion vehicle wasn't a great deal of fun on surfaced roads. Dragging wheels through brush and plowed fields, as this crew had been doing, was like trying to swim with a boat anchor. The company commander had wisely unloaded the pair of mortars as soon as she could.

"Charlie element in position," Captain Garmin reported. His platoons had a shorter route than Coke's, though there'd been a delay as many of the troops and cars crossed the road cautiously to reach their attack positions. *"Charlie out."*

Coke frowned at his display. Eight Heliodoran

vehicles were moving away from the terminal building. Twelve more were in the final stages of loading soldiers from an early-landed transport. A battalion headed toward Potosi to reinforce the patrol engaged there. The squad of infantry he'd left in a blocking position could at best slow them with a hit-and-run ambush, and that would be extremely risky.

On the southern perimeter, three of the combat cars and their associated infantry were short of where he'd wanted them to be able to enfilade the westernmost of the Heliodoran transports. Coke gave the order anyway: "All Team elements. Move into final attack positions."

Johann Vierziger eased *Cutting Edge* forward. His seat was raised so that he looked out of the hatch in the bow slope instead of through the vision displays within the driver's compartment.

"Wait for my command to fire," Coke continued, "unless the enemy engages you first. In the latter case, fire at will. Mortars, when the shooting starts, drop your rounds on concentrations shielded from direct fire. Team One out."

Some troopers felt claustrophobic when they were buttoned up in a vehicle. Coke was pretty sure that Vierziger just wanted to be able to add his own increment to the skein of fire which would shortly enwrap the Heliodorus Regiment.

The bow of *Cutting Edge* nosed up to the perimeter fence. Beside the vehicle, an infantryman was slicing a hole in the fence so that the wire didn't obstruct his line of fire.

The nearest starship — a freighter in the gage trade — was 200 meters away, northward and to the right. The terminal buildings were almost 800 meters distant.

The column of Heliodoran transport, lightly armored ten-wheeled trucks, drove toward the gate and Potosi beyond. Soldiers leaned on the waist-height panels of the cargo boxes, looking like sightseers rather than combat troops.

"Barbour says we've been seen!" Margulies shouted.

"Fire at will!" Coke ordered. He squeezed his thumb trigger as three red flares lifted from the terminal building.

Coke aimed at a detail of soldiers horsing crates from the cargo bay of a Heliodoran transport. The figures went down like bowling pins. A case ruptured, spewing out multicolored smoke from the marking grenades within.

Sten Moden launched one, then the other, of his missiles from the starboard wing of the fighting compartment toward targets far to the left. The backblast cleared swathes of empty scrub.

Coke needn't have worried about the most distant transports. A missile detonated on the boarding ramp of each.

Coke shifted his point of aim to the cargo hold of his chosen freighter. The inertia of the spinning iridium barrels fought the weapon's powered traverse, giving the motion a greasy dynamism.

The open hatch was a foreshortened trapezoid in his sight picture. Coke squeezed the butterfly again. The stream of 2-cm bolts reflected within the starship's dark interior like the pulses of a short circuit.

Ammunition detonated in a series of quivering yellow puffs. The orange flash that followed ripped the vessel apart, blowing the middle third across the port as jagged shrapnel.

The blast hurled Coke back from his tribarrel. The concussion set off stacked munitions previously unloaded from other ships. The shock wave skidded the eight Heliodoran trucks, already raked and burning from the eastern element's gunfire, into a single piled inferno.

Coke got up. He'd lost his helmet. Pilar, white and as stiff-featured as a skull, handed it to him.

A black mushroom mounted a thousand meters

from the crater where the center of the starship had been. The two ends of the vessel lay crumpled, thirty meters from where they rested before the explosion.

Gunfire ceased for an instant. The shock had flattened potential targets as well as stunned the FDF gunners.

The initial eight-round salvo of mortar shells landed amidst the unloaded cargo. The white flashes and blasts would have seemed devastating had they not just followed a cataclysm.

Loudspeakers throughout the terminal buildings blared, "Invading forces, you have been surrounded by soldiers of the Marvelan Confederacy. Throw down your arms and surrender. You are surrounded by troops of the Marvelan Confederacy. There is no escape but surrender!"

Bob Barbour again, using the patches into the PA system he'd prepared weeks earlier. Coke had never doubted the value of intelligence and electronic warfare, but Barbour would make a believer of the most hardened grunt.

A Heliodoran crew-served weapon raked the southern perimeter from a position far enough to the west to have been shielded from the exploding starship. They were using a coil gun, a scaled-up version of the Heliodorans' personal weapons. The gun managed to cough out a dozen half-kg shells. One round lifted a Frisian infantryman twenty meters in the air, shedding limbs as he tumbled.

A storm of fire erased the weapon and its crew. Some of the shots came from nearby Heliodorans who knew their best chance of survival lay in surrender.

Partial silence returned, striated by the crackle of flames and the screams of those injured too badly to crawl from the spreading fires. Bits of cloth fluttered above whatever sparse cover the Heliodoran survivors had found. Some of the makeshift flags were white, but the intention was clear regardless.

"Colonel Shirazi to Marvelan Command!" a voice cried over one of the commo helmet's open channels. *"We're laying down our arms! I repeat, we're laying down our arms! We claim the right of exchange under Bonding Authority regulations! We're laying d—"*

Coke cut away from the Heliodoran commander's bleating. "Team One to all Team elements," he ordered. His throat felt as though somebody'd scaled it with a wood rasp. "Cease fire, but hold your positions. When the other side's sorted itself out a little better, I'll have them leave their weapons in place and march to the west end of the port reservation. Cease fire unless you're in danger. One out."

Coke switched to a general push to contact Colonel Shirazi. Sudden dizziness made him sag against the receiver of his tribarrel. The air above the glowing iridium shimmered. Through the heatwaves, Coke saw Johann Vierziger looking back at him anxiously.

Pilar gripped Coke's shoulder, trying to keep him from falling. Silent tears cleared tracks across the grime on her face.

Sten Moden stared out at the barren killing field. There was no telling how many people had died. There would never be a certain figure: the secondary explosions had been too general and too powerful. Hundreds, perhaps over a thousand; in as little time as it takes to open a poached egg. . . .

"It could have been worse," the logistics officer said. "It could have been us."

Niko Daun was talking sixteen to the dozen in the light of a lantern hanging over the nearby mess table. He wasn't bragging. In fact, he didn't seem to be aware of the presence of the members of the expeditionary force seated with him.

Many of the ex-Slammers were veterans of a score of incidents as hot as the one the young technician had just survived. They listened tolerantly as they ate.

"He's coming along, Matthew," Johann Vierziger said with mild amusement. "And the next time he won't make the mistake of pointing his gun at a pair of thugs and telling them to surrender."

The lantern illuminated only half of Vierziger's face. Shadows hollowed the killer's perfect features into the agony of a 14th century "Pieta."

"Is mercy a mistake, Johann?" Coke asked. They sat on an empty mortar case near the edge of the expeditionary force's Night Defensive Position.

"I used to think so," Vierziger said. He smiled. "Thinking a gun's a magic wand that you wave — that *is* a mistake. When those Astra stragglers stumbled onto the van, he should have cut them down immediately."

The wired-in southwest corner of the port reservation was ablaze with floodlights. The Heliodorus Regiment, disarmed and under the guard of four combat cars, would be repatriated as soon as possible.

One of the transports the regiment landed in was still operable. Several days of work were necessary to repair two more, however.

Three transports would suffice to carry all the survivors comfortably.

"Niko did all right," Coke said. "A lot of veterans would have frozen when somebody shot them square in the chest. Thank the Lord for body armor."

Vierziger stretched his slim, hard form, still smiling. "It has its uses," he said, rather than agreeing.

Coke turned toward the eastern horizon, though there was nothing immediately visible save dark forest which had so recently flamed with the directed lightning of powerguns. "Thanks for taking over organizing a citizen's watch in Potosi," he said. "I've got a platoon backing them up as a reaction force, but the gunmen seem pretty much willing to come in peacefully."

Vierziger nodded. "Sten had some friends in town,"

he said. "Solid people, for civilians. It's not hard to set a structure up if you've got good material. And the locals want a structure."

Matthew Coke's spirit osmosed through the flesh and hovered above the scene. He was aware of sensory stimuli — the laughter of troops relaxing after an action of exceptionally concentrated violence; long-molecule soot from smoldering plastic, masking but not completely hiding the stench of burned flesh; the touch of a breeze on a night that was beginning to turn cool — the way he would have been aware of readings on a console display.

"The Marvelans should've sent along a civil administration unit with the troops," his voice said.

"They didn't have time," Vierziger said. "Alois wasn't going to wait for civilians to get their end together when he already had clearance to deal with the military side."

Vierziger spoke with almost proprietary satisfaction; the tone of a long-time veteran or even friend of President Alois Hammer. Coke looked at the sergeant and said nothing.

"I think, Matthew," Vierziger added mildly, "that you have a visitor coming."

Coke's mind was one again with his body, aches and stresses complete. Pilar's solid figure walked toward the NDP from the terminal building. She'd insisted on trying to put the facilities to rights immediately. It was hard to see that being possible, given the disruption the Heliodorans had caused and the damage from the exploding starship.

They had decisions to make in the near future, both of them.

Coke stood up. "Johann?" he said. "It's quiet now, but the Marvelans will pull us out of here in a few weeks at the longest. Do you think the civilians here will do any better the next time?"

"That's up to them, Matthew," Vierziger said. "The

only thing that matters to our souls is what we've done ourselves."

"*You* believe in souls, then?" Coke snapped.

Vierziger nodded. His smile reminded Coke that Lucifer was a fallen angel. "Oh, yes," the little killer said. "I believe in souls."

Matthew Coke turned and walked to meet Pilar at the guard post. By his own orders as Commanding Officer, troops of the Cantilucca Expedition were required to carry weapons with them at all times.

Coke's sub-machine gun and holstered pistol remained on the crate where he'd been sitting.